# LOVING LAURA

## #4 Ghost Falls

## SARAH HEGGER

# Dedication

*I dedicated my first published book to Chris Kennedy, and she's been with me through all the books between that one and this. More importantly she's been with me through the life shit that happened around writing and for that, I can never adequately express my gratitude. It really was kismet, my friend.*

*And to my girls, Olivia and Caitlin. I wish I could take credit for the awesome women you are, but I suspect most of that was you.*

# Acknowledgments

A big thank you to Debbie Fuller and Anna Sharpe for boldly going where no one has gone before. Your proofreading skills are invaluable and I'm super grateful for your time and effort.

I owe a constant debt of gratitude to Penny Barber for still putting up with me after 18 projects together. The woman deserves her own island for editing my scribbles.

To Renee Rocco for the beautiful covers she produces for me.

# Copyright



❀ Created with Vellum

# Praise for Sarah Hegger

*Praise for Sarah Hegger*

Positively Pippa
"This is the type of romance that makes readers fall in love not just with characters, but with authors as well." Kirkus Review (Starred Review)

"What begins as a simple second-chance romance quickly transforms into a beautiful, frank examination of love, family dynamics, and following one's dreams. Hegger's unflinching, candid portrayal of interpersonal and generational communication elevates the story to the sublime. Shunning clichés and contrived circumstances, she uses realistic, relatable situations to create a world that readers will want to visit time and again." Publisher's Weekly, Starred Review

"Hegger's utterly delightful first Ghost Falls contemporary is what other romance novels want to grow up to be." – Publisher's Weekly, Best Books of 2017

"The very talented Hegger kicks off an enjoyable new series

set in the small Utah town of Ghost Falls. This charming and fun-filled book has everything from passion and humor to betrayal and revenge." – Jill M Smith, RT Books Reviews 2017 – Contemporary Love and Laughter Nominee

Becoming Bella
"Hegger excels at depicting familial relationships and friendships of all kinds, including purely platonic friendships between women and men. Tears, laughter, and a dollop of suspense make a memorable story that readers will want to revisit time and again." Publisher's Weekly, Starred Review

"…you have a terrific new romance that Hegger fans are going to love. Don't miss out!" Jill M. Smith – RT Book Reviews

Nobody's Fool

"Hegger offers a breath of fresh air in the romance genre." – Terri Dukes, RT Book Reviews

Nobody's Princess

"Hegger continues to live up to her rapidly growing reputation for breathing fresh air into the romance genre." – Terri Dukes, RT Book Reviews

"I have read the entire Willow Park Series. I have loved each of the books … Nobody's Princess is my favorite of all time." Harlequin Junkie, Top Pick

# LOVING LAURA

# Chapter One

Laura opened her office door and peered into the after-hours gloom of St. Peters Recreation Center. Her voice intruded loudly on the heavy silence. "There's nobody out there."

The note she had found pushed under her door earlier today had made her jumpier than usual. In the bright light of day, a note threatening to "shut her the fuck up" didn't frighten her, but with flickering fluorescent light doing creepy things to an already Bates Motel worthy corridor, her imagination was staging a takeover. At night, the old church recreation center echoed with the energy of the people who passed through during the day.

"You know you're ridiculous, right?" Her verbal butt kicking got her into the corridor. "It was only a note and it's not like it was the first either." She strongly suspected where the notes were coming from too. Thus far Cole Watts had done nothing but threaten, and there was a significant difference between threatening and doing. A difference that shrunk with each moment she spent in the abandoned corridor.

A large shape loomed out of the murkiness. "Hey, Miz Laura."

"Y-Uri." She got her hammering heart under control as

the tall, hulking silhouette of the rec center janitor moved into the scant light. "You scared me."

"I scared you, coz you shouldn't be here alone." Uri crossed his arms and rested them atop his large belly. "You know you shouldn't be here late, Miz Laura. Reverend Michael says nobody is to be here alone late at night. And you're a lady."

"I know, Uri." When he got that look on his face, she'd have more luck moving the entire rec center than arguing with him. "And you're right. Daniel offered to stay with me, but I didn't think I'd be that late and I lost track of time."

"Still." Uri shook his head, light playing off the shiny pink dome of his head. "You can't be here late."

"I know and you're right." Laura nodded. "And I'm on my way right this minute."

Uri hitched up his toolbelt. "Then I'll come with you."

"No, that's fine." Her car was parked right outside in the parking lot and sweet as he was, she didn't rate Uri's chances if something were to happen. "Isn't it *Supernatural* night?"

"Well, yes it is, Miz Laura, and this is nearly the last season and you know I don't like to miss it." He pointed to the exit door. "So, we need to get you into your car."

"I'll be fine, Uri." She patted his hand. "You go and watch your show."

Indecision played across his features. "But Reverend Michael said—"

"You offered, and I said no." Laura gave him a mental nudge. "You did well, Uri. You did the right thing."

His face cleared into a beaming smile. "I did ask. I did right."

"Yes, you did." She made a show of checking the time on her phone. "And if you go now, you'll have enough time to get your popcorn and soda ready for your show."

Uri nodded. "I like the double butter kind."

"Because that's the best kind." She smiled at him. "I'll be

fine from here." She inched open the exit door and pointed to her car sitting in a pool of yellow light. "See, there's my car, parked right under a light. I bet you I can be in my car and gone before you've even put your popcorn in the microwave."

Giggling, Uri shook his head. "No, you can't, Miz Laura. I live right downstairs and I already put my popcorn in the microwave. I opened the bag just right, and all I gotta do is press start."

Laura eased through the exit door. "Off you go then. I still think I can beat you."

"You're weird." Spinning, Uri lumbered away. "See you tomorrow, Miz Laura."

"See you tomorrow, Uri. You can tell me what Castiel does in this episode. You know how much I like him."

"I will, Miz Laura." Uri waved over his shoulder as he hurried away.

She hadn't lied to Uri. Daniel had offered to stay with her, but with their relationship status unsettled she chose not to muddy the waters. Working late together had led to late night coffees and the possibility of their being more between them. Recently that possibility had clarified itself into a no go. She really liked Daniel, what woman wouldn't, but he didn't do it for her.

The exterior door swung shut behind her with a gentle nudge on her butt and the solid *thunk* of the lock engaging.

Outside, the air carried the dusty leaves and woodsmoke smell of fall. The temperature had cooled, and she hurried across the small, cracked asphalt lot to her car.

"I wanna talk to you." A man appeared in front of her so suddenly she nearly ran into him. Cole Watts topped her five feet eight by half a head, and his bulky jacket framed wide shoulders.

She stopped, and her heart leaped into her throat for the second time in almost as many minutes. Unlike when she had identified Uri, however, her heart still fluttered nervously. Cole was scary and mean, and she was glad she'd sent Uri away. "Cole, hi." Her voice came out breathy, and she took a minute to gather herself. "Can't this wait for the morning? I'm happy to talk about whatever you need to speak to me about during normal office hours, but for now—"

"What I got to say won't take long." He crowded closer to her. "And I'll do the talking." He smirked and raked his gaze from her head to her toes. "You get to do the listening."

"All right." Given she was alone, in the dark, in a crappy part of town with a known criminal who liked to leave her scary notes, letting him have his say seemed her wisest course of action.

"You need to stop filling Karstyn's dumb fucking head with stupid shit." Cole jabbed a finger in her face.

Karstyn was one of the boys she worked with in her after school program. "I'm not sure what stupid, er, shit you're referring to."

Her car was less than twenty feet away, but the distance seemed to yawn longer.

"He ain't going to college." Cole stepped closer to her, forcing her to step back. "You hear me?"

"I hear you." Debating anything in an abandoned parking lot was a truly horrible idea, but for Karstyn, she had to try at least. "But Karstyn is a very bright boy, and there are some wonderful scholarship—"

"You don't listen real good, Miz Turner." He gripped her arm.

"Karstyn loves school." She tried to ease her arm free.

Cole tightened his grip. "Karstyn is fucking done with school. He can graduate, and then he needs to get his fucking ass to work."

Their parents had died ten years earlier, and Cole had been taking care of Karstyn. That would suggest Cole cared about his younger brother and would want the best for him.

"Karstyn is interested in pursuing a medical degree, and he's getting the grades to make that happen."

"I'm not making myself clear." Cole backhanded her.

Laura's ears rang, and there was a split second of numb before pain exploded along her jawline. He'd hit her, and her brain was slow catching up with that fact. She staggered two steps back, not knowing whether to run for her car or the rec center.

"Don't you fucking dare." Cole was on her before she could move. He grabbed her hair and yanked her head back.

"I only want what's best for Karstyn." Maybe she could still reason with him. "We both want what's best for him."

Pushing his face into hers, he yelled, "Get a fucking clue, bitch, and leave this shit alone." His face twisted into an ugly mask. "Karstyn ain't coming back here neither."

"Please." Laura wasn't sure if she was begging for Karstyn or herself, but things had gone horribly bad, and she was painfully aware of how alone she was. "Please don't do this."

"You begging me, bitch?" Cole forced her head back. "Don't matter who you are to start off with, all bitches end up begging."

"Cole." Beating back her panic, she used his name in a deliberate attempt to reach him. "You need to let me go. You came here to talk about Karstyn."

"Yeah, I did." He studied her face, his dark eyes glittering down at her. "And I sure as fuck got your attention now, don't I?"

Agreeing with him, not antagonizing him further seemed like the wisest course. "You have my attention."

His other hand clamped on her breast. "I like it when you beg. Do it again."

"Please." *Please don't hurt me. Please don't do this.*

He squeezed her breast and laughed. "Again."

Tears blurred her vision, and she tried to blink them away.

She was utterly alone. Even if she screamed, nobody would hear her. "P-please."

"Please what?" He licked his lips. Stale alcohol and cigarette breath filled her nostrils.

Her entire being focused on making it out of the situation as best she could, and she'd do what she must to make that happen. "Please don't hurt me."

Nails scratched her breastbone as he yanked down and ripped her shirt open. "Tell you what, Miz Turner." He laughed softly, hot breath hitting her face. "You be nice to me, and I'll be real nice to you."

"I tell you what," a man said as a huge shadow fell over her. "You get your fucking hands off her."

Cole looked past her head, up, and up some more. His Adam's apple bobbed as he swallowed. "Who the fuck are you?"

"Barrows," he said. "Brett Barrows."

The name registered, and she whimpered. She knew Brett Barrows. At least she knew his sister Blythe and his brother Blake and his baby sister Kim, who came to daycare at St. Peters.

Releasing her, Cole lurched back with his arms raised. "You and I don't got no beef, Barrows."

"We do now." Fury etched Brett's harsh features as he stepped around her.

Everything slowed, and her brain kept cycling details she knew about Brett Barrows, including that he was on parole, and in his time had been badder and meaner than Cole. Blythe said he was turning his life around. Getting into a fight wouldn't go well for him. She caught his forearm, her fingers stretched to accommodate its girth. "No. Don't."

With a frown, Brett glanced down at her hand on his arm.

"Fuck this." Seeing his chance, Cole spun and legged it across the parking lot.

Laura tightened her grip on Brett's arm. She couldn't let

him go. Being attacked was her fault. She shouldn't have been there alone and so late, and she should never have stopped to talk to Cole.

Cole leaped the chain-link fence at the back of the parking lot and dropped into the dark on the other side.

"He's gone." Brett peered into her face. "Are you okay?"

"Y-yes." Her teeth chattered so hard she could barely speak. Suddenly chilled, she grabbed the tattered ends of her shirt and tugged them over herself. "I'm f-fine."

"Ah hell!" Brett reached for her.

"I'm fine." At least that's what she tried to say, but it came out in a juddering sob that shook her entire body.

"You're not fine." Brett folded his huge arms around her and drew her against the wide expanse of his chest. "But you are safe now."

"Oh." Her purse slid from her shoulder and thudded to the ground. Of course she hadn't zipped it closed, and the contents spilled on the asphalt. From her position against Brett, Laura stared at a rolling lipstick tube.

Brett's deep bass voice rumbled against her ear. "You're okay, Miz Johnstone." He dipped his head near her ear and gentled his voice. "I got you."

"I'm p-perfectly f-fine." Entire body shakes rippled through her, and she couldn't make them stop.

"Uh-huh." Brett stroked her back with hands large enough to span her waist. "I can tell."

"I just need a minute to catch my breath." Her fingers tightened around the sides of his T-shirt and clung. At some point, she would need to let him go but as soon as the thought surfaced, the rest of her shouted it back down. She was safe.

Brett didn't seem to mind her limpet impersonation and kept stroking her back. Gradually, her breathing slowed to a more normal rhythm, and she was even able to pry her fingers off his shirt. Taking a deep breath, she stepped out of the warmth and security of his hold. "Thank you." It was a bit late but still needed saying. "For everything."

"You need to call Nate," he said.

"No." It came out more forcefully than she intended, and she modulated her tone. "I'm fine, and I don't want to risk Cole taking this out on Karstyn."

"Karstyn?" Brett crouched and picked up her bag.

Laura couldn't let him pick up all her crap, so she kneeled beside him. "His younger brother. That's what tonight was all about." She picked up her wallet and condo keys and dropped them in her bag.

Brett handed her a pack of Kleenex. "Miz Johnstone, I don't mean to upset you, but tonight might have started about his brother, but it sure as sh—hell didn't end that way."

"T-turner. I'm divorced. I'm also f-fine. He didn't do anything to me." If Brett hadn't come along, it could have gotten so much worse, and just thinking like that got her hands shaking again.

"Hey." Brett handed her a bottle of hand sanitizer and a packet of tampons. "What happened here wasn't nothing. You need to tell the sheriff."

"Nate has bigger concerns." It took her three tries to shove her things back in her bag. She forced herself to look at him. "He frightened me, nothing more. I'm just being stupid. He could do a whole lot worse to Karstyn."

"Stop a second." Brett lifted her chin with his fore and middle fingers and turned her face to the light. Frowning, he stroked his thumb along her jaw. "That's gonna leave a bruise."

With him so close, she could see how thick and dark his lashes were and the flecks of gold in his eyes. "It could have been a lot worse." She hated how her voice quavered, and how tears clogged in her throat. "You got here before anything bad could happen."

"What was he doing here?" His knuckle grazed her jaw.

"His brother is one of my kids. Well, not my kids but the kids I work with, and he wants me to stay away from him because he doesn't want him to go to college." The impotent futility of her position almost pushed her over the edge. "But Karstyn is bright. He's so clever. He could do anything. Anything."

Brett's face went harder than the asphalt beneath her knees. "He attacked you because he doesn't want his brother going to college?"

"Yes." Brett must have superhuman powers of perception to make sense of her word vomit. "I think he was only trying to scare me into staying away from Karstyn."

Brett raised his eyebrow. "This Cole jerk have a second name? Karstyn's brother and I need to have a conversation."

"No." She didn't like that determined gleam in Brett's eye. If she gave him Cole's second name, she had the feeling Brett would track him down. Nobody growing up in Ghost Falls didn't know about Brett Barrows and the explosive temper that had repeatedly landed him in prison. Her stupidity tonight in being alone and giving Cole the opportunity to approach her was not going to be the reason Brett went back to jail. "I just want to go home."

"Miz Turner." His gaze bored into her. "If you won't report this to Nate, I need a name from you."

She shook her head to emphasize her point. "No."

"If you don't tell me I'll find out another way."

"You can't." She grabbed his wrist as if she could stop him physically. "You can't."

He cocked his head. "Why not?"

There really was no polite way to say this. "You're on parole."

"What the fu—hell does that have to do with anything?" He looked truly fierce, but she wasn't frightened of him.

Laura got to her feet. "I'm not going to be the reason you go back to prison."

"Pretty sure that motherfu—son of a bitch would be the reason." He raised one large finger. "If he reported our chat, and he's not gonna do that. Not when I get through with him."

Dear Lord, it was going from bad to worse. She'd already done so much harm to everyone around her. She couldn't take one more crappy act on her conscience. "I'm begging you not to do this."

"Fu—dammit!" He scowled. "He put his hands on you. Nobody has the right to do that."

"I just want to go home and forget all about this."

Face inscrutable, he overshadowed her. "Okay, Miz Turner, but on one condition."

"What's your condition?"

"I promise to stay away from that motherfu—bastard, if you promise to stay away from him too."

In as much as her job allowed, but Brett didn't need to know that part, so she held out her hand. "Done."

"Deal." His huge palm engulfed hers.

Warm tingles ran up her arm, and she left her hand in his longer than required for a handshake. She forced her hand to open and let his go. "Thanks for the rescue." That sounded so lame. "And under the circumstances, I think you should call me Laura."

He smiled. "Laura."

The smile and her name out of his mouth pulled the plug on her brain and left very little to work with. "And you can say fuck in front of me. I've not only said it, I've done it as well."

# Chapter Two

Brett climbed in his truck and left Blake a voice message that he'd be late getting to their place.

Classy girls had always been his kryptonite. Ever since he'd first realized there was a them and us setup in Ghost Falls, which must have been around first grade because the Barrows kids hadn't made it to kindergarten. Instead, Barrows kids got to visit bars on their mother's hip, wreathed in a halo of cigarette smoke and recognizing the smell of alcohol from the moment their little brains came online.

He'd only come to pick up Kim's backpack from kindergarten where she'd left it this afternoon. On his way to the kindergarten he'd seen that motherfucking piece of shit with his hands all over Laura. His blood pounded with the familiar Barrows-man rhythm: *hurt them, make them pay.*

Streetlights flashed across Laura's face—delicate and flawless like fine crystal—as she eased her SUV into the empty road outside the church. Damn fool crusading woman to be working late in this neighborhood. Everything from her expensive SUV to her clean Chucks and her shiny hair announced her as a mark. He didn't get how a woman like that had been near enough to crap like her attacker for the attack to go down in the first place. Women like Laura belonged tucked away safely in their silk-lined lives with some suit bringing down a seven-figure income to keep her wrapped up tight.

Her trying so hard not to cry and lose her shit was branded into his brain, right alongside the feel of her tucked safely against him. The need to defend and level justice had near enough choked him. He didn't care what she believed. He knew he'd gotten there before that fucker raped her. Asshole like that was never getting close to something as good and classy as Laura Turner. He had thought to put his dirty hands on all that sparkle and make it filthy and stained like he was.

After putting his truck in gear, he dropped into her shadow. She actually thought he would leave her to go home on her own with that POS still out there somewhere. Even after she'd been attacked, he'd lay his left nut on the line she had no idea he was behind her. If women like her insisted on stepping outside their safe bubble, they needed to learn a few things about self-preservation. One, you don't work late in a fucked part of town when nobody else was around. Two, you check your mirrors for a strange vehicle sitting pretty in your slipstream.

She'd had the crap scared out of her and didn't need him picking on her. Victim blaming is what his sister Blythe called it. At least he thought that's what his sister had said. A man who had seen most of his twenties and thirties in and out of the state's hospitality tended to fall behind on trends.

*Trends.* He had to laugh at himself. The only consistent trend in his life had been about persuading a group of evil badasses that he was eviler and badder than them. It had become habit, and Laura should have run from him, not tried to save his worthless ass from getting into more crap by screwing up his parole. Damn woman should have been spending that time and effort worrying about herself.

That last comment about how he could say fuck in front of her…her eyes had gone wide before she'd hotfooted for her car with her cheeks burning.

For a moment, he'd almost gone with the unholy desire to fuck with her, but then he'd remembered who she was. Or more importantly, what she was.

He'd ask around tomorrow and get that last name he wanted. Pay the fucker a visit and remind him it wasn't okay to smack women around. Brett's gut twisted on his hypocrisy. Who the fuck was he to stand in judgment of anyone? In fact, the biggest, nastiest piece of shit in Ghost Falls was currently on Laura Turner's tail.

When she turned left on Route 20 and not right and up to the expensive houses clinging to the brow of the mountains behind Ghost Falls, he nearly lost her. He'd been sitting in the right lane, waiting for her to return to the magic kingdom of country clubs and private schooling, orthodontists and plastic surgeons, personal trainers and fancy foreign nannies.

Cutting across two lanes, he flipped the bird to the college kid in his new foreign dick extension. Red-faced and ready to lay down, College wound down his window at the next light.

Brett wound down his window and let College feast his eyes on every fuck-ugly, head-shaved, mean-eyed inch of his face.

College drove off, proving the money his parents were spending on his education was not entirely wasted.

He caught up to Laura as she took a right into a neat condo development. It was a perfectly respectable place with pretty duplexes sharing a strip of green lawn, but not what he'd been expecting.

Brett didn't listen to gossip, a lifetime of being the subject of it had cured him of that, but Eric Evans and Laura went way back somehow, and now Blythe was with Eric, and Blythe talked. Then you had Eric being Matt's brother and Matt being married to Pippa St. Amor—Turner when she wasn't on television—who was Laura's sister. Blythe also worked for Pippa on her television show, *Your Best You*. And if that wasn't enough, his kid brother, Wheeler, worked for Diva St. Amor, and Jesus, could that broad talk, and Laura was her granddaughter.

There you had Ghost Falls in a nutshell. Everybody knew everybody else and were all up in each other's business. So, yes, he'd heard rumors Laura had lost out in her divorce. Not that it was any business of his, and if he wanted to know, he'd straight up ask Laura.

She parked and sat in her car doing whatever the hell it was women did in their cars in the five hours it took to park, turn off the ignition and get out of the damn car.

His phone buzzed with a text. Nobody used these damn phones to call each other anymore. Blythe had sent him a text loaded with pictures. There was the man with the red face and horns, who looked royally pissed, flames or a small campfire, and then another face with steam coming out its nose. Brett didn't always know what those things meant, and surely didn't care to find out—hadn't the species evolved from the days of talking through pictures—but Blythe's words had a crystal meaning that made him feel like his face had turned bright red and steam was coming out his nostrils.

Blythe: *Pat is back at the house.*

"Motherfucker." Brett needed to hurry Laura into her condo and make sure she was safe. He had places he needed to be, a reality that didn't like to be ignored. Pat was back, and it bore saying again, "Mother. Fucker."

Once out of his truck, he jogged across the parking lot to Laura's car and knocked on the driver's window.

She turned her face, all eyes, at him and gaped.

With no business to even be noticing, he still liked her eyes. They were large and green and tilted up at the corners like a startled kitten. She had the typical pale skin of a redhead, and it looked soft and silky, begging his touch.

She opened her window. "Are you following me?"

"Yup." He stood back before he gave her a heart attack. She'd had enough shocks for one night. "Needed to see you got home safe."

Frowning, she looked at his truck. "You followed me from the church to make sure I got home safely?"

"Uh-huh." He opened her door. They were running out of time here. Pat was home, and Brett well knew his father's reign would spread nothing but shit and damage in the shortest of time. "You need to get inside."

"I beg your pardon?" The neatest, classiest scowl wrinkled her perfect brow.

Brett amped up the badass. "You need to get inside. Now."

"Oh. Okay." She gathered up her things and stepped out of her car.

Brett waited until she was halfway down the tidy brick walkway before he said, "Lock it."

"What?" She stared at him.

"Your car." He jabbed his thumb at it. He'd put it down to shock that she'd forgotten to lock her car, but his gut whispered she did that often. "You need to lock it."

A splash of color crossed her cheeks. "This development is quite safe."

"Lock it." He held her gaze to make sure she got the message. "I gotta go."

"Please don't let me keep you." She beeped the locks and marched away from him.

Class or not, what Laura Turner's ass did to a pair of jeans was worth writing country songs about.

She stopped suddenly and took a deep breath, her slim shoulders riding up and then down. "Mr. Barrows?"

"Brett will do just fine."

"Brett." She peeked over her shoulder. "I…um…never

mind." She squared her shoulders and marched to her front door.

Trying to fit the keys in the lock, she dropped them and crouched to get them.

He got to them first. "Want me to make sure you get in okay?"

She nodded, the relief on her face gripping his lungs and squeezing.

"How about I check around inside as well?" He should have realized she'd still be afraid. "Make sure everything is okay. All windows and doors locked."

She peered up at him with those cat eyes. "Would you?"

"Yep." He might invade a small country for those eyes, or rip the moon from the sky to have her look at him like she was right now, like she needed his felonious, badass self. Embarrassed about the direction his thoughts had taken, his next words came out brusquer than he'd intended. "Let's do this. I got somewhere to be."

"Oh." She flushed and cleared her throat. "Never mind. You've done enough for me for one night. I can—"

"Had five minutes, got four now." He slid her keys from her slack grip and opened her door. "Wait here."

"But—"

"First I'm going through the whole place and gonna make sure there's nobody here. Then I'll check all your doors and windows." He brushed past her into the house. Again it surprised him. It was modest and respectable but far from the palace he'd expected her to live in.

"No!" She slid into the hallway. "I'd rather wait here."

The woman had been attacked, and of course she didn't want to stand on her doorstep all alone in the middle of the night. He was such a dumbass. "Stay in the kitchen."

"I will." Still clutching her bags to her chest, she nodded.

Her fragility and vulnerability made him feel like Godzilla.

"And you really shouldn't let convicted criminals you hardly know into your home."

The house was decorated in tasteful shades of beige and white. He'd bet Laura had decorated in what Blythe informed him were neutrals. It looked good and restful. Clean lines, comfortable looking furniture. Upstairs were two bedrooms, one all purple and sparkly shit that he guessed belonged to Laura's girl. The other was covered in hockey posters and had a hockey league cover on the bed.

Brett approved of the kid's choices of hockey players. He knew Mark Crowe of course, defense for the LA Strikers. The other guy was a Canadian who played for Ottawa. The guy had a mean cross-check and didn't back down from a fight.

Downstairs, he quickly checked the large open floor plan before joining Laura in the kitchen. "All good."

"Thanks." She blinked up at him. "For everything."

A smile got away from him before he could stop it. "You're welcome."

"I…you…just—"

"You're scared, and you got reason to be." The need to comfort her pulsed in his blood, and he touched the cream silk of her cheek. "That was a shitty thing that happened to you tonight, but you're okay now. There's nobody here—I even looked under the beds and in the closets—and the house is locked up tight."

Her cheeks flushed but she didn't push his hand away. "I don't know what would have happened if you hadn't come along tonight."

He had a damn good idea, but she didn't need to hear that now. "But I did, and you're safe."

"Yes." She slid her arms around his waist and pressed her cheek to his chest. "Thank you."

His voice gummed in his throat, and by the time he got over the surprise enough to hug her back, she'd stepped out of his arms and stood there blushing.

Now he felt like a heel. "You should report it."

"You know why I can't."

"I know why you think you can't." The bruise forming on her cheek and jaw said something different. After he'd tossed Pat's ass back into the cesspit he'd emerged from, Brett would definitely be nosing around. Laura Turner was a unicorn in their world. She was untouchable, and Brett aimed to make sure that asshole from the rec center understood that good.

She folded her arms and raised her chin. "If he gets nasty with Karstyn, there is nobody to take care of Karstyn."

"Sugar." Once more giving in to the need to touch her, he cupped her face between his palms and forced her to look at him. "I came across somebody getting nasty with you, and that gives me a vested interest in making sure nothing like this happens to you again."

She had the most perfect mouth he'd ever seen. It was full and lush and begged a man to dip his head and taste. Brett yanked that thought train off the tracks. She was so far out his league it was laughable.

"I can't." Her breathing quickened and her gaze flickered to his mouth, lingered, and came back up to his eyes. "And I'm begging you not to do so, either. Please."

When she looked at him like that, he would promise her the world. "Okay." Pride made him add, "But I'm not happy about it."

# Chapter Three

Ah, hell no!

Brett let himself into the kitchen of the Barrows family house. With its chipped linoleum floor, cracked tile countertops and crappy sagging cabinets, it told the story of their family's dysfunction; the hole punched through one cabinet, never repaired, the person-size missing chunk of drywall, the knife marks in the scarred kitchen table. A huge reason for that dysfunction was currently sitting at the kitchen table letting Brett's mother fuss around him.

Not in a million years would he ever call Pat his father. Sperm donation didn't make a man a father, and nobody was a better example of that than Pat Barrows. Brett hadn't seen Pat since he'd gone down the last time, and then Pat had only visited him while he was awaiting trial to hit Brett up for money.

"Evening, son." Pat sat back in his chair and smirked.

Bloat and broken blood vessels of a longtime alcoholic marred Pat's boyish good looks. Not that Carly saw it. Pat was the love of her life, and she clung to him with a tenacity that defied all reason. Almost forty years they'd been together, long enough for any woman to see the pattern.

"Hey, Mom." He kissed Carly's cheek. "You okay?"

"I'm fine. Good. Wonderful." Wringing her hands, Carly gave him a nervous smile. "How are you?"

How was he? Fucking pissed might cover it. Red hot with rage would be more like it. He checked his temper and took several deep breaths. Losing it would make him no better than the piece of shit that had sired him. Brett kept his shit under wraps these days. Especially since the last time he'd lost it had nearly cost him his sister's love. He still thanked whatever god was watching that Blythe had forgiven him.

"What are you doing here, Pat?" He shoved his hands in his pockets.

Pat waved his cutlery in the air. "Having dinner."

Carly had let him back in the house and cooked him dinner. She never cooked anymore. When they were kids, she'd barely done so, and now that the littlest Barrows sibling, Kim, was safe and living with Blythe, she didn't bother at all. Until Pat came around, and then it was all domestic bliss.

"You're not welcome here anymore." Brett stared down at Pat.

Bo slid into the kitchen and stopped and gaped at Pat. "What the fuck is he doing here?"

"My question exactly." Brett pinned his younger brother with a stare. He'd told them to let him know if Pat came sniffing around. That he'd had to hear it from Blythe meant they'd not been telling him shit. "You were supposed to let me know if he showed his face here."

"I didn't know." Palms up, Bo backpedaled. "I've been pulling extra shifts on site. Want to get me a place of my own."

Brett believed him. Not because anybody with a trace of brain should believe a word that came out of Bo's mouth, but because Bo was too scared of him to even try to lie to him.

Leaning over in his chair, Pat slapped Carly on the ass.

"Hate to disagree with you, son, but looks like I'm very welcome."

Brett breathed deep, once, twice, three times and still his temper simmered, spat and crackled beneath his skin. Pat putting his hands on Carly was like a dead man's switch in his brain. "Get your fucking hands off her."

"She's my wife." Pat folded his arms and stuck his chin out. "Got rights to put my hands on her whenever I want."

Pat would think that too.

"Yeah, her medical records tell that story loud and clear, you old son of a bitch." Brett leaned on his knuckles and got right up in Pat's face. "But you touch her again and I'll be the one you deal with." Pat had learned that he didn't want to deal with him when Brett had turned fourteen and gotten big enough to drive the point home with his fists.

Pat shoveled meat and potatoes in his face as his cunning little brain went through the variables of the situation. Meat and potatoes one of his kids had paid to put on the table.

With the survival instincts of a cockroach, Pat had spent his lifetime working out when he could push and when he needed to back off. This time he rejected confrontation. His expression melted into one of guilt and self-recrimination. "I've changed, son. Did a lot of thinking while I was away this time, and I want to do right by my family."

Like fucking hell.

But Pat interpreted his silence as softening and went for the jugular. "You know what that's like, Brett. Everyone tells me how you've changed too. That you're not the same nasty, mean bastard you were."

Classic Pat to work an insult into his appeal for clemency. Also, and not to quibble, but Brett's "change" had cost him years of soul searching, years of taking accountability and years of group therapy. He hadn't suddenly woken up and changed, and neither had Pat. "You haven't changed," he said. "You're still as much of an asshole now as you were."

"Hey!" Pat pounded the table. "You watch your fucking mouth."

Carly flinched and ducked out of fist range.

And damned if something in Brett didn't startle to attention as well. When he'd been a kid, Pat hadn't stopped at smacking Carly around. If Brett closed his eyes, he could still feel the open-handed blows across his face and head, and as he grew older and bigger, the fists to his gut and chest. Always out of sight so the school wouldn't report Pat. That he still flinched instinctively, even deep inside, nearly ripped Brett's anger out of control. He fisted Pat's shirt and dragged him out of his seat. "Or what, motherfucker? What are you going to do about it?

Pat must have caught Brett's reflexive flinch because he chose bluster over good sense. "You're not so tough, you cocky shit."

"No?" Brett's voice went silky smooth. "Why don't you try me and find out?"

He'd love to take Pat apart piece by festering piece.

Carly grabbed his arm and tugged. "No fighting, please. We're all back together again. We should celebrate."

"I'm not celebrating with him." Bo sneered at Pat. "And he's not drinking my beer either."

"I am if it's in my fridge," Pat snatched the can away before Bo could grab it.

"We should have a drink together." Carly fluttered her hands, smiling like it was the happiest day of her life. "Let's have a drink to celebrate your father being home."

Not able to produce a word, Brett shook his head. This was how it always went. Pat arrived home from wherever the hell he'd been, and Carly fell into his arms, ecstatic to have him back. Pat always played his part perfectly, the penitent husband, the prodigal returning. He would play nice until the money pool dried up, and then the beatings would start. Now that Blythe had taken Kim and Wheeler out of the house, it was only Carly that Pat could still hit without being hit back.

Fists on flesh had been the soundtrack to his childhood, and it had played over and over again. Pat would stay until life got uncomfortable for him and then he'd split, often leaving Carly with a belly full of another kid when he did.

After Kim, the doctors had told Carly no more children. Honestly, Brett wouldn't put money on her listening. The same doctors had been telling her she needed to quit smoking and drinking, especially when she was pregnant, but Carly had yet to listen. That you couldn't save someone from themselves was the hardest reality to accept.

Like now, Carly would let Pat back in the house, feed him, fuss over him and have him back in her bed. As much as he and Blythe, even his one sister-in-law, Dixie, tried to talk to Carly, it wouldn't change shit until Carly woke the hell up.

Brett had years ago given up on Carly seeing the light. For whatever twisted reason, she chose life with Pat over no Pat every single, goddamn time.

Worst case scenario, Pat would go too far one day with his beatings. If the next kid he gave her didn't finish the job for him. Carly was a crap mother. Straight up, useless. Maybe he was more like her than he cared to admit because even despite that, Brett couldn't give up on her and leave her to reap what she'd sown.

"How many days sober you got now?" Brett said to Carly. Another thing he had no control of until she chose to take care of it.

Carly winced, and Brett knew what that meant. "It's a special occasion, baby. Just one drink to celebrate."

"Only it's not one drink with you." Brett still had to try. "You know that because you're an addict. Your addiction is telling you it'll be only one, but we both know it doesn't work like that."

Pat grabbed Carly's hand and pulled her closer to him.

Face soft and eyes filled with love, he said, "You do what makes you happy, my lady. Nobody's got a right to tell you what you can and cannot do."

Really? Brett rather thought his shitty childhood gave him at least a say there, or perhaps the money he contributed to the household. Pat didn't want Carly healthy and making clear-eyed choices, because a sober and clean Carly might one day choose not to take his sorry ass back again.

Brett used the only leverage he had. "He doesn't stay here," he said to his mother.

"But this is his home. His family is here." Carly put her hand on Pat's shoulder.

Pat gazed up at her. "There's my beautiful lady. Still got that heart of gold."

"I don't care." Brett hated hurting his mother, but Carly was her own worst enemy. "And I pay the bills on this house and put food in that refrigerator. If he stays here, that stops."

Carly gaped at him.

"Come on, son." Pat tried the jolly old man routine. "We both know you're not the kind of man to let your own father starve."

Nope, one of them knew he was exactly that sort of man. "I mean it." He looked at Bo. "You let him finish his meal, and then you sling him out. Got it?"

"Got it." Bo looked more than happy to comply. Yeah, Bo had grown up in the Carly and Pat shit show as well. When Brett had first got out, Bo had been pulling the same useless, lazy shit he'd been doing for years. Lately though, Bo had been making changes, sticking to the job Brett had gotten him at Evans Construction, taking care of stuff around the house when it needed doing, and contributing to the expenses. Brett hadn't even had to beat his ass in months.

Bo sneered at Pat. "Eat up, old man. It might be the last free meal you have in a while."

"This is my house." Pat pounded the table again.

Carly ran for cover and huddled in the farthest corner of the kitchen, next to the broken and lopsided passthrough that was supposed to connect to the dining room. It had been broken since Bo had shoved a drunken Becker through it when they were teens.

"You two dumbasses don't got no say here." Pat glared at Brett and Bo.

Brett nearly laughed in his face. The asshole was straight up delusional. He nodded to Bo. "I'll see you later." He pointed at the hutch. "You think you can fix that?"

"For sure." Bo jerked his chin. "And don't worry about the trash in the kitchen. I got it."

Brett clapped him on the shoulder. Bo had even been venturing into personal hygiene. Probably meant there was a woman involved. "I know you do."

As he strode for the door, Pat called after him. "You let Blythe and little Kimmy know that I'll be around to see them. Say hi."

Red washed his vision, and Brett grabbed hold of the stair rail and held. The wood cracked in his grip as he struggled to control his temper. Pat was baiting him, and he didn't need to take the lure. He could walk away from this. Except, Pat needed to hear him and hear him good, so he strode back into the kitchen.

"You go near Blythe or Kim, and I'll kill you." Brett meant every word. He didn't have much in his younger years to be proud of, but for a while there, before he'd gotten himself eyeball deep in shit, he'd managed to stop Pat from taking his fists to Blythe. He almost didn't mind the beatings he'd taken for her, knowing he was taking them instead of her. Then later, when Blythe had started growing into the sort of beauty Pat had gotten a notion to monetize, Brett had put a stop to that right fucking fast.

Pat swallowed but held his gaze.

The bravado didn't fool Brett. Pat was going to have to

change his shorts when he left. As long as it kept him from Blythe and Kim, Brett was good. He got back in Pat's face. "Do you hear me, motherfucker?"

"I hear you."

"Good." Brett left then. So far, he'd managed to keep it together. Any longer, and he might make good on his threat to Pat right away.

His phone rang as he was getting into his truck. His brother-in-law, Eric Evans, saving him the call he would have made. "Eric," he said by way of greeting.

"Brett," Eric said. "I'm glad I got you."

"Yeah?" He slammed his truck door and wished Pat's head had been in it.

"Can you meet me for a drink?"

Eric wouldn't be asking for nothing. "Where?"

"Cranks?"

And Brett chuckled picturing his smoother than silk brother-in-law in the biker dive bar. But Eric dug the place, and being the charming mofo he was, had even gotten tough old Cruze behind the bar eating out of his hand. "I'll be about ten."

"See you then."

Brett stopped him before he could hang up. "You've heard the news?"

"Pat's back." Eric sighed. "You at the house?"

"Yep."

Eric grunted. "Do I need to remind you you're on parole, or do I need to bring the lime and the shovels?"

It would be funny, except Brett was sorely tempted anyway. "That all you called for?"

"Wow!" Eric chuckled. "I forget what a silver-tongued charmer you are."

This time Brett had to crack a smile. God alone knew how or why, but he and Eric dug each other. They couldn't be more different. Brett strongly suspected his brother-in-law had regular manicures but if Eric didn't tell him, he didn't have to get his head around it. "So?"

"Meet me at Cranks." Eric hung up.

With nothing better to do, and the temptation of beating Pat into a bloody pulp still lurking, Brett got into his truck and drove to Cranks. The truck looked a whole lot better than when he'd bought it. His brother Ben had a knack with engines and had been helping him. Thing still looked like shit, but it ran smooth.

Eric was already there when Brett arrived, his fancy black sedan standing out like dog balls in the rutted earth parking lot.

Cranks was a seedy dive bar in a small town and looked it. Black paint peeled from the cinder block exterior, peppered with the leftover scraps of thousands of posters and flyers. The sign blinked and flickered its way to imminent electronic death. Someone had chucked something at it and broken the outer tube of the N until it more resembled a V. It would stay that way from now on and blend into the fog of crappy hanging over the place.

Seated at the bar, Eric had Razor by his side as he fastidiously wiped the neck of his beer bottle. His brother-in-law was a smart guy.

Beside him, six seven in his socks with barn door shoulders, Razor looked like he was part of the decorating scheme. Thick dark tattoo lines disappeared into a T-shirt straining over the pounds and pounds of muscle that made up Razor. He looked mean. He looked like a bad man to cross. And he was. Until you knew him better, and then you got that Razor wasn't exactly a teddy bear, but more of a pit bull: capable of inflicting damage but loyal to a fault.

Razor spotted him first and nodded.

Eric turned and smiled his greeting. Dude was a good-looking son of a bitch. No wonder Blythe had been hooked on him for so long. He stood and shook Brett's hand. "Thanks for coming."

Razor lifted his chin. Brett lifted his back. Their standard greeting to establish they were each okay, but not great. Since Razor had lost his job as a bouncer a month earlier and was struggling to find something else, him being only okay didn't surprise Brett. And since this was Ghost Falls and news traveled at light speed, Razor would already know that Pat was back and understood all that meant.

Eric ordered him a beer and got a fresh one for himself and Razor. "Got an idea for the two of you."

Raising an eyebrow, Razor looked at him and then Eric. "This legal?"

"Please." Eric shook his head. "I'd have invited you to one of those classy places on the ski hills if we were going to talk about breaking the law."

Razor laughed and Brett with him. Along with his news anchor good looks, Eric was one charming motherfucker. "I already work for you," Brett said.

"This is true, but working as a security grunt is a waste of all you have to offer." Eric wiped the neck of his new beer before he sipped. "And this job is not from me."

"Who then?" Razor bristled.

"The diva," Eric said and jerked his head in the direction of Ghost Falls's one and only mansion, and the home of Diva Philomene St. Amor. In her time, the diva had sung in every major opera house in the world. She was an opera legend who'd been born right here in Ghost Falls. She had come home for her retirement and built the weird Addams family via Westeros style monstrosity she lived in.

Eric's older brother had been in charge of the building. Brett and Matt had gone to school together. Ended up in a bunch of the same classes, given Matt's habit of excelling school and Brett's of failing it. He'd even played defense when Matt was high school QB. Brett had never been that close to that much raw football talent. It had bought Matt a free-ride scholarship to college.

Then old man Evans had died of a heart attack, and Matt had caught the hospital pass. He'd turned his back on a shining future and taken care of his family. At the time Brett had wanted to punch Matt Evans in his perfect, talented throat. He hadn't understood how anyone could turn down a future that bright. But he got it now. There were times in life when you had to do what you had to do, dig deep and tackle the hard shit.

It was after old man Evans's death that Blythe and Eric had first drifted into each other's lives. All of that was ancient history now, but it still proved how far apart the Evans and Barrows families had been, and now they were all up in each other's business.

"What's the job?" Brett cut to the chase.

"It's to do with Laura," Eric said.

Brett blinked, wondering if his thoughts of her had manifested the words coming out Eric's mouth. "What?"

"Laura." Eric looked at him quizzically. "Pippa's sister."

"I know who she is," Brett said. Man oh man, did he ever. "What's she got to do with this job?"

"Phi, that's the diva, is worried about Laura working in that part of town." Eric grimaced.

"She heard about that already?" Of course she had, because this was Ghost Falls.

Eric stilled and looked at him. "Heard about what?"

"Damn." Brett should have kept his mouth shut, but with Eric having that look in his eye, the one that meant he was chasing this to death, he may as well lay it out. "Earlier tonight I caught some asshole giving her a tough time."

Stilling, Eric didn't look so tame and sophisticated anymore. "Is she okay?"

"Yep. I got there and chased the son of a bitch away." Then he turned to Razor. Razor had mad connections in all kinds of places. "You know a kid called Karstyn who goes to the rec center?"

"Is that who attacked Laura?" Eric had the sort of still a rattler got before it struck.

"No." He didn't want Eric going off half-cocked. "I didn't hear all that he said to Laura, but the dickhead who attacked her was the kid's older brother."

"Ah!" Razor knocked his knuckles on the bar. "That kid'll be Karstyn Watts. He's a good kid. His brother is a bona fide asshole. Name of Cole."

"That's the one then." He looked at Razor, and Razor nodded. They would be paying Cole Watts a visit.

Watching them, Eric sipped his beer. "Tell me that look is not what I think it is."

"It's not what you think it is." Brett motioned Cruze for a beer.

"You're lying." Eric shook his head. "You can't go after him, Brett."

Brett didn't see any can't about it, but he wasn't going to waste his breath arguing.

Eric proved his smarts when he played the one card Brett couldn't toss. "Blythe will never forgive either of us if you go back to prison. She needs you, Brett." Then like the evil shit he was, Eric said, "Don't you think she's spent enough of her life without her big brother to back her?"

Hissing like a deflating tire, Razor chuckled. "He's got you there."

"The diva's job for you has just gotten bigger. I was going to tell you about some dickhead who was making threats, nasty letters, texts, that sort of thing." Eric shook his head. "Either Laura's got more than one asshole on her tail or the same guy just upped the stakes. The diva wants Laura kept safe, and she's prepared to pay good money to make her so."

Razor squinted at Eric. "Like a protection detail?"

"More of a keeping an eye on her type of thing." Eric

grimaced. "Making sure what happened tonight doesn't happen again."

Frowning, Razor shook his head. "I'm not sure—"

"We'll do it." If he couldn't go after the prick, Brett could make sure Cole stayed way, way, way away from Laura. "And tell Miz St. Amor to keep her money."

# Chapter Four

Laura parked close to the rec center the following morning. She hadn't slept well the night before, what with the attack, and then collapsing all over Brett Barrows like some forties-movie-style helpless dame.

She couldn't even fathom what someone like Brett must've thought of her weeping all over his admittedly lovely chest. The man probably chewed nails with his morning cornflakes.

Three a.m. had seen her up and baking. The least she could do is thank Brett in some way for being so good to her. Before getting out of her car, she checked all around her. Her hands shook a little as she gathered her things and locked her car. She did another scan of the area before she fast walked into the rec center and got her day started.

As she'd feared, Karstyn didn't come to group that day, and she left a message for Daniel. She didn't want to tell him what had happened last night, but she might have to for Karstyn's sake.

Telling herself she wasn't being a coward, she approached Blake Barrows.

Blake Barrows was sitting on a bench in the middle of the small rec center lawn as he waited for his ride. She could wait beside him and give Brett her thank you herself, but she was too embarrassed after her reaction last night.

"Hi, Blake." She stopped with her Tupperware clutched to her chest.

He looked up at her and smiled. "Hey, Laura."

"Umm…" She felt a bit silly now. "Brett coming to pick you up?"

Blake had been coming to Daniel's group for a couple of months. A few months before Brett had found him and brought him back to Ghost Falls, he'd skipped town after cleaning out Blythe's bank account.

"Like he does every day." Blake gave her a smile so reminiscent of Blythe it was almost uncanny.

From what Daniel had told her in confidence, Brett had broken his parole, hunted his brother down. Ghost Falls's sheriff, Nate Evans, had turned a blind eye and persuaded Brett's parole officer to do the same.

"Could you give him this?" She shoved the Tupperware at Blake before she changed her mind. Everyone liked brownies, right? Saying thank you was the right thing to do.

Blake took the box and frowned down at it. "What is it?"

"Only some brownies." She didn't want to get into a full explanation. "He did me a favor, and this is my way of saying thank you. There's a note for him inside."

At first Blake gaped at her, and then his face split into a wide grin. "You baked Brett brownies?"

She'd been right. This was stupid. She should never have done it. What would someone big, bad and tough like Brett Barrows want with baked goods? She reached for the box. "No. I mean I did, but it's stupid so I'll—"

"He loves brownies." Blake winked at her. "I've just never known anyone bake him anything."

"Oh." She eyed the box Blake held loosely. She could still grab it and make a run back to her office. "It's nothing. Just some brownies."

"You should give them to him yourself." Blake jerked his head. "That's him now."

The only thing worse than having been stupid enough to bake Brett Barrows brownies, was having to see his face as she gave them to him. "Nope." She moved as fast as she could without out and out running. "You give them to him. I'm late. Late for a meeting. A really important meeting."

Laura didn't slow until she reached her office and shut the door. Pressing her back against the door, she forced herself to take a couple of deep, soothing breaths. This was ridiculous. She was behaving worse than her fourteen-year-old daughter, Daisy, with a crush.

About six four and built like he hefted school buses around for fun, Brett was all muscle and one hundred percent intimidating badass. The sort of badass she should have bought a bottle of whisky or a case of beer to say thank you to, but it was done now. Blake would give him the brownies, and they could both put last night behind them.

Staying out of view, she eased up beside the window and peeked out.

Brett climbed out of the pickup and strolled toward Blake. He wore another one of those muscle loving T-shirts and jeans that cupped his ass.

It was more than the sheer size of him and the whole big, bad, mean and moody thing he had going. There was this quality of impenetrability about Brett, like nothing could break him, and nothing could bend him.

The two brothers shook hands and stood speaking.

Blake said something, and Brett laughed.

God, that smile was so unfair. It creased up the serious, no bullshit lines of his face and reminded you that badass Brett was a very handsome man. Blythe said he looked more like their father than their mother. Carly Barrows had once been the most beautiful girl in Ghost Falls in her youth. And despite all the bad choices weighing the Barrows clan down, she had made some beautiful children.

Blythe was straight up gorgeous.

And Brett—Laura sighed—if Brett made a move on you there would be no doubt about it. She could just imagine those hazel eyes fixing on her with keen interest. Crowds would part for those huge shoulders as he made a beeline. Brett would allow nothing in his way if he fixed on a woman.

She was so pathetic. Laura pressed her palms into her eyes and forced herself away from the window. Brett probably liked capable, no bullshit women who could fend for themselves, not a wilting flower who asked him to check under her bed for monsters.

And Laura forced herself to turn and get back to coloring in her posters for a youth social.

A knock on her door startled her. "Come in."

"Hey." Daniel pushed open her door and gave her his awesome smile. "You left a message for me?"

"Yes. It's about Karstyn Watts." Despite Daniel's smile, her pulse stayed normal. She liked Daniel, really liked Daniel, but not in that way. They'd been on a date or two, ran into each other almost daily, but that spark wasn't there. She suspected not for him either.

Hands in his pockets, he sauntered into her office and looked at her poster. "This for the social?"

"Yeah." She looked at her poster. It didn't completely suck. "I know the kids barely look up from their phones, but I'm going old school anyway."

"Old school." He winked. "I like it." Daniel also had hazel eyes but his were browner than Brett's. Daniel had also served time, but had turned his life around, gotten his degree while still in prison and turned his experience with addiction and crime into a great way of helping at-risk teens.

Not that Laura had any grounds to judge either one of them.

She'd made a couple of clangers for mistakes and had ended up with community service. Not even she could have predicted she would like her community service so much that once it was over, she would start working on the same team as Daniel.

Like all towns, Ghost Falls had the charming picturesque front they showed to the tourists. A few blocks away from the gorgeous town hall and Memorial Park, St. Peters church marked the transition to the seedier underbelly of Ghost Falls.

She and Daniel worked out of St Peters on a program paid for by the good tax paying citizens of Ghost Falls. Like similar programs across the country, the demand way outstripped the supply of services, and they were under-funded, overworked and fighting an uphill battle.

"So." Daniel propped his hips on her desk. "Is this the sort of conversation we can have over dinner?"

They really needed to talk their tepid relationship through before it impacted their working environment, but for now she took the conveniently hovering excuse. "I really can't. I have to finish this, and I have Daisy and Sam tomorrow, so I want to get home and tidy up. Maybe bake something."

At least her kids appreciated her baking. She should have stuck to baking for them. It's amazing how things that seemed like a good idea at three a.m., really came up as stupid in the harsh light of day.

Her biggest failure had been to her children by not giving them a mother they could look up to, and her actions had been the major reason she'd split from Patrick. She'd done that to her children, and for some reason she always felt like she needed to bake or mend something. It was like she was trying to win mothering points back. It was pathetic.

Daniel looked at her as if he might call bullshit and then nodded. "Raincheck?"

"For sure." They really did need to talk and soon. "We've got a big problem with Karstyn."

Daniel raised his eyebrow and waited.

"I had a run in with Cole Watts last night." She kept it light.

Frowning, Daniel folded his arms. "And by run in, you mean…"

"He cornered me in the parking lot." She wasn't going into details. "He doesn't want Karstyn in the after-school program anymore."

Daniel was no dummy, and he studied her intently. "When did he corner you?"

"It doesn't matter." She waved a dismissive hand. "The important part is that we need to find a way to get Karstyn back in the program. He's looking seriously at college—"

"When, Laura?" Daniel's easy going exterior concealed an iron will.

"Last night. I was working late and—"

Daniel stepped closer to her. "Did he hurt you?"

"No, he—"

"He tried." Brett took up her entire doorway. "I got there before the idea could grow."

Laura's pulse leaped into overdrive, and heat climbed her cheeks. Her voice came out breathless and girly. "Really, I'm fine. As I said last night."

"How bad?" Daniel turned his back on her and addressed Brett. Like she didn't even exist.

"Bad enough that she shouldn't be working late and alone." Brett stared at Daniel as if he was to blame for what Cole had done. He had her Tupperware tucked next to his hip.

She really needed to put a stop to the testosterone stinking up the room before it escalated, so she stepped between the two men. "This is not necessary. Cole got a bit aggressive, Brett chased him away."

Daniel studied her face and scowled at Brett. "She get that bruise from Cole?

"It's noth—"

"Yup." Brett nodded. "She also got it because she was left alone here at night."

Now Brett was taking this too far. "Daniel offered to stay, and Michael wasn't even—"

"You're right." Daniel stuck his chin out. "It won't happen again."

"What are you talking about?" Laura stared at Daniel. "I often work—"

"Damn straight it won't." Brett leaned into Daniel. "Because I'm going to make sure it doesn't."

What did that mean? Laura gaped at him. "What do—"

"You're going to make sure of that?" Daniel squared up to Brett like he had no idea of self-preservation. "And who the hell are you in all this?"

Oh, God, they might fight. Their aggression was making her jumpy. "This really isn't—"

"I'm the one who's making it my problem."

"Is that right?"

"That's right."

Only an inch separated the two men, and Laura lost her cool. "Enough," she yelled.

They both snapped their heads her way.

Brett opened his mouth to speak but she got there first, before he could interrupt her. Again. "I'm the one who was attacked, and I will say if I work late or not." She jabbed her finger at Daniel. "You are not responsible for what happened to me, so don't even think of taking this on yourself." She turned that same finger on Brett. "And you." She took a breath. "Thank you for last night, but that ends your responsibility to me. Rest assured I will take better care next time."

They both scowled and looked ready to start up again.

"No." She slashed her hand through the air. "I'm going to get some...er...colored markers. For my poster." She was secretly proud of her quick improvisation. "By the time I come back, I would like my office empty. Okay?" With that, she spun on her heel and speed walked it down the corridor.

If they wanted to behave like Neanderthals, they could do so without her as audience. Her ballet flats pattered on the linoleum as she hurried to the supply closet. She could do with more markers.

Pushing a mop around half-heartedly, Uri pulled an ear bud out one ear and gave her his gap toothed grin. "Hey, Miz Laura. You look pretty today, Miz Laura."

"Hi, Uri, and thank you." She slowed her pace for a word with him. Uri would be hurt if she charged right past him. "How are you today?"

"I'm good, Miz Laura." His grin widened. "I got a new set of Yu-Gi-Oh! Cards." Eyes sparkling, he looked at her expectantly. "And guess what?"

"You got the Seal of Orichalcos."

He shook his head, smirking. "Better."

"Silfer?"

Squirming, Uri giggled. "Better."

"No." She gave him a skeptical side eye. "You did not get Exodia."

"I did." He nodded and rapped his mop on the floor. "I got Exodia the Forbidden One."

That was big news, and she smiled. "I'll tell Sam. He'll be so jealous."

When Sam came to work with her, he and Uri often dueled. "You tell him." Uri giggled. "I need to tell you about Castiel."

All was silent from the direction of her office. That could be a good thing or a really bad thing. "Can we do that later?"

"Sure." Uri cocked his head. "Where you off to in such a hurry?"

"Oh." She almost forgot her mission. "I need some colored markers."

"In the supply closet." Uri nodded. "Only be careful of

that lock, Miz Laura, that lock I haven't fixed yet. It gets stuck."

"I'll be careful, Uri."

Uri looked behind her, and his eyes widened. "Who's that?"

"Laura?" Brett's deep voice echoed down the hallway.

"That's Blake's brother. You know Blake, he goes to Daniel's group."

Uri stared past her shoulder. "He sure is big."

"Yes, he is." She smiled to reassure Uri. "But he's very nice. You should tell him about Exodia."

And with that, coward that she was, she turned tail and headed for the supply closet.

Brett's boots pounded the floor and impatience lashed his voice. "Laura, hold up!"

Nope. Not today. She was all full up on making a dick of herself.

"Hey, Blake's brother," Uri said.

Laura slowed. She couldn't leave Uri to handle an angry Brett.

Brett stopped and blinked at Uri. "Er…hi."

"I know Blake." Uri eyed him warily. "He's nice. Blake."

"Yeah." Brett gentled his tone. "Yeah, he is."

"Blake doesn't know Yu-Gi-Oh! Do you know Yu-Gi-Oh!?"

Time to get out of there. As she turned, Brett looked up, and the look in his eye got her moving faster. He was not happy about having to chase her down. Well, they'd said everything that needed to be said between them.

The supply closet door hung ajar. A paper with Daniel's untidy scrawl in red marker read, *Lock is broken. Don't shut door.*

With any luck, Brett would get detained and give up. Yeah, no, that didn't seem much like Brett. Reaching around the corner she flipped the light switch. And nothing happened. "Dammit."

Uri mustn't have gotten around to it yet. He tended to focus on one area, and until he switched that focus, all other areas of maintenance lapsed.

The markers were on the back shelves, second shelf from the bottom, where she'd put them when she had tidied up the supply closet. Already signs people had been looking for stuff abounded. Her OCD twitched to put the staples with the paperclips and not sharing space with the toilet paper.

Nope. She didn't have to fix the world for everyone, and she wound through the shelves to the markers.

She had them in her hand when heavy footsteps sounded outside the supply closet. It could be Uri, if he'd suddenly grown a foot and gained a hundred pounds. Or Daniel on his way out. It could even be Reverend Michael back a day early from his conference. Not strictly speaking hiding, Laura hunkered down behind the front shelving units.

The supply closet door squeaked. "Laura?" Brett called. "I know you're in here."

*Shit, shit, shit.* Uri must have told him where she was going. From where she stood, she could see his huge pair of steel-toed boots and the frayed hem of a pair of often washed jeans.

This really was juvenile. "Back here," she called, and knew when she was beat. "I'll be out in a minute."

"Are you hiding from me in here?" The trace of amusement in his tone was unmistakable.

It almost had her smiling back. "I wasn't hiding." Laura stuck her markers out in front of her as she crawled around the shelving unit between her and Brett. Then it occurred to her she was managing to look more idiotic by the second, and she stood, markers clutched to her chest. "I mean sneaking around."

Brett loomed. His hazel eyes locked on her, and her brain stopped communicating with her mouth. "Or hiding. I wasn't hiding or sneaking I mean. I was getting some markers."

"Ah." Brett stepped into the supply closet. "You baked me brownies."

"I did." Her face crinkled up before she could control the childish impulse. Sam did that when he was feeling awkward. "I know it's dumb, but I wanted to say thank you, and when I want to thank someone, I bake."

"Nobody's ever baked me brownies before." He held up the Tupperware, and his expression softened. "Thank you."

"Thank you," she whispered. "For everything last night."

He looked down at the brownies. His lips twitched.

Laura's face grew hotter. That had sounded loaded with innuendo. "For the timely rescue," she chirped. "And the checking out my house and the being so nice." She made a gesture at the brownies. "That's not nearly enough for all that you did, but—"

"Sugar." He cupped her nape. "You did a real nice thing here. It was sweet of you."

"Th—" She snapped her mouth shut before she thanked him for the millionth time. The combination of his size—his muscles had muscles—his attitude and the bad boy reputation he'd more than earned twisted her loopy. It made no sense. She wasn't one of those women who loved a thug. If you lined all her exes up, you'd have a Brook's Brothers catalogue. And then you had, Brett. Oldest son of the infamous Barrows clan, currently on parole and a man who flat out fascinated her. "Was there anything else?"

"Yeah." Brett's shoulders blocked the light from the hallway, and his face was in shadow. His deep voice sent a hot flush over her skin. "You and I will be seeing a lot more of each other."

More opportunities for her to make an idiot of herself, but she managed a semi-neutral tone. "Why's that?"

"Your grandmother isn't a big fan of you working in this part of town," he said.

Phi wasn't a big fan of a lot of what she did. "Sorry?"

"The diva is worried about you being here and being vulnerable." His gaze swung her way like an interrogation lamp and hit her with a blast of brain beating heat. "And we both know she has something to worry about."

That tasted like criticism. "You came across me once in a compromised position. That doesn't mean it happens all the time, or like I'm trawling abandoned parking lots for trouble." She got a handle on her irritation. "I appreciate your concern, and Phi's, but I can take care of myself."

"Right." His face conveyed the opposite. "Thought about what could have happened if I hadn't come across you?"

"Of course I have." She was not going to ask him how dumb he thought she was. In case she didn't like the answer. "I, more than anyone, don't want a repeat of last night."

His expression softened. "You don't need to be scared, sugar." Brett stepped farther into the closet, eating up all the space and sucking up all the air between them. "That's what I'm telling you—"

*Click*

"—I'm gonna make sure it doesn't happen again."

"Umm." With a sinking feeling in her gut, Laura tried to peer around him. "Did you shut the door?"

"Nope." He glanced over his shoulder. "It swung shut."

"The door to the closet swung shut?" Nope, this couldn't be happening to her. "Well, then." She gave him her best Pollyanna smile. "We might have a problem."

He gave her a look that doubted her sanity. "What kind of problem?"

"No need to worry yet." Flexing her fingers, Laura stood in front of the supply closet door. "I'm going to open the door." It was the moment of truth, when she would discover if she was locked in a supply closet with a sexy as hell man mountain who seemed determined to insert himself into her life. Also, that was at least the third time he'd called her sugar, and she wasn't a big fan of pet names. First things first, however. She grabbed the handle.

Brett crowded in behind her. "Why don't you open the door?"

"Whether I can or not is the million-dollar question." At five eight, Laura was taller than a lot of women, but Brett left her feeling petite. She turned the handle.

It stuck.

On a groan, she dropped her hand and pressed her spine to the wall beside the door before her knees gave out. "Dammit!"

"Ah hell no." Brett grabbed the door handle and yanked. The wood creaked, the handle gave a metallic ping, but the door stayed shut. The effort did interesting tendon and vein things to his forearms. They were the sort of arms you could take a bite out of and keep gnawing up to his shoulder. While you were there, you may as well go for broke and chew on that chest as well. Inappropriate much? She gave a mortifying high-pitched giggle.

He pounded on the door. "Hey! Hello!"

"Uri probably has his music in," she said. He had probably moved far enough down the hall to be out of hearing range.

"Laura?" Brett was looking at her funny. "Are you having a breakdown of some kind?"

Was she? Probably. She gave him a sunny smile that felt more like a snarl. "Nope."

"Are we locked in?" He asked it as if he'd asked before. Probably while she was going full tilt mental carnivore on his muscles.

"The lock is broken." Meaning they couldn't open it. And she'd left her phone in her office. "Do you have a phone?"

"Yeah." He grabbed for his back pocket like he hadn't thought of his phone before. Probably because a lot of his adult life had been spent behind bars where, she had it on good authority, phones were not allowed. He frowned down at the screen. "I've got a signal."

"Great!" Dear God, when was she going to stop sounding like chairperson of the irrationally cheerful committee. "Let's call someone to come and get us out."

"Umm…" He looked sheepish, and she really didn't know how a man this big and bad looking managed a glimmer of adorable, but there it was. "I don't have any numbers on here."

"What do you mean you don't have any numbers?" She wasn't finding his confession quite as adorable.

Brett cleared his throat and rubbed at the stubble at his nape. "I don't use it that much. Mostly for my sister. She texts me. Those little pictures."

"Emojis?"

"Yep." He nodded. "She likes those."

"Well, then, do you have her last text?"

The light went on behind his eyes. "I can text her back."

"You sure can." Pollyanna slipped her leash again. "And ask her to get hold of Daniel or someone else to let us out."

Brett texted with one forefinger, and it took everything in her not to snatch the phone from him and do it faster. If she'd been even a tad less intimidated, she might have.

His hands were big enough to crush her skull, yet they'd cradled her face like it was glass. Lurid images of those big hands on her waist, caressing her thighs, cupping her breasts… She snatched a proper sanitation pamphlet from the rack beside her head and fanned her flushed face.

"You're not claustrophobic or anything are you?" He glanced at her.

"Nope." She wasn't getting into the *or anything*.

He put his phone away in his back pocket. Lucky phone because Brett had a spectacular ass as well. "That's done. Blythe said she'd let someone know."

"Great!" she chirped.

Brett looked at her, his hazel eyes sharp and probing.

*Probing. Snicker. Shut up. Shut up. Shut up.* Perspiration prickled beneath her skin, and she fanned harder.

"If you're not claustrophobic, is the problem me?" He stepped closer. "Do I make you nervous, Laura?"

Her head started nodding, even as she simpered and chattered away. "Of course not. Why would you make me nervous? That's just silly. So silly. Silly." She clenched her molars together to stop the words from carrying on. "Well." She tried to lighten the mood. "At least you're used to confined spaces."

# Chapter Five

Laura had stayed up late the night before cleaning her condo in preparation for the kids. This morning she'd gotten up early and baked chocolate chip cookies, Sam's favorite, and brownies for Daisy. In the oven their favorite pot roast simmered. She'd washed and ironed their bed linen and put fresh towels in the bathroom.

They were her children, and still she prepared for them like they were visiting royalty. It didn't take the degree in child psychology she didn't have to figure out she was overcompensating. She couldn't help it. Her duplex didn't compare to the beautiful house she used to share with them and Patrick.

When Patrick asked to keep the house in the divorce, Laura hadn't argued. Neither had she kicked up a fuss about him having primary care and custody. Given the legal and financial trouble she'd landed her ass in, at the time of her divorce, she'd counted herself lucky Patrick hadn't gotten more vengeful. Her biggest need out of her divorce had been access to her children, and she would have made any concessions to ensure she stayed close to Sam and Daisy. Hindsight being so frustratingly accurate, she could have safeguarded her parental rights better.

Exactly on time, Patrick rang the doorbell.

Excited, and always a little nervous as to her reception, Laura opened the door.

"Mom." Sam barreled into her, wrapping his arms around her waist. Still enough of a little boy to want Mommy hugs and not be embarrassed about it.

Hanging back with an ever-present scowl on her face, Daisy nodded to her and walked into the condo. "What's that smell?"

"Pot roast." Laura wrapped Sam close to her. It broke her heart every time she had to let them return to their father. Missing her children was a physical ache in the most primal part of her. She held on to Sam and inhaled the dusty, sweaty boy smell until he wriggled to get free.

"Oh, man!" Sam dashed into the kitchen. That was Sam for you. He never walked when he could run. "Cookies, and brownies! Daisy, did you see the cookies?"

Patrick chuckled, and they shared a look. It had taken fifteen months for Daisy to get to her feet. Sam had been on his before his first birthday. They hadn't been able to stop him ever since.

"Hello, darling." Ignoring the bad attitude rolling off Daisy in waves, Laura pulled her into a hug and held her for as long as she would allow.

Daisy put up with about point five seconds before she wriggled. "I'm fine. And a vegan."

This was new, and Laura looked at Patrick. He shook his head and grimaced. Daisy was up to her tricks again.

"How are you, Patrick?" Laura made sure to keep things easy and pleasant with Patrick. After all Daisy and Sam had been through, the last thing they needed was feuding parents. Not that she had any grounds to go to war with Patrick. The divorce was her fault, as was her separation from her children. "You look well."

He did, wearing a new pair of slim jeans and an untucked

shirt. Margot, Patrick's new fiancée, had been updating his wardrobe, and the new clothes suited him. He looked younger and more vital than he had in years. By contrast she felt as if she showed every minute of thirty-eight. Exhaustion dragged into her day and followed her to bed at night. Where she didn't sleep that well.

"I'm getting back in the gym." Patrick patted his flat stomach. "Getting back in shape."

"It shows." Not like it showed on Brett Barrows, who looked like he'd spent his entire incarceration working on those muscles of his. She'd like to see what sort of shape he was in. Which was the most inappropriate thought to have in front of her ex. "How's Margot?"

"Good." Patrick's smile widened, and there was the sweet man she'd married. "Busy planning for the wedding."

"I'll bet." Laura really liked Margot. She was a nice woman, and she adored Patrick. She also treated Sam and Daisy really well. The fact that Laura felt no jealousy about Patrick and Margot's upcoming wedding spoke volumes about her marriage to Patrick. At no specific time had Laura been aware of falling out of love with Patrick. She just had, and it had happened a long time before their divorce. Him moving on with his life with another woman was a relief. Also, Margot made Patrick happy, and a happy Patrick was a fair and accommodating Patrick. "Everything good with Daisy and Sam?"

"Sam has some reading to finish for tomorrow," Patrick said and handed her a book.

Laura didn't recognize the book or the author. "I'll do it with him."

"And Daisy has a math test."

"Is she ready?" Laura lowered her voice. She didn't want Daisy knowing they were talking about her. Daisy was hair-trigger at the best of times.

"Who can tell? She throws a fit if I ask." Patrick blew out

a long breath and rolled his eyes. "You're a better man than I am if you can get her to study more."

Daisy's schoolwork had been slacking off since the divorce. Her therapist told them to give it time, but to also keep Daisy accountable for her actions. Allowing their sympathy for her to cloud their judgment wouldn't help Daisy get through this. Another blame to add to Laura's growing tally.

Patrick cleared his throat. "There was some trouble at school."

"With Daisy?"

He nodded. "She's been skipping the odd class. Nothing too much yet, but we need to keep an eye on it."

"Right." Laura's heart sank. Daisy knew exactly who was to blame for the divorce and she didn't hesitate to let Laura feel the burn. Talking to her was a booby-trapped minefield of teen rage and hurt. "I'll have a word."

"I tried." Patrick shrugged. "Maybe her mother will have more luck."

Daisy's mother doubted that very much, but she would certainly try.

"I'll pick them up—" Patrick caught her chin. "What the hell happened to you?"

Dammit! Laura had slathered on the concealer, but her bruise still showed through. "I ran into some trouble last night."

"At that damn church?" Patrick cut straight to the chase. He hated where she worked and the at-risk teens who were her job.

"In the parking lot, but it was late, and it was my fault I was still there. I should have left with everyone else." She kept Patrick sweet as much as possible. He could snatch her contact with her children away from her. In hindsight, she should have listened to her grandmother and used Phi's divorce lawyer. Phi had been willing and ready to pay for her lawyer as well, but at the time guilt had choked Laura to the point she had turned the offer down.

Phi was as much her victim as Patrick and the children. It had seemed like the worst sort of hypocrisy to take money from the same person she'd stolen from. But Phi had been right, and Laura should have thought it through more clearly. Not that she thought Patrick would ever take Sam and Daisy away, but the power balance was heavily skewed to his side.

"Laura." Patrick took on an unmissable pontificating tone. "Working at that place is a risk you shouldn't be taking. Not at your age."

"I'm thirty-eight, Patrick. Not quite an AARP member yet." This was one of the times a little more power on her side of the equation would help. They'd been through this before, but she wanted to avoid a fight. "I love my job, Patrick, and the kids at the center need me."

"The world is full of children." Patrick tsked and dropped her chin. "There is no reason to keep working in that ghetto church."

Not a word of concern for her wellbeing, but then she'd given up any right to his concern. Laura launched a mental ten count and kept her patience. "The church is in a difficult part of town. It's still a great church, and Reverend Bradford does so much good work with the community. He needs all the help he can get." She gave him a conciliatory smile. "I do important work with these kids, Patrick, and it's very rewarding."

Patrick huffed. "They could easily get what you do from someone else." He indicated her face. "Really, Laura, this sort of thing was inevitable. Frankly, I'm surprised it hasn't happened before now."

"I've learned my lesson, and I'll be more careful," she said, wanting for a second to be the old Laura and on equal enough footing with him to argue the point. Not that old Laura had argued much either. Patrick had a way of blocking opposition and moving forward regardless. "No more staying late for me."

"You should take better care of yourself." Patrick nodded and loaded the look he sent her way. "Daisy and Sam still need their mother."

There it was, the heavily veiled threat that wasn't quite a threat, but still put the fear of God into her. If she lost Daisy and Sam, she didn't know how she would find the will to get up in the morning.

After getting a couple more bits of homework and extra-mural info on Daisy and Sam, she closed the door on Patrick and turned to watch her children. She lived for these unseen moments when she could experience them in her space.

They were arguing already, and she moved into her small open plan kitchen to get dinner ready. Daisy had the remote, and Sam wanted it more than his next breath.

"Sam?" She needed to intervene before things got out of hand. "How about you come and help me mash the potatoes?"

Sam hesitated but spending time with her in the kitchen won. He was still young enough to want to spend time doing things with her. In a year or two he would want to spend more time with his peer group than his parents. Her heart already ached for losing her baby. When she had been married to Patrick, they had agreed two children was the perfect number. Fate had blessed them with one of each, and Laura had believed herself content. Even if way, way, way deep inside, in that hidden part of her she'd longed for a large, messy family.

"Here we go." She handed Sam the masher and added butter and milk to the potatoes. "Make them smooth as silk."

Sam grinned up at her. "So, keep 'em lumpy?"

She prodded his skinny belly and was rewarded with a giggle. Taking a fortifying breath, she approached Daisy.

Daisy kept her gaze locked on the screen.

"Daze?" It was wrong to be afraid of your own child's

anger, but Laura hated the scenes Daisy could throw. Daisy could throw a tantrum to rival her great grandmother Diva St. Amor. "Dad says you have a math test in the morning."

Eyes front, Daisy grunted.

"Are you ready for it?" Laura took the remote and turned the television off.

Daisy bristled and scowled. "I was watching that."

"Really? What was it?" Laura called bullshit.

"It's just a test." Daisy went with a quick direction change. "And it's stuff I know anyway."

"Are you sure?" Laura risked another step into possible wrath. "Because you know your grade has slipped recently."

Daisy gave her a scornful glare. "Really, Mom? Because I hadn't noticed."

"You like math, and you're good at it." Laura kept to the script.

Shrugging, Daisy reached for the remote.

Laura kept hold of it. "What's this about skipping classes?"

"It's nothing." Daisy growled her exasperation. "It was two classes, and we weren't even doing work. The teacher was absent."

"That's still no reason to miss school," Laura said. "School is not voluntary."

Daisy stared at the blank television screen, her jaw stuck at a defiant angle that was so Laura's younger sister, Pippa, it almost made her smile. Another relationship Laura had managed to damage. For a woman who had grown up as the good girl, she sure had done a thorough job of screwing up when she had veered to the dark side. "Daisy, this is important. Skipping school can have long reaching repercussions."

"Really?" Daisy turned and faced her, and Laura braced. The look on Daisy's face broadcasted that she was going in for the kill. After months of this, Laura could almost write the words for Daisy. That didn't lessen their sting, however. "Tell me, Mom, did you think about the repercussions when you stole from Phi to pay off your gambling debts?"

And there you had it. Happier now that she'd drawn blood, Daisy took the remote from her hand and clicked on the television.

"No, I didn't." Laura couldn't let it rest there. "I didn't think about anybody or anything but myself. I can say I'm sorry, and I have." She used to be the mother and the moral yard stick in this relationship. Now she was the black sheep. "But those are just words, and I'm doing my best to show you how sorry I am." She took Daisy's hand. "I'm so sorry, darling. I can't fix the past, though, I can only do better going forward."

"Whatever." Daisy yanked her hand away, and Laura felt the ricochet throughout her being.

And she had nobody else to blame but herself.

# Chapter Six

Laura looked up from her desk as footsteps pattered down the hall toward her office.

A pale face beneath a mop of curly dark curls poked around her door. "Miz Laura?"

"Hi, Tate." Tate was a regular at her afterschool program and had his ear to the ground outside the church. The look on his face had her bracing for trouble.

"It's Karstyn, Miz Laura." Tate sidled into her office and edged for her desk.

Laura suppressed her flinch as she heard the name. Karstyn and Tate were friends. In fact, it was Tate who had first brought Karstyn along to the rec center. Since then, Karstyn had been a regular in her program for the last nine months, and Laura had been helping him get his grades up. Karstyn had a dream he'd shared only with her, and apparently his ass of a brother as well, that he wanted to go to med school. "What happened?"

"Cole won't let him go to school." Tate shifted from one foot to the other. "He's saying like how it's time Karstyn pulled his weight."

*Shit*! In the three years until Karstyn turned eighteen, Cole had full control.

"Cole is saying Karstyn gotta work with him," Tate said. He eyed the jar of candies Laura kept on her desk. She slid it closer to him. Not too long ago she would have shuddered in horror at the amount of processed sugar in those things. Now she had better things to expend her energy on. "What did Cole do?"

"First he tore up all Karstyn's applications." Tate pawed through the selection. The reason she also made sure she kept wrapped candy. "Then he burned his schoolbooks."

Damn! She would have to replace those.

"Then he roughed up Karstyn a bit." Tate's cheeks bulged with candy. "Told him he weren't to go nowhere."

Laura's heart stuttered. "How badly did he rough Karstyn up?"

"He's done worse." Tate shrugged.

She'd gotten a taste of Cole's worse firsthand, and she sure as hell didn't wish that on Karstyn. "Where is Karstyn?"

"That's what I came to tell you." Tate abandoned the candy jar. "Karstyn is hiding out at my place. He got away from the house while Cole was sleeping but he doesn't have long. Cole will wake up and want to know where he is. He'll go crazy if he finds Karstyn didn't listen to him."

When Cole found out Karstyn had run, he was going to be angrier than ever. "How long can he stay at your place?"

"Not long." Tate pulled a face. "My dad is on shift right now, but he'll send Karstyn back to Cole if he finds him at home."

Somebody needed to fetch Karstyn. Laura dialed Daniel's number and got voicemail.

"Hi, it's Laura." She left a message explaining the problem and asking Daniel to get back to her ASAP. She looked at Tate. "When does your dad get home?"

Tate checked his phone. "About thirty minutes."

So, scrap the Daniel idea. She tried Michael's cell but that went to voicemail as well. She could call Nate, but no crime had been committed, and he might be obligated to turn Karstyn over to the system before she could find somewhere for Karstyn to go.

"Miz Laura?" Tate raised his eyebrows and sighed. "He can't stay at my place."

Getting anywhere near to Cole again was close to the top in her lexicon of bad ideas, but Karstyn needed help. On the other hand, if she acted quickly, she could fetch Karstyn and be back here before Cole knew anything about it. Grabbing her purse, she scooped up her car keys. "Let's go get him."

"You and me?" Tate gaped at her. "In your car?"

"Yes." Laura chivied him to the door. Best she go now before she chickened out. She had to firmly set aside what Cole was capable of doing to her if he caught her. "You can show me where to go. Come on."

"You can't go there." Tate ran to keep up with her.

Tate wasn't wrong, but unless Daniel or Michael got back to her in the next five minutes, she didn't see an option. Cole had scared the crap out of her the other night, but she was all that stood between him and Karstyn. "Yes, I can. But we need to be quick."

"Miz Laura." Tate got between her and her car door. "No offense, Miz, but you don't fit in there, and you'll be easy to spot."

"Which is why we need to be in and out before Cole even knows Karstyn is gone." She got around him and into the car. She would stand out from her soccer mom car to her designer jeans, still a leftover from her marriage. These days, she couldn't afford not to wear the clothes she had, because God knew, with her salary and the debt to Patrick, she wouldn't be buying any more like them for a good, long time.

Tate leaped around the car and slid into the passenger seat. He gave her the directions, and Laura's heart went even further south. He was taking her right into the sort of place everybody in her life would yell at her for going to. The sort of place Brett must be an expert at navigating. She could only imagine what Brett would have to say about her current plan.

"Reverend Michael is gonna be pissed at you." Tate pointed. "Turn right there."

He would be, so would Daniel, so would Patrick if he ever found out. And so would Brett.

"Reverend Michael didn't answer his phone, or he would be the one doing this."

As they drove past, a cluster of people sitting on the chipped front stoop of a crumbling apartment building gawked at them.

"Yeah." Tate scoffed. "I don't think the reverend is gonna see it like that. He's going to ask why you didn't wait for him."

"You said it was urgent."

"It is." Tate glanced over his shoulder. "You know anyone with a red pickup?"

"Maybe." It had to be a coincidence. Lots of people owned red pickups. "Why?"

"Take a left and then a right straight after." Tate stared over her shoulder.

Laura obeyed his instructions. "Are we getting closer?"

The view outside her car was daunting. A group of young men loitered at an intersection in front of a dilapidated two-story that must have been built at the turn of the century. Now it was a rotting, graffitied hulk with a car graveyard in the front yard.

Pounding bass came from their left as a car cruised by and slowed. Pointing and laughing, they sped off.

Tate shrunk lower into his seat. "Told you we would stand out."

"Yup." Laura tightened her grip on the steering wheel and threaded her car through the potholes on the road. "But we've come this far, so let's finish this."

Tate looked behind him again. "Still there."

"What?" She tried to see what he was looking at through the rearview mirror.

"Red pickup," Tate said. "Saw it pull into the road behind you."

Alarm spiked through Laura. Brett Barrows was not the only person who owned a red pickup in Ghost Falls. Nate owned a pickup. Okay, a black one, but still, pickups were common. "Can you see the driver?"

"Not really." Tate turned and pointed. "Pull over there."

Laura took a long slow look around her before she moved to the side the road. They were on a quieter street, and nobody was about. A field of weeds and scrub was reclaiming an abandoned construction project. On their side of the road, small houses rubbed shoulders over chain-link fences. "He's here?"

"Hmm." Tate stared out his window.

Laura tried to see what he was seeing. "Did we lose him?"

"I'm not sure." Tate swung in his seat until he was facing her. His eyes went wide. "Miz Lau—"

Someone tapped at her window, and Laura jumped. She may have squeaked.

Brett Barrows stood beside her car. One hand on the roof, he bent low as he motioned her to open her window.

"That's Brett Barrows." Tate's eyes went wide. "Do you know him?"

Heart still pounding, Laura hit the button for her window. The soft hydraulics shrieked in the tense silence as Brett's gaze met hers. He did not look happy. "Laura."

"B-brett." She wanted to kick herself as stupid took hold of her jaw again. "Oh my goodness, you gave me such a fright. I jumped a mile." She looked at Tate who was gaping at her. "Did you jump? Because I certainly did."

"Laura." Brett's deep voice growled her name and shut her mouth. "What are you doing?"

"Sitting."

Brett frowned. "In this neighborhood?"

"I'm looking for…er…I'm taking Tate home." She didn't know why she lied other than she was sure Brett wouldn't like the truth. Or worse, he might tell Michael or Daniel, and word might get out. After her attack, both men had lectured her on safety.

Frowning, Brett's gaze flicked to Tate. "That true?"

"No, sir." Tate shook his head. "No, Brett Barrows, she's not taking me home although we are going to my house."

Brett kept his gaze steady on Tate.

Tate kept on talking. "My friend Karstyn is there. He's hiding from his brother, Cole."

Brett kept right on looking and to Laura's chagrin, Tate kept right on chattering.

"Cole don't want Karstyn to go to college. He wants him to be his mule, coz Karstyn is still a minor without a record and can't get into too much trouble. He found out Karstyn was working toward college and lost his shit. Told Karstyn there would be no more college and that meant he didn't need to go to school no more. Then he went to have a nap coz he was out late partying last night, and Karstyn ran away and is hiding at my place." Tate pointed across the road to a neat, worn looking house. "That's my place there."

It took Laura months to get kids like Tate and Karstyn to open up to her, and all Brett had to do was loom and look.

Brett's gaze shifted to her. "Tell me the kid is jerking my chain."

"I'm going to fetch Karstyn."

"No, you aren't." It rumbled like a threat through Brett's big chest. "You're going to turn your car around and go back where you belong."

"No, I'm afraid I can't do that." Truth be told, she'd love to turn right back around and drive out of there, but Karstyn needed her. "I really don't have much time, and I'd like to get

Karstyn and be gone before Cole realizes he's missing." In case he thought she was being stupid—er—than she was, she added, "You know more than anyone how much I don't want to run into Cole."

"Cole in there?" Brett addressed the question to Tate.

Tate's head whipped from side to side. "No, Brett Barrows. Na-ah. Karstyn is hiding from him, and Cole don't know where I live anyway."

"Go home, Laura." Brett dropped his hand and stepped away from the car. "We'll talk about you being here in the first place later."

"Um…Brett." Laura stared at his retreating back. "I need to get Karstyn."

"Go home." He didn't turn around.

"Not without Karstyn." She climbed out her car. Cole was not going to put his hands on Karstyn or her again. "He's one of my kids, and that makes him my responsibility."

He spun around and stalked back to her, stopping toe to toe. Then he said in a painfully controlled voice. "Get back in your car and go home. This is no place for you."

"Karstyn is in that building." She pointed behind him. "And he's alone and scared, and I'm not leaving without him."

Brett's hazel gaze locked her in and held her. "You're gonna be a pain in my ass about this, aren't you?"

"I beg your pardon?" She channeled her best version of her mother.

Brett stared at her, hard. "You've got some damn crusading cape on, and you're here to save the world."

"Karstyn needs help, and I'm the closest thing he has to that." It seemed unwise to taunt the beast always lurking beneath Brett's skin but Karstyn needed her. "I did try Daniel and Michael, but they weren't picking up, and Karstyn is running out of time. In fact, we're wasting time standing here and arguing."

Brett sighed and looked at Tate. "You." He jerked his thumb. "Get in my truck and stay there."

"Yes, Brett Barrows." Tate fumbled with his seatbelt in his haste, and almost threw himself out her SUV. "I'm going now, Brett Barrows."

For a second, she imagined Brett almost laughed but something that approachable didn't match his floor to ceiling badassery. Then the impact of what he'd done hit her. "Hey! I need him to get into the house."

"Nope." Brett shook his head and glowered down at her. "He's not going anywhere further with you."

Surely he didn't think, for one fleeting second, that she was leaving without Karstyn. Not when she was this close. "Yes, he is."

"No." Brett leaned closer. "He isn't."

"He is." Laura held her ground. Karstyn was a special kid, and she wasn't going to be the next in a long line of people to let him down. "Because Karstyn is going to college, whether I have to fight you and his brother to make that happen."

Brett's eyes darkened, and his expression got so forbidding, she nearly dived back into her Lexus and burned rubber the hell outta there. "You stay away from Cole Watts, you hear me, Laura? Far, far away."

"I mean to." Her voice came out in a frightened whisper. She scrunched her toes together inside her Chucks for courage and kept holding his gaze. "I only want Karstyn."

"I'll get him for you." Brett sighed. "You go back to your place, and I'll bring him to you."

Laura stared stupidly before she found her voice. "You will?"

"Yup." Brett stood and jabbed his thumb at her car. "Go straight home. I'll see you there."

She had no idea why he was doing this and spoke to his retreating back. "But—"

"Home, Laura," he said over his shoulder as he strode for his truck. "Right now."

LAURA ALMOST PACED a worn area through her condo floor as she waited for Brett. It occurred to her for the hundredth time that he might have lied to her to get her to go home.

Except she didn't think Brett operated like that. If he didn't want you to do something, he would straight up tell you and then stand and scowl until you did as he told you. She wasn't a big fan of bossy, domineering men, and Brett just might be the biggest, bossiest man she'd ever encountered.

Patrick had always been polite, almost deferential with her. Even when he'd found out how much in debt she'd put them, he'd barely raised his voice. Sending her home like a naughty child wouldn't have occurred to Patrick. Then again, she was now divorced from Mr. Polite and Deferential, and she didn't care to dwell too much on what comparing Brett and Patrick meant.

Pounding on her door made her jump, and she rushed to answer it.

Her relief at seeing Karstyn swept all her irritation away.

Under his messy dark blond hair, Karstyn's face showed the strain he'd been under. With his aquiline bone structure and striking dark eyes, Karstyn would grow to be a handsome man. He gave her a sweet smile. "Hey, Miz Laura."

"Hey, Karstyn." She forced the panic and worry out of her voice and resisted the urge to hug him. Karstyn needed stable and safe right now. "Tate said you were in some trouble."

"I'm sorry I sent him for you." Karstyn glanced over his shoulder at Brett standing behind him.

*Shock! Horror!* Brett was towering again.

Laura opened the door wider and gestured them both into her space.

As he had last time, Brett took up way more room than made her comfortable. Nothing about the man put her at ease, but he had something that kept snagging her attention and holding it. The harsh lines of his face escaped classically handsome, but his craggy, rugged features appealed to her more than she would admit to anyone. As for his big, hard, muscled body…

Well, the less she went there, the better.

She managed to untangle her thoughts enough to speak to him. "Thank you for finding him."

"Don't thank me yet." Brett scowled at Karstyn. "I explained to the kid how much I don't like him tangling you up in his shit."

Now Brett had gone too far, and she forgot all her nerves and tingling around him. "You had no right to do that." She gave him the firmest tone she could manage. "Karstyn and the other kids in my program rely on me."

"You're a woman," Brett said, as if that was explanation enough.

Laura stared at him, waiting for more. When he stayed silent her irritation spiked. It had been a while since she'd walked face first into that much unmitigated sexism and, annoyingly, she couldn't think of anything pithy and humbling to say. So she went with, "My being a woman is irrelevant. I work with Karstyn, and he knows he can call on me if he needs me."

Brett took a deep breath. "I get that, babe, but you're a woman. You live on your own. What's more, you're a class piece and not used to running the same streets this little shit does."

*Oh my— Oh. My. God.*

Back that truck right the hell up and keep on backing it. In a few sentences, Brett had managed to trample on so many of her boundaries she had trouble deciding which one pissed her off more.

"I may be a woman." She drew on her inner Phi. "But I am not your babe, and I am most definitely not a piece."

His lips quirked.

Hot or not, sexy or not, Brett Barrows was a mammoth asshole. "And do not refer to my boys as little shits. Got it?"

Brett's lip curled into an almost smile. "Got it." He grinned. "And you're a total babe."

"I…you…" She had no words, and she ended on a huffy growl with her fists clenched.

To make matters worse Karstyn was looking at Brett as if he'd seen his savior.

"It's okay, Miz Laura," Karstyn said. "He doesn't mean it like it sounds. And he's right about me not sending for you. I should have sent Tate to find Daniel."

"Or me." Brett dropped a hand on Karstyn's shoulder. "That dumb fuck of a brother of yours gives you any more trouble, you've got my number."

Karstyn nodded.

Well, that was…kind, but the mouth on him. These boys needed positive role models. "Watch your language," she said.

Up went Brett's brow as he cocked his head. "Figured my cussing wasn't as a big a deal as making sure the kid got safe."

"Nothing is more important than getting Karstyn safe." She managed a reassuring smile for Karstyn. Setting Brett straight could wait until Karstyn was settled. "But you could be more aware of the example you set." And that women now had the vote and could state opinions outside of the kitchen and everything. Some of those opinions might even be worth listening to. *Who'da thunk it?*

"Noted." Brett shrugged. "Since last time you told me my mouth didn't bother you, maybe you could send me a list of times when it's okay and when it's not."

His sarcasm she could do without, and she added it to her

mental shit list, but she turned her attention to Karstyn. All of fifteen, and built like he was older, already this kid had seen more crap from life than anyone deserved. In that, he was exactly like Brett.

"You can stay here for the night." She pointed at Sam's room. "Take my son's room, and I'll call Daniel in the morning, and we'll find a safe situation for you."

"Like foster care?" Karstyn screwed up his face.

Laura hit a wall. "I'm really not sure, sweetie." She put as much reassurance in her voice as she could. "I'm not a social worker, but Daniel and Reverend Michael will know better what our options are."

"Trust Miz Laura, kid." Brett put his hand on Karstyn's shoulder. He handed Karstyn a battered kit bag. "Go and get showered up for bed. I need to talk to Miz Laura."

Funny that, because she had a word or two for him, but she bit her tongue as Karstyn disappeared into Sam's room. Brett waited until the bathroom door shut and then folded his arms and glared down at her. "He can stay here tonight, but tomorrow, he goes."

"That is not for you to say." Laura kept her voice low. They'd already bickered too much in front of Karstyn, and the events of the night were beginning to tell on her. Karstyn must be exhausted. "In fact, this telling me what to do thing stops now."

"Ba—Laura." He gave her a long-suffering look. "That kid is in a seriously shit situation."

"I know that."

"The sort of shit situation—" He spoke right over her. "—that can, and will, blow back on the people around him. I aim to make sure none of that blows back on you."

That took some of her irritation away, but only a teeny amount. "I know all about Cole. I plan to be very careful."

Brett nodded. "And I aim to make sure you are."

"No, you don't." She maintained eye contact. "What you

do for my grandmother has no bearing on me." Stepping closer she had to tilt her head up to hold his gaze, but he needed to get her and get her good. "You and your overbearing, sexist, Neanderthal bullshit are done here."

He grinned at her. "Ah, sugar. I'm gonna have to give you a hard no on that. I can work on the sexist, but the overbearing and Neanderthal are just getting started."

# Chapter Seven

Laura got dressed for her date with Daniel the following night carefully. A date with a good man always deserved effort, but she also needed to set the right tone—as in a not sexy kind of tone. This conversation had been a few weeks in coming but it had to be had.

Unfortunately, Daniel hadn't been able to sort out a place for Karstyn yet. Brett would certainly not be happy about Karstyn spending the night at her place again. The big prick would just have to suck it up. She'd tell him so next time she saw him too.

"I'm leaving now." She stopped at her living room couch where Karstyn was watching TV. "I have my phone with me, so call if you need anything."

Karstyn smiled shyly. "You look nice, Miz Laura."

"Thank you." Getting dressed for her date had taken longer than she would have liked. She was dreading this evening and Daniel was far too nice a human being for that. "Bye."

She drove to a small Italian restaurant near the expensive property developments on the hills overlooking Ghost Falls. Pippa's husband, Matt, along with his brother, Eric, had built most of those developments and kept them from over-whelming Ghost Falls or destroying the natural beauty surrounding their town.

Daniel was already there and waiting for her. He stood as she approached the table, a smile on his handsome face. He'd tamed his rather unruly hair tonight. He wore a white button-down and jeans, and looked so good in them, it had Laura questioning herself again.

Daniel was a great looking guy, funny and sweet and strong, any girl's dream guy, yet he didn't do it for her.

"Hey." He leaned down and kissed her cheek, smelling of something woodsy and delicious. "You look beautiful."

Laura forced a smile as she took her seat and accepted a menu. She contemplated ordering a glass of wine and then went for water. Daniel didn't drink, and although he said he was fine with others drinking around him, it didn't seem fair.

Daniel looked at her across the table, the dim light high-lighting his strong features. "Karstyn okay?"

"Fine." She nodded and opened her menu. "He's quiet and respectful, no trouble."

"We'll move him as soon as we can," Daniel said. "I don't like him being at your place."

Another man with an opinion about her actions. Maybe she should post her life online and let the entire world weigh in. "He's no bother, and there isn't anywhere else for him right now."

"This is not about Karstyn." Daniel's gaze fixed on her with quiet intensity. "Cole is dangerous, and if he wants to find Karstyn, it won't take him too long to make the connec-tion with you."

"Cole only knows me through the rec center."

Daniel tapped the table. "If you're in Karstyn's life, Cole can find you. He's a man who's made it clear what happens to people when they say no to him. If he wants answers, he'll get them." He sat back and folded his arms. The set look to

Daniel's jaw said it wasn't open for debate. "We'll find somewhere within a day or so."

"Okay." She was getting really tired of the men in her life thinking they could keep pulling this bullshit attitude on her. But tonight, she needed to talk to Daniel about the two of them. Trying to think of the right way to bring it up, she pretended to study her menu. Daniel was a great guy, everyone knew Daniel was a great guy, but she needed to end things before it went past the few careful kisses they'd shared.

Laura didn't want careful, respectful kisses. She wanted to be possessed by a kiss, consumed by it. After a marriage in which she'd become suffocated one predictable and expected year after another, she didn't want tentative or uncertain. She craved wicked and wild, impetuous and powerful. For too many years, she'd pushed herself into a mold that fit what everybody needed her to be. Conformed until the worst of her oozed out of the shape she'd forced it into and took over.

Daniel cleared his throat and motioned the waiter. "A glass of your Malbec, please."

"You don't drink." She looked up.

"But you do, and you look like you might need it." He shrugged. "Want to wait for the wine or get straight into it?"

"What?" Laura should have remembered how intuitive and perceptive Daniel was.

"You know what." He smiled. "The reason you've been putting off this dinner for a week."

Laura nearly told him she'd been busy, but she owed him more than a vapid excuse.

He gestured the air between them. "You and me aren't working for you."

The waiter put a glass of wine in front of her, and Laura took a big sip.

"Daniel." His brutal honesty awed her, but then again, it was one of the things that had drawn her to him in first place. "You really are a great—"

"A great guy?" His lips twisted into a shadow smile. "No offence, Laura, you can do better than that." He didn't seem angry, but more resigned. "And I know I'm a great guy, just like I know I'm not the guy for you."

She wished she could think of anything other than platitudes. "I really wish you could be."

"There's a lot of that going around lately." Daniel sipped his water. "To be honest, I'm not sure if it's really there for me either. I would have liked to give it more time." He shrugged. "But that's not happening."

"I'm sorry." Laura stared at the writing on her menu without making sense of the words. Daniel didn't know how much of a lucky escape he was getting. She wasn't worth his disappointment. "I think I should probably go."

"Why?" Daniel didn't look like he was being sarcastic. He leaned forward. "It's all good, Laura. We were friends before we explored this thing between us. We're still friends." He gestured her menu. "So let's have dinner, as friends, and talk like we always do."

Daniel gave no indication throughout dinner that he was hurt by their parting. After the glass of wine, Laura started to relax. As they ate, Daniel kept conversation easy and comfortable, and she was able to enjoy their evening.

She insisted on splitting the bill, or she tried to, but Daniel was adamant.

Back at her condo, Laura opened her door. First, she heard Karstyn's voice, and then, she spotted her daughter on the couch beside Karstyn, and her heart dropped. "Daisy?"

Out of respect for Patrick and his dislike of what she did, she ruthlessly kept that part of her life from her children.

Both kids looked up at the sound of her voice. A connection shimmered in the air between Daisy and Karstyn. Their shoulders pressed together on the large sofa. Their heads were close, and they were both a bit flushed.

Laura's heart sunk even further. She didn't think something would have happened at this first meeting, but there was a definite spark between those two. Daisy had only recently started taking an interest in boys. As unready as Laura felt for that time in Daisy's life, Patrick was doing even worse. He had his head firmly shoved in the sand about his little girl growing up.

"Hey, Mom." Daisy looked as if she might have been crying. "I thought it would be only you here."

If Daisy was here, it meant she wasn't with Patrick, where she was supposed to be. "Does your father know you're here?"

"He doesn't give a shit." Daisy shrugged.

The language was a red herring, so Laura said, "Yes, he does, and you know it. I'm calling him."

"Why!" Daisy shot to her feet. "He doesn't care about me. He doesn't even want me there." Then her face grew a bit calculating. "And I'd much rather live with you than Dad."

Like hell Daisy would. Pain her as it did to admit, her daughter couldn't stand her condo and spent every visit comparing it to her father's beautiful home. Laura got her cell out and moved to her bedroom to make her call. She had eight missed calls, six of them from Patrick and two from Daisy.

"Laura." Patrick picked up the phone on the first ring. "Is she there?"

"Yes. I came home from dinner with a friend to find her here." Daisy and Karstyn had their heads close together. "What happened?"

"Your daughter's teen angst is what happened." Patrick raised his voice slightly. "Where were you, and why weren't you answering your phone?"

"I was having dinner with a friend." She didn't think Patrick would care if she dated, but she wasn't going to bring up her dating life with him until there was someone who would be around long enough for it to be an issue.

"She scared the life out of me." Patrick sighed. "None of this happened before…before the divorce."

The silent accusation that she had caused the newest wrinkle hung between them, and he was right. "I thought I was the only one getting attitude."

"I wish." Patrick growled. "I suppose we can leave her there for the night and talk this out when calmer heads prevail."

She really had been hoping to not mention Karstyn to Patrick. "Um…that might not be the best idea."

"Why?" Patrick grew impatient. "I have to be up first thing in the morning. I have early appointments. Surely, for once, we can dispense with the perfect parenting and let this one slide."

In these verbal jabs and barbed criticisms, Patrick's hurt and anger found an outlet. Not that Laura blamed him. She had destroyed their marriage and hurt them financially. She had broken her perfect home, and she had only herself to blame for that. Knowing she had earned his anger, she suppressed her desire to defend herself. "It's not that, Patrick. I have a…someone here."

"A boyfriend?"

"What?"

"You have a man there?" Patrick demanded. "Is he who you were having dinner with earlier?"

"I was having dinner with a friend," she said. Patrick had no reason to sound infuriated about the idea of her having a man in her condo. He'd moved on months ago and was all set to marry Margot next summer. The children weren't even supposed to be with her tonight. There was a slight edge to her voice as she answered him. "I would be perfectly entitled to have someone here, but that's not the case." He wasn't going to get any happier with what she had to say. "No, this is one of the kids from the church program."

"In your home?" Patrick's incredulity vibrated down the

line. "What the hell is one of those gangsters doing in your condo?"

It hadn't been so long ago she'd been just as ignorant and bigoted. Again, Patrick stepped into her business, but she kept it calm and firm. "I can't get into the details, but he had nowhere else, and it was an emergency. He'll be gone tomorrow." She crossed her fingers she was right. "He's a good kid."

"Did Daisy meet him?"

Laura hummed her agreement. "And that's why I think it would be better for everyone if she came home."

"Right." Patrick's tone brought a picture of him vividly to mind. The way his jaw grew tight and his eyes narrowed when he was annoyed. "I'll be right there."

Laura hung up picturing Patrick shoving his legs into track pants and muttering to himself. Patrick didn't shout when he got angry, he hissed at you through thin lips and muttered. A lot of muttering.

Putting history aside, she stopped behind the couch. "Your father's on his way."

"I can't stay here?" Daisy's gaze flicked to Karstyn. "Why can't I stay here?"

"Because you're supposed to be at your father's, and it's not your decision where you sleep." She was such a fraud, rebuking her daughter when she had absolutely no moral right to do so. "What happened?"

"Ask Dad." Daisy folded her arms.

Laura breathed deep. "I'm asking you."

"He's pissed at me." She stuck her bottom lip out. "He doesn't want me there. All he wants is Margot." The way she said Patrick's fiancée's name dripped derision.

"Your father is entitled to a life of his own, and that includes Margot." She sat on the sofa arm. "Besides, you like Margot."

"She's a THOT." Daisy snickered at Karstyn.

Karstyn flushed and looked uncomfortable.

"Don't." Laura held Daisy's defiant gaze. "Don't be rude about Margot. She's important to your dad and a thoroughly nice woman."

Daisy jerked her head away. "Whatever."

"What was the fight with your dad about?"

Daisy stared mulishly ahead of her.

After glancing at Laura, Karstyn nudged Daisy. "Tell your mom. She cares about you."

Daisy flushed and dropped her head. "It was a dumb fight, but I'll tell you. If you want."

Apparently, when Karstyn said something, it was gospel. If she had dared to even hint at such a thing, Daisy would have cut her off at the knees. "I do care, Daisy, and I want to know what has upset you enough to bring you here in the middle of the night."

"It's about school." Daisy grumbled. "Dad is on my case about grades."

Before the mess Laura'd made, Daisy had been an excellent student, like she'd been a sweet, clever, imaginative child. "Is he right to be worried?"

"No." Daisy glanced at her. "Okay, maybe a bit, but I plan to catch up."

"It would be a better choice to not fall behind, don't you think?"

Eyes flashing ire, Daisy spun and glared at her. "Are we going to talk about better choices?"

"Daisy." Laura knew that look, and Daisy was about to shove the dagger in.

"Is that what you did, Mother?" Her voice grew vicious. "Was it you making better choices when you gambled away all that money and stole from Phi?" Her expression radiated spite "Was it making better choices that allowed you to screw up everyone's life?"

# Chapter Eight

Laura took Karstyn to work with her the next morning.

In the night, Daniel had called and let her know they'd found a place for Karstyn. She had an early meeting at the rec center, but after that she was free to take Karstyn to his foster home. Daniel had offered to do it for her, but Laura wanted to get a look at the people taking Karstyn in. He was at a critical point, and she didn't want some clumsy handling driving him away from the direction he was taking.

As they walked past the hall, music pounded out from Blythe's exercise class. Karstyn peered in, stopped and stared.

Blythe was enough to stop any teenage boy in his tracks. Blond, hourglass, toned and beautiful, it was clear why Blythe had taken over the health and fitness role in Pippa's makeover show, *Your Best You*.

Mid arm-twirl, hip-swing, Blythe looked over and waved and smiled.

Laura smiled and waved back. It still amazed her that somehow she and Blythe had ended up friends. She even joined in Blythe's class when her schedule allowed.

"Yo!" A man's deep voice came from farther along the passage.

Strongly suspecting she'd identified the yo-er by tone and timbre, Laura took a deep breath and steeled herself for a pre-coffee Brett Barrows encounter.

Karstyn lit up with a shy smile. "Yo, Brett."

"Good morning." Laura kept it old school. Her desire to babble had thankfully disappeared since she'd had more contact with Brett. "You're here early."

Brett's gaze swept from her face down and up again. Fast enough not to be considered leering, but also slow enough to say he didn't give a shit who caught him looking. "Waiting for you."

The look, the words, and her brain stuttered to a halt. Laura blinked at him. "Oh."

"How you doing?" Brett fastened his stare on Karstyn. "You staying out of shit."

"Said I would." Karstyn's chest puffed, and he stuck his hands into his pockets, mirroring Brett. "Not much I can get into at Miz Laura's."

Other than her daughter, but Laura decided against sharing that tidbit with Brett. Instead, she did a mental slap to the side of her head and pasted a pleasant, noncommittal smile on her face. "Is there anything I can help you with?"

"Other way around." Brett clapped a hand on Karstyn's shoulder. "Spoke with Daniel. Gotta take this guy to his foster home." He turned, taking Karstyn with him, and strode away. "See you later," he called over his shoulder.

"Daniel did what?" Laura had to sprint to get in front of them. She only barely made it to the entry doors first and slid between the doors and them. She used her firm, no-nonsense voice. "I'll take Karstyn to his foster home after my meeting this morning."

"Nope." Brett gave her a steady look that managed to convey the endless patience of men everywhere with hysterical women. "Told you. I'm taking him. Daniel called last night and asked. I said I would."

Daniel was going to get an ass kicking when she caught up with him, but one overbearing arrogant male at a time. At least before coffee. "Regardless, Karstyn is my responsibility, and I want to take him to his foster home."

"It's okay, Miz Laura." Karstyn gave her an encouraging smile. "Brett will make sure I get there fine and check it out."

"Not gonna leave him there if I don't like it." Brett shifted to slide past her.

Laura sidestepped into his way again. "That's beside the point. I will take Karstyn after my meeting. I need to see this place for myself."

"Laura." Brett's expression conveyed he was done with the conversation. "Don't want you involved in this."

"I'm already involved in this." She gave Karstyn an apologetic smile for the way they were discussing him as if he wasn't standing right there. "And I want to see it through." She looked at Karstyn. "Please would you wait in my office until I've sorted this with Brett?"

Karstyn looked from her to Brett. "But—"

"Thank you, Karstyn." Her tone stated she wasn't asking but telling. "I won't be long, and then after my meeting, we'll have time to get you properly settled."

"Okay." Karstyn raised his eyebrows and took off for her office. His sneakered feet squeaked against the floor as he sauntered down the corridor.

Laura waited until he'd turned into her office before addressing Brett. "I appreciate your concern, but I will be taking Karstyn." She held his stony gaze, digging her nails into her palms for fortitude. "Further, I don't appreciate you and Daniel discussing my wellbeing behind my back. While I recognize it comes from a good place, I also must ask you to involve me in all decisions concerning me. Especially when it comes to my work with these kids."

Up went one of his eyebrows. "You done?"

Was she done? For now, at least. "I believe so."

"Got a deal for you," he said.

Her mind went some interesting and dangerous places, but she stomped on that hard. "What deal?"

"You have your meeting. Karstyn and I will hang out in your office, and then we'll all go to his foster home."

"I—" That actually sounded like a good idea. "Fine." She forced a smile. "But I'll have your promise that you won't take Karstyn while I'm otherwise engaged."

"Otherwise engaged?" He grinned down at her. "That's a fine way of saying you have a meeting."

She wasn't going to fall for the charm, not much and not visibly anyway. "Your word please, Brett."

"Sure." He shrugged. "I won't take Karstyn while you're —" he leaned close enough to whisper in her ear "—otherwise engaged." He stepped back, taking his delicious leather and sage scent with him.

Concentrating hard on not letting her rubber knees give way, Laura strode to her meeting.

A ninety-minute budget meeting was enough to render anyone brain numbed. Unfortunately, she'd spent a portion of it reliving the warmth of Brett's breath against her cheek and neck. As their accountant went on about charitable contributions, her imagination forayed into what Brett's chest would feel like.

Hard, definitely, and hot. Heat seemed to radiate off the man. She'd like to solve the mystery of his tattoos. She had only ever caught tantalizing glimpses peeking out from under his clothing.

"Laura?"

"Yes?" She jerked her attention back to the room to find Daniel and the other five members of the budget committee staring at her.

"The church family day." Daniel rescued her. "You still planning on doing something for that?"

"Oh, yes." She was still mad at Daniel and needed to set

him right about interfering behind her back as soon as she could. "I wanted to get the kids' input before I put an idea forward. I want their ownership and buy in."

Michael smiled at her. "Great idea. They also might have something more exciting to offer than the usual bingo."

"What's wrong with bingo?" Rowena Griffith glared at Michael. "We have bingo every year. The parishioners look forward to it." She glanced around the table. "I hope you're not thinking of canceling bingo. I can't support that."

"No, Rowena." Michael spread oil on troubled waters. "Nobody would be foolish enough to cancel bingo."

Right this moment, Brett could be out of patience and making a run for it with Karstyn. "Perhaps you'd like to take over bingo?" She managed a smile for Rowena. "And Daniel and I can do something different."

Rowena mulled this over, glancing at her bestie by her side. Patty gave her the nod, and Rowena smiled. "We'll run bingo."

"Although—" Patty had to have her say.

Laura suppressed a groan. It wouldn't be a meeting unless they heard Patty's opinion on everything.

"We will need to okay what the youngsters decide." She fixed Daniel with a stern look. "This is a church run recreation center after all, and whatever we do has to be in line with our parishioners."

"Perfect." Michael smiled at all attendees, demonstrating the saintlike patience that Laura admired. "If that's all?"

Patty gave it some thought, and she and Rowena shared another look before the meeting broke.

"Daniel." Laura stopped him outside the meeting room. She didn't have much time because she didn't trust Brett to stay put if he'd decided he'd waited long enough.

Daniel turned to her with his easy smile. "What's up?"

"You called Brett and told him about Karstyn's foster home?" For politeness' sake, she phrased it as a question, but she didn't think Brett had lied. When you were Brett's size, you didn't need to lie or prevaricate.

Tilting his head, Daniel met her gaze unapologetically. "Yes, I did, and you know why."

"It wasn't your place to do so." Laura kept it calm, but that superciliously raised eyebrow Daniel was giving her was going to get itself stapled to his forehead if he didn't check himself. "If I needed help, I would have asked for it."

"No, you wouldn't, Laura." Daniel didn't look an iota remorseful about his interference, nor bothered by the imminent eyebrow stapling. "You don't ask for help, even when you should. We're friends, Laura, as well as colleagues, and I'm going to make sure you stay safe." He shrugged. "And Brett can make sure you do stay safe."

With that, he hurried off after Michael, and Laura was left to stew and simmer all the way back to her office.

In her office, Brett sat behind her desk, his feet on the window ledge as he chatted with Karstyn, who was lounging in her visitor's chair. They looked very chummy and cozy together.

As she came in, Brett looked up with a smile. "Hey."

"Hi...hello." Her brain damn near short-circuited with the force of his smile, and she forced a calming breath in and out.

Raising an eyebrow, Brett said, "Bad meeting?"

"It was fine." Her heart was still doing weird jumps at the idea of him in her space. "Are you ready to go?"

Standing, Brett nodded. He motioned Karstyn and her to precede him.

Acutely aware of Brett behind her, Laura was glad she made it to the parking lot without tripping.

Brett headed for his truck, she headed for her SUV, and Karstyn stood in the middle and glanced from one to the other.

"We'll take mine." Brett jabbed a thumb at his truck.

She didn't know how she could continue to crush on someone who insisted on trying to boss her around. "Actually, I'm more comfortable in my vehicle."

"Yes." He got an expression of endless patience on his face that dared her to test it. "But mine will fit in better where we're going."

She adopted her own version of that face. "Yes, but Cole might be watching to see where Karstyn goes, and your truck stands out more than my car."

"Cole wouldn't dare."

God, what it must be like to be that convinced of your own invincibility. Of course, you had to survive a couple of stints in the big house to get that infallibility. Did anyone even say big house anymore? "I still would prefer to take mine."

"We're taking mine." Brett tossed the keys to Karstyn. "Get your shit and put it in the back."

Laura breathed deep, and deeper still, and it did nothing. Not a thing. She still wanted to smack him. Granted, she'd need a stepladder to reach his ears, but where there was a will…

Dredging up her best firm but not confrontational voice, she said, "Brett, I think we need to establish some boundaries."

"Uh-huh." He folded his huge arms over that mammoth chest Laura wanted to fall face first into. "We can get to those." He jerked his head. "In my truck."

"No." She held her ground and her temper. "The truck is part of those boundaries."

He frowned. "You don't like my truck?" Then his face cleared, and he nodded. "I get it. You don't want to be seen in that hunk of shit. Classy piece like you."

"No." For a horrible moment, black spots danced across her vision, and she thought her head might explode. "It has nothing to do with the truck, or me being a class—" Nope, not going there. "For whatever reason, you and I are both involved in making sure Karstyn gets to a safe foster home."

"Yep." He took a careful breath.

So far, so good. "And as such, we need to work together."

"Don't wanna be rude here, sugar, but you're kinda stating the obvious, and now I have to state the obvious, which is that we're standing out here for anybody driving past to see."

He was right, and she knew it. "We can discuss boundaries after we drop off Karstyn."

"You got it." He winked at her and strode for his truck. "And you can tune into your awareness and give yourself permission to establish healthy boundaries and limits."

Was he messing with her now?

He yanked open the truck door. "Come on, toots. Get your high maintenance ass in my truck."

# Chapter Nine

Karstyn's foster home was in a modest but respectable neighborhood about an hour's drive from the church. He would need to change schools, but that would be best anyway.

His foster family was a middle-aged couple who already had another two fosters with them. The home wasn't elaborate, and Karstyn would need to share a room with a twelve-year-old boy called Ethan, but it was clean, and the other two foster kids looked happy and settled.

Social Services had already spoken to the parents, but Brett took the father aside and spoke to him about Cole. Nobody wanted to take any chances, and Brett handed him a card. "You see that asshole anywhere near here, you give me a bell."

"Will do." Both foster parents nodded.

Karstyn brought in his stuff, one pitifully small bag and a school backpack. Then there was nothing more to do but say goodbye.

Laura gave him a quick hug. "You take care of yourself and check in when you can. I want to hear all about your new school."

Staring at his feet, Karstyn nodded.

She suspected he was getting emotional, and she retreated for the sake of his teenage pride.

Brett stepped closer to Karstyn and cupped his nape. "These are nice people, you hear me, bud?"

Head still lowered, Karstyn nodded.

"It ain't always easy to let people help you," Brett said. "But don't be a dick like I was. Do better than me."

"You're not a dick," Karstyn whispered.

"Yeah, I am." Brett lowered his head. "I was a dick because I thought I could do it all myself, and that landed me nowhere I want to see you go. Hear me, bud?"

Karstyn nodded.

"You're smart, and that will see you a long way if you use it right," Brett said. "Keep your ass in school, keep it out of trouble and there's no stopping you."

"Got a dream of going to college." Karstyn peeped at Brett. "Miz Laura says I can get there too. My grades are good."

"Laura is a clever lady." Brett smiled at him. "Even if she does bitch at a guy all the time."

Karstyn snort laughed and threw her a guilty look. "She's not that bad."

"Thanks." Laura played along because Karstyn was looking surer of himself.

Brett kept his attention on Karstyn. "You got my number?"

"Yeah."

"You know where to find me?"

"Yeah."

"Then, you need me, you use that knowledge." Brett let go his nape. "You're a good man, Karstyn. You tell me if that asshole brother of yours shows his face."

"Will do." Karstyn nodded.

His foster father came to stand beside Karstyn. "We'll all watch out for him."

As they drove away, Laura had to fight back tears. She stared out the passenger window to hide them. Some of these kids had such a hard road ahead of them, as hard as the road they'd traveled to reach the point they were at then. Life wasn't fair. It made the way she'd damaged her family seem even worse. She'd never had to conquer great obstacles or overcome an impossible situation she was raised in. It made her feel pathetic.

"Hey." Brett's big hand closed around hers. "I got a good feeling about them. He's gonna be fine."

She nodded because she didn't trust her voice yet, but she also had gotten a good feeling around the family.

"Lay those boundaries on me, honey." His voice was warm and teasing. "You know that's gonna make you feel a heap ton better."

Brett Barrows, she was beginning to learn, had a wicked sense of humor beneath all that badassedness. "My name is Laura." She surreptitiously wiped away a tear. "Not toots, or sugar, or babe, or any other endearment you want to toss at me."

"Okay." He nodded and said, "Laura," in that base rasp that shot straight to her lady parts.

Their boundary talk was going better than she'd expected, and she needed to keep her focus out of her jeans. "Also, women should not be referred to as pieces or any other sexist and demeaning term."

"Shorty?"

She glared at him.

He grinned. "Chick?"

"Don't even."

"Bint? Broad? Bitch? Babe? Dame?"

"No, no, no and no, and does anyone say dame anymore?" Yeah, she caught that glint in his eye. "Anyway, I think my point is made."

His smile made her melt. "I take your point…Laura."

"Was that so hard?"

He chuckled. "You've no idea."

They drove in silence for a while, but it wasn't uncomfortable. Laura wouldn't exactly call it peaceful and calm, but her brain had decided to give tripping over itself in front of him a break. Emboldened by his easy capitulation on the other issues, she broached her next boundary.

"Umm…"

He glanced at her and winced. "Another boundary?"

"A big one."

"Boundary?"

"Yes. What else?"

His lips twitched. "Lay it on me."

A weird, crazy thought wormed into her brain and squatted. Brett Barrows might—lots of weight on might—be flirting with her. "So, the bossy thing you do."

"Bossy?" He grunted. "I prefer assertive."

Assertive her ass, bossy was bossy. "Anyway. Your assertiveness, which comes perilously close to bossy, I feel to be misplaced and inappropriate toward me."

"Hmm." He stopped at a red light and stared at the car in front of them. "Gonna have to disagree with you there, babe."

"Argh!"

"Laura." He tossed a wicked grin her way.

And he needn't think he could do that and get himself out of hot water. Even if it kinda did disarm her. And what the hell was she doing? What the hell was she thinking? She wasn't that woman, the sort of woman who indulged sexist and overbearing behavior. She was a self-aware, modern woman who deserved respect and insisted on it. "You're not taking any of this seriously."

"I am." He wiped the grin off his face. "Seriously, Laura, I'm listening to every word you say."

"And?"

"I'm taking notes?"

God, he was impossible, and she needed to get over her asinine crush on him. "Whatever."

The light changed, and he got the truck underway.

"You and Daniel a thing?" Brett broke the silence.

"Eh?" She'd been staring aimlessly out the window, counting the now uncomfortable minutes as they ticked by.

He glanced at her. "Are you and Daniel a thing?"

"I'm not sure what business that is of yours." She nearly winced at how prissy her tone sounded, but she'd had enough of Brett Barrows for one day.

He shrugged one big shoulder. "It's none of my business." With a snap of his wrist, he turned on the radio. Selena Gomez purred and moaned her way over the airwaves.

Enough of that. Laura snapped it off again. They had enough emotional currents in one truck cab as it was. He also needed to explain that question. "If you also think my relationship status is none of your business, why did you ask?"

Brett stared out the windshield, a muscle in his jaw clenching and unclenching.

"Brett?"

He glanced at her. "Hmm?"

She made a face at him to get him to speak.

"I'm thinking," he said.

"Do it out loud."

A slight smile tilted one corner of his mouth. "You sure you want that?"

"Yes." He could have a lot of inconvenient thoughts that might be better not shared. "No. I'm not sure."

He chuckled softly. "I'm thinking whether to answer your question honestly or not."

"Honesty is always the best policy." Except in certain situations, and having trotted that little clichéd gem out, she really hoped this wasn't one of those unfortunate situations.

"Unless you're facing twenty to life," he said and grinned.

She couldn't help but smile back. "Except then."

"So, you and Daniel?"

He really stuck to something doggedly, but she told him anyway. "Not a thing. Anymore." Then she added. "Not really ever a thing. We thought we might…but it didn't work out." And now she'd said a whole helluva lot more than she thought she would. "No."

Chuckling he shook his head. "Good."

All the air left her lungs and got sucked from the truck cab until she struggled to drag in her next breath. Brett Barrows *was* flirting with her. Holy hell, and she hadn't a damn clue how to deal with the situation. On the one hand, inappropriate and out of character crush on big, scary ex-felon, on the other hand big, scary ex-felon flirting back and making her long dead libido want to come out and party.

The truck stopped, and he turned to look at her. They were back at the church, and she couldn't remember getting there.

"Any more boundaries you want to put out there?" He tilted his head.

"Would you respect them?"

"I'd try." His gaze darkened and roamed her face. "And I call you babe and honey because in my head there's a lot less distance between us. There's a little something here between us." He motioned between them with his large blunt fingers. "You feel it too."

"Uhng." Her heart was beating so hard he must have been able to hear it. She was getting an intense lesson in her fight or flight reflex. Or rather her flirt or flight reflex. Before she could stop herself, a hysterical giggle escaped her. She clapped her hands over her mouth before worse came out. "I need to go."

"Yeah." His face turned grave, and he stared out the windshield. "That's definitely for the best."

BRETT WATCHED as she damn near ran across the parking lot to get away from him. Smart girl. If she had any idea what was going on in his head, she'd lock herself in that office of hers and call the police.

The things he wanted to do to Laura Turner. Craved to do to Laura Turner.

Christ, he needed to get laid.

He put the truck in gear and eased out of the parking lot. Instead of getting hard thinking about Laura Turner, he should be finding a woman in the same ballpark as him. Find himself a warm body to sink deep into until he forgot all about all that fresh, clever, feisty, classy as fuck woman that he wanted to get his big, dirty, bloodstained hands on.

When he'd been paroled, he'd thought the first thing he'd do is find himself a willing pussy. Yet, here he was months after his release, still beating it in the shower. He couldn't explain it. Maybe if he got himself some, he wouldn't be so obsessed with a woman he had no business even looking at.

His phone buzzed, and he dug it out of the center console.

"Hey, Blythe."

Her voice quivered down the line, and his gut went tight. "Brett."

"What's wrong?" The tears in his sister's voice made him want to break something.

Blythe took a deep breath. "I'm sorry to call you, but Eric is in Denver for the night."

"Blythe." He softened his tone. "I'm here for you. You know that." At least when his brother-in-law let him be. Eric Evans was a good guy and loved the crap outta Blythe. It couldn't have worked out better for her.

"It's Pat." Her voice went hard and cold in a way he understood. You had to grow up with the Pat and Carly shit show to understand that depth of anger, resignation and despondency. "He's here, and he's demanding to see Kim."

"Fuck!" He pulled a one eighty in the middle of the street,

ignoring the outraged blare of horns all around him. "Call Nate."

"Already done," she said. "I—" She took a deep breath. "But I need you, Brett. Can you come?"

"Always, grub. Every single fucking time." He'd hurt this beautiful baby sister of his more than he could ever repay. "I'll be there in ten." Five if he could make it so.

"Thank you, Brett." Blythe hung up on those whispered words of gratitude that he didn't deserve.

That, that right there, was why he needed to lose any idea of Laura Turner. That was his life, his screw up, his consequences to bear, and the never-ending fuck fest that was the Barrows family.

# Chapter Ten

Blythe and Eric lived in a beautiful house on the outskirts of town that Eric had designed and built. As Brett arrived, the spectacular view was spoiled by the drunken fucktard on the porch.

"Blythie!" Pat lurched for the door and hammered on it. "Come on, baby girl, let Daddy in. I just want to see my girls."

Brett threw the truck in Park and leaped out. Over his dead body would Pat go near those girls.

Blythe had dealt with their father her entire life, but Kim had a blessed escape thus far, and they all aimed to keep it that way. In a rare moment of solidarity between the Barrows siblings, they all kept Pat from Kim.

"You've got no place here, Pat." Brett leaped the four porch stairs and rolled up on Pat.

Pat turned and blinked him into focus. "Hey, son."

"You need to go." Brett was many things to Pat, punching bag when he was small enough, part time scammer when Pat needed it, and fall guy, but son was not in any of those. "Go."

Pat's face grew belligerent, and weaving, he pointed at Brett. "You got an attitude problem, kid."

"What I got is a problem with you being here." Brett

crowded Pat away from the door. "Get in the truck. I'll drive you where you need to go." Straight to hell if Brett had any say in it.

Lurching back toward the door, Pat got redder in the face. "I made those girls, and I got a right to see them."

"You got no rights here." Brett reached for the fraying edges of his patience. Kim was in the house, and she might even be able to hear Pat's shit going on. They had all grown up in fear of Pat, and that's why they were all going to make sure Kim escaped the experience. "Nobody wants you here, Pat, and you're not going near those girls."

"Oh yeah?" Pat wheezed a chuckle. "You gonna make it so."

"If I have to."

Eyes going crafty, Pat laughed harder. "You got some fucking neck coming here and behaving like your shit don't stink, boy."

Pat was trying to bait him, so Brett took a deep breath. Motherfucker would have to try a fuck ton harder than that shit.

"I know what you did." Pat's cunning eyes glittered in the alcoholic flush of his face. "I know what you did to her." He jerked his head at the door. "She sees you. Don't see why she shouldn't see me."

Brett knew what he'd done too, knew it down to his marrow, and Pat's taunt didn't touch him. It merely reminded him that nobody, not even him, was going to make Blythe's life miserable anymore.

Tires crunched on the gravel drive, and Pat spun around.

A police cruiser stopped outside the house, and Nate Evans climbed out. Tall and dark-haired, their sheriff was also Blythe's brother-in-law and another pretty-looking Evans brother. Dixie had informed him Nate was the hottest of the brothers, but the uniform had always ruined Nate's appeal for Brett.

Nate studied the scene on the porch before approaching. He nodded a greeting. "Brett."

"Sheriff."

Nate climbed the porch stairs, sunglasses in place, looking relaxed. Brett knew that could change in a heartbeat. Nate hadn't been elected sheriff because of how pretty he was. Well, maybe not only because of how pretty he was. Word was he always got the female vote around town. "There a problem here?"

"Nope." Pat straightened his shirt and stood straighter. "No problem, Sheriff. Just having a little chat with my kids."

"Then we do have a problem, Pat." Nate tucked his thumbs in his utility belt. The subtle threat not lost on anyone on the porch. "Because Blythe doesn't want you here."

Pat gaped at him and opened and shut his mouth. "Girl wants to see her daddy."

"Not that girl." Nate motioned the cruiser. "Now, I'm in a good mood, Pat. It's a beautiful day, and my wife puts a smile on my face every morning. Don't screw that up."

Pat blinked at Nate, and Brett could hear the gears turning behind Pat's eyes. Pat didn't do subtle. You had to come at him with a jackhammer, and right now, Pat was debating how far he could push Nate.

Stupid shit.

"Get in the cruiser, Pat." Nate's expression hardened. "And you and I can take a drive together."

"I ain't done nothing wrong." Pat glanced at the front door. "Just wanna see my daughters. Tell them their daddy loves them."

Not likely. More like Pat had run out of drink money and needed a soft touch.

"That's not gonna happen." Nate's voice took on an edge of steel. "What is gonna happen, is you're getting in that cruiser. Choice is yours whether you do it cuffed or not."

Pat hesitated. He glanced at the door, then Nate, and

finally the cruiser. Cunning asshole was weighing up options he didn't have.

"Jus' wanna see my girls." He shuffled across the porch and threw Nate a reproachful look. "They're my flesh and blood."

"Yep." Nate stayed on his heels as he walked Pat to the cruiser. "You might have remembered that when you took your hand to them."

"I never—" Pat stuck his chin out. "Ain't got no conviction on that, Sheriff. Make it libel, wouldn't it?"

"Shut up, Pat." Nate yanked the door open and crowded Pat into the cruiser. He slammed the door and walked back to where Brett stood watching. "You good?"

"Yup."

"Blythe call you?"

"Yup."

Nate had the look of a man about to get something off his mind. "I'll have a word with Eric," he said. "Next time, if there is a next time, she calls me and calls you once he's gone."

"I made her a promise." Brett didn't like Nate telling him what to do. "I aim to keep it."

"Yeah." Nate shrugged one shoulder. "But that's gonna be real hard to do if he pisses you off and you break the conditions of your parole."

Son of a bitch had him there, and they both knew it. "He doesn't get to me."

"Bullshit," Nate said.

It was bullshit, and that was another thing they both knew. Pat got under his skin far easier than Brett liked. It was hard to keep a cool head around a man who'd beat the shit out of your mother in front of you, and then started in on you when he could. Brett had stopped that shit when he had gotten big enough to stop Pat, but the anger was a long, slow simmer that never really went away.

"Stay away from him," Nate said. "You got a good thing going here. The work you're doing for Eric, and now keeping an eye on Laura for Phi. You're good at that, and you could make something more of it, but not if you're locked up."

With that, Nate got into his cruiser and backed out the drive.

The door opened behind him.

"Brett!" Barely knee high, a blond torpedo threw herself at him across the porch.

Pivoting, Brett caught his baby sister as she leaped for him and raised her over his head.

She screeched her delight and beamed down at him. "Blythe said you were here, and you were making that smelly man go away."

"Hey, princess." She was so tiny in his arms it felt like he was handling glass. "He's gone now. Sheriff Evans took him away."

Kim leaned closer and whispered in his ear, "I'm going to marry the sheriff when I'm old enough." She smelled like apples and sugar and Play-Doh, and it was perfect.

"Hate to break this to you, princess, but Sheriff Evans is already married." He lowered her to the floor.

"I've got time to worry about that," she said.

Brett gave her a mock glare. "Do you now?"

"Uh-huh." Kim giggled and hung on his arm. "Do the thing, Brett, do the thing."

Who needed weights when you had Kim? Brett lifted her off her feet as she clung to his forearm. She giggled even louder. "He's married to Bella." Kim swung from his arm, green eyes sparkling and so free of worry it made his heart swell. "I like Bella."

"So does the sheriff." Blythe stood in the doorway, one shoulder propped on the doorjamb. They looked so alike she could have been Kim's mother instead of her older sister. Pat was a loser, but he made beautiful girl children. Blythe smiled at him. "Hey."

"Hey yourself." Still swinging Kim, he walked toward Blythe and kissed her cheek. "You okay? He bother you?"

"Nah." She made a face. "But I heard what Nate said, and he's right, I shouldn't have called you. I don't want you getting into trouble over him."

He shook his head. "I can handle Pat."

"Nobody can handle Pat." Blythe turned and walked into the house. "You're staying for dinner."

And it was not a request, so he followed her into the house.

Man, he loved their house. If he had the money, he'd get Eric to build him one just like it. Sheets of glass faced a view of the front range that took your breath away. The living area was open, wide and spacious with cathedral ceilings held up by dark wood beams. More wood gleamed on the floors. Dominating the far wall, a fireplace stood surrounded by natural rock, the same natural rock that had been used in the kitchen.

Blythe was taking something out the oven that smelled all kinds of awesome. She nodded at Kim. "She's been asking about you."

"Yeah?" That made him happy in a way he didn't know how to put into words. When he'd first been released, Blythe hadn't wanted him anywhere near Kim. For his part, all he'd wanted was to meet the little sister who had been born while he was still inside. It had taken a while for Blythe to trust him enough to let him have a relationship with Kim. "She's a good kid."

"I am." Kim's green eyes sparkled up at him. "Everyone says so."

Blythe laughed and shook her head. "Go and put your toys away, and then wash your hands for dinner."

"Are you staying?" Kim peered up at him.

Brett snorted. "Of course I'm staying. Have you smelled what Blythe is cooking?"

"It's a kind of shepherd's pie." Kim leaned into him and whispered. "Only she makes it much nicer than the one we get at play group."

"Go pick up your toys." He gave Kim a gentle nudge.

Blythe opened a beer for him and set it on the counter. She had no idea how that simple gesture hit him where he lived. He'd never expected, and for damn sure, didn't deserve her forgiveness. The way she accepted him as part of their lives, like he had a real and meaningful place there, was a gift he would never take for granted. He motioned Kim. "You're great with her, Blythe."

"So are you." She smiled at him and handed him some plates and mats.

Brett went about setting the large kitchen island for dinner. "You should get one of your own."

"So should you." She raised an eyebrow at him.

"I'd like that." Opening up about himself was like yanking open a door too long jammed shut.

Blythe glanced up at him as she set a bowl of salad on the island. "You want kids? I never thought you would."

"Yeah." It always made him feel stupid to let someone see beyond the tough guy act. "But that's not gonna happen."

"Why not?" Blythe jammed her hands on her hips. "You could meet somebody nice, start a family. You've served your time, Brett."

"I know that." His old cellmate, and the man he credited with saving his sorry ass, Eli, had always bitched at him about letting people in, and it was something he had to work on every day. You grew up Barrows, and you grew up pricklier than a porcupine. "But the sort of women who want to get with me are not the sort of women I would want to raise a child with."

Blythe's smile faded, and she looked sad. "Yeah. But

maybe because you don't believe you ever deserve anything more than that kind of woman."

"Blythe." He needed to set her straight on this. "I'm an ex-con with a history of violence against women." He gave her a pointed stare. "You know that more than anyone. No decent woman could, or should, come anywhere near me."

"Brett." She met his stare and held it. "We both know the truth behind all that, and you're not the same man who went into prison."

No, he wasn't, and he acknowledged the truth of that with a small shrug. Eli had made sure the changes in him stuck. "Regardless, it's the sort of thing that's bound to come up in conversation, don't you think?"

He had her there, and Blythe's grimace confirmed that. "We can change our path," she said and motioned the beautiful house she now called home. "This, right here is proof of that."

"This right here is proof that you're too good to be a Barrows," he said. And she was. The best part of a messed-up gene pool. If she didn't look so much like their mother, he might've thought her a cuckoo in the nest. She was looking like she might start arguing, so he switched the subject. "You hear from Will?"

Will was their youngest brother, the first ever Barrows to go to college, and Brett couldn't be prouder of the kid. Poor little bastard had been named Wheeler by Pat as a joke and preferred being called Will. Brett got why too.

"He's doing great." Blythe smiled, big and happy. She'd done that too, made sure Will got to change their messed-up family tune. Then she giggled. "I think he might have met a girl."

"Yeah."

"Um hmm." Green eyes sparkling with mischief, Blythe nodded. "He's gone all secretive and has asked me to take him clothes shopping."

"You got money for that?"

"Brett!" She stamped her foot at him. "You don't have to pay for every damn thing. We are doing this together."

That's what she thought. "Grub! I'm the oldest, and that makes me responsible. I don't know why I gotta keep telling you."

"You call her grub." Kim climbed onto the stool beside him. "But you call me princess."

"You think that makes you special, huh?" Blythe's look told him their conversation wasn't over.

"Uh-huh." Kim nodded and giggled.

Their conversation was over. Brett had a world of hurt to make up for with his family, and he aimed to do it. Blythe would get used to the idea.

# Chapter Eleven

Unable to settle, Laura wandered around her condo. The days when the children were with Patrick were the worst. Having Karstyn here, even for those couple of days, had helped stave off the loneliness.

He'd sent her a text thirty minutes ago to let her know he was well. He'd sent it along with a picture of himself and his twelve-year-old roommate. He did look well. She forwarded the photo to Blythe and asked her to send it to Brett.

Even that tenuous connection sent a tiny thrill through her. She poured herself a glass of wine and climbed into one of her indulgent bubble baths.

Jasmine scented steam enveloped her as the hot water went to work on her tense muscles. I didn't take long for her thoughts to head where they shouldn't. Brett Barrows was unlike any other man she'd ever met. Not surprising considering their disparate backgrounds. Speaking to him almost felt like trying a foreign language.

Patrick had always been flawlessly polite and considerate of her feelings. There had been times she'd wanted to do something to shock him. Well, she'd certainly managed that in the end. Patrick had been understanding at first, but she had destroyed the trust between them, and Patrick had been right when he had said he felt like he'd never known her.

He hadn't. She hadn't known herself either, it turns out.

She stayed in her bath until her skin pruned. Once she'd dried off, she moisturized and slipped into her robe. Her debate between another glass of wine and a cup of tea was interrupted by a knock on the door.

It was after nine, so late for a social visit but not unheard of. Belting her robe tighter, Laura opened the door.

Standing in the breezeway, Brett stared down at her from beneath the brim of a battered baseball cap so old the logo was indecipherable. "You didn't check."

"What?" For a second, she wondered if her fevered imagination had conjured him there.

"The door," he said. "You didn't check who was on the other side before you opened it."

Dressed in her robe, bare feet catching the night breeze, she felt more than a bit disadvantaged. She dusted off her inner Phi and went with insouciant. "Can I help you?"

"I got your text." He stuck his hands in his pockets, pulled out his phone and showed it to her.

Maybe she was missing something here. "So you came round?"

"This texting thing. Not really something I do." He gave a slight grimace and glanced around him. "Is me being here okay?"

"Yes." Kind of weird, like she'd manifested him, but definitely okay. "Would you like to come in?"

"Not sure." He stared past her into her condo and rubbed his nape. "You're…" He gestured her robe. "Not really dressed."

The flicker of heat in his eyes stroked her skin like a touch. Her voice came out breathy. "I was in the bath."

"Right." He cleared his throat. "I need to level with you here, babe"

"Not calling me babe would be a good place to start."

A grin flashed across his face. "Noted, but you being naked threw me off my game."

Heat flushed over her skin and tightened in her belly. Being attracted to this man was so out of character, but equally as undeniable. The way chemistry prickled in the air between them was surely her overactive imagination. She must have been still channeling Phi, because next she said, "Are you coming in or not?"

"The way I get when you're about." His hazel eyes locked on her and smoldered. "Seems like asking for trouble to come in there and be alone with you."

Her heart missed its next beat, and her breath caught in her throat. If he was implying what she thought, she had no idea how to feel about that. Terrified, for certain, and so, so tempted.

His eyes blazed down at her. "You getting my meaning?"

"I think so." There was something liberating about his honesty. "I'm deciding how I feel about your meaning."

"Huh." Rubbing his nape, he chuckled, and it stroked warm fingers over her suddenly sensitive nerve endings.

"I'll probably regret this." She made an impulsive decision and opened her door wider. "But why don't you come in. I'm sure we can be trusted in a confined space together." She pressed her lips together before she made another unfortunate crack about confined spaces.

Brett crossed the threshold like a man walking a tight rope and glanced about him. "This is not the sort of place I'd imagine you in."

"Really?" It was not the sort of place Laura of a couple of years ago would have deigned to live in. "What did you imagine?"

"Classy," he said, and his gaze drifted over her. "Expensive."

If this had been two years ago, he'd have been dead on. She shrugged. "It's enough for what I need."

"Your kids here?"

"No." He knew a lot about her. Did that mean he'd been asking questions? Probably not. She was getting way, way ahead of herself. "They're with their father."

"No husband and no Daniel." He walked to the large picture window and stared down into the parking lot. "Anybody else I should know about?"

"Why?"

He turned and raised his eyebrow at her. "I think you get why I'm asking."

"You don't like me." The words flew out of her mouth.

"Honey." His smile came slow and sensual and ratcheted up her pulse. "I like you just fine. And I think you like me just fine as well. You're not too happy about that, however."

He must have read her mind. "I…" She didn't know what else to say, and the way he was looking at her made her lose her thoughts. "You're right, I'm not comfortable with it."

"Me neither." He shrugged. "But here we are."

"Where?"

"Here." He smiled. "And here is where we should stay."

That made so much sense, but the pang of disappointment was there as well. "Is there a reason you came here tonight?"

"Yeah." He turned. "I got the message about Karstyn. Thank you."

"You're welcome."

"But I need you to promise me you won't be going alone there to see for yourself." He went on as if he hadn't heard her.

It sounded like they were drifting into bossy and overbearing territory again. "I can't promise that. Boys like Karstyn are my job, and I like my job. I care about him, and the other children like him."

Brett grunted. "That's what I thought you'd say, so I got a counteroffer for you."

"All right?" She wasn't a big fan of his counteroffers thus far, at least the ones he'd leveled on her before today.

"I want to give you my number." He held up his cell, but as if it was a bit of a foreign object to him. "That way, if you get a bug up your ass to go places you know I won't like you going, you call me. I'll come with you."

Laura took a deep breath. He had this way of packing his statements with so much crap she found unacceptable it was hard to know where to start. At least he hadn't called her babe. "I will want to go to see some of my cases," she said, speaking carefully so he got it all and remembered it. "And although it is absolutely none of your business where I go, and it matters even less how you feel about it, I did get a fright the other night outside the church, and I would rather not experience that again." She held her hand up to stop him before he spoke again. She needed to get one of his speeches dealt with before he released any more head-exploding arrogance in her direction. "Therefore, I will text you if I have to go somewhere that makes me nervous, and if you are able to accompany me, we can go together."

"I will be able to go with you, and on the remote chance I can't, I'll send Razor," he said, a smirk playing around his mouth as if she amused the hell out of him.

She'd leave the smirking for another day. "And Blythe could have given me your number."

"No, she couldn't." He shook his head.

Laura was missing something. "Of course, she could. All you had to do was ask her for mine or get her to send me yours. You didn't have to drive over here."

"A couple of things there, sugar." He closed the few feet between them and stood close enough to her that she had to look up. "First off, I don't want Blythe knowing we're in contact. I ain't the sort you need to be seen with." He cupped her cheek with his palm. "And driving over here to see you is the best part of my day so far."

"It is?" Her pulse drummed in her ears, and heat radiated from his gentle touch on her cheek. She wanted to turn her face into his palm and rub against him.

"Umm." His gaze grew more sensual as he studied her face. He looked at her as if he was trying to catch every subtle shift and nuance of her expression. "Pat was with Blythe when I got there."

"Your father?" She wished she had the courage to close the space between them and nestle into his heat and power. But she'd never been that confident with men. Not even with Eric, and they'd been young and crazy in love. The same Eric now married to Brett's sister. This was the problem with living in small towns. Your sins were never too far from catching up with you.

"Father?" Brett chuckled. "I'm damn sure he doesn't deserve that title, but him, yeah."

Blythe had worked long and hard to break free of her childhood. "Is Blythe okay?"

"Yeah." His expression softened. "I like that you ask that."

"I like Blythe." And there was a statement she'd never thought she'd make. She had been so jealous of the bond between Eric and Blythe when they were younger. She had seen what it had taken Eric years and years to realize, that he loved Blythe with a forever, unconditional kind of love. The kind of love Laura had always wanted, but that was now looking impossible.

"She likes you too." Brett dropped his hand. "But she isn't going to hear about this." He gestured between them. "Because then she's going to get all kinds of impossible ideas. Being Blythe and a woman, she won't hesitate to share those ideas with her girl posse. Word will get out, and you don't need the kind of shit in your life a Barrows brings."

Sexist reference to the girl posse aside, he had a point but not for the reasons he thought. "I have to put my children first."

"Yeah, you do." He smiled, and it tugged at her heart strings. There was so much jammed into that smile—regret, resignation, self-loathing—and she wanted to take the time to unpack it.

Gathering her courage, Laura leaped. "For the record, and apropos of nothing, if I didn't have a ton of crap to make up to my children, I wouldn't think it was a bad idea at all."

"Ah, sugar." He grabbed his cap and dropped it, then brought both his hands up to cup her face. "I wish to hell you hadn't said that."

She read the answer in his face before she spoke the question. "Why?"

"You know why?" A half smile came and went before he dipped his head and touched his mouth to hers.

The touch was so gentle it barely registered, but she knew she wanted more. Laura rolled to her toes and increased the pressure of her lips to his.

Brett stilled, explosive in his absolute lack of movement, and sucked her bottom lip into his mouth. "I'm no good for you."

"I'm an even worse idea for you." She wanted more, so she wrapped her arms around his head.

The kiss instantly went from tentative to incendiary.

Brett opened his mouth over hers, his tongue breached her lips and tangled with hers. It wasn't a tender exploration of something new, or a tentative request for more; it was a demand and a devour. He wanted her, and he wanted her to know how much.

His hands dropped, and she mewled her objection to the loss of his touch.

Deepening the kiss, he picked her up and held her pressed into him.

Laura felt every hard, muscular part of him where it

pressed into her. She grew desperate for more of him and chased the taste of him with her tongue and her teeth. Her arms tightened around his head, holding him captive so she could possess him the way he possessed her.

All too soon, he dragged his mouth away and lowered her to her feet. He was panting, color riding the rugged jut of his cheekbones.

And his eyes…the intensity of the way he looked at her almost melted her to the floor. It looked as if it tortured every part of him to let her go. "Yeah." It was more rasp than word. He strode for the front door and yanked it open. He looked behind him before he left. "That's what I was worried about."

# Chapter Twelve

Her phone ringing dragged Laura awake long before she wanted to be the next morning. After Brett had left last night, she'd gone ahead and had a glass or two more of wine. Forcing open her gritty eyes, she peered at the screen.

Pippa.

Rolling over, she took the call, her voice laced with sandpaper as she answered, "Hey."

"And hey yourself," Pippa said, chirpy enough to make Laura's head ache. It had taken a Netflix marathon binge alongside the wine to get to sleep after Brett left. "We're here, where are you?"

"We?" A tendril of something she might have forgotten fluttered, and then she got it. "It's Thursday."

"It is indeed." Pippa laughed. "And your favorite sister is standing outside your door wondering what she has to do to be let in."

The clock by her bedside read past ten, and Pippa was here to plan Phi's surprise birthday party. "I'm coming."

She threw her legs over the side of the bed and creaked to her feet. Sometimes she really missed the days when she'd had her life and her children's lives planned down to the minute.

Her foot caught on her Chucks, and she nearly went ass over tip.

Past Laura would have been stylishly dressed and groomed, hair in place and makeup perfect. She would also have had the coffee ready to pour and something delicious and nutritious straight out of the oven and cooling on the baking rack. Past Laura would also be repeating a mantra on not letting Pippa get under her skin.

Dragging on her robe, present Laura staggered into her bathroom and grabbed a hair tie.

Of course, past Laura would have been doing all this in a lame attempt to compete with her more beautiful, more glamorous, more everything, younger sister.

Flinging open the door, she said, "I'm so sorry. I overslept."

Looking quintessentially Pippa, and thus gorgeous and glamorous and enchanting, in a powder blue trench with her red hair artfully tumbled, her sister grinned at her. "Good morning."

"Let me at her." Laura made grabby hands for Jasmine. Only Pippa could get away with a pale blue trench coat with a toddler.

Dressed in a purple tutu, snow boots, a superman cape over her sparkly unicorn T-shirt and a bright pink hard hat, Jasmine grinned at her. "'Lo!"

"And hello to you." Laura buried her face in Jasmine's neck and sucked in a deep breath of cotton-candy-sweet little girl. Jasmine made her heart ache for Daisy at that age. Of course, past Laura would never have allowed Daisy out of the house in anything less than perfectly coordinated separates. Laura smiled at Pippa over Jasmine's head. "I see we dressed ourself this morning?"

"I have literally spent a fortune on adorable kids' clothes." Pippa rolled her eyes and stepped into the condo. She closed the door with a hip check and dropped an enormous baby bag on the floor. "But the battle is bigger than I am some mornings."

"She looks great." Laura grinned at Jasmine. "You're going to be a fashionista like your mummy, aren't you?"

"No!" Jasmine wriggled to get down.

Pippa strolled into the living room, gracefully shrugging off her trench coat. Trench coat envy twitched in Laura. She missed her beautiful closet in her old house, her beautiful closet filled with beautiful clothes. But her lifestyle now didn't lend itself to those clothes, and her budget certainly didn't cover them, so she'd kept a few pieces she couldn't bear to part with, and the rest she'd donated to a women's organization that provided appropriate clothing for women who were struggling to enter the job market. "I really am sorry I overslept. I didn't get much sleep last night."

Bending, Pippa picked something up and stood with Brett's cap balanced on her forefinger. She twinkled mischievously at Laura. "Was he worth losing sleep over."

Jasmine grabbed her blankie from the bag and stomped into the kitchen. "No!"

Pippa kept grinning, and Laura's face got hotter and hotter. "What your daughter said."

"Really." Pippa wrinkled her nose. "That's disappointing. Why wasn't he worth losing sleep over? No good or false advertising?" Pippa crooked her baby finger and raised her brow.

If she thought she couldn't blush harder, Laura was wrong. These conversations with Pippa were new as well, and as much as she enjoyed the greater ease between them, Pippa's forthrightness took some getting used to. "No, as in I don't know. He didn't stay."

"Really?" Pippa's face lit up. "But there is a he?"

Laura opened her mouth in instant denial but then stopped. She didn't have to hide things from her sister. The facade past Laura had worked so hard to maintain was shattered beyond repair. "I'm not sure." She wrinkled her nose. "Maybe, but it could be a truly horrible idea."

"No." Jasmine bumped Pippa's leg with her sippy cup. "No."

"Now you have to tell me the rest." Pippa uncapped Jasmine's sippy cup and handed it back to her. "My last truly horrible idea turned out to be the best one I'd had in a while."

"Yeah." Laura was happy for Pippa having found and then married Matt, and them having this beautiful child, but she'd had her happy ending and managed to screw it up beyond recognition. "Let me brush my teeth first, but I don't think it's going to be a you and Matt, happily ever after sort of horrible idea."

"Go." Pippa pointed. "And have a shower while you're at it. I'll put coffee on."

"No." Jasmine banged her cup on the floor. "No, no, no."

After taking a quick shower, Laura dragged on jeans and a T-shirt, and scraped her wet hair into a braid before joining Pippa and Jasmine in the kitchen.

Pippa had made coffee and added eggs and toast to the mix. She pushed the plate at Laura. "Eat, and talk while you do it." She cupped her coffee mug in her palms. "First, I'm going to need a name."

Laura laughed. She couldn't help it. Grabbing her courage, she said, "I seem to have developed a ridiculous crush on Brett Barrows."

Pippa sprayed coffee over the kitchen counter and came up coughing and spluttering.

"You see." Laura handed her some paper towels to mop herself up with. She was glad the pale blue trench was still on her couch. "Horrible idea."

"Now, hang on to your horses there." Pippa held up a hand as she dabbed her linen shirt. "Let me process this."

Laura ate her breakfast while Pippa processed.

"In the interest of clarity, let me confirm." Pippa took a

breath and sipped her coffee. "We are talking about *the* Brett Barrows here? Big, bad Brett Barrows?"

"Uh-huh." Laura stuck toast in her mouth before she said something stupid.

"Wow." Pippa widened her eyes. "That is probably the last person I expected you to have a crush on."

"I know." It shouldn't bother her to hear what she already knew, but it did. "He's him, and I'm me."

"But now hang on a minute." Pippa propped her hip against the counter. "The man is hot, in a totally scary and intimidating way, but still hot."

"You think?"

"Totally." Pippa nodded. "You and I have completely different taste in men, but I can see what you see. And he's kinda your type."

Now Pippa was out to lunch. "Brett is nothing like Patrick."

"I was thinking more of Eric," Pippa said. "Same edgy hot thing going on. Same bad boy vibe."

"Eric was years ago." And still not a comfortable topic of conversation for her. "I didn't know what I wanted back then."

"Or maybe you really did know what appealed to you," Pippa said. "This woman in front of me today is a lot more like that girl than the Laura who was married to Patrick."

Whenever her past was mentioned, Laura felt the overwhelming desire to apologize. She'd caused so much damage. "But that didn't end well, did it? You know what I did to Eric."

"Would you do that now?" Pippa cocked her head.

Laura didn't even have to think about it. "Hell to the no."

"There we go." Pippa shrugged. "Does Brett have tattoos?"

"He does." But she'd not seen all of them.

Pippa grinned. "I bet you'd like a closer look."

"This is stupid." Laura shut down that line of thought. "Nothing is going to happen between Brett and me. Let's plan our grandmother's seventieth birthday."

"Aka her eightieth, but nobody tell her." Pippa rolled her eyes. "Any ideas for a theme."

"Sparkle."

"Yeah." Pippa laughed. "And a lot of it. I was thinking a masquerade."

Pippa and Phi had always been so close. "Oh, she'd love that."

"Any chance to play dress up." Pippa looked up, paused, and then said, "You know you deserve happiness, Laura. Same as everyone else, you're allowed to be happy."

BRETT MET Razor at Cranks that night. He'd taken Will shopping for new duds while Blythe was at work. There would be bitching when Blythe found out, but sometimes it was better to ask forgiveness than permission. Blythe could go on and on about how they were doing this together, but while he'd been in jail, Blythe had shouldered the burden for both younger siblings. It was because of Blythe that Will was in college, and due to Blythe and Blythe alone, that Kim would grow up never knowing what it was like to hide from your stoned, drunk parent.

Razor jerked his chin in greeting and motioned Cruze for a second beer for Brett.

A man got between Brett and the bar. "Barrows."

"Ronnie." Brett held the gaze of Ghost Falls's, possibly the entire state's, most dangerous resident. Ronnie Ork, aka Fast Ronnie, aka Hatchet, aka the Cutter. He'd run with Ronnie before he'd gotten sent down, kept Ronnie's hide in one piece, and the guy felt like he owed him. "How you doing?"

"Doing good, Brett." Ronnie picked his teeth with the long nail on his pinkie finger. "You still hold my marker."

"I told you, Ronnie." As much as he didn't relish pissing Ronnie off, he needed to get this straight. "I ain't about that life anymore. Consider the marker null and void."

Ronnie's cold gray eyes went sharky. "Can't do that, Brett. Man's gotta have honor or he ain't nothing. Call that marker, and do it soon." He clapped Brett on the shoulder. He was almost a head shorter, but Brett still wouldn't have wanted to test himself against him. There was nothing Ronnie wouldn't do to win. Nothing. "I don't like to be obligated."

"I hear you." Brett stepped aside so Ronnie could walk past him. Fuck! Ronnie was a complication he didn't need. He wanted distance between himself and his former life.

Razor watched Ronnie leave. "What was that about?"

"His marker."

Shaking his head, Razor sighed. "Then you better make something up and get him off your back."

It wasn't that easy. Ronnie's weird sense of honor would demand an eye for an eye.

"She settled for the night?" Brett had asked Razor to keep his eye on Laura today. The shopping had been partly an excuse and a convenient way to put distance between them. After that kiss last night, Brett did not trust himself within touching distance of her. He wanted to kiss her again and do a whole lot more.

Razor nodded. "Her kids are with her."

"Good." Laura would never do anything to endanger her kids. "She stay out of trouble today?"

"Yup. That sister of hers, the one from television came round. They spent a few hours together, and then your lady ran some chores." Razor sipped his beer.

Brett nodded his thanks to Cruze for his beer. "She's not my lady."

"No?" Razor raised an eyebrow. "Then why aren't we getting paid for this gig?"

"Family." He put his beer to his mouth to stop his mouth from going off.

Razor nodded and chuckled. "Right, family."

"Cole is lying low." After he'd dropped Will at his residence, Brett had gone hunting. Plenty of his old acquaintances knew Cole Watts and were more than happy to hand over info on him. "Fucker's in the wind, but I put out feelers."

"He'll stay in the wind if he's smart," Razor said.

True that. They drank in a companionable silence for a while.

"I checked with Daniel on her schedule." Razor broke the silence. "He was more than happy to let us know when there was a chance she'd be working late."

"I had a word with Karstyn," he said. "He'll call me first next time."

"Good." Razor nodded. He turned to Brett, opened his mouth and shut it. Then went back to his beer.

Brett hated mysterious shit. "What?"

"Nothing."

"Don't nothing me like a goddamn wife. What?" Laura would hate that last thing he'd said. She'd probably bitch at him about it using her classy education words.

Razor plunked his beer bottle on the bar. "Okay, then. You ever think we might be able to do this, like for money?"

"What this?" Brett stared at him.

"Like surveillance and protection. Security." Razor shrugged.

"Buddy." Brett stared at him. Razor must have lost his tiny mind. "We've both got records long as our arms. The only thing we know about security is how to get past it, and the only thing we know about protection is that we're generally what it's there to prevent."

"Exactly." Razor rapped his knuckles on the bar. "You're

already working security for your brother-in-law, and we could use what we know to stop other assholes like us."

"Yeah, but…" It made a certain kind of sense. "Who would trust convicted felons with this sort of thing?"

Razor pulled a face. "There is that, but we could maybe get around it if we had some good references."

"Maybe." Brett let the idea roll in his mind. It was a dumb idea, but not that dumb, and it stuck like gum on your shoe. "Actually, I've been thinking I want to get my high school diploma."

"You never got it?" Razor signaled Cruze for two more.

"Nah." Brett picked the label on his new beer. "Went down for the first time three days after my eighteenth birthday."

"That's rough."

"Yeah." Pat had persuaded him to take the rap for some lifted televisions. Being young and a first offender, according to Pat, had meant he would get a lesser sentence. Maybe he had, but who the fuck put their kid behind bars instead of them?

You know who didn't do that messed up shit to their kids? People like Laura, that's who. She hadn't been raised like that, and she wasn't raising her kids like that either.

He needed to get her out of his mind.

"Hey, baby." A waft of sickly sweet perfume enveloped him as a female body pressed into his side. She slid her arm around his shoulders and brought her mouth to his ear. "You feeling lonely?"

"Hey, Amy." They'd gone to school together way back when. "How you doing?"

"I'm good." She snuggled closer to him.

Brett had always liked Amy, but it had been a long time since they'd hooked up.

In that time, Amy had gotten married and divorced twice, and had four children, one of them after her last divorce. Her baby daddy had been sent down for dealing, but not before giving her the scar on her top lip. Amy's hard life had etched itself into her eyes. She looked good, if you didn't look too closely. Her hair was still black, although now the dull brittle sheen came from a bottle. Her face was unlined, but her skin looked tired and paper thin. "Wanna get outta here?"

"Nah." Brett kept it gentle and slid her arm from around his neck. "Why don't you hang for a while? Have a drink?"

"Seriously?" Amy reeled back, eyes glittering from between her thick eyeliner and fake lashes. "You're hot, baby, but girls don't wanna hang with you. I've got plenty of friends." She laughed and lurched away from him, high or drunk, probably both. "We wanna fuck you, Brett baby. Because that's about all a big bastard like you is good for."

# Chapter Thirteen

Brett arrived a few minutes early to pick Blake up from his support group at the rec center. Being early gave him the advantage of being able to check on Laura.

At least, that was the lame-assed excuse he gave himself for wanting to see her. As much as the other night had been a monumental cock up, the memory of their kiss tormented him. She'd wanted him, near enough as badly as he wanted her.

Still, he had promised Eric he'd keep an eye on Laura, and he was starting to see how stubborn she could be.

She was sitting at her desk, head down, shiny curtain of copper hair obscuring her face. He took a moment to watch her before he said, "Hey."

Startling, she looked up and flushed. "Hi. I didn't see you there."

"I just got here." He propped his shoulder against the doorjamb and forced himself to stay put. Weak sunlight turned her skin to marble, all the way down the long, elegant sweep of her neck and disappearing beneath her plaid shirt. She even made plaid look sophisticated.

She raised an eyebrow. "Is the plan to loom and stare?"

"For starters." Beneath all that class and ice simmered a firecracker, and he wanted to set flame to her and watch her burn. "I'm here to pick up Blake."

"Oh." Her pale cheeks showed every bit of color as they went pink. "I thought you were checking up on me."

He couldn't resist adding a mouthful of gasoline to her flame. "I'm doing that too." And then because it got the better of him, he said, "I'm glad to see you listening and staying put."

*Ka-boom!*

Her spine snapped straight, her cheeks went deeper pink, and those wicked green eyes turned gemstone hard. "I beg your pardon?"

She'd kick him for sure if she knew how much all the hot ice aimed at him made him want to melt it.

"Brett!" Reverend Michael hailed him.

Big boots clomping as he strode down the corridor toward them, Reverend Michael looked more tough guy than neighborhood priest. He held out his hand to Brett and grinned at him. "Good to see you." He poked his head around Laura's doorjamb. "And keeping an eye on Laura for us."

Laura shot to her feet. "I don't need—"

"I never liked her working late on her own." Michael didn't even glance her way, but his eyes twinkled like he knew exactly what he was doing. "And in that vein, I heard a wonderful rumor."

The way Michael looked at him made Brett twitch. It was the same look he'd gotten when Michael had talked him into carrying furniture around for the retirement center, and another time getting him to help set up the bake sale for the women's auxiliary. Michael reminded him of Eli; neither of them would be moved when they were on a mission, and if they were on a mission, you needed to make yourself scarce, or that mission swept you along like a tidal wave. He knew he was going the regret asking, "What rumor is that?"

"Blythe told me you're going to hold a self-defense class here at the rec center." Beaming, Michael tossed an arm around his shoulders. One of a handful of men who could stand eyeball to eyeball with him.

Ah, hell no. "Now, wait a minute. I never—"

"There are so many women around here who would benefit from learning how to protect themselves." Michael looked at Laura.

"Not to mention the elderly." Those witchy eyes glittered at him as she got her own back.

Still, he had committed to no such thing. "Now, listen. Blythe had no business—"

"The women's auxiliary is really excited about this." Michael clapped his shoulder and dropped his arm. "The only self-defense class in town is at the gym, and that's way over on the other side of town."

"And expensive," Laura added with a smirk.

This was getting away from him, so Brett pumped the brakes. "I'm an ex-con."

"Right! That's what makes this so perfect." Michael's eyes sparkled. "Nobody knows more about self-defense than a genuine tough guy."

"Not to mention how most of our community can't afford the class at the gym." Laura grinned at him. Not giving a shit, he knew she was enjoying his discomfort.

"Listen." He held out his hand to stop them. Somebody had to be the goddamn voice of reason around there. "Even if people did come—"

"Oh, they'll come." Laura twinkled at him.

"Some of them to get a look at our biggest, baddest resident." Michael chuckled. "Plus, the ladies of the auxiliary tell me you're not too hard on the eyes."

Heat flooded his cheeks, and he felt like a fucking teenager. "Even if they did come, I'm no teacher."

"There's nothing to it." Michael threw his arms wide.

"And I'm sure Blythe could give you some pointers if you need them."

"I don't need them, because—"

"Great." Michael rubbed his hands together. "I'll have a peek at the schedule and let you know when we can fit you in."

"There is no need to look at the schedule—"

"Yeah, I really need to." Michael grimaced. "The rec center is busier than ever, and we want to make sure we don't create a conflict."

"That's not what I—"

"Last year I mistakenly scheduled a painting class on flower arranging night." He rolled his eyes. "Hoo-ee did I get it for that."

Laura joined them at the door. "I'll send the schedule to your phone."

"You're the best." Michael grinned at her and checked his watch. "And I'm late for a parish meeting. Blessings all round." He hurried off.

Nobody railroaded Brett, nobody. He folded his arms and glared after Michael. "I'm not teaching a self-defense class."

"Hmm." Laura's eyes danced with laughter as she tapped her chin. "I hate to break it to you, tough guy, but it looks like you are."

"Nobody will come." They'd all run him out of town sooner than take a lesson from him.

Laura chuckled, and he fucking loved that sound. "I'm afraid I heard the women's auxiliary, and they'll turn out in droves to get a good look at Brett Barrows."

"Why?" Inside he was straight up squirming, but he'd be damned if he let that show.

"Don't be modest." She grinned up at him. "You're Ghost Falls's most notorious resident. After Phi, that is."

He dug that she'd lost her fear of him. "You're getting a kick out of this, aren't you?"

"Just a teeny bit." She made a gap between her thumb and forefingers. "Seeing this as a bit of payback for all the chest thumping bossiness to be honest."

Damn she was adorable, laughing up at him, her beautiful eyes full of life and light.

He crowded closer to her, trapping her against the opposite doorjamb. "If I'm so big and bad, do you think you should be laughing at me?"

"Think of it more as laughing with you." She giggled, but her gaze stayed on his.

Not able to resist touching her, he cupped her cheek. "Sounds like bullshit to me."

"Maybe." The sparkle in her eye shifted to a gleam that his body recognized instantly. He wanted to kiss her more than he wanted his next breath. Standing there, with her scent surrounding him, the heat of her skin so close to his, he couldn't think of one damn reason why he shouldn't.

She read his intent. Her eyes darkened, and she softened toward him.

A ringing phone made her jump and glance at her desk. She frowned. "That's the ringtone for my ex."

Grabbing her phone, she said, "Hi, Patrick." She listened for a while and said, "No, she's not with me. I'm at the rec center."

Her ex's voice came tinny over the line.

She sighed. "I work here, Patrick."

More chatting from the ex.

"Did you try her cell?"

It sounded like the ex got excited on the other end of the call.

Laura backed right down. "Of course you did, I'm sorry. I'm only trying to think of what we can do."

That must be the first time he'd seen his redhead back down, and he didn't like it one bit. Fire like the one in Laura should always blaze bright. Brett had heard the ex was a doctor, or something. Dentist! That was it. Dentist didn't sound all that intimidating, but it was a reminder that the dentist's ex-wife was so far out of Brett's league they weren't even circling the same sun. He needed to remember that next time he got the urge to put some part of his body on some part of her. And there went his thoughts places they shouldn't again.

"What do you mean?" Laura frowned, her tone sharper. Tension tightened her shoulders.

Whatever it was, he wasn't leaving until he was sure she was okay. He stepped into the room and stood beside her.

She turned her shoulder and listened. "When did you expect her back?"

Yeah, that wasn't going to fly with him, but he stayed where he was and waited.

"But that was two hours ago." She took a deep breath. "No, I'm not blaming you. I'm just worried about her."

There were a few more uh-huh noises, a couple of nods, and Laura gnawing on her lip like she was going to chew that thing right off. Then she hung up and kept her head down as she hunted for her stuff. "I'm sorry I have to go."

"What is it?" Brett got right up in her space. When Blythe wanted to avoid coming clean, she pulled the same diversionary tactic, and he didn't take it from her either. "What's wrong?"

"It's nothing, but I need to go."

"Sugar." He got her by the shoulders and forced her to make eye contact. "Tell me."

For a moment it looked like she might put up more of a fight, and then her shoulders slumped. "That was my exhusband, Patrick. Daisy was supposed to be home a couple of hours ago, and she's not."

"Did he call her friends?"

Laura stopped and looked at him. Actually, she looked

right through him. "Look, Brett, I know you're trying to help, but I need to get home and see if she's there."

He itched to argue with her, convince her to let him help her, take some of the burden from her slim shoulders, but he didn't have that right. All there was between them was a few awkward interactions and one hot as hell kiss, a kiss that shouldn't have happened in the first place. Laura was worried about her daughter and that came first.

Stepping out of her path, he said, "Let me know if there's anything I can do."

"Thank you." She gave him one of those polite smiles that told him more than a string full of cuss words how unlikely it was that she was going to holler for help. Laura had shut him out.

She grabbed her stuff and left, striding down the hallway her phone at her ear as she tried to find her daughter.

He was all kinds of wrong for her, and she might not want his help, but she had it anyway. Brett watched from the rec center lawn as she got into her car.

Blake joined him. "Is that Laura?"

"Yep."

"Why are we staring at Laura?" Blake glanced at him and grinned. "Other than the obvious reasons."

Brett didn't have an answer for him, so he strode for his truck. More like he had an answer, he just didn't like it much.

# Chapter Fourteen

Patrick and Margot lived in the same house that used to be hers and Patrick's. They'd made the decision to keep the house and provide as much stability for Daisy and Sam as they could after the divorce. Ranch-style and immaculate, it sat in a neighborhood of similar houses, each one a showpiece of style and elegance. To think she used to spend so much effort and brainpower on how much curb appeal the house had.

A lot. The house was beautiful, a beautiful prison that had trapped her as surely as the one Brett had lived in.

Margot answered the door to her knock. "She's here," she said by way of greeting, relief showing on her pretty, sweet face. "She arrived about ten minutes ago."

"Laura." Patrick strode down the hallway from the kitchen. A new runner now decorated the dark wood floors, and a pile of shoes and school bags sat on the corner of the stairs. She'd been far too obsessed with neatness to have allowed that, but Margot ran a much more relaxed home. "Thanks for coming. I can't get a word out of her, maybe you can do better."

She doubted that. "I'll try." She moved for the stairs and then stopped and looked at Margot. "If I may?"

"Of course, yes." Margot blushed to her hairline. "This is your house."

"Was my house." She smiled at the other woman. "Now it's yours, and nobody likes the ex-wife barging around."

Patrick's jaw tightened. He hated any reference to their divorce. Patrick came from a devout Catholic family, and he'd gotten married for life. Well, she'd screwed that up for him as well.

Daisy's room was to the left of the top of the stairs. The door was closed. When she'd lived there, she hadn't allowed stickers on the door, but now it was covered in album covers for Black Veiled Brides and My Chemical Romance. A large STAY OUT sign had a purple post-it beneath it that read *That means you, Sam*.

Knocking first, Laura waited to hear Daisy tell her she could come in before she opened the door.

The interior of the room had undergone a turn to the dark side as well. Dark purple curtains draped Daisy's pretty four-poster bed and a lurid graphic of sinister mermaids covered her bedspread.

Daisy glanced up from her laptop. "Oh, it's you."

Graphic art stickers peppered the pretty mirrored dresser Laura and her mother had picked out from Restoration Hardware. A stick-on mural of skulls and flowers covered the wall behind it. Laura shifted aside a pile of black clothes and perched on the round wicker chair. "Yup, it's me."

Daisy pecked away at her laptop.

Nobody could out stubborn a teenager with a grudge, so Laura blinked first. "Dad called me when you were so late coming home."

"Why?" Daisy scoffed and flopped on her back. She propped her laptop open against her raised thighs. "I'm here now."

"But today is a school day, and you know you have a curfew." Laura had put the curfew in place, and Patrick continued it. They wanted Daisy to have time to do her homework without pressure.

"So." Daisy shrugged. "I didn't have any homework."

That was unlikely, given Daisy and Sam still went to Blessed Sacrament, Ghost Falls's expensive, private Catholic school, and competition was fierce. "Are you sure about that?"

"Yes, Mom." Daisy drew the *mom* out like a piece of well-chewed gum. "I'd know if I had homework or not."

"Okay, but that's not the only reason that curfew is in place." Laura kept a tight lid on her impatience. Losing her temper would only weaken her position and play into Daisy's agenda. "And if you're going to be late, you text either me or Dad or Margot."

"Margot's not my parent," Daisy snapped. She glared at Laura, and then went back to her laptop like she was afraid she'd said too much.

"No, she isn't." Laura was grateful Margot was such a thoroughly nice woman that she did give a shit about Daisy and Sam. "But she is an adult responsible for you, and you owe her the courtesy of letting her know where you are." She gentled her tone. "She cares for you, Daisy; we all do. When you're late like you were today, we worry."

"Really?" Daisy's head came up, and her eyes snapped and sparked. "You all care for me?"

Here it came, the meat to the sandwich. "Yes, we do."

"Like you cared for me when you were pushing me on Phi so you could go and gamble?"

Laura could recite Daisy's spiel by now. Any attempt on her part to check Daisy's behavior was met with a catalogue of her sins. "You liked going to Phi's, and we're not talking about me now."

Sensing blood in the water, Daisy put her laptop aside and pinned Laura with a derisive scowl. "But shouldn't we be talking about you, because aren't you the reason this is all happening?"

"My behavior is the reason for the divorce, yes." Her voice shook, and Laura cleared her throat. It never failed to leave a mark when Daisy attacked. She had caused all the misery. Daisy spoke nothing but the God's honest truth. "And we can talk about that if you'd like. After we talk about your behavior today."

Daisy's scowl deepened. "I don't know how you could do it, Mom. You screwed up everything."

The pain behind those words was worse than the anger. "I don't have a good answer for you." And how Laura wished that she did, some sliver of justification that could make things easier for all of them. "I was deeply unhappy, and I acted out. I should have known better, and now everyone is paying the price."

"Right." Sniffing, Daisy glared at her laptop.

Wanting to hold her, Laura got up and perched on the end of her bed. She wrapped her hand around Daisy's ankle.

Daisy allowed the touch for a few seconds before shifting her leg away.

Laura breathed through the pain of what she'd lost. Lost? Nope, Daisy had gotten it right, what she'd screwed up. Not so long ago, she'd been Daisy's safe place, the person Daisy turned to when she needed a person. It had been months since Daisy had done more than tolerate her hugs, and the loss was a physical ache inside her. "I'm sorry, darling." She forced back the tears. Tears were for victims, and she was the cause of all Daisy's anger. "I wish I could go back in time and do things differently." Maybe face her unhappiness and deal with the consequences instead of trying to self-soothe the pain away. "But I can't do that; I can only say I'm sorry and hope you can forgive me."

"What if I can't?" Daisy's voice quavered, and she cleared her throat.

"Then I'll have to live with that."

"Yes, Mom." Daisy's eyes met hers, and tears shimmered

in their depths. "But because of something you did, I have to live with it too."

And Daisy had her there, so Laura just nodded. "You're entitled to be angry with me—"

"Gee, thanks."

"But that doesn't entitle you to take that out on your father or Margot. More importantly, it doesn't entitle you to punish yourself with your anger." When Laura had first started working with at-risk kids as part of her community service, she would never have dreamed Daisy would be one of them. "You matter, Daisy, and whatever stupid things I've done doesn't change that."

Daisy fiddled with the edges of her laptop and then made eye contact. "Do you like it? Working with those kids at the rec center, do you like it?"

"Very much." Laura had never thought she would either. "Most of them need to know someone is on their side." She let that sink in. "Where were you?"

"With friends." Daisy shrugged, pouting. "It's not like I was doing drugs or having sex or anything."

"I'm relieved to hear it." Her work at the rec center had also taught her so much about handling her own children. "But I also want you to know that whatever happens, I'm here for you."

"I know that." Daisy shifted and glanced at her. "Are we done, because I do have some homework?"

"We're done." Laura stood. After a brief hesitation, she leaned over and kissed Daisy's temple. "I love you, flower. You'll always be my girl."

Patrick was waiting in the hallway outside the door as Laura shut it behind her. "Well? Anything?" He was a good dad and a loving one.

"She said she was with friends. I don't think there is anything more to worry about, other than the curfew trans-gression."

Patrick nodded. "Did you set a punishment?"

"I rather think I've lost the right to do that." Laura produced the check and held it out to Patrick. "Here we go. I had a bit extra to work with this month."

Taking the check as if it was poisoned, Patrick said, "You know you don't have to keep doing this."

"But I do." Until all of the three hundred thousand dollars she'd cost him got paid back.

"I took the money out of your portion of the settlement. As per your instructions." He shoved a hand through his hair. "You don't owe me anything."

Wouldn't life be a dream if that were true.

Laura spent ten minutes with Sam before she left. Her phone showed three missed calls and a voicemail from an unknown number.

Voicemail clicked in. "Er…hi, Laura. This is Brett. Barrows. Wondering if everything was okay with your girl."

For reasons she didn't want to examine too closely, she redialed his number. She wanted to hear him call her a ridiculous nickname in that deep, rumbly voice of his.

"Yup." He answered almost immediately.

"Hi, it's Laura."

His tone softened and smoothed, and she got what she'd wanted. "Hey, sugar. Everything okay?"

"It's okay." Talking to Brett meant she never needed to lie, never needed to present the prettiest version of herself. "She's home and safe and says she was hanging with friends."

"You believe her?"

"I do, but I'm not sure which friends. Patrick and Margot called all the usual suspects before they called me."

He hummed. "She say who?"

"No."

"You ask?"

"No."

"Why not?"

She let the car's Bluetooth pick up the call before she answered. "My daughter is angry and hurt by me. I have to pick my battles carefully with her."

"What's she mad with you about?"

No way she was ready to answer that. "That's a discussion for another day."

"Okay." He took a breath. "Where are you now?"

"Just leaving my ex's house and on my way home."

"You go straight home," he said.

The bossiness must go marrow deep. "If I want to go straight home, I will. If I want to stop at a store on my way, I will. Likewise if I wanted to try out for a strip club on my way home or pop in on one of my kids."

"Sugar." He chuckled. "You go near one of your kids, and I'm gonna know about it and show up behind your left shoulder." His voice grew raspier. "And if you audition for a strip club, I'll be showing up there too."

"Some people might consider that stalking." She must be coming down with flu because the bossiness wasn't irritating her quite as much anymore, and it really should.

"They might," he said. "But you wouldn't be one of them, would you, sugar?"

He had her there, and she sighed. "No, I wouldn't, and stop calling me sugar."

"Sugar, you need to put down that guilt burden you're carrying," he said.

His insight surprised her into silence, and she drove without responding for a while. "It's not that easy."

"Eli always used to say we need to forgive ourselves first, so we can teach others how to do it."

"Who's Eli?"

"A friend." His voice gentled. "I was lucky enough to share a cell with him for a few years. He's part of the reason I turned my ship around."

First evening stars hung in an indigo and orange sky as she

pulled into her condo complex. The night didn't seem quite so long or lonely anymore.

"You're right," she said, and then went with her gut. "I do need to put my burden down. Right after you put yours down."

He laughed. "Yeah. I'm gonna have to get back to you on that." His voice stroked deep and rich across her senses. "Good night, sugar."

# Chapter Fifteen

Brett drove to Cranks to meet Razor later that night. It wasn't like his social calendar was busting at the seams anyhow.

He'd gone years without sex when he was inside and been more or less okay. Yeah, really, people survived without sex. It did happen. Since spending time with Laura, however, the lack of sex nagged at him.

At the risk of sounding like Eric, he would have to admit it was the intimacy that he craved more than the physical act. The urge for that physical release was there, no doubt about that, but he really wanted the other shit that came with having Laura in his life.

He parked between a Chevy rust bucket and pimped out F-150. If he wanted to share his need for intimacy, he was in one hundred percent the wrong place.

"Brett." Cruze was taking a smoke break outside and gave him a nod. Not that the smoking ban had made much impact on Cranks, but Cruze took the downtime. "Razor's already inside."

"Thanks." He skirted the hogs parked near the door.

As he opened the door, the noise of a Friday night in full swing smacked into him. The combo-pack smell of beer, cheap perfume, weed and hot grease always took him back to his early teens. He couldn't have been older than thirteen the first time he'd followed Pat into Cranks. Back then, Pat had been pleased as shit to have a hulking kid who looked like he might grow into being muscle.

A couple members of the local MC looked up as he edged past their table and nodded.

"Hey, Brett." A curvy girl with scarlet-red hair gave him the eye. "Buy me a drink?"

"Maybe another time." He smiled to ease the sting. "Gotta take a meeting with my boy Razor."

She pouted and batted her lashes at him. "Another time, then. I'm gonna hold you to that."

There, that proved his point. If he wanted to get laid, he could.

Razor was perched on his regular stool, studying the crowd around him with a scowl.

The guy sitting next to Razor saw Brett coming, scrambled off the barstool, snatched up his beer and melted into the crowd. There were times when Brett's reputation came in handy. He took the seat next to Razor. "What's up?"

"This." Razor sighed and gestured the crowd ebbing and flowing around them. High pitched female laughter punctuated the low bass murmur of male voices. "Ever wonder why you and I come here?"

"Cruze's pretty smile?" Brett accepted a beer from a skinny barman they only used on busy nights.

Razor snorted and sipped his beer. "We come here out of habit, my man."

"Yeah?" Brett didn't know where Razor was going with that. He'd give Razor time to get there, however. There was the thing he really liked about Razor. Despite the thug-life exterior, Razor had a philosopher's soul. Unlike most of the people they'd grown up with, Razor thought shit out. He questioned others, himself, the world around them. A few trips upstate had only made him more of a thinker. Razor had spent his time inside reading everything and anything he could get his hands on.

"The thing is, Brett—" Razor sighed. "We came here as kids because it's all we knew. This shitty bar was the best we could do."

"Hey!" Cruze caught that on his way back behind the bar.

Razor grimaced. "Sorry, Cruze, but even you call this place shitty."

"This is true." Cruze laid down three shot glasses and poured them all a Jack. "But the drinks are wet and the barman available."

They laughed and Brett took his shot. He motioned no to the next one before Cruze could pour. Since he'd been out, he never liked to get wasted. Growing up seeing what alcohol did to Pat and Carly, and then later what he had done under the influence of alcohol and a few other substances, he never wanted to go there again.

"To continue," Razor said as Cruze drifted to the far side of the bar, "we were raised to expect certain outcomes. In our case mostly bad outcomes, but familiar outcomes all the same." Razor gestured with his beer bottle. "And this place, it fits that version of our futures."

"But?" Because Brett knew it was coming.

"But we're not those guys anymore. We've changed; therefore, our outcomes have changed. Yet, we still come here."

Razor might be onto something.

"And the reason we come here, I think—" Razor nodded as if the matter was decided "—is because we don't believe, deep down, that we have really changed. Deep inside we still predict the same outcomes for ourselves."

Did he do that? Some part of him couldn't dismiss the idea out of hand, and Brett rolled it around his mind for a couple of sips of beers. "Is this some kind of manifestation thing?"

"It could be." Razor tapped his bottle on the bar top to indicate he needed another. "It might be that by clinging to the vestiges of our past, we are clinging to our past. Makes me wonder what we could do if we let go of our past and went all in on a different version of our futures."

"Maybe." Brett sipped his beer. He looked around him at Cranks at how Laura would see it. Only way she'd come in here was after one of her kids, and even then, it would involve a bucket of Purell.

Razor tapped his knuckles on the bar. "Your boy, one Cole Watts, has been seen around."

Razor had his instant attention. "Where?"

"Here and there." Razor shrugged. "He's still making himself scarce, but word is he's looking for his brother."

"How likely would you say he is to find his brother?"

Razor grimaced. "You know how it is. Anybody can be found if the person wants to bad enough."

"Yeah." And that's what continued to worry Brett. If Cole had an ass itch to find Karstyn, he would guess Laura was the gatekeeper to finding Karstyn. Sooner or later, Cole would come looking for Laura, and Brett needed to make sure he was there when that happened. Regardless of what the stubborn woman had to say about it. "You keep an eye on that?"

"Will do." Razor sipped his beer. "Been keeping my eye on the kid as well."

"I appreciate that."

"Introduced myself, said I was a friend of yours and gave him my number," Razor said. "Figured with a brother like Cole, Karstyn was due all the help he can get. The kid's smart too."

"Laura said."

"Wants to go to college, become a doctor."

Brett nodded. Few enough kids made a break from their shitty beginnings, and if this one had big enough dreams and enough determination to make them happen, Brett was there for that. All in.

"Something else about Karstyn though." Razor picked the label off his bottle. "There's been this girl hanging around with him."

Brett wasn't sure he liked the sound of that. "What girl? Could she be a plant for Cole?"

"Nah." Razor shook his head. "Not that kind of girl at all. Young girl, about the same age as Karstyn and real class. Dresses well, clean, shiny hair, that sort of thing."

Brett was impressed. Clearly, Karstyn's dreams included the right kind of girl by his side as well. "You know her?"

"Nope." Razor wheeze laughed. "This is the kind of girl if I came near, her daddy would reach for the shotgun, and Mom would call 911. This is a nice girl, man, way nice."

There didn't seem to be anything to worry about there. Probably a girl Karstyn went to school with, but Brett had given the kid his word he'd look out for him, and sometimes that meant checking harmless shit out, just in case. "Can you get a picture of her? Let's see who she is."

"Consider it done." Razor clapped him on the shoulder. "This is what I mean." He flicked his hand between them. "We make a good team, you and I."

Before he could respond, Brett's phone rang. Caller ID told him the call came from St. Peters. With a sinking feeling he answered. "Yup."

"Hey, Brett." Michael sounded his usual unflappable positive. "Michael Bradford here."

"How are you?" Brett had the nasty feeling Michael was calling to twist his arm further.

"Good, good. Calling to set up that time for the self-defense class."

There you had it. They were all out of their minds if they thought a bunch of women would show up to learn self-defense from him. If they showed up at all, it would be to Mace him. "I really don't think this will work."

"Don't say that." Michael sounded crestfallen. "We've already had a bunch of sign-ups."

"You have?" He looked at Razor, but Razor had no clue and shrugged.

Michael laughed. "We sure have. And I'm not going to be the one to disappoint these ladies."

Fucking hell! Only for Reverend Michael would he do that class. "When?"

"Thursday, seven p.m. work for you?"

Nope, no time ever worked for him. "Sure. Tell the… students to wear something they can move in."

"Awesome," Michael said. "And Brett, I appreciate you doing this."

"No trouble." As in so goddamn much trouble.

Razor indicated his phone with his beer bottle. "That Reverend Michael?"

"Yup." He should have shut it down in Laura's office, but he'd been lulled by her shiny hair and big green eyes, and Michael had taken the gap. He braced for Razor's reaction as he said, "Turns out I'll be teaching a self-defense class on Thursday at seven p.m."

Razor paused, bottle halfway to his mouth. "Say what now?"

Through gritted teeth, Brett repeated what he'd said.

Except, Razor didn't immediately fall off his stool laughing. He shrugged and said, "He's a good man, the Reverend Michael. Keeps that community together with bubblegum and grit, but he does it somehow."

This was true and also why Brett had allowed the self-defense class idea that much traction.

"He walks his talk, the reverend." Razor leaned his elbows on the bar and stared at the bottles racked on the other side.

"When I first got out, he made sure to spend time with me, get me on the right track. He's a good man."

Michael never seemed to take time for himself or run out of energy and enthusiasm for his community. "That he is."

"Man like that asks for your help—" Razor shrugged "—you give it."

There it was, the wisdom of Razor, straight from the barstool. "Which is why I am now about to teach a bunch of women how to kick balls and gouge eyes out."

Razor chose then to start up with his annoying wheezing, hissing sort of laugh, like letting air out of a tire. "I would pay good money to see that."

Brett could do better than that. "I tell you what, you teach this class with me."

"What?" That wiped the smirk off Razor's face fast enough. "I'm not doing that."

If Razor had all these big ideas, it was time for him to start walking his talk. "You teach it with me." Brett spoke slowly and clearly to make sure the mofo got it. "You teach this class with me, and we can see how well we work together."

"That's not fair." Razor scowled at him. "You can't use my business idea against me."

Brett smirked around the neck of his beer bottle. "Appears I just did."

"You're serious?" Razor studied him. "I teach this class with you, and you'll think more about my idea."

"Yup." He'd think about it, probably go ahead and reject it, but he would think about it. "Meet you at St. Peters, Thursday, seven p.m. Oh, and wear something you can move in."

# Chapter Sixteen

When you got a diva decree to present yourself at lunch, that's what you did. Laura drove to her grandmother's house that Saturday, the familiar knot of guilt, shame and resentment all tangled in her belly.

When Philomene St. Amor had retired from her illustrious career as the world's premier dramatic soprano, she'd returned to her hometown of Ghost Falls. Not content with any of the houses available, Phi had built the perfect backdrop for her personality.

Laura turned into the long, tree-lined driveway leading up to the house. Phi had insisted on adding a few twists and turns to the drive so it seemed as if you were driving deep into the woods, and then *wallop*, you came around the bend, and the house assaulted your eyeballs.

Stone turrets, gargoyle drain spouts, fountains and stables all smashed together in a tasteless mishmash of gothic and medieval with a healthy serving of fantasy tossed in.

Laura took the drive around to the kitchen entrance and parked next to the large horse trough. A family of ducks took exception to her disturbing their noon splash and squawked and waddled back to the stable.

Also parked in the kitchen yard was Pippa's sporty SUV and her mother's sensible one. This was going to be a girl's lunch, and that ratcheted the dread quotient all the way up. The four of them never played nicely together, all their characters too disparate.

"Phi?" She let herself in through the kitchen door.

A vibrato exclamation sounded from deeper inside the house. The baize door to the hallway beyond the kitchen flew open, and Phi posed in the doorway. One hand on the doorjamb, the other pressed to her considerable bosom, Phi grinned at her. "Laura, dahling, how thrilling that you are here."

"Hey, Phi." She obediently kissed the proffered cheek. The familiar Phi-scent of patchouli wrapped around her. It was a scent she associated with adventure and flights of imagination. It was also a scent she associated with her greatest guilt. "You look…sparkly."

"I know." Phi giggled and twirled. "This came only this morning, but I just had to wear it."

*This* was a rainbow-striped onesie with huge colored gems for buttons marching down to Phi's crotch. More multicolored gems littered the rest of the onesie, each corresponding with their color stripe.

"Hello, darling." Her mother slid past Phi and kissed Laura's cheek. She studied her for a moment. "You look tired. Are they overworking you at that place?"

Mom was not a big fan of the rec center either. Her relationship with Mom—once so close—was now awkward and strained. Mom didn't know how to adjust to this new version of Laura. Where once they'd been able to finish each other's sentences, they now skirted each other like polite, confused strangers. "I'm fine," she said. "It's just been a long week."

Over Mom's head, Phi watched her with those knowing green eyes. Phi saw so much more than people gave her credit for. It was easy to overlook her keen brain and warm heart under all the drama and flamboyance, but if Phi cared for you, she went to the wall for you.

Guilt ass-kicked Laura, because she'd betrayed Phi's special brand of love.

"No." Phi shook her finger, talonlike nails sporting paisley. "I don't want that face here. Not today and not ever."

As far as Phi was concerned, it was over. Laura wished she could be more like that, but she'd stolen from Phi and attempted to sell her precious treasures to pay off her gambling debts. She couldn't fathom how Phi had found it within herself to forgive her theft.

"Matt's with Jasmine." Pippa floated into the kitchen in a gorgeous, deep green maxi dress. She looked like a sexy earth goddess. "So, I can play."

"Good." Laura kissed Pippa hello and then hugged her because it felt right. "You need to take time off from being a mommy."

Pippa grinned. "Too right, and Phi's been making Moscow mules."

"Oh, boy." Laura's heart lifted as she laughed along with her sister. Phi was a demon with a heavy pouring hand at the cocktails. "Last time we had one of these lunches, it took me all of Sunday to recover."

"Why can't we have a nice bottle of chilled white wine?" Mom frowned at Phi.

"We can." Phi twirled her hand in the air. "After we drink Moscow mules. *Pashli!*"

They obediently followed her into the living room. There really wasn't much alternative with Phi. Diva led, and the rest of them dropped into her wake.

Phi took a copper mug from the cocktail bar and went to perch on her monstrous wooden throne. Elegant and under-stated in linen trousers and a cashmere sweater, Mom bypassed the bar and slid on to the floral sofa. Covered in sateen, the thing was slippery as hell, so Laura sat on the arm. Pippa took her usual place, cross-legged on the floor.

"Now." Phi sipped her mule and smacked her lips. "What have you been up to?"

Which brought up a bone she had to pick with Phi. "You know what I've been up to, because you put a bodyguard on me."

"Oh, Mother." Mom sighed and shook her head. "Why do you always do things like that?"

"Because that's who I am." Phi drew herself up straight. "And at eighty, I've earned the right to be exactly who I am."

Phi's age fluctuated with the point she was trying to make.

Pippa turned to her with accusing eyes. "You never told me about a bodyguard."

"He's not strictly speaking a bodyguard. He just keeps an eye on me. Makes sure I'm not at the rec center late at night, or that I don't go to bad parts of town alone."

"I can't believe I'm saying this, but I agree with Mother," Mom said. "I hate that rec center, and I'm scared witless something will happen to you."

Phi stared at her, piercing green eyes demanding a response. "You didn't tell her?"

"No." Laura squirmed inside and stood. "It was nothing."

Mom's eyes locked on her, so like Phi's, it was disconcerting to be getting it from both of them. "What didn't you tell me?"

"Tell her," Phi said, and sipped her drink. "Or I will."

Pippa glanced at Phi, then Mom and finally her. "Tell both of us."

"There was an incident. At the rec center."

Mom sucked in a breath, and Pippa gaped.

"What sort of incident?" Pippa got in before Mom.

Laura glared at Phi before she answered. Phi knew how much Mom worried about the rec center, and none of her business needed to come out.

Phi looked arch. "There have been entirely too many secrets between us, petal. Now fess up."

"A man. A brother of one of the children I work with. He was waiting outside for me, and he got a bit aggressive with me." She tried to downplay it as much as possible.

Mom paled.

"Motherfucker!" Pippa exploded to her feet. "Are you all right? Did you tell Nate? What did he do to you? Who is this asshole? Why didn't you tell me? Wait." She held up a hand. "Did this happen before or after I came around the other day?"

"Which question would you like answered first?" Laura tried to play for time.

Pippa folded her arms. "All of them."

"Yes, it happened before you came around. He just threatened me and got a bit shovey. I was fine because Brett was there, and he chased him away. And I didn't tell you because I didn't want to make a fuss."

"Too late." Pippa stuck her chin out. "Because now I'm pissed, and I am going to make a fuss."

Laura didn't bother to hide her groan. "I'm sorry, Pippa. I didn't want this to become a big thing."

"But it is a big thing." Mom looked pissed too. "When a daughter of mine gets attacked by some street thug, it's a big thing. And then to be rescued by that...Barrows lout." Mom shuddered.

"Brett is not a lout." Phi stood and freshened her drink. "At least, he's not a lout anymore."

"I'm not sure anyone can change that much." Mom sniffed and picked a speck of lint off her trousers. "He comes from bad seed, that one. The whole family is..." She grimaced.

"Blythe is lovely." Pippa rose to her friend's defense. "She got her baby sister and Will out of that house. Will is going to college now."

Mom pursed her lips. "That's true. Blythe reminds me so much of her mother when she was younger. I went to school with Carly Pryors, as she was then. She was the prettiest girl in school."

"*La la la la-la,*" Phi trilled and waggled a hand. "She was the prettiest girl after you, Emily, my sweet."

Mom laughed and rolled her eyes. "You only say that because I'm your daughter."

"Exactly." Phi's eyes twinkled with mischief. "And I could never have a homely daughter. My daughter is always the prettiest and the best."

"Just a pity I couldn't hold a musical note in a bucket." Mom got up and poured herself a glass of white wine. "I'm still a little bitter I never inherited your talent."

Phi preened. "And it is a prodigious talent."

"None of us did." Pippa wrinkled her nose. Then turned to Laura. "You used to sing, didn't you?"

"A bit." She'd stopped because it seemed to upset her mother. "But I didn't have a voice like Phi's."

"So few do." Phi sighed. After a fortifying drink, she clapped her hands. "Shall we eat?"

"Where's June?" Pippa looked around her as if Phi's grumpy old housekeeper would leap out from behind the couch. June was more likely to be hiding somewhere, pretending to work and texting the details of their conversation to her contact list.

"I sent her home." Phi led the way into the dining room. "She's not as young as she used to be, and her arthritis is bothering her."

Laura eyed the table with suspicion. "Did you cook?"

"Please, God, no." Pippa went pale.

"I did not." Phi glared at both of them. "But had I cooked, it would have been excellent, and you would have enjoyed it immensely."

Highly doubtful, as Phi considered following a recipe to be

mundane and settling for mediocrity. The memory of grape and brie mac 'n' cheese loomed large and ugly.

Mom took a seat opposite Phi at one end of the long, heavy, twenty-seat table. "I cooked. A smoked salmon frittata with a green salad."

"Salad." Phi pulled a face. "Wretched rabbit food."

"It's good for you." Mom stared Phi down. "And you eat far too many saturated fats."

"I am an artiste." Phi cut into the frittata. "Food is a sensual experience for me."

"Most thing are a sensual experience for you," Pippa said and handed Phi the salad. "Eat it; it's good for you."

Phi pulled a face and put two lettuce leaves on her plate. "Speaking of sensual experiences, let us return to the subject of the delicious Brett."

"That segue didn't even make sense," Pippa said. "But Brett is rather delicious." She grinned at Laura. "Don't you think, Laura?"

Damn Pippa! Laura's face heated. "I suppose so."

"Oh my." Phi broke into another trill. "Do I detect a frisson?"

"Does she?" Pippa's grin widened. "Does Phi detect a frisson?"

Mom looked aghast, pausing with her slice of frittata halfway from the serving dish to her plate. "Laura couldn't possibly be attracted to that man. Dear God." She plunked her frittata on her plate and stared at it. "The man's a criminal."

"He was a criminal." Laura didn't want to get angry, but her mom was being super judgmental. "And he served his time. He's a completely different person from the one who went to prison."

"This is true." Pippa gesticulated with her knife. "He's made amends where he needs to and is always there to help Blythe."

"Don't wave your cutlery around, Pippa." Mom frowned. "But he beats women."

"Once." Laura jumped to Brett's defense. "And if you ask Blythe about it, she'll tell you there were extenuating circumstances."

"Aren't there always?" Mom's lips tightened, and her frown deepened. "Once is enough, thank you very much."

A lot of people thought that, herself included. Then she'd gotten to know Brett better. Still, their conversation wasn't relevant. "It doesn't matter, Brett and I are not a thing."

"Thank God for that." Mom took a hefty sip of wine. "Because I shudder to think of that creature around my grandchildren."

"Mom." Pippa raised her eyebrow. "You're being a bit small minded there. People can change, and those people deserve forgiveness."

Not everyone deserved forgiveness, and Laura pushed salad around her plate, her appetite gone.

Phi stared straight at her. "Everyone."

# Chapter Seventeen

Babble of female voices hit Brett before he even opened the door to the rec center hall. As he pushed through the doors, all gazes snapped his way. He'd never wanted to fidget more. That much female attention focused on a guy made you nervous.

And what the actual hell? The hall was heaving, packed with women for his self-defense class. His and Razor's self-defense class, that was, and buddy better show.

"Brett." Laura approached him from a knot of women to one side, including Pippa, Mrs. Turner, the sheriff's wife, Bella and her crazy friend Liz. "Your class is ready for you."

Also there was Blythe and his sister-in-law, Dixie. Blythe waggled her fingers at him and mouthed *I told you so*.

The hall doors flew open and crashed into the wall behind them. Wearing lime green sweats and a sparkling headband, Diva Phi swept into the hall. "Did I miss it? Am I too late for the shirtless part?"

"Shirtless part?" Brett sent Blythe the evil eye.

A laughing Laura looked up at him. "Phi has one of her things in her head."

Damn, she was pretty like this with her glowing, smiling eyes and flushed cheeks.

"Not just Phi," Liz called over. "All in favor of shirtless instructors say aye."

"Aye!" roared the hall.

Had these women never seen a chest before? Cheeks hot, he shut that shit down. "This is a self-defense class, and there will be no shirtless instruction. Now." He clapped his hands to cut through the deflated murmuring. "What is the first thing you should know about self-defense?"

Phi's hand shot up.

"Yes."

"Why won't there be shirtless instruction?"

A couple of women nodded along with her, and all eyes snapped his way again.

"I'm not an object." He tried not to sound prissy. "Now, are you taking this seriously or not?"

"I could take it a lot more seriously if he was shirtless," someone muttered from Liz's direction.

Blythe was pink cheeked she was laughing so hard. Yeah, he'd get some payback on her too.

He looked around the room. "First thing you should know about self-defense?"

Blythe got her hand up this time. "You should, as much as you can, avoid having to use it."

"Correct. The first rule to any of this is not getting yourself into a bad situation in the first place. Avoid bad situations, and for the most part, they won't come looking for you." Blythe needn't think she was all the way forgiven. "The second thing I want to tell you is your money, your designer purse, your wallet, these things are not worth your life. Let them go. The guy snatching your purse is a lot more focused on getting it and getting away before the cops arrive. Make it easy for him, and it might be the reason that's all he does." They were all silent and looking at him now. Some with doubt about what he was saying. "Any questions?"

Phi's hand shot up.

"Not about shirtless instruction."

Phi's hand disappeared.

"Now, I can see some of you looking unhappy about what I just said." He paced from one side of the group to the other. All gazes tracked him. "But let me explain something to you in the simplest terms: your stuff isn't worth your life."

"Sorry I'm late." Razor strolled into the hallway, wearing the tiniest workout tank Brett had ever seen. The damn thing looked like it was hanging from Razor's shoulders by a piece of string.

His class perked up immediately. Next time he'd pay Razor to wear less.

Brett was amazed at how fast the rest of the class went. There was, of course, a lineup to spar with Razor when it came time to practice their techniques. All in all, it went a helluva lot better than he'd expected.

Blythe approached him as he stood watching Liz go to town on Razor. "You did great." She hugged him. "I'm so proud of you."

An annoying lump wedged its stupid ass in his throat, and he had to swallow. Laura in her yoga pants helped distract him. She had partnered with her sister, and they were practicing on each other. Phi sat on a foldout chair she'd brought with her and offered her opinion. Brett simply didn't have big enough balls to tackle the diva.

"It went okay," he said to Blythe. Apparently he didn't suck as an instructor, and who knew Razor had the soft touch?

As the women left the hall at the end of class, most of them stopped by to thank him or ask him something.

Liz got straight to the point. "You coming back next week?"

"We are." He got Razor in a headlock.

Laura trailed behind her mother, Phi and Pippa.

Mrs. Turner gave him an assessing look. "I enjoyed your class. Thank you."

"You're welcome."

She hesitated, still studying him, and then moved on.

Laura took her place and whispered, "Sorry about my mother."

"People are suspicious of me." It was no less than he expected. "I made it that way, remember?"

"Yes." She nodded, then cleared her throat. Her cheeks flushed. "Would you like to come for dinner? We could talk."

Shit, he'd like few things more. And the things he would like more all centered on being alone with Laura, a woman he had no business fantasizing about, which is why he said, "I'd really like that, sugar, but it's not a good idea. Not after the other night."

"Right." She went redder and hurt flashed through her lovely eyes. "Of course you're right. I just thought…well, I don't know what I thought. I was going on instinct."

He wanted to hold her, soothe away the hurt he'd caused. "Sugar."

"No, it's fine." She slapped a jaunty smile on her face. "And don't call me sugar."

He couldn't help but watch her incredible ass walk away from him. Until he'd met Laura, he would have pegged himself as a tit man all the way. But with Laura and those legs of hers, he was seeing the light.

Razor joined him and winked. "You been keeping something to yourself?"

"What?" He tried to head Razor off.

"Yeah." Razor smiled and nodded goodbye to a group of women. "If I had a woman that fine, I'd also want to keep her all to myself."

Inside, he felt like she was his, so it scraped him raw to say, "She's not my woman."

"Seriously?" Razor gaped at him. "You should get on that."

"I'm not getting on that." He wanted to howl and pound his fists into the ground.

Razor shook his head. "Please tell me this is not some stupid feeling of inferiority on your part."

"It's not that."

"Then what is it?" Razor folded his arms.

"I'm an ex-con with a nasty record, and she's…" He didn't have enough of the right words. "Beautiful and classy." It was the best he could do. "She deserves so much more than me."

"This is totally an inferiority thing." Razor snorted. "From what I saw, you're the one who thinks you aren't good enough for her. She seems to like you fine the way you are."

"I don't wanna talk about it." Because he would beat something, possibly even Razor, if they did.

Shrugging, Razor dug his phone out his gym bag. "I got that pic you were looking for. The girl with Karstyn."

Brett studied the girl in the photo. She was lanky, still more child than woman, with deep red hair and a pretty face. An uneasy prickle ran down his spine. The girl pictured with Karstyn was a dead ringer for Pippa, and that couldn't be a coincidence. "Keep your eye on that situation." His step had a spring to it as he strode for his car. He now had the perfect excuse for showing up at Laura's place.

*IDIOT! Stupid idiot!* Laura wanted to punch her face and keep going until she felt better, and by better, she meant less humiliated. God only knew what pig stupid impulse had pressed her to invite Brett to dinner.

He'd made it more than clear the other night that while he

was attracted to her, they were not going to go there. So what did she do? She went and invited him to dinner.

"Idiot!"

"What?" Pippa stared at her. "Are you talking to me?"

"No, me." She flapped her hand. "I did something stupid."

"With our yummy self-defense instructor?" Pippa winked at her.

"No." And disappointment and irritation made her brusquer than she intended. "And you really need to stop talking about Brett and me being a thing."

Pippa's brows lifted. "What's got you all bent out of shape?"

"Nothing." She tried to recover, but she was still riled up inside. "You keep saying there's something between Brett and me, and there isn't. There's nothing there. Nothing."

"Oh-kay." Pippa pulled a face. "But he did spend most of class staring at you."

"Argh!" She couldn't win with Pippa, so she stomped off. "You're impossible."

"He's right to stare though," Pippa yelled after her. "You do have a great ass."

# Chapter Eighteen

Laura had somewhat recovered her equilibrium by the time she got home. She'd issued the invitation without even thinking what food she had in her condo. As it was, she laughed as she looked at the contents of her fridge: bread, milk, eggs, bacon, and half a dark chocolate and intense orange candy bar.

It was a damn good thing Brett had turned her down. She took a huge bite of her chocolate bar as she grabbed her TV remote and scanned the channels.

Her doorbell rang, and she checked the time. It wouldn't be any of her family at this time.

Maybe…

Nope, that was stupid thinking.

She opened the door and nearly choked on a mouthful of chocolate. "Brett?"

"Did you even check who was there before you opened the door?" He scowled down at her.

She wanted to ask if he'd changed his mind, but he could be checking up on her for Phi, and she liked to limit her rejections to one per day. "Is there anything you needed?"

"There's a lot I need, sugar." His mouth quirked. "But I keep promising myself not to go there."

It didn't help when he flirted with her. The push-pull was getting tired, and she was newly stung by it. "What are you doing here?"

"Yeah." He rubbed his nape. "Sorry about that. I wanted to ask if you had a picture of Daisy around that I could see."

"Sure." She inched the door open. "But why?"

"I need to make sure of something." He shut the door behind him. "But I don't want to say anything to you until I know for sure."

"Know what for sure?" If he was talking about Daisy, then he needed to tell her more.

"That picture?" He raised an eyebrow.

She stood her ground and raised her eyebrow right back. "That reason?"

"Okay." He huffed. "But I don't want you to freak out."

"Then tell me something before I do." Her irritation got the better of her. "And what does that mean anyway? Has anyone who was going to freak out not freaked out because someone asked them not to freak out before they told them the thing that made them freak out?"

"Er...not sure." He side-eyed her. "But Razor has been keeping an eye on Karstyn the last couple of days, and there is this girl who he's seen hanging with Karstyn. Classy girl, sweet and pretty, and not like the girls at Karstyn's old school."

That might not have been the last thing she'd expected him to say but near enough. "Daisy doesn't know Karstyn."

"Could she have met him?"

"No." And then she remembered. "Actually yes." And there had been a definite vibe between them. But Daisy wouldn't go behind their backs, would she? Laura didn't like the answer that shot right into her brain. Damn straight Daisy would. "Karstyn had to stay here before we found a foster family for him, and Daisy came here that night."

"Right." He nodded. "But let's not go leaping to conclusions. Show me her photo, and I'll see if it matches the girl Razor took a picture of. Then, I want to check it out for myself."

"Okay." She led him to the mantel and showed him her most recent picture of Daisy.

Daisy was grinning at the camera, her arm wrapped around Phi.

Brett sighed. "Looks like the same girl. Sorry to tell you that, sugar."

"That's okay." Her mind cycled through the possibilities. Daisy lying to her concerned her more than anything else. "Karstyn is a good kid. I'm not worried about her spending time with him."

"But you didn't know." He moved closer to her. "And that smarts."

She nodded. It was hard to keep her defenses in place when he was being compassionate, and he smelled so freaking good. "She's so angry at me all the time. Every time she does something like this, I can't help but think I caused it."

"Sugar." He tipped her chin up. "Even the best kids from perfect families get into shit."

"Don't call me sugar." But she was kind of liking it more and more. "And Daisy had the perfect family until I screwed it all up."

"That's a fuck ton of responsibility you're hauling around there."

"But it's true." She grabbed the wine from the kitchen and poured herself a glass. She raised the bottle at Brett. "This or beer?"

He hesitated and then nodded, as if he'd made a decision. "I'll have a beer." He strode to the fridge and got one for himself. "And I'll take that dinner invitation if it's still open."

"Because you feel sorry for me?" Laura swallowed her bitterness with a hefty mouthful of Malbec. "Because my kid is screwed up, and I made her that way? Because I have this pitiful lonely existence in this horrible condo?"

Brett's eyebrows shot to his hairline. "That's a lot of baggage to unpack, sugar."

"Don't call—"

"Sugar." He enunciated the word slowly. "I call you sugar, and I'm gonna keep right on doing it."

Laura huffed, but the embarrassment after her little tirade swamped her mock outrage. "Sorry about the emotional dumping."

"I don't feel sorry for you." Brett's gym shoe toes intruded on her vision, bumping against the toe of hers. "Can you look at me, please?"

She shook her head. She'd really rather not.

"Sugar." His low grumble brought her head up. "I want to have dinner with you. I want to spend time with you. I keep having to remind myself not to. I wanted to say yes before, and now I'm out of willpower, and I want to stay."

"But you think we're too different."

He chuckled and stroked her cheek with a thumb. "I think you're way too fucking good for me, and I'm right about that."

"I'm not." She lifted her chin out of his grasp. If she was going to air her dirty laundry, she needed some distance to do it. "You think I'm perfect, but how do you think I ended up in this shitty little condo, being a part-time mother?"

"Why don't you tell me?" He leaned his hips against the counter and sipped his beer. "Tell me how big and bad you really are, Laura Turner."

Laura needed more wine. She didn't often share the details of what she'd done. Shame had become a familiar companion, like an old friend who you knew so well you could finish their sentences for them, the sort of friend who needed no backstory when you told them something, the sort of friend who constantly reminded you of your faults. So more a frenemy than anything else.

Brett watched her with his beautiful hazel eyes, and it occurred to her he might be the only person she knew who genuinely wouldn't judge her.

"A couple of years ago, I got into some trouble. Gambling." She took a hefty sip of wine. "I used to lie to my husband, lie to everyone really, and go to the casino." The incongruity of it made her want to laugh. "While other moms were doing the weekly groceries or going to Pilates, I was playing poker."

Brett sipped his beer. "You got into debt."

"Er…yes." It didn't take a genius to put that together. "As I'd been lying to my husband about where I was, I thought I couldn't go to him and tell him." To this day, she didn't know why she hadn't gone to Patrick when she'd first started to see trouble coming. If she'd gone to him before things had gotten too bad—no point going down that road, because she hadn't done that.

"How much?" Brett caught her hands.

She hadn't been conscious of their anxious movements until he took hold of them. "Over three hundred thousand." She'd left a lot of real estate there for interpretation. "Closer to four hundred thousand than three."

Brett whistled. "Not gonna lie here, sugar, that's a lot of cake."

"I know." She finished her wine. "By the time it got to be that much, I was getting desperate, and there was no way I felt I could go to Patrick and confess what I'd done."

"Is there more?"

"Oh, yes." She started laughing and couldn't seem to stop. "The best part is how I tried to make the money back."

"I'm guessing you didn't change your mind about letting your man know."

She shook her head. "That's what I should have done. That's what anybody with half a brain would have done. First I tried to win the money back."

Brett winced.

"Yeah." He got it and how that had gone. "And when that didn't work, I stole some antiques from my grandmother and sold them in Denver to an antiques dealer."

He raised an eyebrow. "A legit dealer?"

"Yup."

Shaking his head, he chuckled. "And that's what tripped you up."

"Yeah, how did you guess that?"

"Sugar." He gave her a loaded look. "Legit dealers are gonna report that to the cops every damn time. They don't want to be stuck with shit they can't move because they can't prove provenance."

She wasn't detecting any judgment from him. "It's almost like you know about this stuff."

"You could say that." He gave her a gentle smile that wriggled right beneath her defenses. "Is there more to this story, sugar?"

"The things I stole from Phi. They were things given to her over the course of her career. They were irreplaceable, and I took them anyway." The pain of that wouldn't go away. "I didn't give a shit about any of that. I took them because I needed them."

"Laura." He slid a hand around her nape and pulled her closer to him.

His broad, white T-shirt covered chest looked like the sort of place a girl could rest her head and put her troubles down for a bit. He was warm against her cheek, his heartbeat a steady, reassuring thump, his hand at her nape, warm and comforting. It had been so long since she'd felt anything less than isolated that she surrendered to the sensation. "Pippa first noticed some of Phi's stuff missing. She and Matt went to Nate about it." He massaged the building tension in her neck. "Nate tracked down the dealer, and that led straight to me."

She pressed closer to him, molding them from head to

thigh. "Patrick was shocked, and at first, we tried to make it work."

"Your man pay up?"

"He did." His other hand rested on the curve of her spine. "He really is a good guy. He paid my debts, and even tried his best to get over it. But in the end, the trust was destroyed." She shrugged. "He wanted the divorce, and I didn't fight him. It seemed the least I could do."

"You got a record?"

She nodded. "Nate did his best for me, and the DA agreed to community service. That's how I first started working with my kids at the rec center."

"Not gonna lie, sugar, that's a fucked-up story."

Being pressed against him, his deep voice reverberating through her, helped push back the weight of her transgressions.

His hand in the small of her back was warm and comforting as he said, "Can I ask something?"

She nodded.

"Why did you start gambling?" He stroked up her spine. "In my experience people go down that road for a reason. I'm asking for yours."

Laura had spent many sleepless nights and hours in therapy working out exactly that. "Phi always says I lost my way."

"Is she right?"

"Partly." She closed her eyes and concentrated on the feel of him. "The women in my family, our relationships, are complicated."

His chuckle bounced her head. "There have to be people out there who don't have complicated relationships with their families but can't say as I've ever met one."

"Could be the company you keep."

He chuckled harder. "You make a good point." His hand

at her nape massaged the base of her skull. "Tell me about complicated."

"I'm the oldest, you know."

"Mm-hmm."

"And I don't really know when it started, or when I first became aware of this, but my mother wasn't happy. I adored my mother, and I wanted to make her life better for her. I was her perfect little girl. Then Pippa was born." She shrugged. "And Pippa was everything I wasn't. She was so like Phi. Those two are twin souls. Pippa was this explosion of noise and mess and life in our ordered and pretty existence. She was a firecracker."

Brett smelled of laundry detergent and clean skin, and the heat of him wrapped her in a safe bubble.

"Phi was away a lot when my mom was a little girl, pursuing her career, so Mom has always had these abandonment issues around Phi. I guess my kid's brain decided my mother needed an ally. Then, with Pippa being so like Phi, they became this opposing team."

"We oldest kids do that a lot," Brett said. "Take care of our mothers."

She raised her head to make eye contact. "Did you?"

"For sure." He let her read the truth in his eyes. "I put myself between Carly and Pat from the moment I figured out he was hurting her."

That sounded so much worse than her story, and she put her cheek back against his chest, but she'd started her confession, so he may as well hear it to its pathetic conclusion. "Somehow being the girl my mother needed became a habit. I made myself into whatever someone needed me to be to make them love me. Except, apparently, there's more of Phi in me than any of us realized. I think my gambling was some kind of messed up cry for help."

"Any more to this story of yours?"

She may as well toss all the skeletons out her closet. "Other than what happened between Eric and me?"

"You and Eric had a thing?"

"Oh, yes. I was in love with him." Eric Evans had been the most beautiful and exotic thing in her life. Gorgeous and wild and able to nurture that hidden part of her, Eric had been a lifeline. "I was seventeen and crazy about him. He was the first person I could ever truly be myself in front of. He was like oxygen." Knowing how protective Brett was about his sisters, she took a breath. "You're not going to like this next bit."

"How about you let me decide about that?"

"It involves Blythe."

He tensed, and she straightened away from him.

"Eric fell in love with Blythe about the same time Blythe did with him." It had been so wrenchingly painful to her at the time. "I could feel Eric slipping away even before he and Blythe connected. I was so desperate to hold on to him, and I…" This part made her cringe. "I faked a pregnancy to hang on to him."

Brett raised an eyebrow. "And Eric tried to do the right thing?"

"Of course he did." She had messed with one of the world's truly nice guys. Because beneath his looks and his wild child, Eric was true blue. "We got engaged."

"And?"

"In the end, I couldn't follow through with it." That was not quite the truth. "Actually Phi wised up to me and confronted me. She told me to break it off with Eric, or she would tell him."

"Blythe knew?"

"She and Eric first became friends the night I told Eric what I'd done. He took himself off to Cranks to get wasted and forget what I'd done." Watching Eric with Blythe had been like salt on her open wound of losing him. In her head, it had all been Phi's fault, and her shame had kept her from ever being able to talk to Blythe. Instead of facing what she'd done, it had been so much easier to blame Phi for forcing her to tell Eric, and to hate Blythe for being there to give Eric what she couldn't. "Now I'm done."

Brett cupped her face and made her look at him. "You sure?"

She nodded.

"I'll always be straight with you, sugar."

Laura couldn't imagine him being anything less than that. "Okay."

"You did wrong," he said. "You fucked up, and you're gonna live with that for the rest of your life."

That was about as straight as she'd heard from anyone. "I know that."

"But that doesn't mean you gotta carry that guilt around with you."

People trotted that one out all the time, and it made her want to scream. "That's easy for you—"

He raised an eyebrow.

And she got who she was talking to, and it made her laugh. "Okay, so you get that."

"I do, and even more, I live that." He kissed her forehead. "But we can't carry our guilt around forever. You sorry for what you done?"

"Yes."

"You done what you could to make it right?"

"I have, and I will pay Patrick back every cent."

"There you go." He pressed his lips to her temple. "You planning on doing it again?"

"God, no!"

"Then we're good." He nuzzled her cheek. "If you were standing here telling me about how you've done what you done because life was too hard on you, and everyone owed you something, then I wouldn't still be standing here."

Her skin felt super sensitized where he brushed against it.

"You done wrong, you owned it, you're trying to make it right."

He made it sound stupidly easy. "Just like that."

"Well, no." He breathed in her ear and sucked her earlobe into his mouth.

Sensation prickled down her neck and shot down her spine. Her breathing deepened, and her muscles grew pliant, liquid.

"There are some who aren't ever gonna get over what you've done to them." His voice grew raspier, deeper, as he sucked on the pulse point in her throat. "And that hurts, but there's nothing you can do about them. You gotta move on and know that you've cleaned your side of the road, and you ain't responsible for their side of the road."

Heat gathered beneath her skin. Her world narrowed to his mouth on her neck, working back up to her jawline. "Is that what you do?"

"Mostly." His lips hovered a breath away from hers. "It's a work in progress."

Laura fisted his T-shirt, anticipation burgeoning in the tiny space between them. Her senses were full of him. The feel of his hot skin, the smell of something woodsy, the possessive press of his hands on her back, the hardness of him against her breasts and pressed at the junction of her thighs. His name whispered from her like a plea. "Brett."

"Wanna know what I'm thinking?"

"So much."

"I'm thinking how much I wanna reach deep inside and find that wild you got tucked in there." He sucked her bottom lip. "Give me your wild, sugar."

# Chapter Nineteen

Laura stilled. Inside, deep within, way below the parts of herself she shared with the world, she went quiet and waited.

His arresting eyes, true hazel, and not merely an ambitious shade of brown, watched her. He saw her. Really saw her. Down to that part she'd kept hidden all her life.

Realization came with a fear knee-jerk. There was a reason she kept that part of her so well camouflaged. Caught in the heated gleam of his gaze, those reasons slunk into the dark. They'd be back to whisper their poison-caution to her, but they had no place there.

Brett waited for her. Forehead pressed against hers, big hands spanning her waist, he was giving her the lead. So much strength and power, held in control for her.

"You sure there is a wild inside me?"

He chuckled. "I know she's there."

His mouth was so close to hers, and Laura brushed his lips with hers.

Breathing deep, his hands flexed on her hips, but he stayed still.

Laura sucked on the pillowy softness of his bottom lip,

drawing it into her mouth. His top lip was beautifully etched, and she explored the shape with her teeth and her tongue.

"Are we doing this, sugar?" His voice had grown deeper and hoarser, and knowing she did that to him was an aphrodisiac through her veins.

She laughed. A lush feminine sound, the laugh of a woman who knew what she wanted and took it without fear. "We're doing this. Nervous?"

"Damn straight." He pulled her hips flush with his and let her feel what she did to him. "It's been a long, long time, and there's a more than average chance I embarrass myself."

There was something thrilling about his admission. "How long?"

He blushed and dropped his gaze.

Damn but that was adorable. Such a big, tough bastard, he didn't seem capable of vulnerability.

"My last stretch was ten years, got out in eight." He shrugged. "Got out, and hooking up with some random woman didn't have much appeal."

Eight years was a large passage of time. "Not even once since you made parole?"

"Came close when I first got out, but this time when I made parole, I made a promise to myself and Eli that I would live a different life. Finding some available woman and doing her didn't fit the new version of me."

Brett exuded sexuality, like a large apex predator. It would never have occurred to her he could be celibate. On the heels of that came the realization that if he was here with her now, somehow she wasn't some meaningless hookup to him. "I'll be gentle with you, big guy."

"Uh-huh." The sound vibrated through his cavernous chest. "All you classy chicks talk so much?"

"Always." She assured him with a nod. "Unless we can find other things to do with our mouths."

Heat flared in his eyes. "There she is."

And there she was. Laura wanted to toss her hands in the air and shout her victory. With this man she didn't need to pretend to be what she wasn't. He already knew the worst of her, and he accepted that without judgment. "Don't call me a chick."

"I'll make a note." He caught both her wrists in one hand and held them at the small of her back. "Anything else?"

His grip was light, and she could have broken free at any time, but something in her thrilled at the easy way he contained her. "Yes. Kiss me."

"Please." He used her gripped hands to press her closer to him. "You classy girls are all about good manners. Say please."

"Please." Laura rolled to her tiptoes and nipped at his bottom lip.

Brett hissed and licked the spot. "That wasn't nice."

"No." She sucked the lip she'd nipped.

His free hand tangled in her hair at the base of her neck and held her still. Slowly, so slowly she wanted to bite him again, he lowered his head to hers. "While we're getting shit straight, I have a few conditions of my own."

"What?" Her gaze stuck on his mouth and willed it to take hers. When she tried to close the distance, he tightened his grip on her wrists and kept her at bay.

"I'm in charge here."

A primal thrill rolled through her. Patrick had always been such a polite almost deferential lover. She hadn't known how to tell him what she wanted, and he would have been deeply uncomfortable had she ever told him. "Is that so?"

"Yep."

She raised her chin. "Show me."

Fisting his hand in her hair, just shy of painful, he fastened his mouth over hers. Rudely, boldly, thrillingly dominant, he pushed his tongue into her mouth. He took what he wanted from her and demanded a response. His grip on her wrists pushed her higher on her toes until she was forced to use him for balance.

He consumed her, and it was exhilarating. Here was a man who could take whatever she handed out and give it back tenfold.

Laura wanted her hands free, and she twisted them in his grip.

He tore his mouth from hers. "Ask me nicely."

"I want to touch you." She craved the feel of him, to imprint through touch every inch of him on her. "Please."

Groaning, he released her hands.

Laura gripped his head and kissed him. The taste of him spread through her cells and ignited beneath her skin. She couldn't get close enough.

He grabbed her hips and lifted her.

With a moan of satisfaction, she wrapped her legs around his waist, digging her heels into his butt to push him against her. He was so hard it made her crazy.

Brett took control of the kiss.

It was like fever ruled her, and her breath hitched. Her heart thundered, and she cleaved to him with every part of her.

Holding her easily, he moved with her across the kitchen. His fingers dug into her ass and ground her against him.

He reached her bedroom and tossed her.

She hit the bed with a bounce and shrieked.

But he was right there, crawling over her, using his weight to pin her to mattress. "You okay, sugar?"

"Yes." She stretched her arms above her head, more than okay. "I want you naked."

"You want?" He raised an eyebrow.

Laura laughed at the sheer excitement of it all. "Please."

"That's better." He pushed away from her and stood by her bed, so large and male in her feminine bedroom.

He fisted the back of his T-shirt.

Laura propped herself on her elbows as inch after inch of gorgeous man was revealed. There was nothing subtle about Brett. Slabs of muscle stacked upon his large frame. Lighter scars and marks told the story of his life. He was beautiful.

His big hands went to his belt, slid it through the belt loops and dropped it to the floor. Those blunt tipped fingers snapped button after button.

Laura held her breath.

He left his jeans unfastened and bent to untie his boots. Standing again, he looked down at her as he toed them off. His eyes, hotly possessive, roamed her as if he was cataloging all of her and deciding what to do with her.

That made two of them.

He gripped his jeans waistband and raised his eyebrows at her.

"Off," she said, and then laughed. "Please."

He slid his jeans off, and he was naked underneath, standing still for her. His eyes dared her to look.

Laura stared down the ribbed ridges of his stomach to the hard jut of his cock, down the bulge of his thick thigh muscles to the swell of his calves.

Brett prowled closer and gripped one of her feet. He pulled off one shoe and then the other. Then he peeled off her socks. "This is a bit one sided."

He peeled her yoga pants off her legs and tossed them. Pointing at her top, he said, "Off."

Laura wriggled out of her shirt. She went for the clasp of her bra.

"Uh-uh." Brett shook his head and climbed over her. "I want to do that."

Skin to skin, heat blazed wherever they touched.

Eyes intent and focused, he lay over her, braced on one

elbow. He watched his hand as he pushed her bra strap aside. He leaned down and kissed the marks left by her bra strap. First one side and then the other.

This new gentleness made her squirm, but he ignored her attempts to hurry him, his entire attention on what he was doing.

He stroked her breast, learning the shape before cupping it.

Laura arched into his touch.

Lowering his head, he sucked her nipple through the bra fabric, wetting it until it clung to her erect flesh. He moved his mouth to her other breast and did the same.

She moved beneath him, pressing against the hard ridge of his cock, rubbing against him and trying to ease her wanting.

Brett slid his hand beneath her bra cup and pushed it aside. He blew on her wet nipple before taking it into his mouth. He sucked, gently.

It wasn't enough, and she gripped his hair. It was frustratingly short, so she pressed her fingertips into his scalp. She didn't want to be treated like a breakable china doll.

He sucked her nipple hard into his mouth and Laura arched off the bed. Sensation shot from the wet heat of his mouth straight between her thighs.

Sitting up on his haunches, he unclipped her bra and pulled it off. Those big hands of his cupped both her breasts. "So pretty." Heat flushed across the hard ridge of his cheekbones. His gaze consumed her. He slid his hand over her ribcage, spreading his fingers wide over her torso.

So powerful, his hands could break her, but they branded her instead, learning her shape and reveling in it. His fingers twisted in the waistband of her panties.

His gaze met hers as he rocked back and pulled her underwear down her legs.

Only once he'd dropped her panties on the floor, did he lower his gaze to between her thighs.

He groaned and squeezed his eyes shut. "Look at you."

Laura spread her thighs wider.

Heat blazed in his eyes as he looked at her. He pressed her thighs wider apart, wide enough to accommodate his shoulders.

Oral sex had always felt uncomfortable with Patrick. It was like Patrick had a mental checklist that he went through every time they made love.

"Fuck, sugar." He lowered his head to her. "How did I live without this?"

There was nothing sweet or tentative about the way Brett used his mouth on her. She'd always hated the expression ate her out, but she'd never understood it until now or how it could leave her writhing under him and panting for completion.

He drove her there ruthlessly, wringing an orgasm out of her that left her weak and boneless.

Wiping his mouth with the back of his hand, he rose over her. "Damn, sugar, you make me crazy."

Laura wound her arms about his neck and drew his mouth down to hers.

His cock pressed hard against her thigh. Tension radiated from the muscles beneath her hand.

"Condom?" Already she craved the rest of him.

Brett pushed away from her and reached for his jeans. He pulled a condom from his wallet and slid it on. He stood there a moment and shook his head. "This bit is going to go humiliatingly fast."

"You can make it up to me afterwards." Laura held her arms out to him.

Brett lowered himself over her as she wrapped her legs around his hips.

He nocked his cock against her and pushed into her.

With a hiss, he grimaced, tendons in his neck standing out. "Shit! I'm sorry, but I can't…" And he thrust into her, hard, crude and rough, and he was right, it didn't last long. He came driving into her with a harsh shout.

Laura wrapped her arms and legs around him and held him tight.

His chest heaved up and down with his harsh breathing. He pressed his sweaty face into her neck. "Yeah." He pushed himself to his elbows and looked down at her sheepishly. "That was faster than even I thought it would be."

"Eight years is a long time." And then she laughed. She couldn't help it. She felt so good, despite everything. What he'd given her, despite coming so quickly, had been so much better than anything she'd ever experienced.

Brett gave her his tough guy stare. "Are you laughing at me?"

"More like laughing with you." He didn't scare her one tiny bit.

"Keep laughing, sugar." He pushed to his feet and strolled through to her adjoining bathroom.

She sat up and scooted to the edge of the bed. Maybe they could revisit this later. She really hoped so.

"Where the hell do you think you're going?" Brett stood in the bathroom doorway.

"I'm thirsty."

The challenge was back in his eyes, and it was a siren song straight to the core of her. He couldn't be ready for round two. Her eyes drifted south, and apparently he was.

He looked down at his hardening cock. "Like you said, eight years is a long time." He walked closer, taking his time, letting her look her fill.

From her bedside table, he snagged the half-empty bottle of water she'd left there the night before and tossed it to her. "You said you were thirsty."

With his eyes thrillingly hot on her, she sipped water. Then she handed him the bottle. He drank and dropped the empty bottle to the floor.

"Now." He gripped her ankles and flipped her to her stomach. "I'm gonna teach you a lesson about laughing at me."

# Chapter Twenty

Laura woke to the magical smell of cooking bacon. Her mouth was watering before she opened her eyes.

Except for the head shaped indent on the other pillow, the other side of her bed showed no sign it had been recently occupied. After Brett had showed her what happened to women who laughed at him, they'd gone to sleep. Neither of them had opened the conversation about whether he should stay or not. It had felt right enough not to need words.

She'd woken in the middle of the night to his hands already stoking a new fire in her, and there had been more showing. Her body felt relaxed but well used, and she stretched and enjoyed the popping of sinews. Rolling out of bed, she grabbed her robe and shrugged into it. A quick stop for tooth brushing and bathroom needs and she wandered into the kitchen.

Brett had his back to her as he stood at the stove wearing only his jeans.

Laura took a moment to thank the gods he wasn't scared of hot grease splatters. Coming up behind him she slid her arms around his waist. "Hi."

"Sugar," he said, with a smile in his voice. "Anybody ever tell you that you sleep like the dead?"

She laughed. "No, but then I can't remember being quite that worn out before."

"Damn." Shaking his head, he clicked his tongue. "We're going to have to work on your stamina."

"Are we?" Liking that more than she probably should, she took another few breaths with her cheek pressed to the warm, silky skin of his back and then went in search of coffee.

He'd already put the coffee on, and she poured herself a cup. Spotting his mug, she refilled it and doctored her own coffee. No surprise, Brett took his coffee black and strong.

Propping her hips on the counter she watched him cook bacon and eggs in her kitchen. It felt right to have him there, and maybe that should have concerned her that things were moving too fast. For the next couple of hours, it was just them, and she didn't want to worry about the future or spend time dissecting her behavior and trying to do better than she had in the past. In a strange way, she'd swapped one cage for another.

The coffee was hot and stronger than she would have made, but it was helping clear the morning fog, so she added more creamer.

When she'd been married to Patrick, she'd felt trapped. It had crept up on her over the course of their marriage, until she had felt as if she couldn't breathe. She'd known on her wedding day that she was making the wrong decision in marrying Patrick, but she'd lacked the vocabulary to express why. In the end, it had been easier to go through with a marriage that came close enough to seem like the real thing.

Since her fall from grace, she'd been freer to be herself, but there was always the watching for bad habits to reemerge. Between counseling and group therapy, she had the tools to make sure she didn't drift back into destructive behaviors, but within those guidelines, she was constantly watching, evaluating herself.

With Brett she could be. It was the most incredibly freeing feeling.

"Hey." He had turned and was watching her. "What's going on?"

"Thinking." She didn't really understand what was going through her mind herself, and she would much rather be in the present moment. "Nothing important."

He sauntered across the kitchen toward her. "Would it help if I greeted you properly?" The look in his eyes told her what he regarded as a proper greeting.

"We could certainly give that a try."

Pinning her with his hands on either side of her hips, he leaned down and kissed her. It was a sweet kiss, with a touch of heat at the end. "Good morning."

"Good morning." She put her coffee down and hooked her fingers in his belt loops. She tugged his hips flush with hers. "Are you cooking me breakfast?"

"I am." He buried his face in the crook of her shoulder and sniffed. "Sugar, you smell wicked good."

His stubble tickled her neck, and she giggled. "Not as good as that bacon smells."

"Rejected, already." His deep, rumbling chuckle made her smile broaden. It was a sound a woman could get used to. "Come, let me feed you."

They ate sitting on the stools at her kitchen island. Along with his other talents, Brett could really cook. He also provided a great view to enjoy her meal by. When they were done, she cleared their plates and went about putting the kitchen to rights.

Disappointingly, Brett pulled on his T-shirt before topping up their coffee cups. "You going to speak to your girl today?"

"About Karstyn?"

Cradling his mug between his palms, he leaned his elbows on the counter. "Might be a good idea."

"Definitely a good idea." Reality had crept into their morning idyll, and she wanted to stamp her feet and shake her fist at it. "Her father is not going to like this."

"He protective?"

She nodded but didn't want to give him the wrong impression. "Dads and their little girls, I think protective comes with the territory."

"Not always." He grimaced. "But let's agree that's the way it should be."

Until she'd spoken about fathers and daughters, it had been easy to forget how different their worlds and experiences were. "I don't think he's going to like who Karstyn is."

"He met him?" Brett paused with his mug halfway to his mouth.

"No." The way Patrick went on about her work at the rec center gave her a hint about how he would react to Karstyn. "But Patrick definitely won't like that Karstyn has Cole for a brother, and also that he comes from the wrong side of town." She shrugged. "And he does have a point, but more in the way of them having very little in common."

Brett's stillness made her look at him.

She'd said something wrong, but she didn't know what it was. "What?"

"Like me," he said and picked up his coffee cup.

It took her a second to work out he was comparing himself to Karstyn. "Well, I suppose so, yes."

"No suppose about it, Laura." He rinsed his coffee cup and put it in the dishwasher.

Something had happened, and she didn't know what it was, but his face had shut down, and his taut muscles yelled *keep your distance*. "What's going on here, Brett? We were talking about Patrick's reaction to Karstyn."

"I know that." He strode into her bedroom, grabbed his socks and tugged them on.

She stood in the doorway as he pulled on his boots with sharp tugs. "You're leaving."

"Yup."

"Care to tell me why?" His attitude was beginning to piss her off. If she knew what she'd done, she could make it right.

He tugged his bootlaces into place so hard it was a miracle they didn't snap. "Got shit to do today."

"But you're leaving now has nothing to do with your shit to do." Her traitorous awareness noticed the flex of muscle and vein across his forearms as he tied his laces.

He stood. "Sure it does."

"Right." Sarcasm loaded the word. With his face locked into neutral and his shoulders back, he looked every inch of his considerable height. She didn't know how tall he was, but above average for sure. "Or you could tell me what this is about."

He stopped abreast of her and stared down at her. Taking a breath, he said, "You and me, we aren't any different from your daughter and Karstyn."

"Of course we are." Is that what he was bent out of shape about? "And we were talking about Patrick's reaction, not mine. I don't have a problem with Daisy spending time with Karstyn. He's a good kid, and he's going far."

"You got no problem dating outside your class?" He scoffed.

His attitude had now thoroughly pissed her off. "Dating outside my class?" She struggled to keep from yelling at him. Her inner Emily took over and reminded her that ladies did not yell. "Are we stuck in a Jane Austen novel? You're the one talking about class and dating outside of it. And I was talking about Daisy and Karstyn. This doesn't have to be about us."

"Uh-huh." Making sure no part of him brushed against her, he moved into the kitchen and grabbed his truck keys from the counter. "This." He flicked his fore and middle fingers between them. "This is a shit idea for the same reasons your kid and Karstyn is a shit idea."

*Ouch*! "Funny you should say that now, in the cold light of day." Emily's inner voice faded under the blast of Laura's hurt and anger. Closing the distance between them, she met and held his gaze. "Because you sure as fuck had no issue with it last night."

He winced. "That's not fair."

"That's my fucking line." She wanted to shake him, smack him, kick him. She wanted to go back to the part where they sat in the kitchen together and everything felt so right between them. "You're taking my words and twisting them."

None of his thoughts or emotions showed on his face. "I'm being a realist."

"Really?" Tears stung her eyelids, part frustration, part hurt, and she turned away from him. "That sounds remarkably like an excuse. Instead of standing there telling me what I think and feel, how about you ask yourself why you're having this reaction to a harmless comment I made? About. My. Daughter."

"Harmless." Anger gleamed in his eyes. "It's only harmless for you, sugar."

"Don't call me that." She slapped her palm on the counter and made it sting. "Especially not as you're making excuses for why you're running away." Not wanting him to see how her palm smarted, she curled her fingers into a fist. She needed to hit back. "Of all the things I've heard said of you, Brett Barrows, nobody ever called you a coward."

"You calling me a coward now? Sugar?" His voice went deadly silky and for the first time she saw the man who had earned his reputation.

Well, it didn't impress her, and he could take his badassery and shove it. "I'm not scared of you, Brett Barrows, so don't even try that intimidating crap on me."

"You should be," he said. "You should be glad I'm leaving. You should never have let me through your fucking door in the first place." He ripped the door open. "I'm no good for you. You know it, and it won't be long before you see what I see. Guys like me have no business coming near women like you. Just like Karstyn and Daisy. I come from the wrong side of the tracks, and I'm an ex-con. We have nothing in common because there is no way I'm anywhere close to your league." He paused and looked at her, and for a moment, she could have read regret in his expression, but then it disappeared. "And sooner or later you're gonna realize that and send me right back where I belong."

Laura stared at the door he'd slammed behind him, one heartbeat, another, and she burst into tears. The son of a bitch had choked them before they had even gotten a chance to get started. And he'd done that because of something he'd decided she would do.

The injustice made her cry harder. She was so angry, and she had nowhere to vent that, and beneath the anger, she hurt. Yes, they were not from the same background. Yes, they had issues they needed to get through. The difference was that she had been more than willing to try.

# Chapter Twenty-One

Brett was in no mood to play nice as he slammed into his condo after coming straight from Laura's place. He didn't know who he thought he was fooling by being with Laura. She was a classy girl, a rich girl as he used to call types like her, and they were more than happy to tangle with rough, but they didn't want it hanging around dirtying their pretty lives.

Jesus, Whitney had taught him that lesson way back when, and he didn't need a revisit to affirm what he already knew. Except, other than coming from money, the similarities between Laura and Whitney ended there.

"Brett?" Blake came through from his bedroom. He and Brett shared what used to be Blythe's old condo. Already showered and dressed, he studied Brett. "You okay?"

With the smell of Laura still on his skin, he didn't have a simple answer. "Why wouldn't I be?"

"You didn't come home last night." Blake followed him to the bathroom door.

"Sorry." He damn sure didn't want to get into his whereabouts. "I should have texted."

Shutting the bathroom door, he turned on the shower and brushed his teeth while he waited for the water to heat.

"Did you remember Kim and Blythe are coming by this morning?" Blake called through the door.

"Right." He hadn't actually. His head had been too full of Laura. Blythe brought Kim around to the condo to see Blake a couple of times a week. After Blake had disappeared with the contents of her bank account and Will's college savings, Blythe was slow in trusting Blake again. Brett didn't blame her; she and Will had worked hard to save their money, and Blake had stolen it. By the time he'd caught up with Blake, the money had been gone. Still, Blake seemed to be genuinely trying to turn a corner, and Brett was cautiously optimistic. In their family, words were cheap and actions rare. "I won't be long."

"No hurry," Blake said. "I already dusted and vacuumed. I also got some of that ice cream Kim likes."

"Great." Brett shucked his clothes and stepped into the shower.

Blake was genuinely fond of Kim, and she was too young to be wary of Blake yet. He might be her favorite brother, but Blake ran a close second.

The doorbell rang and Blake yelled, "They're here."

As he finished his shower and got dressed, he could hear the chatter from the living room.

"No, Blake." Kim had her bossy voice on. "Not like that, like this."

"Hey." Blythe looked up as he walked in. "I was just about to send Kim to find you."

"Brett." Kim hopped off her barstool and launched herself at him. "Brett, Brett, Brett! Blythe and me are here. We came to visit."

"Hey, princess." He caught her and hefted her over his shoulder. "Where'd you go?"

Kim shrieked her delight. "I'm here."

"Where?" He spun in a circle.

She kicked her legs and giggled. "Here. Behind you."

"Where?" He turned in the opposite direction.

"Behind you," Kim bellowed.

He did it a couple more times before right siding Kim and greeting Blythe properly.

Blythe was a dead ringer for Carly when she'd been younger. Always a pretty girl, happiness made Blythe beautiful. It may have taken Eric a while to get his head out his ass where Blythe was concerned, but now that he had, his world revolved around making her happy.

"You look different." Blythe studied him. "What did you do?"

Blake snorted. "Or maybe who did he do?"

"Really?" Blythe raised her eyebrows and stared at him. "Is there something you'd like to tell us, Brett?"

He glared at Blake. He only let Blake live with him so he could keep an eye on him, not the other way around. "Nope."

"He didn't come home last night." Blake smirked at Blythe. "Only got here a few minutes before you."

"Seriously?" He scowled at Blake. He had better watch his goddamn mouth.

Blake grinned back.

That was the problem with no longer being an asshole; people forgot what it was like when you went medieval on their asses.

"Hmm." Eyes sparkling, Blythe tapped her chin. "Let me guess. Do I know her?"

"I'm not playing this game." He stomped into the kitchen. "Coffee?"

"Yes, please." She perched on one of the barstools.

Kim looked up from the puzzle she and Blake where putting together. "I'll take a coffee."

"You'll take a hot chocolate, but I'll put it in a coffee mug for you," he said to Kim.

"So, I do know her." Like a terrier, Blythe got right back on that bone.

He kept his face blank. "Milk?"

"Cream." She drummed her nails on the countertop. "So, if I know her, and you know her…does Blake know her?"

"Blake!" He was going to have a long talk with Blake about minding his own business and what they did and did not tell Blythe. "Coffee?"

"I'll take a hot chocolate," Blake said, and he and Kim giggled.

"Intriguing." Blythe made a thinking face. "All three of us know her."

He lost his patience. "I never said that."

"But if we didn't know her, you would have said no straight away." Blythe looked smug.

Turning away, he put the coffee on and got some milk from the fridge for hot chocolate. "That's not even logical. I said nothing."

"I'm a genius at reading between the lines." Blythe grinned. "I've narrowed it down to two places we could know her from, Cranks or the rec center, and I don't go to Cranks much."

"I haven't been there since I got back," Blake said.

Blythe clapped. "Ah ha! So you have to have met her at the rec center."

"I go to the rec center," Kim said as she tried to pound a puzzle piece into the wrong place. "I go to school there."

Blake rescued the abused piece. "Yes, you do. And do you know who else is at the rec center all the time?"

"Who?" Kim blinked at him.

Blake turned and grinned at Brett. "Miz Laura is at the rec center all the time."

"Fuck," Brett whispered but too softly for Kim to hear.

"Really?" Blythe made a banquet out of the word. "You don't say."

"True as the day is long," Blake said.

"Gimme the piece." Kim held her hand out to Blake.

"Please." Blythe fixed her with a stare. "Say please."

Kim turned a disarming grin on Blake. "Please?"

"That's better." Blythe turned back to him. Her eyes danced with mischief. "Do you know what else, Blake?"

"No, tell me." Blake's smirk was pissing him off.

"Our Brett has been spending a lot of time in Laura's company lately."

Blake gasped and looked shocked. "You don't say?"

"True story." Blythe laughed. "Brett is keeping an eye on her, making sure she's safe."

"Is that what Brett's doing?" Blake snort laughed.

The two of them were having a whale of a fucking time. At his expense. "Explain how any of this is your business."

"We're family." Blythe shrugged. "Comes with the territory."

His anger popped and dissipated. They were a family now, and they had Blythe to thank for that. She'd stepped in and taken care of Kim when Carly was too blasted to do it, and she'd made sure Will went to college, and she'd moved him and Kim out of that toxic house as soon as she could afford it. Because of Blythe, all the disparate Barrows had started to form their own, hell-born clan.

"Speaking of family." Blake got to his feet and sauntered into the kitchen. He took down two mugs and started making his and Kim's hot chocolate. "Anybody heard if Pat is still around?"

Blythe grimaced. "According to Dixie, he still is. He and Carly are still in their honeymoon period."

All three of them knew what that meant. When Pat came back, he made a point of being charming and loving with Carly. At first. It was all so predictable, and it had played out so many times over the course of their lives.

"I wish she would wise up and kick him out for good." Blythe rubbed her forehead. "She can't still believe he's changed after all this time."

"She has to believe it." Blake shook his head. "If she confronts the truth then she also has to confront a whole lot of other shit she doesn't want to face."

Unlike their other brothers, Blake actually had a brain and saw things clearly. When the honeymoon ended, Pat would get punchy again, and Brett wasn't about to let that happen. "Is Dixie keeping an eye on Pat?"

"She goes around every second day and makes Ben go the other," Blythe said.

Ben had gotten so lucky when Dixie had married him. For once in his life, Ben had swung for the fences and scored. Dixie didn't put up with any of Ben's shit, and she had more or less strong-armed him into being a decent human being.

"Let me know if anything changes," he said to Blythe.

She nodded. "I will, but you have to be careful of your parole. You can't kick his ass."

Brett didn't agree, but Blythe only got upset when he spoke about it, so he said nothing.

"Speaking of parole." Blake squirted whipped cream on top of Kim's hot chocolate. "Anybody got any idea how Barron is doing?"

Barron was serving time for aggravated assault. Pat had passed his shitty genes down to his sons. That was the toxic Barrows legacy and why he had no right being near Laura.

"He wrote to me," Blythe said.

Brett tensed. Barron had a mean streak, and last he'd heard, hadn't had any sort of revelation. "What did he want?"

"A photo of Kim."

Over his frozen corpse would Barron get near Kim until he sorted his life out. "Did you send him one?"

"No." Blythe snorted.

"Good." When Barron got out, they'd have a chat, and based on that chat, Brett would explain his options to him. "She doesn't need that in her life."

He put a mug of coffee in front of Blythe and poured one for himself.

Blake took the hot chocolates over to Kim, and they went back to the puzzle.

Blythe watched him over her mug rim. "So? Laura, hmm?"

"Drop it." He had really hoped they were done with that.

She laughed at him. "You don't scare me, brother. Apparently you don't scare Laura either."

"You're really not going to drop this, are you?"

Shaking her head, she grinned at him. "This is way too good to drop."

"All right." He cleared his throat. "Something did happen with Laura." He held his hand up before she could reply. "But it's not going to happen again. It shouldn't have happened in the first place."

"Why?" Blythe shrugged. "If you like her, and she likes you, which clearly you both do."

Deep inside where Blythe couldn't see, he squirmed. "She's like Whitney."

"Whitney?" Blythe frowned. "That rich girl you were seeing when you were twenty? Whatever happened to her? You had a massive thing for her."

"I thought I was in love with her." Whitney had been the center of his life. "And she went back to her rich boys after she got tired of playing with a kid from the wrong side of town."

Blythe's face dropped. "I'm so sorry. I had no idea."

"You wouldn't." He kept it light. Right after Whitney had dumped him, he'd started on a path that had ultimately led him into the darkest part of his life. "You were just a kid."

"Sounds like a real princess." Blythe made rings with her coffee mug on the counter. "But Laura isn't like that. And I know her better than most."

"She told me." He sipped his coffee. "About you and the thing with Eric."

She raised her eyebrows. "She did? That must mean something."

"It means she wanted to clear the air between us before things went much further." He admired Laura's honesty, and that brought him right back to standing in her kitchen, holding her while she told him about her screw up. Her honesty and rawness had reached deep inside him and wrapped around his soul. The connection between them had felt so real and so special.

Blythe thought his response over. "You know, a year ago if you'd told me this, I would have agreed Laura was exactly like Whitney, but now…" She shrugged. "She's changed. What she did and her owning up to it forced her to get real with herself. I think if she liked you, sharing her story with you would be a genuine attempt to build an honest foundation. And as far as I know, she hasn't been with anyone since her divorce."

An uncomfortable thought wormed its way into his head. Nothing about Laura last night had given him any reason to believe she was like Whitney. Laura had been genuine, and so open and courageous she'd touched a part of him that he reserved for few people.

Then this morning, she'd said that thing about Karstyn being from the wrong side of the tracks and how he and Daisy had nothing in common, and it had reminded Brett so much of another conversation. Too much like a conversation that had broken his heart all those years ago, but not a conversation that had taken place in Laura's kitchen this morning. "Damn."

He didn't realize he'd spoken out loud until Blythe looked at him. "What did you do?"

"I may have overreacted." He still didn't think he was good enough for her, and their worlds couldn't be farther apart, but Laura didn't belong in the same cesspool as Whitney. "I messed up."

"Well then, big brother, you need to do what you do so well."

"Meaning?"

Blythe came around the island and hugged him. "Make it right, Brett."

## Chapter Twenty-Two

Laura was having a crappy day. It had started out badly with Brett and his bullshit in her kitchen and gotten steadily worse. Budget cuts threatened her afterschool programs. Done delivering a verbal landmine, Rowena had spent the rest of the budget meeting vetoing any and all ideas Laura and Daniel suggested for the youth group contribution to family fun day.

Despite both of them putting their best faces forward, there was still a lingering awkwardness between her and Daniel. They would get past it and be able to work comfortably together again, but for now, their interactions felt brittle.

On her way back from the budget meeting, she passed Uri in the hallway, where he was crouched in front of the supply room door and mending it. "Hi, Uri."

His broad face went pink, and he grinned. "Hi, Miz Laura. You're looking pretty today."

"Thank you, Uri. You getting that lock fixed?"

"Sure am, Miz Laura." He waved a screwdriver at her and giggled. "Can't have anybody else getting stuck in there."

Uri could always brighten her day. "I guess it was just my dumb luck to get caught in there."

"No, Miz Laura." Uri shook his head. "You didn't shut the door. It was the big one that shut the door."

Brett. The author of her crappy day and the last person she wanted to talk about right now. "You're right." She smiled at Uri. "We can blame him."

"You can do that now," he said. "He's in your office."

Uri must have misunderstood. *Please, let Uri have misunderstood.* She really didn't have it in her to go another ten rounds with Brett today. "The big—Brett is in my office?"

"That's the one." Uri flipped his screwdriver in his hand, gunslinger style and shoved it in his back pocket. "Blake's brother. I know because he said hi to me when he came past."

Some days rolled right over you and flattened you, and she was picking Daisy and Sam up from school in a little while. It would be great if for once, Daisy didn't feel the need to take a piece out of her hide, but the chances of that were lower than nonexistent. Bracing herself, she walked into her office.

Standing with his back to her and his hands in his pockets, Brett looked out the window. Unfortunately, the physical appeal of him hadn't abated. Probably gotten even worse since last night, and she now knew what he looked like naked. She cleared her throat. "Brett. Can I help you?"

"Hey." He turned and gave her a sheepish smile. "It's my turn to make sure you get out of here safely."

Ah, well that explained his presence in her office. "Okay, but I'm leaving early today to get my children."

She fast-tracked her plans into leaving in the next five minutes. Waiting outside the school if she got there too early suddenly became a better option than this awkward interaction with Brett. Even a run-in with judgy school mothers beat the excruciating atmosphere clogging her office.

Brett rubbed his nape, his bicep fighting to escape the sleeve of his dark green T-shirt. "Um…about this morning."

"I think the less we say about that the better." She channeled her inner Emily, chilly and aloof and protecting her underbelly. Moving to her desk, she started gathering her things. There was nothing more she could do there anyway, until Rowena decided to get over herself.

Backlit as he was, she couldn't be sure, but it felt like he was watching her.

It was unnerving, and she gave him a frosty stare. "Was there anything else?"

"Damn, sugar." He laughed ruefully. "When you get pissed, you're like a glacier. I'm thinking I'd like it better if you yelled and threw something at me."

"Because I should care so much about what you'd prefer?" She crossed her arms and stepped back from the betraying weakness of her knees to his smile. "And would it do me any good to point out, again, how I feel about that ridiculous name you call me?"

"Yeah." He shrugged. "I might take that more seriously if you had a problem with it when I was buried inside you."

Words failed her, and she gaped at him. She couldn't believe some of the crap that came out of his mouth. And somehow, she'd managed to convince herself she liked Brett Barrows. The man was an anachronism, a sexist throwback that she was for damn sure throwing back. Tossing him a withering look, she snatched up her purse and gym bag and stalked out of her office.

"Do you mind?" She jangled her keys at him. "I need to lock my office."

"Too far?" He grimaced. "Yeah, I definitely went too far there."

Laura held her keys aloft and waited.

"When you look at me like something you'd like to Lysol, it makes me want to shake you up." He strolled out her office, took the keys from her and locked the door. "Sorry about that. It's a gut reaction."

She took her keys back without any part of her hand

making contact with any part of his. "Well, I don't believe there is much I can say to that."

Spinning, she walked away, careful not to run or to dawdle. Brett did not deserve her changing her usual pace. Everything was normal with her, nothing different and nothing disturbed.

"Actually, I'm not done." He strolled after her. "I got something more to say."

Based on the most recent assholery to escape his lips, she didn't want to hear it. Laura quickened her pace and pushed through the doors to the parking lot.

"Were you such a ball breaker with your ex as well?" He kept up with her. "Could you slow down a second and give a guy a chance to explain and apologize."

"No." It was super childish, but she kept right on walking. "There is nothing you have to say that I want to hear."

"Even if I tell you I'm a dickhead and I fucked up this morning?"

It was enough to get her to stop walking, and she stared up at him. "You were an unmitigated dickhead this morning."

"Fine." He nodded. "An unmitigated dickhead. Would you care to know why?"

As much as she'd like to keep storming away, she did want to know. "Yes."

"When I was not much more than a kid, I was involved with a girl like you."

"Girl like me?" She dared him to answer that and not piss her off.

Brett cleared his throat and glanced over her shoulder. "Classy, rich, came from the right kind of family."

"I'm not rich."

"But you were, and you were raised that way," he said. "Anyway, Whitney was with me because she liked a bit of rough in her life. I was with her because I thought I'd met my one."

"Ah." Some inkling of understanding dawned. "She dumped you for being from the wrong side of town."

He nodded. "Yup. And I guess it's still a sore spot, because when you said what you said about Karstyn this morning, I was thinking Whitney."

"I'm not Whitney." It might be stating the obvious, but she didn't like being lumped in with a woman she'd never met, and one who sounded like a total bitch. "And if you'd stayed around long enough this morning, we could have had this conversation then."

"I know that." He shifted closer to her. "But I guess I panicked and ran."

Now he'd lost her. "Panicked?"

"Last night." He flushed. "It meant a lot to me, sugar. You got under my skin."

"It meant a lot to me too. Up until enter the dickhead." His admission took some of the heat out of her anger and soothed her feelings. "You hurt me this morning, Brett, and I don't have a lot of capacity right now for being hurt."

"Laura." He took her hand. "I'm not so good at this sort of thing." He gestured between them. "I've spent the last eight years protecting myself and watching my back. You took me by surprise. I never saw you coming."

That made two of them. "I didn't either. I've been going through the motions of life since my divorce."

"I'm sorry, sug—Laura. Last night meant a lot to me, maybe too much, and I hate that I fucked it all up."

"Maybe you didn't fuck everything up." His honesty disarmed her. It was hard to picture Brett as vulnerable, but standing in front of her, admitting he had feelings for her, was devastating to her anger and resentment.

He grinned, and his face cleared of tension. "Yeah?"

"I said maybe." Her girl card would be revoked if she completely rolled over.

"I'll take it."

They walked in silence to her car. Suddenly her frustrating day didn't feel so crappy anymore. She put her stuff in her car and turned to him. "Okay, thank you for coming to see me and saying what you did."

"Had to make it right." He shrugged. "Now go and fetch your kids."

"Will you be following me?"

"You know I will be." He shoved his hands in his pockets. "Me or Razor will be keeping an eye on you until we know where Cole is at and what he's doing."

"Right." She opened her door and climbed in. His apology had been great, but he also hadn't mentioned anything about seeing her again. It had been so long since she'd dated, she didn't know the rules anymore. What she and Daniel had dabbled in had been far too tentative to even be called dating.

The moment stretched between them, and she toyed with suggesting another date, but she didn't even know if they were dating. Plus she had Emily in her mind lecturing her about girls never chasing boys. "Well." She cleared her throat to break the silence. "I should go." She sounded overly chipper as she added. "Have a great afternoon."

Brett nodded and stepped back from her car.

"Bye." She waggled her fingers.

"Laura?" He stepped forward.

Heart pounding, she met his gaze. "Yes?"

"Last night." He shoved his hands in his back pockets. "Best night of my life."

# Chapter Twenty-Three

Laura wasn't feeling exactly happy as she drove to Blessed Sacrament to fetch Daisy and Sam, but Brett's apology and his closing remark had improved her outlook. The cloud in her day was the way her mind kept insisted on dwelling on where they went from there. She'd had a taste of how things could be with Brett, and she wanted more.

Not only the sex, which was also the best of her life, but the deeper connection between them. She could talk to Brett. Despite their completely different backgrounds, they had found common ground. Brett had dragged himself out of the gutter, and she respected that. It was easy to be herself with him, and that self was a version she liked. He understood how it felt to confront the worst of himself. So many people walked around with this idea that given a certain situation they would behave better than anybody else. Well, she and Brett knew that they'd had those opportunities, and they had not behaved their best. It gave you a different outlook on life, and one they shared.

Parking outside the school, Laura braced for the mommy gauntlet. She joined the periphery of a group of waiting mothers. They stood in the shade of a spreading oak on the manicured lawns outside Blessed Sacrament, like they had when she'd been part of them. Thank God Patrick was still happy to pay to keep the children there, because she certainly couldn't afford it anymore.

An attractive blonde wearing LuLuLemon and a full face of subtle makeup gave her a frosty smile. "Laura."

"Penny." She smiled back. Nobody would guess that she and Penny had regularly gone to lunch, and even shopped for Penny's wedding dress for her fourth marriage together. Now they skirted each other like polite strangers.

Frances, whom she'd met at a Mommy 'n' Me playgroup when Daisy was two, gave her a curt nod.

A thin corridor of grass opened between her and the other mothers. They might not know all the details of her divorce, but they knew she'd fallen from grace, and even worse, fallen out of their socioeconomic bracket. As if they feared her contagious, they kept a subtle distance between them and her. It used to hurt. Now it stung, but she'd quit fighting her isolation.

Sam came out first, his face alight with the joy of ending his school day. "Hey, Mom." He grinned up at her. "Guess what?"

"What?"

"We played dodgeball in gym today and I nailed Preston right in the nose." Sam rocked back and forth on his toes.

Suppressing the desire to cheer because Preston could be an entitled little snot, she said, "Is he okay?"

"He's fine." Sam rolled his eyes. "It didn't even bleed, and I thought it would because Preston cried for so long."

A good mother would take this teachable moment and deliver a gentle remonstration about nailing people in the nose with a ball. Then again, Preston had been a biter, and Sam had worn his dental imprints on more than one occasion.

Older children came out much slower. Deliberately

dawdling so as not to risk being confused with the younger children.

Daisy strolled out with two other girls from her class. She'd also had to make new friends after the divorce. Her former best friend happened to be Penny's oldest, and the split had happened to the girls as well.

"I painted a horse as well," Sam chattered on about his day. "And we did reading today and I read out loud."

Sam was a book lover. "You did? What was the book?"

When she'd done the school run before, she'd never stopped to appreciate the precious insight it gave her into how her children were.

"Hey." Daisy gave her a chin jerk, turned and waved goodbye to her girls.

"Daisy, guess what?" Sam trotted along beside Daisy.

"No." Daisy gave her brother a look of teen scorn.

But Sam was not so easily deterred. "No, this is good. You're gonna want to hear it."

Daisy sneered at him. "What?"

"Guess."

She rolled her eyes. "Just tell me already and stop being so annoying."

Laura led the way to her car with them in her wake.

Sam's teacher almost contorted her neck to avoid making eye contact with her. Before her screw up, teachers had been a lot friendlier too.

"Bullshit!" Daisy responded to Sam's story but with enough enthusiasm to give Sam encouragement.

Sam spared her no detail in the retelling of the dodgeball incident.

Being a social pariah had some advantages, and Preston's mother, Caroline, would not be cornering her for an excruciatingly polite expression of her displeasure over the incident. Of course, she wouldn't come right out and criticize Sam, because that would break the civilized and flawless polite mommy code, but under the guise of a shared laugh about the darnedest things kids did, she would ask for and expect the requisite apology.

Daisy took the passenger seat and shoved her backpack into the floorboard.

"What sort of day did you have?"

"Okay." Daisy shrugged.

Laura joined the snake of traffic crawling away from the school. "Didn't you have a math test today?"

"Yup."

"How did it go?" It hadn't been that long ago Daisy had chattered away to her like Sam. She missed those days.

Daisy smiled at her. "Really well. I got an A."

"You did?" The smile made Laura happier than the A. It seemed like forever since Daisy had smiled at her with that unrestrained delight. Normally she got a sneer or a smirk, but a big, beautiful smile, hardly ever.

Still grinning, Daisy nodded. "Actually Karstyn has been helping me with my math."

"Oh?" She kept it light. She didn't want to go against Patrick if he was, as she suspected, against Karstyn. But Karstyn was a good kid and a smart one, and she wasn't about to nip a friendship between him and Daisy in the bud because of where he came from.

"We were FaceTiming, and I needed to study, so he said he'd help me."

Laura turned onto the road outside the school. "Sounds like you should get him to help you again."

"Yeah?" Daisy said it softly, her smile growing mistier.

So, she and Karstyn were more than friends, and Laura had mixed feelings about that. Daisy was young for a romantic relationship, but forbidding it would only make it sweeter fruit. As long as she kept the lines of communication open, she could keep an eye on things.

"I have a test tomorrow," Sam said. "A spelling test, but I already know my words."

"Look at you, all ahead of the curve." She winked at him through the rearview mirror and Sam giggled.

Daisy cocked her head and studied her. "Did you do something different today?"

"What do you mean?" Laura hated that she braced for rough weather when Daisy spoke to her voluntarily.

"Like your hair or your makeup." Daisy shrugged. "You look pretty."

"Thank you." And just like that, her day zoomed into wonderful. "But I can't think of anything I did differently."

Sam leaned forward. "I always think you look pretty."

"Which is why you're my favorite man in the whole wide world." She motioned him to sit back.

Back at her condo, Daisy's good mood continued. She had no complaints as Laura served them pasta. She even unbent enough to tell Laura a story about two classmates who had gotten into an argument about a boy.

While Laura helped Sam with his homework, Daisy disappeared into her bedroom with her phone. A few minutes later, the low murmur of her voice meant she was on a call.

"When can I have a phone?" Sam glared at Daisy's door.

Laura wanted to listen, but Daisy was also entitled to her privacy. "You know when."

"But that's three years from now." Sam stuck his bottom lip out.

She and Patrick had agreed the children would only have a phone when they turned thirteen. "Yup." She tapped his workbook. "Let's finish this last problem."

"Everybody else in my class has a phone," Sam whined. "Even Preston."

"Well, Preston also got nailed in the nose by a ball today. Do you want one of those too?"

"No." Sam chortled and went back to his homework.

Laura left him to finish on his own and puttered around the condo. During her marriage, she'd been a stay at home mother. Times like this, with the kids around, had been her daily normal. Now it felt like there was constantly a hole in her life when they weren't with her.

Daisy wandered into the kitchen and took a stool at the counter. She had the look of a girl who wanted a chat. "Mom?"

"Yes. What's up?"

"You like Karstyn, right?" Daisy picked the polish off her thumbnail. A lurid shade of orange that would have made old Laura shudder.

Treading as carefully as she could, she said, "Yes, I got to know him quite well at the rec center, and I do like him. Is he doing okay?"

"Yeah." Daisy nodded. "He likes the family he's with, and one of the younger kids has a kind of crush on him and follows him around."

To keep her hands busy, Laura filled the kettle and put it on to boil. Aside from not wanting to fall foul of Patrick, it was also so long since Daisy had allowed her in her life. She was nervous. "I'm glad." Without endangering Karstyn's trust in her, she added, "Because you know where he came from wasn't that great?"

"He told me." She frowned. "He's scared of his older brother."

"And he's right to be." Laura needed Daisy to understand well, even if it risked alienating her. "Cole is dangerous, and I don't want you going anywhere near him."

Daisy nodded. "I know. Karstyn says the same thing. He doesn't want me anywhere near Cole."

Laura absorbed the relief of that. Clearly, Karstyn had been honest with Daisy about his family.

"Mom?"

Here came the meat of the discussion. Laura made herself a cup of tea. "Yes."

"Do you think Dad would like Karstyn?"

She hunted for how to answer best. "I don't think your father would like where Karstyn comes from."

"That's what I thought." Daisy grimaced. "But you don't mind?"

"Cole scares me," she said. "But Karstyn isn't to blame for his brother or the way he was born." Any more than Brett was to blame for having been born a Barrows. "I have the advantage of having worked with Karstyn, and I know who he really is."

"So, that's a no." Daisy raised her chin.

"It's more of a Dad would like him if he knew him like we did." Probably. Patrick, for all his good points, did have a healthy dollop of snob in him. "I think Dad should have the chance to get to know him. Start by telling him about Karstyn."

"Mo-o-om." Daisy rolled her eyes. "There's nothing to tell. Karstyn and I are friends."

"Then there won't be a problem telling Dad about your new friend."

Daisy growled her irritation and flounced out of the kitchen.

For the rest of the afternoon, Daisy stayed in her room, and Sam helped Laura bake cookies.

Patrick arrived right on time to pick them up.

"Hi." He studied her. "Did you have your hair done?"

"No." Her days of biweekly salon appointments were long gone. She didn't miss them either.

"Huh." He smiled. "You look good."

Apparently good sex had additional benefits. Not that she was going to share that with her ex. "Thank you."

Sam threw his arms around her middle and squeezed. "Bye, Mom."

"Bye, Sam. I love you." This was the part Laura hated. It hurt like ripping out her heart and handing it to Patrick.

Sam pressed his face into her arm and then let go. "Love you too."

"Bye." Daisy stopped in the doorway.

"Bye, darling. I love you." Laura ached for the little girl who would hug first and cling to her.

After an awkward moment, Daisy opened her arms and hugged her. "Love you, Mom."

# Chapter Twenty-Four

Before being locked up, Brett would have rather pulled his nails out with a pair of rusty pliers than go grocery shopping. Prison had given him a new appreciation for the simple things people took for granted. Being able to choose what you ate, when you ate it, and how you ate it was a privilege he'd never take for granted again.

Bent over with both arms folded on the handle, Blake pushed the shopping cart.

They shopped together because he hadn't yet trusted Blake with money. Blake had been back for a few months now and Brett needed to consider loosening the reins. Unfortunately, the only way to know if Blake was really in recovery was to give him enough rope to hang himself.

Brett picked out some apples and put them in the cart.

"Brett?" A woman, around fifty, plumpish and short, and vaguely familiar stopped him. She flushed. "Hi."

"Hi." Brett tried to place her.

She pointed at her chest. "Jennifer, Jen, from your self-defense class."

Now he got it. "How are you?"

"I'm good." She blushed deeper red and cleared her

throat. "I was going to talk to you after class, but…do you have five minutes."

"Sure." For what, he couldn't begin to guess. Women like Jen normally gave him the side-eye and a wide berth.

"Could I buy you a cup of coffee?" Jen pointed to a Starbucks at the front of the store.

Whatever had a woman like Jen wanting to buy him a cup of coffee had to be big enough to get him intrigued. No time like the present to give Blake some rope. He looked at Blake. "You finish up here?"

"Yeah." Blake looked surprised and straightened. "Sure."

"Good." Brett handed over his debit card. "Code is Kim's birthday. Know it?"

"Er…yeah." Blake blinked at the debit card. "Sure."

"Come and find me when you're done." Brett motioned to Jen. "Let's have that coffee."

As they stood in the line for coffee, Jen fidgeted with her purse strap, cleared her throat, and looked everywhere but at him. He got it. He made nice women nervous. They also desperately wanted to know what had landed him in prison but were too scared or polite to ask.

Once they'd gotten their coffees, his straight black, and hers some kind of whatchamachino coffee corruption in a cup, they took a seat at a small table overlooking the parking lot.

"I really appreciate this." Jen smiled wanly. "I hope I'm not taking you away from anything important."

"Just groceries." He did his best to look reassuring. "Blake's got it." At least, he hoped like hell Blake had it. "What can I do for you?"

"Well, it's like this." She adjusted the sleeve on her cup. "When I was in class, you seemed to know an awful lot about how the…er…criminal element thinks."

Brett hid his smile behind sipping his coffee. "Jen, I understand how they think because I used to be one of them."

"Oh!" Her cheeks pinked. "I knew that of course, but I never meant…that is to say—" She groaned and rolled her eyes. "I'm making a mess of this."

Brett was getting curiouser. Whatever had her stopping him in the grocery store was greater than her fear of him.

"It's about my husband. Ex-husband." She shifted her cup on the table. "He's not a criminal."

Not one with a record at least. Sometimes the difference between a con and not was one conviction. "Right."

"Only he is being rather…difficult." Jen's eyes had that haunted quality he'd spent so long dispelling from Blythe's. Those were the eyes of a woman frightened of a man who had the ability and will to hurt her.

He kept his tone even, but men who picked on women sat high up on his shit list. And yes, he did get the irony of that, fuck you very much. "How difficult?"

"He calls." She cleared her throat. "And texts. A lot. Sometimes he's not very nice."

As in being an aggressive asshole, if he read between lines well. "Are you divorced or separated?"

"Divorced." Jen sighed. "I left him, and he was very angry about it."

That made Brett twitchy as hell because it probably meant Jen's ex was escalating. "Other than the calls and texts, does he make any other attempts to contact you?"

"He shows up at our—my house. Often when I'm not there and lets himself in. Well, he did until I had the locks changed, and now, he more stands out front and waits for me."

"How often?"

She swallowed and tears glittered in her eyes. "A couple of times a week." Her hand shook as she smoothed her hair back. "He also follows me around. When I'm driving, he pops up in my mirrors, or when I go places, he's often there watching me, sometimes worse."

"How much worse?" Motherfucker was breathing down the neck of getting physical with his ex-wife, who from what Brett could see, was a nice lady. Wouldn't have made a difference if Jen was a bitch from hell, you didn't do that shit to a woman.

"He shouts." She flushed red. "Obscene things. Embarrassing things. He makes the most awful scenes."

Brett had heard enough to see the pattern clear as day. "You need to tell the police."

"I did." Her face tightened with frustration. "And Sheriff Evans was lovely about it and very supportive. I have a restraining order in place, but Art—that's my ex-husband—will stand right at the edge of it. He stopped calling and texting me from his phone, but he got another one, and I can't prove it's his."

Jen needed someone on her side because the law dragged its fucking ass on stalking exes. "How can I help?"

"I was thinking there might be things I could do that will help." Jen sipped her coffee but didn't look like she even tasted it. "Practical things that might make me feel safer."

"First off, Jen." He risked taking her hand. He didn't want to spook her, but she looked like she needed the reassurance. "You need to leave this with Nate, Sheriff Evans. Don't confront your ex, don't speak to him and don't communicate with him in any way. Changing your locks was smart, but you need to install a security system as well."

"Like an alarm?" She wrinkled her nose. "Art wanted to put one of those in when we first moved to Ghost Falls, but I refused." Her laugh lacked amusement. "I said we were safe in this town."

"And you will be again." He met her gaze and held it. "We just need to get Art off your back, and you will be safe again. To do that, you also need to gather evidence. All the calls, all the texts, if he emails you, if he leaves you written notes, you keep everything."

She nodded. "I have been."

"That's good, Jen, and real smart too." He wished he could lie to her and tell her everything would be fine, but she had a long row to plow here. "If he stands at the mark of his restraining order, take pictures of that and keep it. Whatever you can do to prove this abuse will help you in the long run."

"Okay." She nodded and stared at him.

"Now this next part sucks, and it's not fair that you're going to have to do all this to get rid of him." He squeezed and released her hand. "If you haven't done so already, and I'm sure Nate would have advised you to do all this, change your cell number, change your landline, get a new email address. Change it all and make it impossible for him to contact you."

"I did that." Jen worried her bottom lip. "But he found it all out."

"Then you do it again, and this time you only give your deets to people who would ride or die for you." People made him want to punch shit sometimes. "Someone gave those deets to your ex, and that person ain't your friend, Jen." He grabbed the sleeve off his coffee. "You got a pen?"

Jen dug in her bag and handed him a ballpoint.

"This is my number." He wrote it on the cardboard sleeve. And then for good measure. "And this is Razor's number. If you can't get me, you call him. I'd trust him with my life, and more importantly, I'd trust him with my sister's life."

Jen looked like she might cry as she whispered, "Thank you."

"First you call 911, always," he said. "And your next call is to Razor or me." He kept it cool as he asked, "What's your ex's full name?"

"Art." She waved a hand. "Arthur York."

"I'm gonna chat with Nate and find out where the sheriff is with this." He couldn't go off like some half-cocked vigilante motherfucker, and Nate was a good cop. He cared about the people in this burg. But Nate was also a really busy cop, and the squeaky wheel got the most grease. Jen wasn't a squeaky wheel, and it must have taken her hours to work up the courage to speak to him. "Then, if you don't mind, Razor and I are coming around to your place to check out the house, the security, where you're most vulnerable—that sort of thing."

"You can do that?" Jen looked cautiously hopeful.

"We can do that." He leaned in and lowered his voice. "Razor used to jack houses, and he was really good at it, until he went down because his fence turned state's evidence."

Jen blinked at him, not at all sure how to take that information.

"What I mean is, if Razor makes it so he can't get into your house, no way Art is sliding his calling card in there."

"Oh." She perked up and even managed a wobbly smile. "He'd do that for me?"

"He'd be happy to." Razor didn't like bullies with an eye on girls either. "But what you gotta do in the meantime is keep sharp. If you're driving, you know who's behind you all the time. If I stop you and pull you over, I want to know what cars are behind you, and if you can, who is in them."

Jen nodded, looking like a kid taking notes in class. "Know who's driving behind me."

"This next part is especially important. You know who's around when you approach your house or anywhere you need to climb out of your car. Getting out of your car, you're at your most vulnerable, and you don't want to stop, and you don't want to get out until you can see your way clear to do it."

Now Jen was looking alarmed. "All the time?"

"Yeah." He couldn't go soft on her. "The more alert you are, the less chance he has to catch you unaware. And you listen to your gut as well. You're a woman, and your gut is good. If something feels off, don't question it, you drive to somewhere safe and you call Razor or me, and we'll check it out for you."

She blinked at him. "I didn't expect you to do this much."

"Razor and I will do all that and more because we really fucking don't like men who bully women." Fuck! He shouldn't have said fucking.

"Well, I never expected this much." Jen sat back in her chair. "And I can't tell you how grateful I am."

"Don't need to be grateful." The way she was looking at him like he was some kind of hero made him squirm, and he sounded a bit brusque as he said, "Be alert rather than grateful."

"I will." She looked determined, like she'd made a decision and planned to stick with it. For her sake, Brett hoped she had. Dealing with dicks like her ex-husband wasn't easy, and dicks often made things worse before they got better. Glancing over his shoulder, she pointed. "Your brother is back, and he looks like he's looking for you."

Frowning, Blake was checking out Starbucks.

Brett waved him over. It didn't look like Blake had groceries with him, and Brett's gut tightened.

"Hey." Blake smiled at Jen, but he looked tense. He looked at Brett. "We need to get going."

Brett really didn't like the look on Blake's face, but he'd already freaked Jen out enough, so he stood. "I gotta go, but you be smart." He pushed the sleeve he'd written his coordinates on closer to her. "And you keep these numbers safe." Then he softened his tone. "We got this, Jen. We're gonna make this go away."

"Thank you," she whispered, and for a nasty moment, Brett thought she might cry.

He backed away with what he hoped was a reassuring smile. "I'll be in touch." As they left Starbucks, he turned to Blake. "Where are the groceries?"

"I left the cart back there." Blake jerked his thumb at the interior of the store. "Ben called."

"And?" His hackles went up as he got it before Blake needed to say a word. "Pat's been at Ma."

Face stiff with anger, Blake nodded.

White-hot rage surged through him, and he had to breathe to get it under control. "Wanna break that down for me?"

"Dixie is with her, and Ben says it's bad. She's refusing to go to the hospital." Blake dropped into place beside him as Brett strode for the parking lot.

He yanked his truck door open. "Pat still there?"

"No." Blake's eyes blazed. "Fucker took off and left her there, hurt. Dixie found her when she went round to check on Ma."

"How long she been hurt?"

Blake took a deep breath as if struggling for composure. "Two days."

"Motherfucker!" The shit show of being a Barrows kept rolling on and on. "Call Ben, Bo, and Becker and tell them to find Pat. You and I are taking Ma to the hospital."

# Chapter Twenty-Five

Bo was waiting for him outside the house when Brett pulled up. They'd been keeping the place looking better since he'd had a this-is-how-we're-gonna-do-shit-from-now-on moment with his brothers.

He hopped out of his truck. "Where is she?"

"Bedroom." Bo trailed him into the house. "Ben couldn't make it yesterday, and Becker and I worked a night shift and slept at a friend's close to site. Dixie got here this morning to check on her and found her lying on the bathroom floor. Ma got that far and collapsed in there, but she can't tell us when that happened."

Tension tightened his chest muscles as Brett strode into his mother's bedroom. He'd been doing this for as long as he could remember. The corridor between the entrance and the bedroom was like his personal highway to hell.

Somebody, Dixie he guessed, had straightened the room and opened the curtains. Fresh air coming through the open windows did its best to dispel years and years of cigarette smoke and spilled vodka.

Carly lay propped against the pillows with her eyes closed.

Stark bruises marred her paper-white complexion, and her breath constricted through what he guessed was a busted nose.

"She's sleeping." Dixie came into the room with a damp cloth and a bottle of orange juice. "As near as I can work out, he left her like this. She tried to take care of herself and collapsed in the bathroom."

Even as he asked the next question, he guessed the answer. "You didn't take her to the hospital?"

"She won't go." Dixie straightened Carly's bedclothes. His mother looked so frail and was finally showing signs of her age and the hard life she'd lived. The black eye, and split lip were all too fucking familiar, and he wanted to rage against the impossible.

"And she needs to go. I'm thinking she's got a couple of busted ribs, at least." Dixie pressed the cloth to the swelling on Carly's jaw. "She won't go since the ER doctors started taking note of the damage to her. Her last X-ray showed more broken bones than a prize fighter."

Each one of those injuries, old and current, were courtesy of Pat. To his living shame, and before Eli had gotten hold of him, Brett had been heading exactly the same way, taking his anger and life disappointments out on the weak and defenseless. When you were six five and weighed two eighty, there were a lot of people weaker than you.

"Ma." Keeping his tone gentle but insistent, he perched gingerly on the edge of the bed, "Ma, it's Brett."

Carly's eyes moved beneath her eyelids, and then the unswollen one opened. She blinked him into focus. "Brett?"

"Hey, Ma." As mad as he got about how she wouldn't learn and kick Pat out, Carly still broke his heart. The way she looked at him like he could save her. That's all she'd been looking for her entire life: a savior, a knight. Instead, she'd gotten Pat and her stubborn belief that cruelty meant passion, and anger was strength. "How you doing?"

"Okay." She coughed and then sucked in a breath on a pained grimaced. "I fell in the bathroom."

"Yeah, you did. Dixie found you this morning." Brett needed to keep his eye on the prize. He'd prefer she agree, but he was prepared to carry her into the emergency room if he had to. "We need to get you checked out."

She looked appalled. "No, honey, I really don't need that. Some sleep and a couple Tylenol, and I'll be right as rain."

"No, Ma." He kept it gentle but firm. "We need to make sure you got nothing broken or any internal injuries."

Shaking her head, Carly predictably got that stubborn look in her eyes. "If I say I'm fine, then I'm fine. You can't come in here and start telling people what to do. Pat says—" Her gaze darted to Dixie. "You shouldn't have called him."

"Yes, I should've." Dixie handed Carly the orange juice.

Brett kept his rage on a tight leash. "What did Pat say?"

"Nothing." Face averted, Carly sipped the orange juice. "I don't know why you ask, because you only get mad when I tell you."

"I'm not mad." Ready to rip the house apart with his bare hands wasn't mad; it was fucking incandescent with rage. He spread his arms wide. "Do I look mad?"

"No-o-o." Carly studied him.

He had to give her credit for not being convinced. As a woman whose survival depended on accurately reading the level of anger in a man, she instinctively sensed what he kept under wraps. "Did he say where he was going?"

"No." She shook her head, so adept at lying for Pat, she could do it without a tell.

"Right." He nodded, because he'd known as much, but fucking hope always sprang eternal, and for once he'd like her to tell the truth and save herself. "What happened this time?"

Dixie shot him a look to say he needed to watch it.

Carly sipped her juice and stared out the window. "Why is the window open?" She shivered. "It's freezing in here, and

I'm not well." She looked at her side table "Where are my smokes? I need a smoke."

"I took them away." Dixie added a blanket to Carly's bed. "The window is staying open because it stinks in here, and that's not good for you either. And I'm not giving your smokes back until I know your ribs aren't messing with your lungs."

"Bitch." Carly glared at her. "You're not even my daughter. You don't get to say what happens here." She turned to him for support, saw his refusal on his face and pouted.

"But I am your daughter." Blythe walked through the door. "Hey, Dixie." Blythe gave her a quick hug. "You're amazing. Thank you for everything."

Dixie winked at her. "You know I do it for you, sweet cheeks."

Blythe came over, put her hand on his shoulder and squeezed. "Nate's outside with the ambulance."

He had to give Blythe credit. She'd grown up around Carly and absorbed Carly's life lessons and still turned out to be the strong, independent woman she was. When Blythe had felt Eric wasn't giving her what she wanted, and even though she had loved the crap out of him, Blythe had been ready to cut Eric lose. She didn't want half measures and love with a hella price tag for herself, and Brett respected the shit out of that. So had Eric, as it turned out, and Blythe had gotten her happily ever after.

He could trust her with Ma, so he stood, and she took his seat beside Carly.

Blythe smoothed hair off Carly's face. "You're not looking so good, Ma."

"It's nothing." Carly glanced at Blythe, then Dixie and then him. Tears filled her eyes and leaked down her cheeks. "I hate all this fuss being made over me. You know that, baby. Make everyone go away so I can sleep."

"No, Ma." Blythe took Carly's hand. "The ambulance is here for you, and you need to let them take you to the hospital. Then you're going to tell Nate where Pat is, so he can find him."

Carly scowled. "I'm not going to any hospital."

"Yes, you are," Blythe said, gentle but implacable. "Because Kim needs her mother, and I need my mother, and we need to make sure you're all right."

Looking coy, Carly fiddled with her sheet. "You don't really need me."

"Of course we do, Ma." Blythe glanced up at him. She had this, and she wanted him to let her handle Ma her way.

Nodding to Blythe, he left the room. He didn't know how Blythe kept her patience, but she was much better at that shit than him.

"Hey." Eric had arrived and stood beside his brother Nate. "Blythe in with Carly?"

"Yeah. She needs to get to a hospital."

Eric shoved his hands in his pockets and sighed. "Ben said. Blythe has the best chance of getting through to her."

"I see that." Anger and frustration churned in him. If he'd been near a gym, he could have burned some of it off.

Nate stood in front of him. "Brett?"

"Yep."

"Brett." Nate's tone grew insistent. "Look me in the eye."

Brett knew what was coming, and he really didn't want to go there. "What?"

"In the eye." Nate didn't back down easily.

Brett met his gaze. "What?"

"You're not going after Pat. If you find out where he is, you call me and tell me. I want your word on that."

Scoffing, he went for distraction. "The word of an ex-con mean anything to you?"

"Your word does." Nate held his gaze. "The man you are now, that man is worth too much to throw his life away on a piece of shit like Pat Barrows."

Eric flanked Nate. "I love Blythe," he said. "And she loves

you. That means we all got a vested interest in you not screwing up your parole."

Impotent fury churned in his gut. Pat needed stopping, but the only person who could make him stop for good kept making excuses for her abuser.

"If you can't find Pat, your hands are tied." Carly would never give up Pat.

Nate shrugged. "You know how this goes. And I still haven't gotten your word."

"Don't push this." Brett couldn't give his word. If he ran into Pat, he wasn't going to give a shit about his parole or anything else.

Eric backed Nate. "Think this through, Brett. You go down again, and they're going to throw away the key. Then who is going to be here for Kim and Will and Blythe?"

"And these assholes." Dixie jabbed her thumb at Ben and Bo. "With your foot on their throats, they've got a halfway decent chance of not being oxygen thieves."

Bo frowned, but Ben just took it. He knew how lucky he'd gotten to get Dixie to marry him.

Brett before Eli would have torn out of there and satisfied the urge to hurt something. He would have ripped Ghost Falls apart until he got his hands on Pat. Then he would have made Pat pay and pay some more. He would exorcise his demon by feeding it blood.

"Okay." Blythe walked out of Carly's room. "She's ready to go."

Blythe had the magic touch all right. She moved into Eric's arms and he held her.

Brett was thrilled for her that she had that kind of happy in her life. The sort of happy that came with love, support and understanding. His mind veered toward Laura before he could stop it. His ache to see her surprised him. It had to do with the way when she was around, she could pause the world and its bullshit for him and give him a moment to catch his breath.

Eric had his head next to Blythe's and was speaking quietly to her.

Whatever he said worked, because Blythe nodded and straightened away from him.

"All right." Eric gestured the EMTs to get moving. "Let's get her underway before she changes her mind."

"Brett?" Blythe slid her hand into his. "Don't do it. Please."

Jesus! They'd brought out the huge guns. He couldn't say no to Blythe. He owed her too much. Through gritted teeth, he managed the best he could do. "You have my word if I find Pat, I will call Nate."

"More than that." Blythe was too canny to let him slide out that easily. "I want your word you won't do anything to hurt your parole."

"Blythe." His anger writhed in him. "He could kill her one of these times."

She kept hold of his forearms. "I know that, Brett. We all know that, but we can't make her wise up."

"But I can remove her problem." The world wouldn't shed one tear for the loss of Pat Barrows.

"You can." Blythe's eyes glinted with unshed tears. "We both know you've got the kind of contacts in this town to find him much faster than even Nate."

Nate hitched his thumbs in his utility belt and shrugged.

"You can find him, and you can make him pay." Blythe's fingers dug into his forearm. "You can make it so Pat is too shit scared or damaged to even yell at a bird."

Brett could tell she was heading somewhere with that.

"After that happens, you're going back to prison. But hey —" she faked a carefree shrug "—it doesn't matter because you know when you go back you've made sure Pat won't lift a finger to anyone ever again." She leaned forward and lowered her voice. "And what does it matter anyway, right? It's not like society would ever miss a man like you."

That hurt more than it should because it was only the damn truth. "You got a point here, grub?"

"Only this: How do you suggest I tell Kim that her favorite brother is going away for the rest of his life? That if she wants to see him again, she's going to have to make visitor's day."

Wow. She didn't fuck around.

"And should we leave a place for you at the table during Christmas and Thanksgiving? Or would you rather we sent you a care package?"

"Blythe…" But he didn't really know what to say because what she was laying down was the damn truth, and he had to swallow it. If he went down again, he would never see freedom this side of the grave again.

"I'll also be telling Will you won't be at his graduation. First Barrows ever to make it to college. Maybe they'll let us show you the video when we visit." Her eyes narrowed, and she looked mean. "But you'll be fine, Brett. You'll be tucked behind bars making best friends with some fuckwit called Bubba and insulated from life. We'll be the ones living with your absence."

"You know I'd miss the fuck out of you."

"I hear you say that, but I need your actions to back that up." Then she touched her belly with her left hand. "Because I don't want to tell this baby they're short one of the best brothers a child could have."

# Chapter Twenty-Six

Laura first got suspicious that all was not well when Blythe didn't show to teach her class. Later, Michael popped into said class with the news she'd had to cancel for the day. Typical Michael, he deflected any nosy questions and went about his day.

"Hey." Daniel stuck his head around her office door. "You heard about Carly Barrows?"

She didn't like the sound of that or Daniel's grim expression. "I heard Blythe's class was canceled."

"Yeah, Blythe's at the hospital."

She was out of her seat before she could stop herself. "Is Brett okay?"

"Brett's fine." Daniel raised an eyebrow. "Carly is not so good. It looks like Pat beat her up again."

Laura's heart sank. It would kill Brett, especially with his own guilt about what he'd done to Blythe. "That's awful."

"Yeah. I got it straight from Dixie. She seemed to think you should know." Daniel's one eyebrow was still poised higher than the other in a silent question. "She asked me to let you know."

Her face heated. "Oh. Thanks."

"Yeah." Daniel propped his shoulder against the door-jamb and played it cool. "Apparently Brett is not taking it too well. The rest of the family is worried about him taking off after Pat."

That sounded like Brett, dammit. "He can't do that. It'll violate the conditions of his parole."

"You're right." Daniel crossed his arms and pinned her with his hard gaze. "It will screw his parole up three ways to next Sunday, and with his record, he's pretty much on his last chance as it is."

Worry for Brett squeezed out other thoughts. He mustn't go after Pat.

The answer was standing right in front of her. "You should talk to him." She came around her desk. "You understand what he's going through. You can give him the right advice."

Daniel looked at her.

"We have to stop him." She wanted to shake Daniel and make him take Brett's stakes more seriously.

After a long moment, Daniel nodded.

"You'll do it?" She knew she could rely on Daniel.

"No, Laura." Daniel straightened, his good-looking face uncharacteristically aloof. "That's not my place, but it looks like it might be yours."

"What do you—"

Daniel's expression called her on her bullshit and stopped her. He was too good of a guy for her to pretend. With a stomach lurch she realized she'd given her feelings for Brett away, and to Daniel, a man she'd only recently rejected.

Tense silence stretched between them. "I'm sorry," she said.

"How long have you been seeing Brett?" Daniel kept it casual, but beneath the surface, Laura sensed the emotion he kept a lid on.

She didn't want him thinking she'd toyed with him and

been seeing Brett on the side. "It's not like that. We're not really anything."

"Really?" Daniel shoved his hands in his pockets. "Because you're not wearing the face of a woman who feels nothing."

"I…" And what could she really say. "This thing with Brett…whatever it is. Only happened recently. After you and I decided…"

He dropped his head and stared at the floor. "It shouldn't matter, but it does."

"I'm sorry," she said, and she was. Daniel was the best man, and he deserved better.

"Brett's a good guy." Daniel turned and glanced at her over his shoulder. "He's also a very lucky one."

Laura stared at the empty doorway.

Daniel's sneakers squeaked against the floor as he walked away down the hall.

"Shit." She sat on the end of her desk. He hadn't deserved to find out like that. She should have told him, but then, she wasn't even sure what to tell him. One night with Brett, however incredible, didn't make much of anything.

She tried calling Brett, but her call went to voicemail, and she didn't leave a message.

That evening, as she walked to her car, Razor was sitting in his truck. She waved to him and stopped as an idea hit her. Before she could overthink it, she walked over to Razor's truck.

"Hey." He rolled down his window and smiled at her. As intimidating as Razor was, his smile softened his face.

"Hey." Now she felt silly for going with her impulse. "I… um…heard about Carly."

Razor winced. "Yeah, that situation is all kinds of bad."

"Is she…okay?"

"I'm not sure." Razor shrugged. "Brett hasn't called."

Laura didn't know if Brett not calling was a good or a bad

thing. She didn't know because she didn't know Brett that well. "Thanks." She stepped away from the truck. "Have a good evening."

"And you." Razor called after her.

All through her dinner of leftover pasta, she kept thinking of Brett. She had no real place in his life, but they were friends. Of a sort.

Throwing herself on her couch, she tried to get interested in something on television.

The situation sucked for the whole Barrows family. Funny, in her past life with Patrick, she had been part of the town who talked about the Barrows family with derision. Knowing some of the family members and more about their awful family life as they grew up and how that spilled into their adult lives made her realize she'd never had any room to judge.

Blythe would have Eric by her side. Eric was great at being supportive, and he would be there for Blythe, and by extension, Kim and Will. Dixie would stand by Ben. Blake, Bo and Becker would all look to Brett for direction. And Brett? Who did he have?

She flipped the TV off and sat up. If this had been her, and Brett had heard about something happening to her, what would he do? Laughing despite the seriousness of the situation, she knew exactly what Brett would do. He'd barge into her life, calling her sugar and handing out the best hugs known to man.

Well, she didn't need to barge in, and Brett had liked her hugs just fine. Laura palmed her car keys and grabbed her purse. She could go by the hospital, check out the situation and make herself useful if she could.

BRETT'S HEIGHT made him easily identifiable outside the emergency room. The wide bubble of space surrounding him probably had to do with his ferocious scowl. Looking every inch the scary ex-felon, he stood slightly apart from his brothers in a waiting area.

As his glance skimmed her, he stilled, and then his gaze snapped back. His hazel eyes were so cold they stopped her mid stride down the hallway.

Under his frigid stare, part of her wanted to turn around and disappear. Then Blake caught sight of her and waved. "Hey, Laura."

She waved back and forced herself closer. "Hi. Dixie let me know you were here."

"Right." Blake looked angry but also upset.

Finally, she risked another look at Brett.

Nope, no friendlier than the last time she'd looked, and it irked. They might not have named this thing between them, but there was something. They'd been intimate, for God's sake, and it wasn't like she was there to demand a white wedding and a picket fence. "How is your mom?"

Silence stretched uncomfortably until Blake, with a glance at Brett, answered, "We're waiting to hear. Blythe is in there with her."

"I came to see if any of you needed anything."

Blake smiled, and his similarity to Blythe was startling. "That's kind of you, Laura."

"No trouble," she said.

Crossing his arms, Brett stared past her as if she weren't even there.

Blake cleared his throat. "The others are out looking for Pat."

That's what worried her, because if they were looking for Pat, then they were probably going to tell Brett when they found him. She crept into what might be a no-fly zone. "Is Nate also looking for him?"

"Yeah." Blake shrugged. "But our family has the sort of connections Nate doesn't have, and we can find him faster."

Brett growled and glared at Blake.

"What?" Blake shrugged. "It's not like any of this is a secret from this town."

Finally, Brett spoke. "This is Barrows business."

"Um…okay." For a weird moment she was sure he was joking and almost laughed.

Blake gaped at him. "Seriously."

If Brett wasn't joking, she rather wished he'd kept his big mouth shut. "Well, I was concerned, and I came to see if I could help."

"We're fine." Brett barely glanced at her.

"Right." She was really regretting the impulse that had brought her there. "Can I get anybody anything? You probably didn't have a chance to have dinner. Something to eat? A cup of coffee?"

Blake looked grateful. "That would be really—"

"No." Brett shook his head. "We're fine."

She met his frigid stare as he stood there, shoulders back, jaw jutting out like he was ready to take one on the chin. The desire to kick him rose swift and hot. His outright rudeness shocked her, and when the numb wore off, she knew she was going to have a whole mess of hurt feelings. She didn't need to stay there and get more crap loaded on her shoulders. "Right." She nodded to him. "I get it."

As she turned to go, Blythe came out of a room down the corridor. She smiled and looked pleased to see her. "Laura. What are you doing here?"

"I heard about your mom." The weight of Brett's displeasure bored between her shoulder blades. "I wanted to see if there was anything I could do." Brett had made it crystal clear she had no place there. "I'm sorry, I didn't mean to intrude."

"You're not intruding." Blythe took her hands. "It's nice of you to come."

"I won't stay." If she did, she might start throwing throat

punches. "But I could get everybody a drink, or something before I leave. Or maybe there's something else you need?"

Blythe squeezed her hand. "That really is very nice of you. The doctor's in with Mom now."

"Shouldn't you be in there with them?" Brett folded his arms.

Giving him a what the hell look, Blythe said, "She asked me to leave, and I can't force her to let me stay."

Laura wanted to ask if Carly would be okay, but Brett's glowering was only getting worse. "Well. If there's nothing?"

"There's nothing." Brett snapped that death glare her way. "You should go home."

It took a couple of breaths to formulate a reply. "Right, I will. Go home."

Why she'd thought she could be of some use was beyond her. She'd put her foot right where it didn't belong, and all because she had imagined there was something between her and Brett. With some stupid half-baked notion of being a support to him, she'd strapped into her armor and come down to save the day. Let this be a goddamn lesson to her. No good deed goes unpunished.

"You don't have to go." Blythe glared at Brett. "I could do with—"

"Yes, she does." Brett got between her and Blythe and motioned Laura to precede him. "This will only take a minute."

"Bye, Laura." Blake was also staring at his brother like Brett had come unhinged. Good, then it wasn't only her who found his behavior unacceptable. "Thanks so much for coming. It looks like Mom is going to be fine. We appreciate your concern."

Some of them did at any rate.

Blythe hugged her. "It was lovely of you to come."

"Laura." Brett's tone made it clear he'd run out of patience.

So had she, and she followed him out of earshot of Blythe and Blake. Gathering her hurt and tucking it away, she said, "I'm sorry, I know you're upset, and I didn't mean to intrude, but that's no reason to be rude."

"Why are you here?"

Looking into his cold, hard eyes and his implacable face, she had no damn clue. "It doesn't matter. It was a mistake."

"Yeah, it was." He crowded closer to her. "You don't belong here. This is not your problem."

He couldn't be any clearer than that, and it hit her like a gut punch. The rudeness was one thing, but the curt dismissal hurt even more. Before she went, though, he could do with a reality check. All this stupid towering over people and scowling shit was so passé. He didn't intimidate everyone. "I came as a friend." She raised her chin and met his angry gaze. "I had some stupid idea that you might need a friend. Clearly, I was wrong."

Leaning closer, he got in her face. "You think I want you to see this?"

"Which part?" She held her ground. "The part where your mother is hurt, or the part where you're a horse's ass?"

"SHE'S RIGHT." Blythe joined him as Laura stalked down the hospital corridor. "You are being a horse's ass."

Even knowing that, he couldn't stop his reaction. Seeing Laura walking into the Barrows' mess had infuriated him. "She has no place here."

"She thought you might need a friend." Blythe sneered at him. "I thought you might need a friend, which is why I asked Dixie to let her know what was happening."

That made no sense. "You told Dixie to tell her? Why?"

"Because of that." She jabbed her forefinger at his face.

"Because I'm seeing a lot of the old Brett right now, and it's freaking me out."

She didn't get it. None of them did. The old version of Brett was the safest place he could be right now. Old Brett knew what to do with the steady poison of anger coursing through his veins. "You fucked up, Blythe. She should never have come here."

"Oooh!" Blythe wagged her head and sang it like a brat. "Are we being big, bad, scary Brett Barrows now? Is that what we're doing? Shall we all run and hide? Should I call the cops?"

Damn, but she had completely lost her fear of him. "Watch it, Blythe."

"Or what." And then she went and poked his arm. "You going to hit me? Break my other arm?"

Oh, no. She did not just go there. Completely at a loss for words, he glared at her.

Blake snickered. "Careful, Blythe. He might get weally, weally, cwoss and be wude to you."

Brett switched his glower to Blake. Kid needed to learn a thing or two. "Watch it."

"No, you watch it, Brett." Blythe lost patience with him and rolled her eyes. "You're not going to hit me or Blake. You're not going to do anything other than stand there and scowl at the world."

She couldn't know that for sure. "Unless Pat walks in here."

"Pat's not going to walk in here," Blythe said. "He has the self-preservation instinct of a rat. He's going to stay far, far away from anywhere you might be."

At least Pat had a handle on what he was capable of. Unlike the rest of his family.

Blythe turned and gaped at him. "Is that why you were such an asshole to Laura? You're worried you're going to go bat-shit crazy?"

Weird, but it had sounded a lot more plausible in his head. "It could happen."

"No, it couldn't." Blake scoffed. "Ask me how I know this?"

He'd play, and then he'd break some shit. "How do you know this?"

"Because." Blake straightened from leaning on the wall. "Even when you found me, after I'd stolen from Blythe and spent all of Will's college money, what did you do?"

"I brought you home." He didn't get what Blake was driving at.

"You brought me home." Blake looked at him expectantly. "You brought me home without beating the crap out of me, or even one good smack to the back of my head."

Blythe snorted. "I'd have hit you."

"I know." Blake winced. "And I deserved it."

Brett had never thought of smacking Blake around, despite how enraged he'd been. At the time, he'd been far more concerned with getting Blythe and Will's money back and getting Blake back on track. "I should have ripped your head off and shit down your neck."

Blake laughed. "But you didn't."

"No, you didn't." Blythe patted one of his folded forearms. "Face it, Barrows, you're just a pussycat now."

Blake held up a hand for attention. "A pussycat who now owes a very kind and sexy lady an apology."

The truth hurt, and he scowled at Blake. "I should have beaten the crap out of you."

# Chapter Twenty-Seven

Brett left the hospital after midnight with the vague notion of finding Laura in the morning and doing some groveling. His truck, however, had other ideas, and he pulled up outside her condo fifteen minutes later.

Not surprising given the time, but all the lights were off in her condo. Already on her shit list, the best thing would be to turn around and go home. He sat and stared at her dark windows.

He'd spent ten minutes with Carly before he'd left, and the drugs they'd given her had kicked in. In addition to the split lip and the shiner, Pat had broken two of her ribs and left a kaleidoscope of bruises and scrapes over her torso and arms. Her arms showed the clear imprint of Pat's fingertips. She'd refused to speak to the policewoman the hospital had sent for, like she'd refused to speak to a really nice young woman from a domestic violence coalition.

Aaand…that was the good news.

Brett climbed out of his truck and stopped outside Laura's door. He really had no right or business waking her up. Especially not after he'd near enough tossed her out of the hospital. If she slammed the door in his face, he wouldn't blame her. In fact, he might slam it in his own face. But the idea of going back to his place with his head so full of bad news, made him lift his hand and ring the doorbell.

He needed Laura, like he'd needed her earlier when she'd shown up at the hospital, only he'd been too much of a jackass to let it show.

Carly was pregnant, which meant the newest love fest with Pat had been going on for longer than any of them had been aware. Carly must have been sneaking out to meet up with him before they decided to bring their show back to the house.

Life deep exhaustion snuck up on him. Bringing Kim into this world had nearly killed her. In her fifties, she shouldn't even be able to get pregnant. Christ, Brett couldn't deal with the possible repercussions of such a late pregnancy.

He pressed the bell again, harder this time.

The thing he hated to admit to himself, even a tiny bit, was there had been a split second when he'd first seen Laura at the hospital that had made him so fucking happy to see her. Then he'd realized her being there meant his mess had spilled out and threatened to taint her.

Carrying that new baby might kill Carly. After a life of utter shit, a high-risk pregnancy was the future his mother was facing.

He jabbed the bell.

And that was what fate had in store for Carly. God alone knew what kind of future this baby had. Would it even be born with all the right parts? Then who was going to take care of a special needs kid? Or any kid, for that matter? Not Carly, for damn sure. She hadn't managed to care for any of her other kids and showed no sign of change. Nope, this poor little fucker would be raised on a deadly combo of cigarette smoke, alcohol and neglect.

The same fucking story. Again and again and again.

Of course, Blythe would never let that happen. Blythe, who should be looking forward to the birth of her first child, would be once again picking up the broken pieces of children that Carly and Pat scattered around.

He reached for the bell, but the door ripped open and Laura stood there glaring at him. "What?"

Hair mussed, wearing some kind of shorts and top pj combo and glaring at him like she wanted to make holes in him, she was still the best thing about this entire clusterfuck.

LAURA COULDN'T BELIEVE he was standing on her doorstep at one fifteen in the morning. She couldn't believe he had the balls to be there at all. She'd only opened the door when it became clear he was going to keep at her doorbell until she answered. "What do you want, Brett?"

"You." He stepped into her, forcing her to give way and let him in. "I need you, Laura." He held up his hands in surrender. "I know I sure as shit don't deserve you, or have any right to be saying that, but I need you anyway."

She stepped back to give herself room to let him have it. To let him know he couldn't come there like that, demanding her attention, especially not after the way he'd treated her at the hospital. Then she saw his face, his eyes more specifically, and her outrage subsided to a simmer.

Brett looked defeated. He looked like a man reaching out with his last gasp, and her heart twisted in her chest and refused to let her ignore his pain.

"What happened? Is your mother all right?" She closed the gap between them.

"Nah." He scrubbed his palms over his face. "She's okay. Well, as okay as she gets."

Her next fear rose sharp and swift. "Did you find Pat? Is that why you're here?" Dear God, she wasn't sure how these things worked. "Do you need me to give you an alibi?"

Brett barked a short laugh and shook his head. "Sugar, how are you making me laugh right now?"

"Well, I'm not trying to make you laugh." And had she really offered to be his alibi? She'd have a word with herself about that later, but him in her condo was the priority. "So, if everything is okay, why are you here?" Unless—

"Blythe and Blake are fine too, everybody else is fine. We're all in one piece." He answered her thought. "I'm here for me."

Simmering outrage took permission to reassert herself. "In that case, I'm not sure we have much to say to each other."

"Gonna have to disagree with you there, sugar, but can't tell you how much I appreciate you putting all the shit aside when you thought you needed to take my back." He walked into her kitchen and poured himself a glass of water.

Maybe he'd like her to whip up a five-course meal for him. "Brett—"

"I didn't want you at the hospital." He downed his glass of water.

She certainly didn't need a rehashing of the hospital scene. "You made that clear. It won't happen again."

"Sugar." He held one huge hand palm up. "Can you give me a minute here? I'm not good at this shit."

Well, that cleared things up nicely. She folded her arms and waited, but she tapped her foot to let him know time was ticking by. "Nothing coming out of your mouth right now is worth my time."

"You and me." He motioned between them. "We don't make a lot of sense. The way we were raised, our lives, couldn't be more different." He cleared his throat. "To be honest, sugar, I haven't a clue what you see in me, let alone why you let me into your bed. You can do so much better."

Rebuttals and arguments crowded her mind, but it all felt like emotional whiplash. "I don't understand."

"Yeah, I know." He blew a big breath out. "I'm trying to find the right words to explain it to you."

"At one thirty?"

He grimaced. "My timing sucks too."

It looked like it might take some time, and she was awake anyway. She put the kettle on. "Tea?"

"Sure." He smiled ruefully. "You're taking this better than I hoped."

"I'm not sure I am," she said. "You haven't said much of anything."

"Right." He rubbed his face. "You being at the hospital, it was like two parts of me colliding when I didn't want them to meet."

"Why not?"

"The man I am when I'm with you." He cleared his throat. "That man has hope. He's a man who can escape the shit show of his life, get his GED, maybe go further. That man might even be worthy of a woman like you some day."

"Let me get this straight." She studied his face. Later, when she'd got an explanation about the hospital, she wanted to revisit the GED mention. It burrowed into her soft spot for him that Brett, for all his physical dominance and confidence, could want something as simple and simultaneously massive as to finish high school. "You were mad about me being at the hospital because you didn't want me to see that side of your life?"

He nodded. "Partly."

"Well." She wanted to shake him. "I hate to break this to you, but I already knew about that part of your history. Pretty much everyone in town knows."

"It's more than that." He growled. "Blythe said I was an asshole to you. Blake agreed."

She made a mental note to thank them and nodded and let him speak.

"You being at the hospital reminded me we don't belong

together." He met her gaze with searing honesty. "I wasn't ready for this thing between us to be over."

"If it's over, then you made it that way with your behavior." Perhaps they should have had this conversation before he left her condo the other night. "And what is this between us anyway?"

"This is you and me exploring something that feels a whole lot more than sex to me." He held her gaze. "And as for it being over, I think that's your call."

"This is the second time you've walked away from me and been an asshole about it. And we haven't even known each other that long."

He grimaced. "Yeah. I know."

"You were an asshole about that Karstyn conversation, but you were an even bigger one at the hospital." She didn't totally understand why he thought she was so much better than him. She didn't see it that way at all. They were two broken halves who made a surprisingly good whole. "And I don't really know what we're doing either." A physically huge man, desperately uncomfortable with this conversation but standing in her kitchen in the wee hours because he needed to sort the problem between them, was her kryptonite. Being vulnerable, she would guess, was a new experience for Brett, and not an easy lesson to learn. "But it feels like more than sex to me too."

Because she couldn't resist any longer, she slid her arms around his waist.

He tensed, but his arms came up and looped around her. "Yeah?"

"Yeah." She shifted until she was pressed front to front with him. When they touched, they made instant sense, like their bodies recognized what the rest of them struggled to comprehend. "I came to the hospital because I thought maybe you'd need a friend."

"I did. I do." He pressed his forehead to hers. "It kills me to see her like that. It kills me that she won't do anything to change shit."

"I'm so sorry." She nestled deeper into him, resting her cheek to his chest. "I can't imagine how that feels."

He folded around her and held her like she was his life raft. "She's pregnant."

Laura held on to him, not knowing what to say because nothing seemed right. For Carly, it could be disastrous. The Barrowses certainly didn't need another mouth to feed or another child to be responsible for. Carly was too old to be having another baby.

"And Blythe is pregnant," he said. "She can't—shouldn't have to—raise another woman's baby again."

"But she has you now." Laura separated enough to see his face. "I don't have the answers; nobody does. This is all new, and you need time to absorb it. All of you do. But this time, Blythe has you and Blake by her side. Eric will also back whatever she does. It's not like she's the only one who can step up. You'll work it out, Brett." She held his gaze. "You'll do it as a family, you and your siblings. Because that's what you're building for all of them, a sense of family."

"I don't know about that." He looked exhausted.

Laura disentangled and took his hand. She turned the kettle off. "Let's go to bed. Phi always swears a night's sleep brings a whole lot more clarity." Actually Phi's bedtime solution definitely involved bedrooms but had nothing to do with sleeping. Laura decided against mentioning that. "Nobody can make decisions when they're exhausted."

"You should kick me out." He let her lead him into her bedroom.

"Probably." Laura pointed him to the bathroom. "Toothbrush under the sink and towel in the cupboard if you'd like to take a shower."

He caught her hand before she could move away. "Why?"

"Why am I letting you stay the night?"

He nodded.

"For the same reason I came to the hospital." She rolled to her toes and kissed his cheek. "You need that friend more than ever right now, and I want to be that friend."

His face softened, and he kissed her forehead. "Sugar, I've never been more grateful for your crappy taste in men."

Laura laughed and got herself into bed. The shower went on, and she must have drifted off because she next became aware of him sliding into bed beside her and arranging her to suit him: her plastered to his side, head on his shoulder.

She woke to the slow stroke of his hand down her spine, and over her bottom. Only half awake, she responded to his touch and his nearness.

"Sugar?"

She undulated into the heat of his touch. "Yes."

He slid his hand between her thighs and found her ready for him.

Laura crawled onto him, his large body hers for the taking.

With a groan, he gripped her ass and pressed her against his erection.

"Condom." She grabbed one from her night table drawer and sat up to slide it over his cock. This big, beautiful man was hers, eyes glittering at her, daring her to take what she wanted.

Brett stroked between her thighs.

Desire took over and made her clumsy in her need to get him inside her.

She slid onto his cock, absorbing all of him on a soft gasp. He filled her so completely and perfectly.

"Yes, Laura." He palmed her breasts, thumbs playing with her nipples. "Take us both there."

She loved being in charge, and she took it slowly, enjoying the sensation of the slide of his cock in and out of her, the rub and press of her clit against his rock hard stomach.

"You like that, don't you?" A flush rode his cheeks as he watched where they joined.

"Yes." She ground down on him, making him moan, relishing that she could.

"Ah." He bowed off the bed. "You're gonna kill me for sure."

Knowledge of what she did to him quickened her to completion. Her orgasm built, and she tightened around him. It swept through her, taking her mind with it.

Brett grabbed her hips and held her still as he thrust deep into her. He joined her moments later, and they rode the wave down together.

She collapsed on him, his chest slick beneath her cheek and his heart drumming under her ear. Like this, they made absolute sense.

# Chapter Twenty-Eight

Laura left Brett sleeping and went to shower. She had an hour or two before Sam and Daisy came, and she had plans for Brett in that time.

The shower door opened, and he stepped in beside her. "We should save water."

She laughed as he pulled her closer, but her laughter ended with the wet slide of his naked skin over hers. She'd never thought of herself as a particularly sexual person, but with Brett, she couldn't get enough. "How very responsible of you."

He dipped his head to kiss her. "Good morning."

"It is—"

Pulling away from her, he cocked his head. "Is that your door?"

Laura listened, and the doorbell rang. "The only people I'm expecting are Daisy and Sam but they're not due—"

Her phone rang, and then her doorbell again.

Brett opened the shower door. "You better get that."

God, this was not good if Daisy and Sam were at her door. She didn't even know where this thing with Brett was going, let alone having to explain it to her kids. And God alone knew what Patrick would make of her seeing someone. If she and Brett were even seeing each other, given his propensity to run hot and cold.

She dried her hands before snatching up her phone.

It shouldn't make any difference to Patrick, because he'd already moved on. But things with them were so tricky, and she really didn't want to risk upsetting him.

Sure enough, there was a text from Daisy saying they were being dropped off early.

It would have been nice if Patrick had let her know yesterday or even texted her this morning. Her mind went numb, refusing to calculate the ramifications of what was about to happen. "It's Daisy and Sam."

"You have to let them in." Brett jerked his head toward the door. "We're gonna have to play this through, sugar." He pointed behind her. "I'm never getting through that window."

"I know." Her mind cycled as she texted Daisy she was on her way.

Sam might buy a story about Brett being here to help her with something, but Daisy was getting past that age. She hurried into a pair of jeans and a sweatshirt then she took a deep breath and went to get the door.

None of them were ready for this, but here it was.

"Mom!" Sam looked as delighted to see her as he always did. "Guess what?"

"What?" She returned his hug.

"We're early." Sam giggled. "But you already know that."

"Dork." Daisy waited for Sam to let her go and then gave Laura a quick hug.

Laura felt sick. She'd only just gotten through to her daughter, and this morning could screw all that up. Daisy hadn't forgiven her for breaking up her marriage to Patrick. No way would she be okay with another man in Laura's life.

"I'm hungry." Sam clambered onto a stool by the island

and spread his hands on the island. "Can you make me breakfast?"

"Sure." She busied herself taking stuff from the fridge, ears pricked and listening as the shower shut off. "What would you like?"

"French toast," Sam said.

Laura almost dropped the eggs she was so freaked out, but she tried to keep it together. "And you, Daisy? Are you hungry?"

Daisy looked toward her bedroom and cocked her head. "Sure. French toast would be great."

"With berries?" Laura almost yelled, trying to drown out the sound of someone else in the condo and knowing it was futile.

"Yes." Daisy glanced at her and then back to the bedroom. "Is there someone here?"

"Um…" Laura hunted through her brain for the best way to drop the bomb. Her face heated, and she wanted to crawl into the fridge.

"Mom!" Daisy's eyes went huge as she whispered, "There is somebody here."

"Who's here?" Sam turned to see what Daisy was looking at. "Is it Pippa or Phi?"

"No." Laura managed to get that out. "It's…um…" Oh God, Daisy would never forgive her for this.

"A friend," Daisy said to Sam, shooting her a shocked glance. "Mom has a friend over. A special friend."

She'd give anything—anything—to start this morning over. At some point she might meet someone she wanted to introduce to her children. That someone might even be Brett, and if things kept going like they were, that was looking more than likely. But she hadn't planned on introducing her sleep-over to her children over French toast.

Sam frowned. "Like Dad and Margot are special friends?"

"Mom?" Daisy lifted an eyebrow. "Are you special friends like Dad and Margot?"

"Not really." Laura didn't want them getting the wrong idea, and she was having trouble reading Daisy's reaction. It almost looked like Daisy was trying not to laugh.

The bedroom door opened, and Brett stepped out. Hair slick from the shower and fully dressed, he nodded to Daisy and then Sam. "Hi, I'm Brett."

"I've seen you at the rec center." Sam looked thrilled at making the connection, but Sam had never met a person he didn't want to befriend. "You're like Blake and Blythe's brother."

"That's me." Brett looked like he was dealing with it a whole lot better than her. Then again, he didn't have as much to lose.

Laura dared not look at Daisy.

"Are you having French toast?" Sam grinned at Brett. "My mom makes the best French toast."

"Thanks, but maybe next time." Brett looked at her. His steady gaze tried to convey it was going to be all right.

Laura wished she could be so sure. "Actually, Brett has to get to work. He can't stay."

"Right." Brett looked at her and then nodded. "Nice to meet you, Daisy and Sam. I hope I'll see you around."

They all watched as he walked to the door, grabbed his keys from the table beside it and left.

Daisy cleared her throat and looked at Laura. "Wow, Mom, Brett Barrows? Way to go, you badass, you."


BRETT HAD SHIT TO DO, and Razor was blowing up his phone reminding him to get to it. Twenty minutes after leaving Laura's house, he pulled up outside Razor's building to pick him up.

Some kid had tagged the front of the building, and weeds pushed their way through the cracked asphalt. The glass entrance doors hung ajar, one side boarded with plywood. Razor lived in a shithole, but the rent was cheap, and he was saving to find something better and more permanent.

Razor appeared in the doorway with a scared-looking kid. He pointed to the tagged wall. "You did that shit, now you make it go away. You feel me?"

The kid nodded and slunk over to the tagging, his pants hanging almost as low as his lip.

"Hey." Razor jumped into the passenger side.

Brett watched the kid fill a bucket with water. "You making friends and influencing people?"

"Little shit is a good kid. Got a great mom, and she could do with some help keeping him in line."

They drove off. Laura might not think so, but she was also a great mom. Her panic this morning was all about not wanting to freak her kids out, and he appreciated that about her. That morning had been an abrupt end to an incredible night, as well as any plans he'd had for morning sex. Just the possibility of Laura and morning sex in the same thought bubble got him smiling.

He stopped at a light and caught Razor staring at him. "What?"

"You're whistling." Razor studied him. "And you look awful chipper this morning."

"It's a nice day." Brett motioned outside the truck.

An overcast sky made Razor's part of town look even more ghetto than normal. A light drizzle misted the windscreen.

Razor folded his arms. "Uh-huh. How's Carly?"

"Pregnant."

"Fuck." Razor shook his head.

They didn't need to say any more; they both got it.

Hunching over, Razor dug in his backpack. "Okay, so

while you were at the hospital yesterday, I did some digging on Artie York."

"Thanks, man." With Brett splitting his time between Laura, Blythe, Blake and the rest of his family, Razor had been doing the heavy lifting on Jen's douchebag ex.

"No, worries." Razor punched his shoulder. "I got your back, and you got mine."

Yeah, he did. Razor was the best thing Brett had taken away from his time spent in the hole. "So, what you got?"

"Artie has money." Razor flipped through some paperwork. "A lot more money than the shit sandwich he handed to our girl in their divorce."

Jesus! Why the fuck did women bother with assholes like Artie? People probably would think the same if he and Laura ever took their act public. "Is he paying up?"

"Sporadically." Razor made a face. "There's no pattern to the payments, and if I had to make an educated guess, I'd say he was using the money as another stick to beat our girl with."

Life had earned him and Razor master's degrees in assholery. They could spot one at forty paces. Razor had done the legwork, so he got to call that one. "What's the play then?"

"Art is a typical chickenshit loudmouth from what I can see." Razor read from his paperwork. "When he's not stalking his ex, he's a tax accountant by day and likes the strip clubs at night."

"What a prince." Brett followed Razor's pointed directions. "Maybe he needs a reminder to fight someone his own size."

Razor chuckled. "You read my mind. I had a chat with Jen yesterday, and she had that new alarm system installed. I got Gerry to give her a good deal."

"I think Art should be paying for that, don't you?"

Spreading his arms over the back of the seat, Razor grinned. "I think Art would be honored to buy his ex a security system."

"How did you get all that on Art?" Neither of them could afford to step out of line again.

Razor grinned at him. "That kid?"

"The tagger."

"Yeah, he knows his way around a computer and spent last night finding what he could."

Brett needed this clarified. "Legally?"

"Always." Razor nodded. "You don't have to break the law to get the stuff on someone."

Under Razor's direction, he parked outside a three-story office building, and the tallest building in Ghost Falls. Built of steel and glass, it screamed delusions of grandeur.

Razor tapped his shoulder. "There's our boy."

A black Audi sedan slid into a spot about four down from them. A tallish, slim guy stepped out. His salt-and-pepper hair was slicked back, and he wore a charcoal suit that fit his slim frame perfectly. "He doesn't look like any accountant I know."

"To be fair you only know the ones who operate on the wrong side of the law," Razor said.

Brett had to give him that one, and he chuckled.

Art York disappeared into the glass building. "Right." Razor tapped the dashboard. "We've got until about ten thirty. Artie will then grab a coffee. Sometimes he takes it to go and fucks up Jen's morning, sometimes not."

Most people would be amazed at how predictable they were. He used to do this sort of surveillance to pull an entirely different sort of job. "Breakfast?"

"You buying?"

He owed Razor that much. "Sure."

Over breakfast, Razor gave him more information on Art. No big surprises there, but more proof of Art being the sort of gaslighting control freak who would justify doing what he was doing to Jen.

Putting his fork down, Razor leaned back in the booth and spread his arms wide. "So, what about that whistling?"

"Nothing." Brett shut Razor down. Laura was not open for discussion "Any sign of Cole?"

"Nope." Razor frowned. "And that worries me. Fucker like Cole suddenly giving up and disappearing, I don't buy it."

"Me neither." Which meant he still had to keep an eye on Laura. Them's the breaks. He couldn't stop the smile if he tried.

Razor shook his head. "I'm glad you took my advice."

"Like hell I did." Brett sipped his coffee. "You give shit advice."

They both knew that was a lie, and Razor snorted.

At ten thirty-two, Art pushed through the glass doors of his building and strode for the coffee shop where they were sitting.

He held the door open for a pretty girl leaving as he was coming in and turned and watched her walk away.

At the counter, he ordered his coffee and waited with his eyes on his phone. Smartphones made watching people almost too easy. Entire attention focused on the small rectangle in their hands, they forgot to look up and look around. It almost took the fun out of surveillance.

Once his coffee was ready, Art took it and went back to his building.

"So if he's not stalking today, he won't move until lunchtime." Razor eased out of the booth. "I thought we should swing by Karstyn's, make sure shit's still under control there."

Karstyn was doing great and hadn't seen Cole. They tapped a couple of contacts. Nobody had seen Cole, and Pat was still in the wind. As Art appeared for lunch, which he took to go, Brett let Razor drop him at the hospital so Razor could stay on Art.

Ben and Dixie were sitting with Carly. He didn't stay long, and Razor was back after Art had disappeared back into his building.

Back in his truck, he and Razor went to grab a bite. "We're good at this." Razor motioned around them. "You know we are."

"Yeah." Because they were, and it fit with the security work he did for Eric. After grabbing a burger, they went out to a couple of Eric's sites, made sure everything looked good from a security point of view and were outside Art's swanky new condo by the time he came home.

Art's Audi glided to a stop next to Brett's truck like a thoroughbred cozying up to a rescue donkey.

Climbing out, Art eyed them. "Hi."

"Hey." Brett leaned against the front fender of his truck. They'd parked in the visitor spot, so Art couldn't even accuse them of trespassing.

"How you doing, Art?" Razor leaned his elbows on the truck's hood.

Art started and gaped at Razor. "How did you know my name?"

"Razor knows a lot of shit." Brett tucked his hands into his armpits and made his biceps pop. A flash of Laura and how much she liked his arms almost threw him. Yeah, his lady liked the way he looked just fine. *Focus, Barrows.*

"Right now, you're wondering if you might know us. Let me save you some trouble. You don't." Razor tossed a piece of gum in his mouth.

"Well, I'll wish you good evening." Art took a mental grip on his balls.

Pity Brett wasn't going to allow that. "Nah, Art. You're gonna stand there while Razor explains a few things to you."

Razor nodded. He was doing brain to Brett's brawn. "Turns out you and us have a mutual acquaintance."

"Yes?" Art looked as if that couldn't be possible. He was also doing the eye slide and calculating his chances of getting to his front door before they could get to him.

Brett straightened.

Art froze.

"You see, we're very fond of this mutual acquaintance, aren't we, Brett?"

On a subtle bicep flex, he grunted. Brawn didn't do a lot of talking.

Razor shrugged and crossed his ankles. "This mutual acquaintance is a bit disturbed, right, Brett?"

Grunt.

"She, and—spoiler alert, Art—it's a woman. She's been explaining to Brett and me how she doesn't feel safe."

Art paled and sidled closer to his door.

"I think he's getting it." Brett mirrored Art's sidle.

Art stilled.

Brett sent him an *attaboy* wink.

"I'll call the police." Art palmed his cell phone.

"You do that." Razor beamed at him. "And while we're waiting for Sheriff Evans, you and Brett and I can keep chatting."

"I mean it." Art's voice grew shriller.

"I believe you, Art." Razor yawned. "Let me help you. Dial nine and then a one and another one. When the nice person on the other side answers, you should go right ahead and tell them two men are standing beside their truck asking about a mutual acquaintance. Be sure to stress how this all looks."

Art deflated. "Did my bitch of an ex send you?"

"Nah." Brett fisted his hands. This scene was losing its entertainment value.

"Piece of advice here, Art?" Razor added a second piece of gum. "Don't call her the B-word in front of my boy over there." Razor shrugged *go figure*. "Who knew an ex-con could have such a thing about chivalry, but there you have it."

Time to stop toying with their food. Brett got close enough for Art to appreciate their size difference. "Jen doesn't appreciate being harassed. And if Jen doesn't appreciate it, you can be damn sure Razor and I don't appreciate it either." He got an inch closer.

Art flinched, paper pale and sweating.

"Let me make this real fucking simple for you, Art."

Razor shrugged. "You shouldn't have called her a bitch."

"You listening, Art?" Brett leaned in.

Eyes huge, Art nodded.

"You stay the fuck away from my girl, Jen. You bother her, and you'll be bothering me. You harass her, and you'll be harassing me. You piss her off, and you'll be pissing me off. Read me here, Art?"

Razor wrapped it up. "Now you're a smart guy, Art, I can see that. Got yourself a good job, make yourself a nice living in that building on the corner of Seventh and First. But for your sake, I want you to be good and sure you don't want Brett pissed off at you."

"I didn't touch her." Art made an effort to save face.

"And you're not going to either, am I right?" Razor smiled at him. "Also, we'll be sending you the bill for a new security system and a little something for our time."

Money was Art's trigger to find his balls. "You can't make me do shit."

This was always the critical part of persuading someone to see matters your way. At first you had the advantage of surprise and they folded, but then there was a moment when they sensed you were winding down, and they made a last stand.

"Do you really think that, Art?" Brett wound his hand in Art's tie and tugged him to his toes, and then tugged some more until Art was pinwheeling his arms to keep his balance and stop himself from landing face first in Brett's chest. "Because that would be a big mistake."

"Uh-oh." Razor tutted. "Now you've gone and got him snarly."

"You're not going to get close enough to her to breathe on

her, and if I hear you did, I'm going to be back." Brett dropped Art and stepped back. "Don't make me hurt you, Art." He smoothed Art's tie as he gave him back a bit of his own gaslighting medicine. "I really don't want to rearrange your face, pretty boy, but if you make me, I'm gonna enjoy the fuck out of doing it."

# Chapter Twenty-Nine

For the first time in months, Laura had a good time with both Sam and Daisy, and by the time Patrick came to pick them up the following evening, there was total peace in her condo.

"Laura." Patrick stood in her entrance hall as the kids loaded their gear into his car. "How were things?"

For the first time, she could answer honestly, "Good. Really good."

He looked taken aback. "Even with Daisy?"

"Especially with Daisy. We got all the homework for Monday done. I don't know if Sam told you, but he needs his skates sharpened."

Patrick shook his head. "This hockey is an expensive sport."

"True that."

Sam snuck between them with his bag. He wrapped his arms around Laura's waist. "Bye, Mom."

"Bye, sweet boy. I'll be at your hockey game next weekend, okay?"

Sam nodded. "I'm gonna score a goal."

"It's not all about scoring goals, Sam." Patrick grabbed the teachable moment.

"Just do your best." Laura kissed the top of Sam's head. He loved his hockey, but the chances of Sam scoring were not huge. That didn't deter him from giving it his all.

"Bye, Mom." Daisy stood in the doorway. "I'll see you in a couple of days."

Laura initiated the hug and Daisy reciprocated. "Count on it."

"I'm sure you'll have enough to keep you busy until then." Daisy giggled and slid past Patrick and went to the car.

Frowning, Patrick watched her go. "What was that about?"

For a giddy, irresponsible moment, Laura nearly lied, but then her adult reasserted itself. If Patrick found out another way, it would be worst. "Um…when you dropped the kids off early, I wasn't alone."

"Sorry?" Patrick blinked at her. "What do you mean— oh!" He looked aghast.

Laura took the gap his silence provided before he could get the wrong impression. "It was unfortunate, and I would never have allowed that to happen. The kids took me by surprise being early."

"That's not good, Laura." Patrick sniffed. "It's important not to give the kids the wrong impression."

This from the man who'd moved his girlfriend into their old family home within six months of their divorce being finalized. Although, she wasn't being entirely fair to Patrick or Margot, but then she wasn't the one standing in front of their ex with her mouth pursed in disapproval. However, they were getting married and it's not like Patrick had exposed the children to a revolving door of women. "I told them he was a friend of mine and left it at that. I thought the less I made of it the better."

"Right." Patrick cleared his throat and shoved his hands in his pockets. "I…um…didn't realize you were seeing someone."

"It's very recent." Laura deliberately kept it light. "And not at the stage where I would want to introduce him to Daisy and Sam."

Patrick nodded and sniffed. "Anyone I know?"

"Probably not." She didn't want to tell Patrick about Brett. Now she got why Brett had been so opposed to letting the two parts of his life mingle. What she and Brett had was special, and new and shiny, and she didn't want reality to tarnish it yet. "Really, it's not at that stage."

"Well, what stage is it at?" Patrick puffed his chest. "It appears to be at the sleepover stage. You know a woman in your position should be more careful of her reputation. What if Daisy and Sam carry tales to school?"

Patrick was so out of line it took her a moment to come up with a reply. "Patrick, I'm divorced not committed to a convent. I'm entitled to have adult relationships. As for school, those women haven't a leg to stand on. I know exactly what happens behind closed doors with most of them."

"Well, of course…" Patrick rubbed his nape and gave a rueful laugh. "I'm not handling this very well."

She got it, she totally did, and she laughed with him. "It's not easy, is it?"

"Nope." Patrick blushed. "You know it's not because…"

"You don't want me back, but the idea of someone else being with me makes you feel possessive?" She'd felt the same when Patrick had first told her about Margot.

"Exactly." He smiled and squeezed her shoulder. "Despite everything, Laura, I do want you to be happy. If this…guy makes you happy, then I say go for it." He chuckled. "And I'll text you next time I decide to drop the kids off early."

"I'd appreciate that."

The moment felt bittersweet between them. Patrick had been the man she'd chosen, the one she'd stood in front of all her family and friends and made vows to. They had shared a life, produced two children, and there was history between them, not all of it bad. "Have a good night and say hello to Margot for me."

"I will." Patrick left, and Laura closed the door behind him.

"Well," she said to her empty condo. "That went a lot better than expected."

She had the rest of the night free, and before she could overthink it, she dialed Brett's number.

He picked up almost immediately. "Sugar."

His deep bass voice thrilled her. "Hi there. Are you busy?"

"In a general or specific sense?" He chuckled over the traffic sounds coming from his side.

The lighthearted banter between them was nice, normal. "As in would you like to come around for dinner?"

"I would like that a helluva lot," he said. "I'll bring beer and some of that fancy girl wine you like so much."

She laughed. "You do that."

"Later, sugar." He ended the call.

A quick shower and change, and some makeup later, Laura stared at the contents of her fridge. Brett seemed like a steak man to her, which was lucky for him because she cooked a mean steak. She prepped some potatoes for oven roasting and put the steak on the counter to reach room temperature. In the middle of making a salad, the doorbell rang.

Heart quick timing, palms prickling, Laura opened the door.

Brett stood on her doorstep in jeans and a plaid shirt over a white T-shirt. His hands were full of beer and a couple of bottles of wine, and she took a moment to drink him all in. Tall, broad and muscular, she could see why he had intimidated her so much. It was more than his size though. Brett wore his life experience in an aura around him that yelled *approach with caution.*

He raised a brow at her. "You gonna let me in or stand there and stare at me."

"Dunno." She shrugged and propped a shoulder on her doorjamb. "View is rather good from where I'm standing."

His gaze heated. "That so?"

"Uh-huh." She nodded.

He crowded her back into her condo. "Let me help you make up your mind."

"You big bully." Laughing, Laura toed the door shut behind him as he strode through to the kitchen and put the wine and beer on her island.

"Now." Brett spun and came for her. "Let's do this right."

Catching her around the waist, he yanked her into him.

Breath whooshed out her mouth as she made contact with his front.

Brett dipped his head and took her mouth in a kiss so hungry and carnal she wilted under its steady onslaught.

Twining her hands around his neck, she rose on her tiptoes and gave as good as she got. Tongues tangled, teeth scraped as the kiss heated.

His hands fastened on her ass and ground her against his hardening cock.

"Sugar." Breathing hard he broke the kiss. "For future reference that's the way you greet your man."

"Taking notes." She nipped at his bottom lip. "And for your future reference that's exactly how a girl likes to be greeted."

He slapped her ass. "Feed me, woman, or I won't be much good to you."

Laura doubted that but she turned and went back to preparing dinner.

A wine cork popped, and Brett poured her a glass of wine and handed it to her. He twisted the cap off a beer for himself. "Things go okay with your kids after I left?"

"Fine." She picked her way carefully through what needed saying next. "But we need to be careful. I mean I don't—"

"Sugar." He came around the island and gripped her

nape. Pressing his forehead to hers, he said, "Your kids come first. Always. I get that. No need to get them involved in this until you and I know where it's going."

Relief swept through her. "Exactly. I mean, at some stage, there will be another man in my life."

"Gonna give it to you straight up, sugar." Brett pressed a kiss to her lips before stepping away. "I got ambitions on being that man, the one you introduce to your kids, but let's take this one step at a time."

The last of her misgivings melted. He really did get it, and it was early days, but she had ambitions in the same direction. "Okay."

"Okay?" He moved away. "Still hungry over here."

Laura heated the pan for the steak. "Tell me what you've been up to."

"I like that." He grinned and took a seat at her island. "A how was your day kind of deal."

She liked it too, and she returned his smile.

"Spent most of it with Razor." He sipped his beer. "We did a favor for one of the gals from the self-defense course."

"Oh?" A tiny twist of jealousy got her. "Which girl?"

"Jen," he said. "A little bit older, kinda short." He held his hand about five feet from the ground.

To Brett, a lot of people would be short, but Laura vaguely remembered someone of that description. "What sort of favor?"

"Her ex is giving her shit. Stalking." He shook his head. "Had to explain to the asshole why that wasn't cool."

If anyone could change someone's mind, it would be Razor and Brett. "You probably scared the crap out of him."

"I hope so." He picked at his beer label. "Sugar, can I ask you something?"

His serious tone stopped her, and she looked at him. "Sure."

"Razor thinks we should go into business." A flush rode his harsh cheekbones as if he was bashful.

It was so incongruous in that huge man that she nearly gave in to the urge to hug him. "What kind of business?"

"Security." He shrugged. "Clients like Jen who need someone on her team."

It was a bold idea, two ex-cons swapping sides, but she loved it. "I think you should do it."

"Really?" He pulled a face. "You're not just saying that to get into my pants?"

"I've already gotten into your pants." She laughed. "I'm saying that because I think you can do it, and you're far too driven and intelligent to be working security for Eric for the rest of your life."

"I'm not intelligent, sugar." He gave a rueful laugh. "I didn't even finish school."

"That has nothing to do with intelligence." It struck her that the kids she worked with were exactly like Brett had been way back when. What she did at the rec center could prevent someone experiencing what Brett was experiencing now, and that made her glad she did what she did. "And you can finish school anytime you like."

"I'm doing that." His flush deepened. "I'm getting my GED."

That impressed the hell out of her. Going back to school at their age was no joke. She didn't want to make it awkward, and Brett had his fair share of pride, so she kept it light. "Let me know if you need any help. There are a lot of resources available for adult learners."

"That's it?" He stared at her. "I tell you I didn't finish school, and you offer to help me?"

"What else?" She turned the steaks, and they hit the pan with a spit and sizzle. "My community service was working with adult learners as well and helping them get their GEDs."

She gave him a lascivious wink. "Maybe we can study together some time."

As she finished the steaks, he told her more about Razor's idea. Over dinner, the chat expanded into getting to know you stuff. It felt comfortable and like she'd known him for years. It felt normal and domestic, and she wanted more of it.

Brett helped her clear up, and they finished their drinks in front of the television. When bedtime came, he got up and followed her into the bedroom, like he belonged there, and Laura was beginning to think he did belong there.

# Chapter Thirty

Brett's cell rang in the middle of the night. As he blinked awake in the dark room, it took him a moment to orient himself. He was at Laura's, lying in her high thread count sheets with the scent of her lavender body lotion in his nostrils.

With a sleepy murmur, she rolled closer to him. "Brett?"

"It's just my phone." He grabbed it off the bedside table and answered the call. Phone calls at this time didn't bode well. "Yep."

"Brett?" The voice was young and male and sounded hesitant.

It took his groggy brain a moment to connect the dots. "Karstyn?"

"Karstyn?" Laura stirred beside him and opened her eyes.

He motioned he had this and sat up. "What's up, kid?"

"You said I should call if—"

"And I meant it." Kid calling at this time could only mean trouble. "What's going on?"

"Um…it's my brother. Cole."

"Right." Brett slid out of bed and tugged on his jeans. "Is he there now?"

Laura sat up, gaze fixed on him intently.

A man could get used to waking up to that much sweet, soft and sexy.

"He's sitting outside my house." Karstyn sounded freaked out and scared.

Brett grabbed his jeans. If Cole had surfaced, he wanted in. "Are you inside?"

"No." Karstyn cleared his throat. "I was out, and I came back late. I was about to go in when I saw him sitting outside."

He pulled his shirt over his head and checked his watch. It was after midnight and late for Karstyn to be out, but first things first. "He still sitting there?"

"Yes. He's waiting for me, and I don't wanna go in," Karstyn said. "My little brother is in there and—"

"You stay put and stay out of sight. I'm on my way." He sat and pulled on his socks and boots. "I'm gonna hang up now, but the situation changes, you call me. Yep?"

"Yeah." Karstyn breathed out a sigh. "Thanks, Brett. I didn't want to bother you."

"I told you, bother me if you need to. You did good, kid. You kept your head, and you protected your people." This kid was going far. Laura was right about that, and Brett aimed to keep his shithead of a brother from derailing that. "I'm on my way."

Laura jumped out of bed and headed for her clothes.

"No." Brett did not have time to argue. Cole was obviously waiting for Karstyn, but who knows how long he would wait patiently. "You're not coming."

Jamming her legs into her jeans, Laura said, "Yes, I am."

"Sugar." He grabbed her wrists as she tried to fasten her jeans and held them. "I'm begging you don't give me a hard time about this right now. Stay here, and I'll call you when I know more."

Hesitation played across her face. Without makeup, she

looked so much like her daughter. "I'm worried about him and now with Daisy—"

"I know that, but I got no time to talk this through with you." He dialed Razor as he spoke. "Please, stay here and let me deal with this. I can't give Cole my full attention if I'm worried about you."

"What?" Razor answered his phone.

"Be ready. I'm on my way."

Laura stared at him and then nodded. "Promise to call me when things are settled."

"I swear it." He kissed her forehead. "Now get back in bed and stay there."

She didn't look like she was going to do that, but at least she wasn't insisting on coming with him.

In the small hours' stillness, he made good time to Razor's place. As he'd expected, Razor waited outside, hoodie pulled up against the chill. He trotted over and climbed into Brett's truck. "Pat, Cole or Art?"

They had a regular convention of assholes they were watching. "Cole. Got a call from Karstyn that Cole is staking out his house."

"Karstyn in it?" Razor pulled out his phone and texted.

"Nope. Kid made him before Cole spotted him. He's holed up outside somewhere waiting for us." Brett chafed at keeping to the speed limit. However, with both him and Razor sitting on fat priors, speeding through town in the middle of the night was an invitation to the police to pay attention.

Razor checked his phone. "Just texted Karstyn. Let him know we're on our way."

"I like that kid."

"He's smart." Razor nodded. "Smart enough not to end up like his brother."

They stayed silent until they drew closer to Karstyn's foster home.

Razor peered through the windshield, looking for any sign of Cole. "How do you wanna play this?"

"Ronnie's marker."

Turning in his seat, Razor whistled. "You sure you want to play that ace?"

"Yeah." He was. As he continued to build this new life for himself, he wanted to put more distance between himself and his past. He didn't want to live in a world where people like Ronnie owed him a favor anymore. "Time to get free."

Razor nodded and said quietly, "Yeah."

Brett killed his lights and eased around the corner into Karstyn's street. Parked cars lined both sides of the road. Edging up beside a fire hydrant, Brett looked around. Karstyn must have been switched on to make Cole.

"There." Razor nudged him.

Inside a sedan about four cars down and to the left, a lighter flared orange as Cole lit a cigarette.

Brett might be going legit, but the hunt thrill prickled beneath his skin. He'd tracked the fucker down. He grabbed a heavy black flashlight and nodded to Razor. Opening his truck door slowly he slid out, keeping his head low.

On the other side, Razor did the same thing.

Using the parked cars as cover, they approached Cole. The low thump of music bass coming from the car helped them get closer.

Motioning Razor to stay that side, he slid around the trunk of the car and came up on the driver's side. He palmed the flashlight. If Cole had the door locked, he was going to need another way inside.

Standing, he yanked the door open.

Cole gaped at him, cigarette halfway to his mouth. "You!"

Razor opened his side and slid into the passenger seat. "How you doing, Cole? We've been looking for you."

"Wha—" Comprehension dawned on Cole's face, and he paled. "I was gonna come see you, I swear it."

"Really?" Brett stepped back. "Get out."

"Why?" Cole eyed the space he'd made between him and the car suspiciously. Then he scowled up at Brett. "I didn't go nowhere near that bit—Miz Turner."

Brett gave him points for not being totally stupid and calling Laura a bitch in front of him. Not many points, but one or two.

"Well, lookee what I found?" Razor rooted beneath the seat and pulled out a gun. "I'm guessing there's no license on this. Cops would be real interested to know you had it."

Cole looked at the gun and then Brett. Sweat beaded his forehead, and his gaze darted between Razor and Brett. "That's not mine."

"Sure, it isn't. You're just holding it for a friend." Brett leaned in and hauled him out of the car. "And it's mine now."

Razor shot him a look. Neither of them could carry.

But Cole didn't know that, or that he and Razor gave a crap about their parole. Cole tried to pull his arm away. "Hey!"

"Shhh!" Brett got into his face. "People are sleeping, and I want to keep it that way."

Cole shut his mouth, but sweat slid down the side of his face. "I don't know what you want."

"Yeah, you do." Razor shifted closer. "You know Brett was not happy about you putting your fucking hands on his woman."

"His woman!" Cole yelped and then immediately lowered his voice. "You never said." He blanched. "I didn't hurt her, not really. I wasn't gonna do anything."

"You calling my lady a liar?" Brett tightened his grip and hauled Cole to his toes.

Cole shook his head. "No, Brett. I didn't know she was your woman."

"Now you do." Brett didn't have to feign the surge of protective rage that went through him. If this bastard went anywhere near Laura again, fuck his parole, Cole was dead. "You stay away from her. Far, far away."

"I swear it." Cole licked his lips and glanced at Razor. "I swear on my mother's life."

"You didn't give a shit about your mother when she was alive." Razor curled his lip. "But we came to find you for another reason."

"You're going to stay far away from your brother." Brett shifted his other hand to Cole's throat. "You're gonna stay so far away from your brother that both of you forget you even have a brother."

Cole's mouth opened and closed, and a calculating gleam started in his eyes. "You can't make me do that. I got rights, legal rights. I'm his guardian."

"What you are is a piece of shit." Brett tightened his hold on Cole's neck. "And you're not gonna be the reason that kid doesn't go to college and change the miserable fucking hand he was dealt."

Discovering his balls, Cole stuck his chin out. "You can't say shit about my brother."

"Yeah, I can." Brett choked off enough air for Cole to have to work for his next breath. "And I'm saying it. Now, you fuck with me, and I'm not gonna come after you. Am I, Razor?"

"Nah. Piece of shit like that not worth screwing up your parole."

The cunning glint in Cole's eyes said he'd suddenly seen a small advantage to press home. "You're not gonna do shit."

"No, I'm not." Brett leaned down and whispered into his ear, "But I hold Ronnie's marker, and he'd love to get it back. Guess who is going to be that marker?"

Cole snapped his mouth shut. Genuine terror took over his expression. "Fast Ronnie?"

"Yeah, that Ronnie." Brett smiled. "He owes me, and

word is he don't like motherfuckers who put their hands on kids."

Looking ready to piss himself, Cole spat the words out. "I won't go near Karstyn or your woman. Tell Ronnie I give my word."

"Good, because I'm gonna ask Ronnie to make sure you do." Brett dropped him. "Now get in your car and forget this address."

Lurching into the car, Cole yanked the door closed and started the engine. Tires squealed, and the acrid stench of burned rubber followed his hasty exit.

Razor came up beside Brett. "Think he'll listen?"

"For a while. Ronnie will certainly keep him listening for even longer." Brett wasn't born yesterday. "Until Ronnie regards his debt as paid and our Cole gets to thinking about what he deserves and how he's been screwed over. Then he's going to talk himself into what he believes is his by right and come looking for it."

Nodding, Razor sighed. They'd both seen it happen too many times to be under any illusions.

A shoe scraped on concrete and Karstyn jogged across the road. He was grinning at them. "That was awesome. I've never seen Cole that shit scared."

"He's scared now." Brett didn't want to spend his life relying on a reputation for being the baddest ass out there. And he didn't want Karstyn thinking that might make a good career alternative. "But there's nothing cool about any of this. You get the grades you need, and you get the hell outta here. Hear me?"

Karstyn's grin faded. "I will, Brett, I promise."

"You do that." And because he didn't want to go too heavy on the kid, he grabbed his nape and shook him gently. "Make all of us proud."

Dropping his head, Karstyn nodded.

"And stay sharp." The kid needed to know he was still not

out of the woods. "Cole is going to stay away for now, but I don't know how long that's gonna last. Stay sharp, like you did tonight, and you can call me anytime."

Karstyn nodded and squared his shoulders. "Thanks, Brett." He nodded to Razor. "Razor. You were totally badass too."

"Get your ass inside." Razor mock lunged at him. "It's late, and you shouldn't be out here."

"I had shit to do." Laughing, Karstyn melted into the night and slipped around the side of the house.

"That's a good kid." Razor nodded. "I'll still keep an eye on him."

"Yeah." Brett led the way back to the truck. He was seriously tempted to go back to Laura's and slide into bed beside her, maybe wake her up and…

A large black SUV was parked behind his truck, and it hadn't been there before. The driver flipped on the light and illuminated the interior. A Black man dressed in a T-shirt and leather jacket nodded to them. Then he turned off the light and eased the SUV into the street.

Both Brett and Razor watched its taillights disappear into the night. Whoever that driver was, he wanted them to know he was there, and Brett wasn't going to risk leading him anywhere near Laura until he knew more.

# Chapter Thirty-One

It hadn't been the best of days. Laura hadn't gone back to sleep after Brett had left in the early hours. She was worried about Karstyn, and she'd waited up to hear from Brett.

He'd texted her and let her know everything was okay. She would have liked a few more details but Brett was not much of a texting man. Not sure whether he'd be back or not she'd waited around and dozed.

Mindful that Cole had resurfaced, she wasn't going to risk a late night at the rec center. Laura left work at her official end-of-day time.

Brett and Razor stood in the corridor outside the large hall talking to an older woman.

He looked up as she approached and gave her a slow, lazy smile that she liked to think he saved for her.

More women streamed past them into the hall, and from the buzz of voices, there were a fair number inside already.

"Hey." He stepped away from the conversation and into her path. "You okay?"

She was a lot better now. "Just a bit tired. You?"

"Good." He looked hesitant and shoved his hands in his pockets. "You look beautiful."

The man seriously needed to get his eyes checked. "I look tired and grumpy."

"It's a good look on you." His gazed roved her face. "I nearly came back this morning."

Heat rushed beneath her skin. "You should have."

"Brett." Razor joined them as the woman they'd been speaking to disappeared into the hall. He jerked his head at the hall. "We should get started."

Laura peered into the hall, and it was full of women. Then she remembered. "Self-defense course."

"Yup." Brett looked grim. "And nobody is taking their shirt off."

Razor smirked. "Don't be such a big baby. I'll catch you in there, and we can talk about Gail after."

She wanted to ask who Gail was, she guessed the woman they'd been talking to, but she didn't think that was what she and Brett had. At least not yet.

"Gail." Brett jerked his head at the woman who had joined the group in the hall. "She asked Razor and me to have a look at her security system. She lives in a shitty part of town."

"Right." From the hero worship currently being beamed at Razor as he walked to the front of the class, he and Brett might be doing a lot of that sort of thing.

Brett stepped into her space, his delicious heat enveloping her. "I'd really like to see you later, but I can't."

"That's fine." It wasn't at all, and her disappointment required a talking to once she reached home.

"I gotta do this Gail thing," he said. "Tomorrow?"

And the sun broke through her clouds. "That works."

"I really want to kiss you right now." He murmured quiet enough for only her to hear.

Gazes turned their way from the hall was reason enough why he couldn't, but it didn't stop her from whispering, "Probably about as much as I'd like you to."

The flare of heat in his eyes warmed her from within. "See you real soon, sugar."

"Make sure you do." She put a little sassy in her step as she strolled away.

Even though she wouldn't be seeing Brett later, her mood was vastly improved. She even sang along to the radio as she drove home.

Patrick sitting on the stairs outside her condo and looking grim brought her mood crashing down.

"What is it?" She grabbed her stuff from her car and hurried toward him. "What's wrong? Is it one of the kids?"

Standing, he shoved his hands in his pockets. "The children are fine. I suggest we take this inside."

That really didn't bode well. For Patrick "taking this inside" was fighting talk. She didn't know what she'd done to piss him off, but she was about to find out.

Letting them into her condo, she offered him a drink.

"No. Thank you." He strode into her kitchen and motioned her to follow. "If you would?"

A polite Patrick was a furious Patrick. She put her stuff down and poured herself a glass of wine. This was looking worse and worse.

"Something disturbing has come to my attention," he said.

Laura turned and propped her hips against the counter. "Okay."

"How much do you know about this new man in your life?" Patrick scowled at her.

Her heart sank as she got an inkling. She took a bracing sip of wine before she said, "A lot. How much do you know?"

"He went to prison." Patrick spat the words. "More than once."

"I'm aware of that," she said. "Who told you?"

"Who told me?" His frowned deepened, and he appeared to be struggling for words. "Shouldn't you have told me?"

Patrick had a right to know who was in his children's lives, but things with Brett hadn't progressed to that point. "He and I are not at that stage." She drank more wine. "I didn't think it was necessary."

"You didn't think it was necessary." Patrick threw up his hands and paced away from her. "You let a goddamn criminal into our children's lives, and you didn't think it was necessary to tell me?"

Now that was taking too much leeway. "He's served time, true, but he's not a criminal anymore. He's paid his debt to society."

"Don't be so fucking stupid." Patrick's voice grew colder and more controlled. "The man went to prison for beating a woman. His sister, no less."

"I understand you're upset, but you have no call to speak to me like that." The fucking stupid comment almost shredded her control, but if she lost her temper with Patrick, it would only put her at a disadvantage. Patrick won arguments by staying in control while others lost their cool. "I know all about Brett's history, Patrick, but—"

"And you let that...thug near my daughter." He leaned on the island and glowered at her. "What if he hits Daisy, or worse? What if he hits you?"

"He's not going to hit either of us." She understood Patrick's concern, but he was going to the dark side really fast. "Perhaps if you met him—"

"Met him!" Patrick looked flabbergasted. "Why the hell would I want to meet someone like that?"

It took her a second to recalibrate. "What do you mean someone like that?"

"A criminal, Laura." He stalked around the island. "A violent criminal."

She kept a lid on her building irritation. Standing there yelling and tossing around accusations wasn't productive. "Brett is not a violent criminal. He has a bad history—"

"And that awful goddamn family. I've heard about them

too." Patrick rolled his eyes and paced to the window and back. "The father is an alcoholic wife beater and petty criminal. The mother is a helpless addict, who I understand recently ended up in the hospital under suspicious circumstances. How do you know your Romeo didn't put her there?"

"Of course he didn't put her there." Laura couldn't believe Patrick would suggest Brett had beaten up his mother.

"Of course?" Patrick shook his head. "Of course because he told you he didn't. Really, Laura, I would have thought after your last brush with those sort of people, you'd learned your lesson."

Patrick had whipped the rug out from beneath her, and she stood there and gaped at him. She should know by now, Patrick liked to toss the past at her when it suited his purpose, but it still left her incredulous. "There is no link between me seeing Brett now and my gambling."

"Yes, Laura, there is a link." He jabbed a finger at her. "And I'm looking at her. You're the link. Or rather should I say your questionable judgment is the link?"

No words. She stood there catching flies.

"And frankly, I've had enough of cleaning up after you." Patrick shoved his hands in his pockets and took a deep breath. "End it, Laura, and come to your senses, or I will be forced to question if your judgment can be trusted around the children."

Buzzing filled her ears. "What did you say?"

"You heard me." He smoothed the placket of his shirt and cleared his throat. "I don't want to do it, Laura, but I will if you give me no choice."

"Are you—" The words wouldn't come out.

"I'm not doing anything yet." He nodded like a man who had accomplished his mission. "Regard this as a warning."

After the door shut behind him, Laura stood there with her empty wineglass in her hand. She had no idea for how long. Patrick had threatened to take her children away from her, because he didn't approve of Brett. Part of her, the part that had been married to Patrick understood his concern. Until she had worked with at-risk kids and their families, she hadn't understood how crime and poverty walked hand in hand. She hadn't gotten how frustration, boredom and hopelessness could drive people to do bad things.

Of course she knew not everyone needed an excuse to turn to crime. There were some people who were wired that way. Cole Watts came to mind.

But Brett, he was different.

*Why?* a tiny voice in the back of her mind asked. Maybe Patrick was right, and her judgment wasn't to be trusted. Maybe she only saw what she wanted to see.

Her phone was in her hand, and she hit Pippa's number.

"Laura?" Pippa came on the line with laughter in her voice. "What's up?"

Words caught in her throat. If she lost her children, that would be the end of her. They were the reason she'd fought to recover. They were the reason she drew breath. "P-pippa."

"Laura?" Pippa's voice softened. "Are you okay?"

"No." She couldn't speak above a whisper. "I..." She couldn't say the words aloud, in case that made it real.

"I'm on my way," Pippa said. "And I'm bringing wine."


LAURA DIDN'T TAKE a decent breath until Pippa arrived with a clanking bag. "Matt's watching Jazzie."

"Thank you for coming." Laura let her in.

"Are you kidding me?" Pippa took a hard look at her face. "You phone me and sound like that, and you think I'm not coming right over."

"I...I..." The tears took her by surprise. Sobs shook her so hard she could barely draw breath.

"Jesus." Pippa wrapped her in her arms and rocked her.

Laura tried to tell her what was wrong, but all she could do was make racking, pained noises.

"*Belle filles*," Phi said, and she was shifted from Pippa's arms to Phi's. The smell of patchouli, a smell she associated with hugs and laughter and wild, impetuous adventures, made her cry even harder. "You cry it all out." Phi stroked her spine and rocked her. "That's it, darling. You cry your river for Phi."

"I'll get the wine," Pippa said.

"Stat," Phi said. "I hope you brought enough."

"I brought three bottles," Pippa said.

"Hmm." Phi separated enough to look into her face. "Is that going to be enough, Lolly?"

Phi's emerald green eyes staring at her from layers of purple glittery eye makeup grounded her.

Laura dragged in a deep breath.

"Here." Pippa handed her a glass. "Only, make sure you're not sobbing when you sip. I did that once and inhaled wine through the nose."

"That's nasty, Agripinna." Phi shuddered and wiped Laura's face with a tissue.

The look on Pippa's face as Phi said her full name almost made Laura laugh. It calmed her enough for her to take a sip of her wine. Pippa hated her full name. Phi had given it to her when she was born, filling in the birth certificate while their mother was still high on post C-section drugs.

"Now." Phi took a glass from Pippa and sashayed into the living room. "Is this your salon?"

"I suppose." Laura was momentarily dazzled by Phi's rhinestone purple velvet onesie.

Phi took a seat and patted the sofa beside her. "Come and tell us all about it." She twirled a hand in the air. "Find us some sustenance would you, Agripinna."

"How about I just lock you in a home?" Pippa muttered, but she was opening cupboards as she spoke.

"Nothing wrong with my hearing, Agripinna." Phi winked

at Laura. "It's always a mistake to drink on an empty stomach."

They were so silly and so familiar that she laughed even harder.

Pippa brought cheese, cold cuts and crackers. She shoved them at Phi. "Here. Now." She took a seat with her wine and nodded at Laura. "Lay it on us."

Laura had never had the sort of relationship with Pippa or Phi, where she confided in them. For most of her adult life, she'd been estranged from Phi and Pippa, but sipping wine and nibbling crackers and cheese with them as she unburdened her soul made her feel supported. Loved.

When Laura finished, Pippa said, "Patrick is being a dick." "He has no right to threaten to take your children away from you."

Laura shook her head. "Not really. Not after what I put him through."

"You've made amends. At some point, he needs to get over it and move on. He doesn't get to help himself to your internal organs as recompense for the rest of your life." Pippa refilled her glass. "And you're paying him back."

Phi stuffed a loaded cracker in her mouth. "You're trying to pay him back?"

"Yup."

"How?" Phi looked around her. "No offence, my chicken, but this is not the Ritz, and you hardly make enough money to do that."

"I make enough." Discussing money made her squirm. "And it's the right thing to do."

Phi snorted. "If I have moved past this, and I was by far the most wronged party, that boring ex-husband of yours should as well."

"He's not boring." Laura's defense of Patrick was more knee jerk than anything else. Patrick was a total snore fest.

"Darling." Phi raised her painted-on eyebrows. "The man eats pizza with a knife and fork."

"He irons his jeans." Pippa pulled a face.

"He refuses to dress up for my parties." Phi let that sink in. By far the worst crime in Phi's eyes. "And portion controls."

"Ye—wait." Pippa turned too Phi. "I know I'm going to regret this, but how does portion control fit into this?"

Phi rolled her eyes and wrapped cheese slices in cold cuts and ate them. "Even at celebrations, he controls how much food he eats."

Pippa made a face at Laura. "What's wrong with that?"

"Food is a sensual experience." Phi threw up a hand as if the answer was obvious. "You should never trust anyone who doesn't lavish the sensuality of food."

The way Pippa and Phi glared at each other made Laura want to laugh. Phi was Pippa in about sixty years.

"Phi, that's just wrong." Pippa smirked. "Lots of people watch what they eat. It's healthier."

"I'll tell you what's healthy." Phi tapped Pippa's knee. "And I've lived a lot longer, so I know better than you." She winked at Laura. "Throwing yourself into the joy and sumptuousness of life, that's healthy. Living this one life we have as if it is all we get, that's healthy. Food is healthy. It's like sex."

Pippa sighed and turned back to Laura. "It was only a matter of time before she turned this around to sex."

"You're telling me you and Matthieu are not making the camel with two backs at every opportunity?" Phi looked affronted. "Because if you aren't, I need to have a chat with Matthieu."

"You leave Matt alone." Pippa looked horrified. "And I'm not discussing my sex life with you."

"Hmph!" Phi refilled their glasses. "You're such a prude."

"No—" Pippa growled. "Never mind that. Can we get back to Laura's problem?"

"Some of us never left it." Phi looked arch as she took

Laura's hand. "Do not concern yourself Lollypop Princess. We shall find a way through this together."

Fresh tears pricked beneath Laura's eyelids. When she'd been a very little girl, a friend of Phi's had written a children's book about her, *The Lollypop Princess*. She'd spent so many years resenting Pippa and Phi's relationship she'd forgotten the lovely things Phi had done for her. "Thanks, Phi."

"I am one hundred percent in your corner, my darling." She sat back with a smug smile. "Now, if you are really bumping boots with that delicious slab of a man—and darling, you make me so proud—perhaps you could take a picture of him shirtless?"

# Chapter Thirty-Two

By the time Matt—with Jasmine in tow and still yelling no at everything—came to fetch Pippa and Phi, Laura was feeling much better and a little drunk.

"Matthieu, my darling boy." Phi twinkled at Pippa's husband. "You should take us home."

"That's what I'm here to do, Phi." Matt leaned down and kissed Laura's cheek. He had a rough edge to him that added attitude to his classically tall, dark and handsome. "You doing okay?"

"Better now." She smiled back. An evening with Phi and Pippa had been the medicine she didn't know she needed.

On her way out, Phi trilled, "Well, hello there."

"Er…hi." Brett sidled past Phi and walked into Laura's condo.

Laura didn't know what he was doing there, but she was thrilled to see him. "Hi."

"We were just leaving." Pippa smiled at him. "Enjoy your evening."

She and Matt hustled Phi out of the condo. She could be heard objecting all the way to the car.

"Sorry." Brett stood just inside her door and looked

around at the empty wine bottles and crackers and cheese remains. "I didn't mean to interrupt."

"You didn't interrupt." Laura closed the distance between them and put her arms around his waist. "I thought you had a thing tonight."

"Razor and I got done quickly, and now I'm here." He looped his arms around her.

"I'm very glad you're here."

The side of his mouth tilted up, and his gaze warmed. "Yeah?"

"Yeah."

"I texted, but you didn't answer, so I took a chance."

"You texted?" She widened her eyes at him. "So you can teach an old dog new tricks."

He grinned down at her. "Next I'm gonna get me a Face-Time profile."

"You do that." She patted his chest. Baby steps. "Phi and Pippa came around to cheer me up."

"You okay?" He focused on her face. "Anything wrong, sugar?"

As much as she didn't want to go back there, Patrick's objections might not go away and would have to be dealt with. "Patrick was here."

"Your ex?" Brett frowned and pulled her closer to him. "It's not one of your days to have the kids is it?"

"Nope. He paid me a special visit." Laura laid her cheek against his wide chest. It was like having her very own warm, breathing wall between her and the world. "He's not happy."

Brett stiffened. "About?"

"Us."

"Sugar." He separated them so he could look at her. "You better tell me."

She sighed and tried to push away the upset that Phi and Pippa had waylaid while they were there. "Daisy said something about you the other day when he came to pick them up."

Brett barely moved a muscle. "And?"

"And Patrick found out about your past." She wanted to get back to the part where he held her and made the bad thing go away. "About your record and your family."

Face heart-attack serious, he moved them both to the sofa and sat her down. "I'm guessing he wasn't happy about you spending time with me."

"Yep." Laura reached for her wine glass. "He's not being fair."

"Laura." Brett's tone chilled her, and she didn't want to hear what he said next.

She should have kept her mouth shut about Patrick, but it was out there now. "Let's not talk about that. I'll work it out."

"Sugar." Brett took the glass out her hand and put it on the table. "These are your kids. We need to talk about this. Tell me the rest."

"I'd prefer not to." She reached for her glass again. "How do you know there's more?"

"Because if an ex-con, and one with my record, was hanging around Blythe and Kim, you can bet your sweet ass there'd be more."

That almost made her laugh. "But you know better than most that because somebody has stuff in their past doesn't mean they're still that way."

"I do know that." He leaned his elbows on his knees and clasped his hands. "But I'd also want to meet that man for myself, look him in the eyes, and know that he'd changed as much as he said."

Brett talking to Patrick would not work out. "That's not going to happen. Patrick is not feeling reasonable about this."

"He say anything else?" Brett was unnaturally still. His serious gaze cut through her wine buzz.

Talking about it made her panic all over again. "It doesn't matter."

"Yes, it does." Brett's jaw set in a line. "He tell you he didn't want you seeing me?"

She couldn't speak, so she nodded.

"He make that a condition of you seeing your children again?"

Not knowing how Brett had guessed that, and resenting him for doing so, she shrugged. "Not quite as directly as that. He called my judgment into doubt and made some veiled threat about that being a factor in me seeing my children."

Despite Phi and Pippa, the awfulness of that possibility crashed into her, and she wanted to cry again.

"Sugar, listen to me." Brett's tone gentled.

Laura felt too vulnerable and shook her head.

Sighing, Brett picked her up and put her in his lap. He tucked her head beneath his chin. "This thing between us, Laura, I've never had anything so sweet." The sadness in his voice brought her tears back. "We were always too good to be true, and I've always known it had an end date."

She didn't want what he was saying to be true, and she resented him for making her face the truth. "Patrick has no right to tell me who I can see."

"Maybe not, but he does get to say who is part of his kids' lives." He tightened his arms around her and rested his cheek against the top of her head. "We both know what we gotta do here."

"No." She shook her head and grabbed his forearm. It had been so long since she'd felt happy, and she didn't want it to end. "I can talk to Patrick, appeal to him to be more reasonable about us."

Brett kept speaking as if he hadn't heard a word she'd said. "We both accept your kids come first. That's the way it should be, and you know that." He tilted her chin up and kissed her soft and sweet. "Maybe with some time, Patrick will see things different, but until he does, you cannot risk your kids." His deep hazel eyes stared into her soul. "Those kids are your everything, sugar, and they need you as much as you need them."

More tears welled, and she knew the truth of what she was hearing. She hated it, but it was her reality. Her gut knotted as she guessed where he was going.

"I'm never going to stand between a mother and her kids." He hugged her closer to him. "Your kids deserve the best you can give them. I'm never going to be the reason you don't get to do that. I can't. Not with the way I grew up."

"Brett." They had only started exploring this thing between them, and already, he was grafted to her in a way that made losing him excruciating. She hadn't even had time to sort out how she felt about him. "This is so unfair."

"I made this life, Laura." Brett stood and put her on her feet. "This is what I reap."

She shivered at the loss of his warmth. "You've already paid the price."

"You and I both know some prices demand you pay them more than once."

Their understanding of that was one of the things that bound them. "I hate this."

"I'm not loving it either." He took a deep breath and looked pained. "I don't regret a damn fucking thing, sugar. This thing with you—" He gestured between them. "Pure fucking heaven, and walking away is going to leave a hole a mile wide straight through the middle of me."

Even as she said it, she knew the answer. "Surely, there's a way we can work this out."

"Don't." He turned for the door. "Thinking about what can't be isn't going to make this any easier."

Anger rose swiftly in her, and she lashed out at him. "So, that's it. Shit gets hard, and you walk?"

Opening the door, he turned. "You're the best thing ever

happened to my sorry ass, sugar. I can't fuck that sweet up." His jaw firmed. "I won't fuck up your life, and the best way I can see not to do that is to walk."

The door shut behind him. Silence descended, and his truck started up and drove away. He was right. She couldn't risk losing her children for anything. Or anyone.

# Chapter Thirty-Three

Blythe's car was parked in front of the house when Brett pulled up to check on Carly. She'd been released from hospital yesterday, and Dixie and Ben had taken her home.

With Pat in the wind though, he didn't want to take any chances.

One of his brothers had been gardening, and he stopped a moment to appreciate the beds now fronting the house. Honest to God, he didn't think they had it in them. Bracing himself for bad, he opened the front door. "Hello?"

"Brett." Blythe appeared through the doorway to the living room. "I thought you'd be by."

He leaned down and kissed her cheek. "Something smells good."

"Yeah." She grimaced. "I'm getting some meals in the freezer. Hopefully she'll eat some of them." She lowered her voice. "Blake is here."

"Really?" That was news to him. "What's he doing here?"

"He's been helping out." She shrugged. "Dixie says he's been coming around and fixing stuff up for when Carly came home."

With all he had going on lately, he hadn't been paying enough attention to Blake. "You believe him?"

"I do." Blythe shrugged as if she couldn't believe she was saying as much. "Maybe seeing how much you've turned your life around has had a positive influence on him."

Brett barely suppressed the snort her words created. He may have turned his life around, but that didn't mean he got his happy ending.

Blythe studied him. "I heard about Laura."

"What the fuck?" The words came out louder than he intended, and he lowered his voice. "How?"

"Well, Phi told Will, and he told me." She grinned. "And Pippa told Matt who then told Eric."

"Who then told you." He finished that thought for her. Forcing himself to do so, he shrugged. "So?"

She riled right up and stepped closer to him. "So, it's not fair. You and Laura have something good together."

"Had." It hurt more than he liked. "We had something good, but her kids come first."

Blythe huffed. "And that's it?"

"What else?"

"For someone who likes her as much as you do, you sure are keen to put roadblocks in your way." Blythe shook her head.

He couldn't believe Blythe didn't get it. "I care for Laura, which means I want her to be happy, and there is no fucking way she's getting happy if she don't have her kids." He moved around her and into the kitchen.

Blake sat at the kitchen table peeling potatoes. He looked up when Brett came in. "Hey."

"Blythe says you've been coming around?"

"Yeah." Blake cleared his throat. "I wanted to talk to you about that."

Bracing himself for shit he didn't want to deal with, Brett took a chair at the table. "So talk."

"I was thinking that I could be more use here." Blake kept his eyes on his peeling. "I mean, if I lived here and not with you." He jerked his chin toward the front of the house. "Mom listens to me, and I can get her to eat properly. Take care of herself."

His knee jerk was to kill that idea.

Over Blake's shoulder, Blythe shook her head and stopped him.

Instead he said, "I'm not sure that's a great idea."

"And I know why you would say that." Blake put a peeled potato into the pot of water at his elbow. "There are a lot of triggers here that might make me use again, go back to my old life."

Brett couldn't have put it better, so instead he said, "I don't want to see you screw up again, Blake."

"Me neither." Blake gave a wry chuckle. "But I feel like I can handle it." He shrugged. "When I'm here I feel useful, needed. Less like I'm always taking from everyone."

Last time someone had trusted Blake, he had stolen Blythe's money and emptied Will's college account. Brett had tracked him down and brought him home. He'd pretty much been keeping a foot on his throat since then. "I dunno, Blake."

"I know there's no reason for you to trust me." Blake spoke quickly as if afraid Brett wouldn't let him get the words out. "I've fucked up more times than not. And also we're not really the trusting kind of family."

Blake could say that again, and they'd all gotten not trusting for damn good reasons. "I'm waiting for a point that makes me comfortable letting you do this."

"You can't babysit me for the rest of your life," Blake said and glanced at Blythe. "I've either got it in me to turn it around like you did, or I don't." He leaned forward, face eager. "You deserve your own life, and I'm ready to test myself. Bo and Becker are here, and they can keep an eye on me. They also managed to make more of themselves, so I reckon somewhere deep inside—and with me it's been buried deep until now—I give enough of a shit about myself to change my future." Blake's voice gentled. "She needs me, Brett. And she knows I understand her better than the rest of you."

Blythe took the potatoes from Blake and put them on the stove to boil. "Why do you say that?"

Brett wanted to know as well.

Blake cleared his throat. "The rest of you don't keep making the same mistakes over and over again like we do." He jerked his head in the direction of Carly's room. "We have this thing inside us that keeps us sabotaging ourselves."

"This is sounding more like an enabling situation to me." Brett couldn't see how two sick people made a healthy one.

"But I've changed." Blake carried on, "I'm not going to make the same mistakes again, but that doesn't mean I don't understand the compulsion to do it. Mom knows that about me." He huffed a soft laugh. "I probably inherited it from her. Blythe." He jabbed his thumb at Blythe. "She was always the strong one. She made her own way, carved her own path." Blake nodded to him. "Even you managed to stop the runaway train you were on and get off it. Mom and I, we have a real hard time with that."

"What about Pat?" Blythe joined them at the table. "We all know he'll be back."

"That's another reason I should stay here," Blake said. "I can keep an eye out for him. Bo and Becker are working long hours. Ben has Dixie. Even Bart got himself into the army." He shrugged. "I'm the only one with less on my plate." He leaned his elbows on the table. "I want to do my part, Brett. I want to see if I can do something for this family that is good and useful."

With their family legacy of fucked up, it was easy to say people didn't change. It was easy to believe that people kept spinning their wheels in the same circles of destructive behavior. But Blythe had taught them all you could rewrite the script. She'd gone ahead and done it, and in the process, made a new future for herself and Kim and Will.

Eli had taught him how to do it for himself. Laura's husband might think he was a deadbeat, but the guy was wrong. Brett had turned his life around, and people like Blythe and Laura had put their faith in him. Even Jen and Gail had come to him for help. It was hypocritical to ask the world to give him a second chance, and not be prepared to do the same for Blake. He had also been thinking Blake needed to take on more responsibility.

"Okay." He glanced at Blythe, and she nodded. "We can give it a try."

Blake's face cleared and he grinned. "Really?"

"But." Brett held up a finger to stop Blake from going off half-cocked. "This is a trial period only. You even think you're gonna backslide, you call me."

"Done." Blake nodded.

"And I don't want you taking on Pat alone. He shows up here, I want to know."

Blake nodded again. "I'll call you first."

"Um…no." Blythe scowled at him and then Blake. "You'll call Nate first."

Blake glanced at him before he nodded to Blythe.

"Hey." Becker stomped into the kitchen with Bo on his heels.

They both took off their boots before they came any farther.

Brett just stared. Neither of them had ever been house trained before. "Hey."

"We came by to see if Carly needed anything." Bo walked into the kitchen and washed his hands. "We're on our lunch break."

If a flying pig winged its way past the kitchen window, Brett could not have been more surprised. He'd had the devil's own time trying to get these two to take some responsibility and live productive lives. "How's work?"

"Good." Becker opened the fridge and took out a pitcher of water. He poured himself a glass and then offered the pitcher to everyone in the kitchen.

Blythe shook her head and gaped at him. "What the hell happened to you?"

"Nothing." Becker looked offended and pulled a chair out and sat. "It's the polite thing to do."

"I know that." Blythe chuckled. "But I was willing to bet you didn't."

"I can learn."

All the times he'd tried to bully Bo and Becker onto the straight and narrow would suggest otherwise, but he kept that to himself. They were trying, just like Blake was, and he couldn't ask any more of them. "Blake says he wants to stay here."

"Okay." Bo squinted at Blake. "But there are no free rides in this house. He stays here, he contributes to expenses, and he does his fair share of chores."

"Sure." Blake shrugged.

Brett sat back in his chair and stared at his siblings. He couldn't believe he was actually having this thought, but it looked like the Barrows clan was going respectable.

# Chapter Thirty-Four

During the day, Laura could stow her worry about Patrick taking the kids away from her. She could even distract herself from the ever-present ache Brett's absence in her life had caused. At night, however, alone in her condo with the children at Patrick's, emotion crept up on her.

She'd really screwed up and lost her marriage because of her mistakes. Not for a moment, was she making excuses for what she'd done, but at some point, the penance had to end. The rest of her life couldn't be spent with her not allowed to be happy. Patrick had moved on with his life, and as far as she could see, was happy with Margot.

Was this how it was going to be? Her asking Patrick to sanction what her happiness looked like.

It had been over a week since that conversation with Brett where he'd walked out the door. She missed him more than ever, and her resentment grew along with her sadness. She had done all she could to own her mistakes and take responsibility. She had asked for Patrick's forgiveness and received it, or so she had chosen to believe. She was also doing what she could to pay the money back.

Her phone rang, dragging her off the highway to self-pity.

"Laura," Patrick said, barely waiting for her to answer. "You had better get over here."

"Now?" She checked the time. It was well after ten at night. Her heart pounded uncomfortably. "Is somebody hurt?"

"Not like that," Patrick said, his tone loaded. "But you better get over here and help me deal with this."

On the drive over to Patrick's, Laura rapidly went through every scenario that could have Patrick sounding that mad. The weight of his displeasure hung around her neck. She'd been carrying it ever since their divorce. Maybe even while they had been married, if she was honest.

She pulled up to the house and the door opened as she climbed out of her car.

"Mom?" Dressed in his red and white plaid pjs, face pinched and anxious, Sam trotted down the walkway toward her. He flung himself into her arms.

Laura hugged him to her. "Shouldn't you be in bed?"

"They're shouting at each other." Sam pressed his face into her. "And Daisy is crying."

Her mama bear rose to the surface. Nobody made her girl cry. "Let's get in the house."

Margot waited inside the door. She gave Laura a wan smile. "Hi. Thanks for coming."

"What's going on?" Margot was pale and wringing her hands.

"Um…" Margot glanced up the stairs. "There's been a problem with Daisy."

Laura's heart sank. "What kind of problem?"

Between them, Sam was looking from one to the other, taking everything in.

"Sam." She kissed his forehead. "I want you in bed."

Sensing weakness in the system, Sam said, "Can you read me a story?"

"I can." Margot looked at Laura for approval. "If you don't mind."

"I don't mind." Laura was grateful she could concentrate on Daisy, and Margot was always good to Sam. She gave Sam a nudge. "Off you go, and I'll come and see you before I leave."

"They're in Daisy's room," Margot whispered on her way upstairs with Sam.

"No, Dad." Daisy's raised voice reached Laura as she was halfway up the stairs. "You can't do that."

Patrick's response was as close to shouting as she'd ever heard. "I can, and I will. While you live in this house, you are my responsibility, and it's up to me to make sure you don't do anything you'll regret."

Laura nudged open Daisy's door. "Hi."

"Thank, Christ." Patrick scowled at her. "Talk to your daughter."

"Daisy?"

Pale, with tear-streaked cheeks, Daisy flung herself off her bed and into Laura's arms. "Mom! He can't do this to me."

No stranger to teen histrionics, Laura glanced at Patrick. "What's going on?"

"I'm glad you asked." He glared at her. "Because you're going to help me fix this."

Of course she'd help him fix whatever was wrong. Daisy was her daughter. The attitude being beamed her way, however, was wearing thin. "Am I missing something?"

"He says I can't see Karstyn anymore," Daisy sobbed. "He's telling me he'll ground me if I don't promise not to see Karstyn."

Patrick knew better than to handle Daisy with a heavy-handed Victorian father routine. Except, he was standing there, hands on his hips, scowling at both of them like something out of a soap opera.

"Daisy, can I speak to your father for a minute? I'll be right back."

"Don't listen to him." Daisy scrubbed her face with her palms. "All he says is how Karstyn is bad for me, and I can't see him anymore."

"I'm going to talk to your father." Laura kept a tight rein on her irritation. Patrick had mishandled the situation. A calm conversation could allay his worst fears.

Patrick led the way out of Daisy's room and downstairs into his study. After closing the doors, he turned to her with arms folded. "This is on you, Laura."

"What?" She was definitely missing something. "She met him at my condo, but I don't see how any of today is my fault."

Patrick huffed. "No, you wouldn't. Because you always do what suits you, and damn the rest of us."

His anger left her wrong footed and reeling. She had her faults, but she didn't recognize the woman he was describing. "That's not fair."

"I'll tell you what's not fair." Patrick stalked behind his desk and snatched up a stress ball. She'd given it to him on his fortieth as a gag gift. "What's not fair is you leaving me to be the bad parent and tell her she can't see this boy."

"I thought you knew she was seeing him," she said, struggling for calm. "When I found out they were…friends, I asked her to tell you."

"You should have told me." Patrick clenched the stress ball. "But you didn't. You know why?"

She'd bet she was about to find out. "Why?"

"Because you knew I would never approve of some ghetto kid hanging around my daughter, leading her into trouble." Patrick sneered at her. "Is this because of that criminal you're screwing? What's good enough for the mother is good enough for the daughter?"

Laura tried to respond, but choked, and it came out as a

garbled cough. It took her long moments to sort everything that'd come out of his mouth. First off, she was struggling to comprehend that Patrick had said all that. Throttled anger made her hoarse as she managed to say, "You are so out of line right now, Patrick."

He swallowed and squeezed his stress ball.

"Let me address your concerns one at a time." A lifetime of being her mother's perfect daughter came to her rescue, and she kept it together. "Karstyn is not a ghetto kid. In fact, I'm not even sure what a ghetto kid is, but putting that aside, Karstyn gets better grades than Daisy. Since she's been chatting with him, she's doing better at school and getting her homework done."

"I—"

"I'm not done." If she heard any more crap out of him, she would stuff that stress ball where the sun didn't shine. "He is trying his desperate best to make it into med school, and I'm doing my best to help him get there. I fail to see how that can be a negative influence on our daughter. The same daughter who has no idea what she wants to do when she leaves high school beyond the vague notion of having fun at college."

Patrick flushed. "His brother is a known criminal."

"Yes, he is, and I can tell you from personal experience, he is a scary and dangerous man. Which is why Karstyn has been separated from him and put with a family who can help him."

"Yes, but—"

"Still not done." She pounded the desk to relieve some of her fury. "Daisy told me about him in confidence. Should I have told you? Maybe, but I didn't see anything bad in their relationship. I like Karstyn, and I think it shows excellent judgment on her part."

Patrick huffed and crossed his arms. "Done now?"

"Nope." She shoved her hands in her pockets before she strangled him. "How dare you call Brett a criminal? He's paid for his crimes and emerged a better man for it. Certainly, someone who knows better than to judge other people for circumstances beyond their control."

Clearing his throat, Patrick dropped his gaze.

"And who I screw or don't screw has nothing to do with you. You lost the right to comment on my behavior when you divorced me."

"Like you gave me any choice." Patrick glowered at her but buried in his anger was hurt as well.

She hadn't wanted to hurt him. "You're right, Patrick. I fucked up our marriage and our family. I fucked up my life, your life and the kids' lives, and I'm more sorry than I can say for that. But I can't invent a time machine and fix what I broke. I can only tell all of you how deeply sorry I am and try to move forward in a way that demonstrates that to you." She took a breath. "You're angry, and I hurt you. I know that. But I'm done getting kicked about it."

Patrick's voice reached her as she got to the door. "What does that mean?"

"It means my life is my own to live on my terms. I don't know how I feel about Brett because we never had the chance to work it out. But we ended our relationship because that's what you wanted."

"Good." He nodded. "Now you can tell Daisy to end things with this boy. He might be a good kid, but he's not for her."

Laura stared at him as the truth sunk in. Patrick would never hear her, because he couldn't hear her. "No, I'm not going to do that. I like Karstyn, and they're young. The less fuss we make about this, the easier it will be." She tried one more time to appeal to his logical brain. "She's fourteen, and he's only a year older. Chances are this thing won't even make the end of the year."

Patrick opened and closed his mouth again.

"And one more thing." Laura dredged up her inner Phi.

"Next time you threaten to take my children away from me, do it with your lawyer present."

She marched from his study with her legs shaking but her head held high.

Daisy was waiting at the bottom of the stairs with Margot.

Margot jerked her head at the overnight bag at Daisy's feet. "I thought some mother-daughter time would be a good idea."

"Thank you." Laura didn't know what else to say. "I'll just say good night to Sam before we go."

"Mom?" Daisy blinked at her. "Are you going to say I can't see Karstyn?"

"No, I'm not." Laura pulled her daughter in for a fierce hug and kissed the top of her head. "But we do need to talk about you standing by the promises you make me. It may take pizza and a lot of ice cream before we're done."

As she turned to go to Sam's room, Margot stopped her. "I'll talk to him when he's calmer. He's a good man, Laura." She grimaced. "Most of the time." Then she surprised Laura by hugging her. "But you're a good woman and a wonderful mother."

## Chapter Thirty-Five

Waking up the next morning with only her and Daisy almost made up for the scene with Patrick the day before. It had been way too long since she'd spent this sort of time with her daughter.

"Hey, Mom?" Daisy pushed her pancakes around her plate.

Laura braced for a big question as she sipped her coffee. "Yup."

"I heard Dad yelling about Brett. Are you still seeing him?"

"Um…no." It smarted more to say than it should.

"Because of me?" Daisy looked stricken.

Rounding the island, Laura reached for her and hugged her. "No. Absolutely not. None of this is your fault."

"Okay." Daisy sniffed. "But I shouldn't have said anything to Dad about him."

"It's not your job to keep secrets for me." She squeezed Daisy tighter. "Your father and I will talk about this and sort it out between us." Separating enough so that she could see Daisy's face, she said, "There is nothing for you to worry about."

Daisy didn't look entirely convinced but nodded.

"Now, finish your breakfast, and let's get you to school."

Laura tidied up the kitchen. In the bustle of daily life that she'd lived before her divorce, she would never have thought how much she could miss something like making breakfast for her children.

"Mom." Daisy took her dish to the dishwasher. "Don't get all emotional or anything, but this was nice." She indicated the two of them. "Spending time together."

Laura kept her emotional buried inside and smiled. "I think so too. We should do it again."

"Totally." Daisy picked up her backpack. "Ready?"

On the drive to school, Daisy selected the music station, and they drove in near silence. It was so sweet to have nothing big hanging between them. Laura breathed deep and enjoyed the moment. God knew, with teens, it could change in a millisecond.

They stopped at the traffic light on the corner of the school.

The car chimed that a door was open. At first, she thought Daisy had opened her door, and she turned to look at her.

"Drive, bitch." A gun appeared at Daisy's temple. "Just drive and keep it easy. Don't draw any attention to us."

Daisy was pale as milk, her eyes huge in her face. Her voice wavered. "Mom?"

Laura's brain had slowed, and it took painful seconds for the pieces to slot into a comprehensible whole. There was a gun against Daisy's head, and Cole Watts was sitting in the backseat holding the gun.

"Light's green." He jerked his head forward. "Drive."

Instinct took over, and she pressed the accelerator and drove smoothly forward.

"Keep going," Cole said. "Right past the school. No speeding, nothing heroic, and we'll get along fine."

Her own voice was surprisingly cool as she said, "What do you want?"

"We'll get to that. You keep doing as I say, and there won't be no problem."

Daisy was crying silently, tears streaming down her face.

Deadly calm spread through Laura. For her daughter, she would do whatever this animal wanted. Nothing else mattered except getting that gun away from Daisy's head.

"Daisy." She injected as much calm as she could in her voice. "I want you to take a deep breath."

Daisy glanced at her and hitched in an uneven breath.

"That's it, darling. Everything is going to be all right. I'm not going to let anything happen to you."

Cole smirked at her in the rearview mirror. "That's a good girl. You keep this up, and we're going to all get on real well." He studied Daisy. "She looks like you."

Laura kept her eye on the traffic. She didn't want Cole looking at her daughter. They stopped at another light and a car pulled up beside them.

Lowering the gun, Cole leaned forward. "Don't do anything stupid, Miz Laura. I would hate to shoot a pretty little thing like this, but I'll do it if you give me reason."

"I'm not doing anything stupid." The light changed, and she drove forward. "Where to?"

Cole checked around them. "Take a left into Elm, and then a right into Eighth."

"Left on Elm, right on Eighth." Laura tried to keep his attention on her. "Can you please put the gun away? You're frightening my daughter."

"You scared, sweet thing?" Cole stroked the gun barrel down Daisy's cheek.

Primal rage surged through Laura, and she breathed deep. She tucked it away and drew strength from it. That ugly gun was a fucking abomination on her child, and she would rip the world apart before she let Cole Watts hurt Daisy.

Daisy sobbed. "Y-yes."

"I'm doing exactly what you want," Laura said. "Take that gun away from her. Put it on me if you don't trust me, but I'm not going to risk my child."

Cole chuckled. "You got fire, Miz Laura. No wonder Brett Barrows got his dick in a twist about you."

"You're okay, Daisy." Laura ignored the fucking animal in her backseat and concentrated on her daughter. It was imperative they both stayed calm. "You keep breathing in and out. I'm here. Nothing is going to happen to you."

"Listen to your ma." Cole sat back. "She's got the right idea."

Laura didn't know where the gun was. She took the right on Eighth. "Where to now?"

"Right on Seventeenth." Cole spread his arms over the backseat. "Where's your boy?"

He must have been watching her. A chill ran through her. "With his father."

"Better this way anyhow." Cole sniffed. "Keep driving down here."

Moving slowly, she took Daisy's hand and squeezed it.

With a terrified side eye, Daisy squeezed back, but she was holding it together.

"I presume we're driving somewhere particular?"

"I'll let you know." Cole kept checking the road outside the car. "Where's Barrows?"

"I don't know." She didn't normally leave the house this early on days when she didn't have her children. Razor or Brett, whoever was supposed to be watching her today, would have no idea where she'd gone.

Cole snorted. "You expect me to believe Barrows doesn't keep an eye on a prime piece like you?"

"Where to?"

He kept giving her directions until they were in a part of town she didn't recognize.

Leaning forward between the seats, Cole used the gun to point. "That yellow house on the right. Pull into the drive."

Laura did as she was told. She left the car in gear. If he gave her half a chance she would go through the house if she had to.

"Get your phone." Cole tapped Daisy's shoulder.

Daisy glanced at her, and Laura nodded.

"Because of you, Miz Laura, my kid brother won't answer my calls. But he'll answer her calls." He smirked and nudged Daisy again. "Call Karstyn."

"Why?" Daisy stiffened.

Cole's voice went deadly. "Call him."

"Do it," Laura said.

"Put the call on speaker." Cole tapped Laura with the gun. "And turn the car off. You're not going anywhere until I decide you are."

Laura killed the engine. She refused to give up hope. He'd make a mistake, and she'd get her and Daisy out of there. Razor and Brett would look for her.

Daisy's phone rang.

"Hey, Daze." Karstyn sounded happy. "What's up?"

"K-Karstyn." Daisy started crying.

"Hey, little fucker," Cole said.

There was silence from the phone before Karstyn said, "Cole?"

"So now you remember you got a brother?" Cole laughed.

"What's going on?" Remarkably, Karstyn sounded calm.

"I'm glad you asked, little bro," Cole said. "Because I've got your sweet thing right here with her mother."

"Miz Laura?"

Daisy's hand was shaking so much trying to hold the phone, so Laura took it from her. "I'm here, Karstyn. Daisy and I are okay."

"And we want to keep it that way, don't we, kid?" Cole

leaned closer to the phone. "So, here's what's going to happen."

"I'm listening." Karstyn was moving, the background noises growing quieter. "I'll do whatever you want me to. You don't need to hurt them, Cole."

"Don't be telling me what I need to do." Cole growled. "I've had a fuck ton of your thinking you're smarter than me."

"I don't think that, Cole." Karstyn moved somewhere quiet. "I just want Daisy and Miz Laura to be okay."

"Then here's what you do. I'm gonna text you an address, and you're going to come to that address. Then you and me are getting the fuck out of Dodge. You do like I say, and nobody gets hurt." Cole's voice grew more menacing. "But you tell Barrows or that big fucking friend of his, you go to the police or anyone else, and your little sweet thing is not gonna be that sweet anymore. You hear me?"

Daisy's breath hitched, and Laura took her hand again. "It's going to be fine," she murmured.

"Now, I got friends here to help me watch for anybody what don't need to be around," Cole said. "And I don't want to hurt nobody, but you are going to get back in line, and do it in a way what means I'm not going down for shit. Hear me?"

"I hear you," Karstyn said. "Text me the address."

Cole ended the call and motioned Daisy. "Get out of the car and do it real slow." He put the gun to Laura's head. "You run, and you're going to be fucking motherless, got it?"

Nodding, Daisy fumbled with the door handle before getting it open. "Don't hurt my mother."

The front door opened, and a guy of medium height, built thick and muscular trotted toward them.

"That's Truly." Cole jerked his head at the man. "And he likes them young."

Rage bubbled to the surface. "If he touches her, I'll kill both of you."

"Whoo-ee!" Cole snickered. "You got that redhead fire in

you. He ain't gonna do shit unless I tell him to. So you keep it cool and doing like I want you to, and your gal is going to be fine."

"You could let her go." She would do anything—anything—to get Daisy free. "And keep me. Karstyn's a good kid. He'd come if it was only me."

"I don't need to test that theory." Cole slid out of the car and came to the driver's door. He jerked it open and motioned her out with the gun. "I got you, and I got her, and you will both do what I say until Karstyn gets here." He motioned them toward the house. "You cook?"

"Yes."

"Good because Truly and me is hungry."

"Daisy stays by my side."

Cole jerked her up short by the arm. "You mind your manners, Laura." He dragged out her name. "You don't get to tell me what's what. Get it?"

Laura nodded and forced the words through her tight jaw. "Please can Daisy stay with me while I cook?"

"That's better." Cole shoved her through the front door.

Truly had Daisy by the arm and dragged her into the house.

"Just to show you I'm a good man, she can help you cook," Cole said.

# Chapter Thirty-Six

Brett had never met Laura's ex, but he was damn sure that's who he was looking at climbing out of Nate's official SUV.

"Hey." He climbed down the remaining stairs from his condo and met them in the parking lot. "I was just on my way to work."

"Brett." Nate shook his hand. "This is Patrick Johnston."

"Laura's ex?" He dropped that in because he didn't want them misunderstanding each other. Everybody knew everybody else here, and best they all get with that.

Patrick nodded. "Yes." He glanced at Nate and cleared his throat. "I've got a problem, and Nate suggested I come to you."

You could have blown him away with that one. He looked at Nate. "Is that right?"

"I can't move on this through official channels yet." Nate shrugged. "But there is more than one way to skin a cat."

Brett folded his arms and eyeballed Patrick. He understood why a father wouldn't want a guy like him around his daughter, but that didn't mean he had to like it. "You got a cat needs skinning?"

"It's Daisy. And Laura." Patrick dropped the act and

showed Brett how freaked out he really was. "I got a call from Daisy's school that she never showed up this morning."

They had Brett's attention now. "That ever happen before?"

"No. I mean, she's skipped a class or two, but she's never missed homeroom." Patrick clenched his jaw like he was trying like hell to hold it all together. "She spent the night with Laura last night." He cleared his throat. "We had a bit of a thing, and Laura took her with her."

Brett didn't like the sound of that, but he was still listening.

"Laura was supposed to drop her at school this morning, but she didn't." Patrick shoved a shaking hand through his hair. "I called the rec center and spoke to Daniel. Nobody's seen Laura this morning either."

Brett stared at Nate. "I do not fucking like the sound of this."

"Me neither." Nate jerked his head at Patrick. "Officially, not enough time has passed for me to issue a missing persons, but we all three know there's more at play here."

Long ago, Brett had stopped trying to figure out how Nate knew what Nate knew. Their sheriff had ears to the ground like nobody he knew. He pulled his cell out. "I'll call Razor."

"Will you help me?" Patrick stood in front of him with his heart in his eyes.

Man's little girl had gone missing, and Brett could only guess how that would feel. If Kim or Blythe went missing, he would move mountains, make nice with the devil, sell his soul to get them back. He nodded to Patrick as he dialed Razor. "I'll find them."

"You thinking Cole?" Nate folded his arms and dropped his chin to his chest.

"Razor." Brett nodded at Nate as Razor answered. "I'd be surprised if he wasn't in this."

"Brett? What's up?" Razor's tone got sharp.

Nate sighed. "Yeah. That's what I figured."

Razor must have been listening, because he said. "We got trouble?"

"Cole."

"Fuck! I just got to Laura's condo, but her car isn't here."

"Right." Brett looked at Patrick. "I gotta go, but I will find them. You can bet your life on it." He nodded a goodbye to Nate. "You can wait for me at Laura's place. I'll bring them back there."

He clued Razor in as he climbed into his truck. Laura with that fucker made his blood run cold, and then heat to fury, but she needed him to keep it together and think.

With Razor working his contacts, Brett called Karstyn.

"Brett." Karstyn's voice was tight with stress. "I can't talk right now."

"Then don't talk. Listen." He put the call on Bluetooth and drove for Laura's place. "Daisy and Laura are missing, and I'm ready to bet the farm Cole has something to do with that." He gave Karstyn a beat to respond. "Am I right?"

Karstyn went silent for so long, Brett worried he'd hung up on him, and then he said, "Yes."

"And the reason you're not telling me is because you've been told what will happen if you get anyone else involved."

The answer came faster this time. "Yes."

"He wants you, doesn't he?" You didn't have to be a genius to realize Cole Watts did not like to lose, and he was not going to let his younger brother out from under his thumb.

Brett pulled up outside Laura's, and Razor hopped in. He motioned Razor to silence.

"He tell you where yet?"

Karstyn cleared his throat and then whispered, "Yes."

"You gotta give me those deets, Karstyn." Brett kept his voice firm but gentle. "Then it's on me. Something happens to either of those girls, it's on me. And kid?"

"Yeah?"

"Miz Laura is just about the best thing to happen to me, and I'm going to make damn sure there's no blowback on her, which means I'm also going to make damn sure there's no blowback on Daisy or you."

Karstyn breathed deep, making the phone crackle. "Okay, I'll text you the address."

"Good. You're doing the right thing, Karstyn."

"Yeah." Karstyn didn't sound convinced. "Can I come with you?"

"That's a hard no," he said. "But I want you to wait at Miz Laura's condo."

Brett ended the call.

"You think he'll go to Laura's?"

Brett had to laugh. "Would you?"

"Hell no."

"Which means we gotta move fast. Tell me that address he sent. We gotta make sure we get there before our teen hero decides to ride to the rescue."

Razor read the address out to him and shook his head. "Cole Watts really is a stupid fucker."

"True that, and as much as I'd like to break him wide open, I'm gonna be smarter than that and deliver him tied up with a pretty ribbon to our sheriff."

Chuckling, Razor said, "And there's a thing I never thought I'd hear Brett Barrows say."

"That makes two of us."

LAURA HAD no idea how much time had passed, but she cooked them a full breakfast and kept Daisy as out of sight as she could.

Truly terrified her. Watching TV with Cole, every now and then his cold, gray eyes would linger on Daisy. Cole was pretty much ignoring them, and she really wished Truly would do the same.

She made Daisy sit in the shadows on the far side of the filthy kitchen. Laura didn't know who owned the house, but grime and sticky dirt covered the countertops, and the oven was encrusted with years' of burned food spills. The stove top was no longer white but covered in dark brown baked-on grease. If she'd have been cooking for anyone else, she would have cleaned the kitchen first, but these assholes deserved food poisoning.

A knock on the front door made her jump.

Truly leaped to his feet and pulled a gun from his back.

"Cover them." Cole motioned her and Daisy with his gun. "Anything don't look right, and you shoot the girl."

"I like that one," Truly whined.

"Jesus." Cole strode for the door. "Then shoot the older bitch; I don't give a shit."

Truly smiled, revealing startlingly beautiful white teeth in his pockmarked face. "That would be my pleasure."

Laura put herself between him and Daisy. Desperately, she tried to remember anything from Brett's self-defense class. Brett had said that staying alive was the most important thing. She really wanted to make sure she did that for her and Daisy.

"I can't see nothing." Cole tried to peer through the frosted glass panels on either side of the door. He raised his voice. "Who's there?"

Karstyn said from the other side, "It's me."

"Looks like it's your lucky day." Cole grinned at them. "You're right; the kid is smart."

He yanked open the door.

Razor stood on the other side. "Surprise!"

"Fuck." Cole tried to slam the door shut.

Truly gaped and then pointed the gun at her head.

"Don't you fucking dare." Brett materialized right behind

Truly. He had the gun away from him, and Truly on the floor before Laura could yell at him to watch out.

Daisy screamed and clung to her.

"It's okay." Laura hugged her so tightly it was difficult for either of them to breathe. "It's all right. Brett's here. He's got us."

Brett had Truly on his stomach and his knee in Truly's spine. He tapped the back of his head with Truly's gun. "You made one huge fucking mistake, asshole."

"Jesus Christ!" Cole yelped. "You'll break my arm."

"Aww." Razor jerked Cole's arms harder behind his back. He shoved Cole so hard against the wall his head clunked. "You're just saying that to cheer me up."

Karstyn peered around the door. He looked at her and Daisy, and relief lit his face.

Wriggling free of her, Daisy ran to Karstyn and threw her arms around his neck.

"You okay?" Karstyn whispered against her hair. It might be young love, and the odds against it lasting were huge, but what Karstyn felt for Daisy was real and written all over his face.

Daisy nodded. "I'm okay. My mom said to stay calm, and we did."

Brett was looking at Laura, his focus grim and intense. "Sugar?"

"I'm fine." She nodded. Her voice quivered, and tears threatened. "I really am fine. Scared, but fine. Fine."

"Uh-huh." Brett zip-tied Truly's wrists together. "I know Sheriff Evans is going to want to talk to you."

Razor had his phone out and was talking to Nate. He hung up. "Won't be long."

"I'll kill you." Cole glowered at Karstyn. "Don't matter how long it takes, but I'm going to make you pay for this. And that little bitch with you."

He lunged for Daisy, and Razor yanked him back, but

Laura lost her shit. "You fucking animal." Her mama rage went supersonic, and she went for Cole's eyes with her nails. How dare he look at her child. At the same time, her knee came up and crunched into his groin.

Cole hissed, went red and dropped to his knees.

Laura didn't give a shit. She wanted him dead. He'd threatened her child and made Daisy scared for her life.

She went for him again, but strong arms folded around her and held her back. "You gotta get it under control, sugar. The cops are on their way."

Laura didn't care. She wanted him dead, and she struggled against Brett's hold.

"Listen to me." His deep calm voice came from right beside her ear. "I get that you want to take a piece of him. I get you want payback, but you need to calm down."

She snarled and struggled harder.

"Sugar, please. You're going to hurt yourself, and I can't see that happen. Nate will take care of this now. You've done the hard part. You held it together, and you kept you and your girl safe. You did it, sugar. Now it's time to let the cops make these two go away for a long time."

Sirens wailed in the distance.

Brett kept talking to her and holding her. She clawed at his hands holding her captive and thrashed in his arms. Still he held her, not hurting her, but not allowing her to break free either. It took Daisy's look of horror to calm her down.

Her fury drained as quickly as it had risen, and she burst into tears.

Turning her in his arms, Brett held her. His big hand rubbed slow soothing strokes up and down her spine. He murmured sweet words against her hair, about how brave she'd been and how he had her now, and nothing was going to hurt her.

She stayed like that as Nate and his deputies arrived and took Truly and Cole into custody.

Nate looked apologetic as he said, "I'm going to need you to come down to the station and make a statement."

"She'll be there," Brett said. "Razor called Patrick and told him his girl was safe. We'll head for Laura's straight after we give you your statement."

Exhaustion made her lean into Brett. She was happy to let him take control. He led her out of the house and to his truck.

"Daisy." She turned and looked for her daughter.

"Right behind us," Brett said, and then he tensed.

Laura's heart missed a beat. "What is it?"

"Maybe nothing." Brett's hard gaze tracked an expensive, shiny SUV as it slowed outside the house and then accelerated away.

Razor stared after the car as well. "I've seen that SUV before."

"Yeah." Brett nodded. "I'm going to take my lady to Nate's and then home."

And Laura really liked the sound of all of that, especially the *my lady* part.

# Chapter Thirty-Seven

It took Laura giving her statement and then the drive back to her condo to calm down. As she grew more composed, exhaustion set in. Brett drove her car while Karstyn and Daisy sat in the back. Daisy had her head on Karstyn's shoulder and seemed about ready to drop.

Laura turned in her seat. "Tired?"

Daisy nodded.

"It's a reaction to the stress," Karstyn said and then flushed. "I read about it."

A strange, disconnected calm blanketed Laura and left her numb. The only part of her still alive was the hand Brett held against his thigh.

Behind them in Brett's truck, Razor followed. She saw a batch of chocolate chip cookies in his future, because she owed Razor as well as Brett. "How long have you known Razor?"

"We go way back." Brett glanced at her. "Of course the first time we met, we got into it."

"You fought?"

He nodded. "Can't even remember what about, but we

kept going until both of us almost passed out." He smiled at her. "I still say I won."

"That must have been quite the fight."

Brett chuckled. "I can tell you I felt it for days after."

He turned into her condo complex. Cars were parked outside her condo and a ways down the road. Laura groaned aloud. "It looks like everyone is here."

"Is that grandma's car?" Daisy leaned forward between the seats.

"It looks like it." Mom's car nestled next to Patrick's, which was behind Matt's truck.

Brett parked, and she turned to Daisy. "You okay, sweetheart?"

"I'm okay." Daisy clung to Karstyn's hand. "It feels kinda weird, like all this happened to someone else."

Laura nodded, because she got what Daisy meant. "I know."

Mom, Pippa and Phi stepped out of her condo and approached the car. Matt came behind them with Jasmine in his arms. Blythe and Eric also spilled out of her condo.

"Everyone is here."

Daisy's breath hitched. "Do I have to talk to them?"

"Not if you don't want to." Daisy had been through enough today. Her family would just have to understand.

Patrick stepped out of her condo and hurried to the car. "Daisy!" Concern creased his face. "They said you were okay." He opened the back door and tugged Daisy out and into a hug. "Thank you, Jesus."

"Daddy." Daisy sobbed against his shoulder.

"You're okay now." Patrick rubbed her back. "You're safe and sound."

Karstyn climbed out slowly and stood beside the car watching Daisy and Patrick.

Opening her door, Brett held out his hand. "Come on,

sugar. There are a whole heap of people who want to see for themselves you're okay."

"Thank you." She stepped out of the car and wrapped her arms around his waist. Some part of her had known Brett would come for her, that she could count on Brett getting her out.

He wrapped his arms around her. "You don't need to thank me. I couldn't have not come if I tried."

For what seemed like the first time since Cole had climbed into her car, Laura drew a clear breath. Being in Brett's arms filled her with an inherent sense of right that she got nowhere else. For her kids' sake, she'd let him go and tucked the hurt deep, but with him holding her now, she was exactly where she needed to be.

"Umm…" Patrick spoke from behind her. "Thank you."

"You're welcome." Brett's deep voice rumbled through her. "No disrespect, but I didn't do it for you."

Patrick cleared his throat. "Nevertheless, thank you."

Turning in Brett's arms, Laura looked at her ex. He dropped her gaze and shifted away. "I'm glad you're okay, Laura."

"Me too." She kept an arm around Brett's waist. With him close, it felt like nothing could hurt her. "I think Daisy wants to go inside."

Patrick nodded. "I'll take her."

"Laura!" Her mother rushed toward her and pulled her into a tight hug. "Thank God."

As if on a secret signal, the rest of her family descended on her. She was hugged and kissed and cried over and she lost track of Brett in the process.

She finally made her way into her condo, which was bursting at the seams with all those people.

Patrick came out of the bathroom and closed the door. "Daisy said she wanted to shower."

Laura nodded, because she felt grubby too, like Cole and

Truly had left their mark on her skin and in her hair. Neither she nor Daisy had been touched, and the relief of that made her shudder, but they both still felt fouled. "I'll take one after her. I think she might want to stay here for the night."

"Okay." Patrick nodded. "I called Margot and told her you're safe."

"And Sam?" Laura was glad he hadn't been in the car with them.

Patrick shrugged. "He's in school, and he doesn't know anything. It's up to you whether you tell him or not."

Checking the time, Laura was amazed to see it was only a little after eleven in the morning. It seemed so much later.

"Miz Laura?" Karstyn stood in front of her, his hands shoved in his pockets. "I'm sorry, Miz Laura, about everything."

"Oh, Karstyn." It hadn't occurred to her he would blame himself, but he stood there looking as guilty as sin. "You have nothing to apologize for. None of this is your fault."

"Yes, but—"

Brett cupped Karstyn's nape. "Hey, kid. This is all on Cole, not you. You manned up and did the right thing, and because of you, we found them before anything worse could happen."

Swallowing, Karstyn dropped his head. "She got hurt because Cole wanted me."

"It's true." Patrick pushed himself into their conversation. "If Daisy hadn't been seeing Karstyn, none of this would have happened to her." He glanced at Laura. "I told you no good would come of you encouraging that relationship."

Laura's level of rage almost matched what she'd felt with Cole, but she managed to keep an inside voice. "Karstyn told Brett where to find us."

Conversation around them stopped, and all eyes locked on her and Patrick.

Pippa glanced at Matt and shook her head.

"Still, none of this would have happened if Daisy had chosen to spend time with a boy from our kind of people." Patrick folded his arms and sunk his chin to his chest—his tell for when he was going to dig his heels in about something.

Brett stilled. His intense silence yelled louder than anything.

Beside him, Razor looked at Patrick as if he wanted to shoot and wall-mount him.

He'd have to pick a number. Karstyn was no more responsible for his brother's behavior than Brett was for his father's. Neither could Karstyn help what family he came from. Like Blythe, Will, Kim and Brett, in fact all the Barrows kids, they'd been dealt a bum hand, and each of them had decided how to play that hand. Laura was proud she managed a calm tone as she said, "You're way out of line, Patrick."

"Really?" Patrick sneered, glanced at Brett and dropped his expression and his voice. "Then how do you account for us standing here after my daughter had to be recovered from a kidnapping?"

"Patrick." Matt put his arm around Pippa. From the look on Pippa's face, more as a protection for Patrick than comfort for Pippa. "You've had a shock, and we understand that's influencing you're thinking right now."

"Of course I've had a shock, but my thinking isn't muddled." Patrick stuck his chin out mulishly.

"Regardless." Matt leveled a hard stare at him. "Nobody wants to hear what's coming out of your mouth."

Pippa said what Laura was thinking. "The very kid you're vilifying is the one who helped Brett find Daisy. And my sister has had enough to contend with this morning without you trying to make this her fault."

"Indeed." Phi's jowls quivered, and she managed to load the word with double the syllables. "You're being judgmental, Patrick, and I'm not fond of judgmental people." She thrust her bosom out and raised one hand. "I saw that in you on your wedding day. I didn't like it then either."

Laura could barely remember her wedding day anymore. It had passed in a frenzy of tuber roses, tulle and wanting everything to be perfect. Strange, but she'd only recently realized that Patrick had been largely inconsequential on that day. It seemed to her that the groom should take up more space in a bride's mind than the placement of the centerpieces or the precise arrangement of the flowers.

Brett stood backlit by the window. Limned by weak sunlight, he looked taller and broader than ever, but even had he not had his physical size, he already took up a much larger space in her awareness than Patrick ever had.

After today, would they go back to living separate lives? She loved her children, and would do anything for them, but keeping Brett out of her life was more about making Patrick happy than her children.

With his face in shadow, she couldn't read Brett's expression.

"Well, I'm sorry," Patrick said in a tone that made a lie of that statement. "But Laura should have thought about her responsibility to Daisy when she encouraged this harmful relationship."

Brett put his hand on Karstyn's shoulder. Pale, but head raised and looking remorseful as hell, Karstyn shifted closer to Brett.

From his other side, Razor bracketed him as if he and Brett were running interference on Karstyn's behalf, but their physical presence couldn't stop the hurtful impact of Patrick's words.

Laura was torn between wanting to comfort Karstyn and a burning need to set Patrick straight.

"How dare you?" Mom stepped up to Patrick. "How dare you use what happened to Daisy and Laura to grind your own ax?"

"This had nothing to do with me." Patrick held his hands out. "Emily, surely you can understand where I'm coming from?"

"You're probably the only one who does get where you're coming from," Matt said.

"Why the hell would you think I'd understand?" Mom gaped at him. "Laura is my daughter. You are merely someone she happened to share her life with for a brief time."

Brett chuckled.

Laura gaped at her mother. Even Pippa stared, while Phi stood there grinning. "Give 'em hell, peanut."

"We quite possibly both owe our daughters' lives to men whom you are happy to condemn, along with that wonderful young man." Emily gestured to Karstyn, and her expression softened as she spoke to him. "Karstyn, you are a wonderful young man, and don't let any bigoted shit tell you otherwise."

Karstyn blinked at her.

Mom rounded back on Patrick. "And while we're on the subject of men, who you judged unsuitable, let me make myself clear. You have no right to tell Laura who she may or may not have in her life. I owe my daughter's and my granddaughter's wellbeing, possibly even their lives, to Razor and Brett."

Brett held up a hand. "Mrs. Turner, if you—"

"I am not addressing you, Brett Barrows." Mom swung an arctic gaze his way. "Wait your turn."

He dropped his hand. "Yes, ma'am."

"She gets her fire from me," Phi said to Brett with a smirk.

Brett shook his head. "Then you gave it to both your granddaughters as well."

"Do you mind?" Mom glared at Phi before she swung her glare back on Patrick. "I have held my tongue for the sake of my grandchildren, but I'm done with this bullshit."

The bathroom door opened, and Daisy stepped out. She glanced around the room and tensed. "What's going on?"

Mom motioned to Pippa. "Pippa, if you would take the young people for a short walk? They don't need to hear this."

"Of course." Pippa rounded up Daisy and Karstyn and herded them out of the condo.

"Do we have to go?" Daisy trailed her reluctantly. "It's getting good."

"I'll get the details from Matt later." Pippa shut the condo door behind them.

"I think I should go too." Razor was out the door before anyone could think to stop him.

"Laura made some mistakes." Mom squared up to Patrick again. "God knows she did, but she has also paid for them over and over again. The woman she is today is partly because of those mistakes, and I couldn't be prouder of her."

Patrick hissed in a sharp breath and drew back. "Let's not discuss that."

"No, let's discuss it." Mom jabbed him in the chest. "And while we're talking about it, let's call it like it is. You're not angry with Karstyn or Brett or even Laura."

Patrick looked furious. "I couldn't disagree more."

"You're angry with yourself." Mom swept right along as if he hadn't spoken. "You're angry with yourself because deep down you have always wondered if the reason she did what she did was because you had failed her in some way."

Patrick flinched and paled.

"Mom." Laura needed to step in before her mother drew blood. "Patrick is not the guilty party here."

"And neither are you." Mom nodded.

Phi clapped and grinned. "Well said, darling, well said."

"You did a terrible thing, Laura, and I'm not excusing that." Mom took Laura's face between her palms. "But you don't need to keep paying and paying for it. It's about time Patrick stopped punishing you."

"I'm not—"

"And stopped trying to control your life." She ran right

over Patrick's protests. "Who my daughter chooses to have in her life is none of your business. And if you choose to make it so—" Mom got nose to nose with him "—I will fight you, and my mother will fight you. If you even think of trying to take her children away from her, you will find yourself knee deep in lawyers for the rest of your natural life."

"It's true." Phi patted her bouffant hair. "I do know a lot of lawyers. They make terrible lovers, but they have other uses."

"You're being a bully, Patrick." Mom drew all attention back to her. "And it stops today."

Patrick opened and shut his mouth, turned on his heel and strode out of the condo.

"Mom." Laura didn't know whether to laugh or to cry. "You might have just made everything worse."

Emily snorted. "You can't go on like this, Laura, and if you won't stand up for yourself, then I'll have to do it for you."

"And I stand right beside her." Phi matched her words with the physical action and posed her chin at a heroic angle. "I am sure Pippa stands with us."

"I know for a fact she does," Matt said.

"And now." Mom clapped her hands. "Laura and Daisy have had more than enough to contend with today. It's time for Phi's girls to circle the wagons."

Matt chuckled and glanced at Brett. "That means we're getting kicked out."

"Right." Brett nodded and moved for the door.

"Brett Barrows?" Mom turned and watched him go.

Brett turned and waited.

"You need to man up as well," Mom said. "Anything worth having is worth fighting for, and both of my daughters are worth more than gold."

# Chapter Thirty-Eight

Brett went straight to Cranks and parked it on a stool in front of the bar. He wasn't surprised when Razor joined him within ten minutes.

Looking around, Razor sniffed. "This shithole again?"

"Hey!" Cruze yelled from the far end of the bar. "Nobody's forcing your loser ass to drink here. You know that, right?"

"Don't get your panties in a wad," Razor yelled back. "You don't even drink here when you're not working."

Razor had a point, and Cruze simmered down on a mutter.

"So." Razor smoothed the condensation on his beer bottle with his thumb. "Good result day."

Brett nodded. "Yeah."

A woman with sprayed on jeans and an MC cut sashayed over to the jukebox and put a song on Brett didn't recognize. Some guy started singing about what he had to do to get some chick. One of those boy bands that wrote those catchy tunes that grafted themselves into your brain. He motioned the speakers with his beer. "Who is this?"

"Jonas Brothers." Razor shrugged.

"They actually brothers?"

"So they say."

"Huh."

Women had always equaled sex to Brett. He'd never let a woman get beneath his skin. Until now.

"We really not gonna talk about it?" Razor turned on his stool and propped his head on his hand.

Shrugging, Brett sipped his beer. "Cole is getting what's coming to him, and everyone is home safe and sound."

"That's not what I mean."

"I know." They'd been friends for too long, and gone through too much shit together, for either of them not to know what the other was thinking. Still, a guy could hope.

The woman who'd put the song on slunk onto the dance floor arms raised and swaying her hips. She caught him and Razor watching and crooked a finger.

Brett shook his head. She was a nice-looking woman, but he didn't want her.

"Your woman okay now? After what happened to her."

"She's not—"

"Yeah, Brett, she's your woman." Razor rapped the bar with his fist. "She's your woman because you light up when she's around, and she does the same when you're near. She's your woman because, even now, you're sitting here all sad sack because you want her, and you've got some half-assed notion that you're not good enough for her."

Brett didn't like feeling stupid, and Razor needed to watch himself. "Shut your fucking mouth."

"You gonna make me?" Razor smirked.

They both knew he wasn't going to do anything about it, so Brett sipped his beer and let it drop. Razor was a good friend and deserved better than him getting pissy. "Her ex has an issue with me being near their kids."

"Her ex is a bit of dick," Razor said. "And her mama opened a can of whup-ass on him."

Not really the point. "If her ex decides to make an issue of this, then it makes life difficult for her. I'm never going to stand between Laura and her children."

Razor shrugged. "I don't think she'd let you. The woman I've met has her head screwed on right and knows how to prioritize her kids. Reading between the lines here, I think you both have the same problem."

"And what's that?" Brett braced for the wisdom of Razor.

Turning to look at him, Razor said, "Neither of you believe you deserve to be happy."

The statement clanged to the floor like an anvil between them, and as much as Brett would have liked to tell Razor he was talking shit, he couldn't. Razor's assessment of the situation was bang on the money.

Razor glanced behind him and stiffened. "Motherfucker," he whispered.

"What is it?" Brett turned in the direction of Razor's gaze.

Looking like his crap didn't stink, Pat was taking a seat at a table of men about his age.

Brett vaguely recognized the men from the days when he used to run cons with Pat.

"Take it easy." Razor gave him a hard stare. "Don't do anything you'll regret."

Separating Pat's head from his neck wouldn't be something he'd regret at all. The world should throw whoever did that a parade.

A tall, well-built man walked into Cranks and strolled over to the bar. He looked familiar, and Brett tried to place him.

His pressed chinos and crisp button down would have made him stand out in that shithole, but it was the undeniable sheen of badassery, don't-fuck-with-me that every hard ass in there recognized instantly.

It took Brett a moment, and then, he recognized the guy from the shiny black SUV he'd seen more than once. Was this fucker following him?

First things first, though. He put his beer on the bar. "Call Nate."

"That's a Texas-size ten-four, good buddy." Razor whipped his phone out so quickly, if he hadn't been about to confront Pat, Brett might have laughed. Also, Razor must have been binge watching that Canadian show he dug so much again.

Seeing him coming, Pat lounged in his chair and draped his arm over the back of another, full of bravado now that he was surrounded by his posse. "Son." He jerked his chin. "Heard you been looking for me."

"And now I've found you." Brett yanked out a chair and parked it. "Thought I might explain a few things to you."

Pat sneered. "You think you got the right to explain anything to anyone, boy?"

"You put her in the hospital again." Brett breathed deep and refused to be baited. "For the last time."

"This ain't none of my business." The crony sitting beside Brett stood up and left.

The other two did as well, one of them muttering about family shit.

Jabbing his forefinger into the table, Pat sat forward. "This ain't none of your business neither. What happens between a man and his lawful wife is nothing to do with nobody but them."

"She's also pregnant again." Rage swept through him as he told Pat the news. Carly had no business having another baby, and especially not given her age. "And even you aren't stupid enough to think this pregnancy is going to be easy."

Pat shifted in his chair and stared over Brett's shoulder. "I ain't gonna discuss this with you, boy."

"Good, because I got a shit ton to say." Brett leaned forward. "I haven't got a clue why, but she loves you, and she's always going to take you back. But that all ends. Today."

"You—"

"Shut the fuck up, Pat. Before you make it worth my while to screw up my parole and make you hurt."

"You couldn't take me." Pat swallowed and sweat beaded his forehead.

"We both know I can," Brett said. "But you're not worth screwing up my life and my future over. So, here's how this is gonna go."

"I don't need to listen to this." Scraping his chair, Pat stood.

"Sit." Brett stayed where he was.

Pat hesitated, opened his mouth, shut it, and then sat. "I don't know why you got beef with me."

"Because you took your hand to a woman, a woman who happens to be my mother, and you've been doing that for as long as I've been alive." He leaned forward to make sure Pat got this good. "And it stops now, or next time, I'm going to make sure she presses charges. You and I both know if you go down again, you're never seeing daylight again as a free man."

Grinning, Pat sat back and folded his arms. "She'll never do it."

"She will, because if I have to sit with her through counseling, or whatever the hell else it is she needs to finally get through to her that she's worth more, I'm gonna do it." Brett shared Pat's doubt, but Pat didn't need to know that. "And this time, she knows she's got all us kids behind her. She's not alone anymore, and she doesn't need you."

"That woman will always need me." Pat smirked. "Because I got what she needs right here." He cupped his crotch.

Brett nearly lost it then, but Razor standing behind Pat gave him the ability to claw back his anger. "This baby might need special care." Pat was too good at throwing out distractions. You needed to keep it straight with him. "And that means money. You're getting a job."

"No, I'm not." Pat scoffed. "I'm not some stupid mark, working for the man all my life."

"You are now." Brett was far from done. "You're going to get a job and bring in a regular paycheck. Then you're going to give half of that to Blake, and he's going to make sure Carly and the baby are well taken care of."

Pat looked at him as if he'd lost his mind.

"I'm allowing you one supervised visit to Carly, and that's gonna be it for the rest of your miserable life." He was breaking Carly's heart, but it was her heart or her life, and he was done playing.

Pat laughed. "I don't have to listen to this." He stood.

Razor pushed him right back down again and kept his hand on Pat's shoulder. "Brett isn't finished yet."

"You're going to do all of this from another part of the country," Brett said. "And that visit I'm allowing you is to cut Carly loose."

"You can't make any of this stick." Pat glanced at Razor. "You said yourself you don't want to fuck up your parole. You lay a hand on me, and it's back to jail for you, sonny boy."

"Oh, I'm not going to lay a hand on you." Brett had saved the best for last. "But I have markers going back twenty years, and I'll call every one of them in."

The chair between him and Pat was pulled back, and the SUV guy took a load off.

"Excuse me?" Brett had to blink at the nerve of the guy.

"Simon." He held out his hand. "Simon Walker, and I've got a proposition for you, but let's take out the trash first."

Brett glanced at Razor, who shrugged.

Simon locked his dark eyes on Pat, and they went colder than any eyes Brett had ever seen. It was like looking into the darkest part of the human soul, and Brett thanked God they were not directed at him.

"You don't know me, Pat." Simon kept his voice low and

calm. "But I know you, and I know plenty of pieces of shit like you."

"Hey—"

"And I really don't like your brand of fuckery, Pat. It disturbs me, and that means I don't sleep well at night." He circled his face with his hand. "And this kind of pretty needs a lot of sleep."

Pat gaped at him.

Razor stared.

"You're wondering who I am." Simon smiled, but combined with those dead eyes, it made Brett's flesh crawl.

Pat's gaze darted around the room. The thing with living your life eyebrow deep in the dregs of humanity, you got real good at recognizing a scary badass motherfucker when you saw one.

"In my former employment, I worked for the government," Simon said. "I tell people it was the FBI, because we all know what would have to happen if I told them what I really did." He leaned forward and lowered his voice.

Brett leaned in with him, and so did Razor.

"Now I freelance, and I take care of what needs to be taken care of. I try to keep it within the law, but that's not always possible." He smiled that death grin again. "Unlike you, Pat, I know how to operate outside the law and get away with it." He paused and rested his intertwined hands on the table. "Why am I telling you all this?"

Pat glanced at Brett. "You know this asshole?"

"Not yet." But Brett got the sense that was going to change. He was also curious as all hell as to where it was going. The last five minutes had gotten surreal.

"I'm telling you this because I want you to understand that you can't run fast or far enough from me, Paddy-boy. I will always know what you're doing, and how and when you're doing it. I will know each paycheck you split with your wife, and I will also know each cent you try to hold back." He winked. "We both know you're going to give it a try, and we also both know I'm going to bring fury and hellfire down on your head when you do."

It sounded like Simon really did get Pat's fuckery.

"You're going to do exactly what Brett told you to do." Simon leaned back. "And I'm going to watch and make sure you do. When you fuck up, I'm going to be the one coming after you, and you'll never see me coming."

Pat squinted at him. "This is bullshit."

"Is it?" Simon raised an eyebrow. "There really is only one way to find out for sure."

"I don't have to listen to this." Pat rose jerkily from his chair. "You assholes can't tell me what to do."

"Looks like they just did," Razor said. "And not that it will make any difference, but I would take them seriously."

Pat opened his mouth, looked at Simon and then Brett, snapped his jaw shut and stormed out.

"Think it'll work?" Razor watched him go.

"It'll work," Simon said. "He'll toe the line for a week or so, then start thinking he's safe, and then I'll have to persuade him otherwise."

Brett didn't know what to make of this guy. "What will you do?"

"If you don't know, then it's not a parole violation." Simon smiled, and this time it was genuine. "Now you must be wondering who I am, and what the hell I think I'm doing."

"Yup."

"Simon Walker." He held his hand out again. "Personal friend of Philomene St. Amor." He winced. "Actually, my father is more her personal friend, but I do not want to ask her about that again." He shuddered. "And I have a proposition for you."

"What kind of proposition?" Brett had heard all about how Simon liked to operate above the law.

"I've been following you for a few weeks now," Simon said.

"I'm in the market for a business partner, and Nate suggested you. I did a bit of work with Nate a while back, and this funny little town grew on me. I've been looking for a way to make coming back work." He gestured Razor to sit. "I trust Nate, but I still wanted to see who I was thinking of getting into bed with before I made my approach." He glanced up at still-standing Razor. "You may as well join us because this involves you too."

Razor took a seat, glanced at Brett and shrugged.

Simon clasped his hands on the table in front of him and leaned forward. "The three of us have some complimentary skills, and I think we could do very well together."

"Why did you intervene with Pat?" Brett needed that explained before they went any further.

"I watched to see if you would lose your shit with him. When you didn't, I knew you were the sort of man I wanted to do business with." He shrugged. "And as a gesture of good faith, I helped you out with your problem."

Brett went with his gut, put his hands on the table and leaned forward. "I'm listening. Give me your angle."

# Chapter Thirty-Nine

Brett didn't know how things would go, but he had to try, for Laura. He waited outside a beautiful home in a well-heeled neighborhood for Patrick to get home from work. A BMW turned the corner and eased down the street.

Patrick caught sight of him before he pulled into his driveway, and their eyes met through the windshield.

Outside his truck, Brett leaned against the door and waited. He didn't want to walk on to Patrick's property without an invitation and get the man all bent out of shape.

Dressed in a shirt and tie with his jacket over his arm, Patrick stood beside his car. "Brett."

"Patrick." Brett returned the nod. "I thought we should talk."

Patrick dropped his head and then raised it. "You're probably right. Want to come in?"

"Sure." Green velvet, crisply mowed grass bordered the paved driveway. It must be nice to grow up in a nice house, live in a neighborhood where you didn't have to lock your neighbors out.

Opening the front door, Patrick motioned him into the

house. "Margot," Patrick called. "I'm home, and I have company."

"Oh? How nice." Of average height with shiny brown hair and a sweet face, the owner of the voice walked on gleaming wooden floors toward them. Her smile of welcome was unrestrained as she held out her hand. "Hello, I'm Margot, Patrick's fiancée. And you must be Brett."

"Must I?" Brett shook her soft, finely boned hand.

She laughed and looked prettier when she did. "Oh, yes. You won't remember me, but I went to school with Blythe. We knew all about her big, bad brothers, and you were the biggest and baddest of the lot."

"Not anymore." Her honesty was refreshing, and Brett saw what attracted Patrick. Margot was sweet all the way through, and she didn't play games or bullshit. This was the kind of woman who wouldn't have many nasty surprises for you to trip over.

Margot looked at him with her head tilted. "So I believe." Her smile widened. "Can I offer you a drink? Beer? Glass of wine? Coffee?"

"A beer would be good." Patrick might not give him the chance to drink it, but Margot looked like she'd be disappointed if he didn't take something.

She beamed at him and then turned to Patrick. "Sweetheart?"

"Beer sounds great." Patrick nodded to her, and she bustled away.

Brett would lay dollars to donuts she came back with one of those fancy, microbrew IPAs.

"Let's talk in my study." Patrick led the way in the opposite direction Margot had gone.

If Brett had aspirations to own a study, it would look like Patrick's. Large wooden desk, comfy leather chair behind the desk, and big ass leather sofa facing a wall-mounted TV that looked big enough to show you the quarterback's nose hairs as he fired one downfield on game day.

Patrick gestured the sofa. "Have a seat?"

Easing into the leather sofa, Brett let Patrick take his power-play seat behind his desk. Fair enough. He'd come into the man's house, and Patrick had to have some idea why he was there. Brett didn't waste either of their time with small talk. "I came to talk to you face to face. I'm hoping you'll hear me out, ask anything you want to know, and I can walk away from here with us on the same page."

"This is about Laura." Patrick folded his arms. The chair creaked beneath him as he leaned back.

"Yeah." Brett leaned forward, too antsy to sink into the deep sofa. "First, I'm gonna level with you. The way I feel about Laura sees me in her life for as long as she'll have me."

Patrick winced. "I thought things weren't that serious."

"Right now, they're nonexistent," he said and then got over the first hurdle. "But I want to change that. I want to be in Laura's life, and I'm fairly sure she'd be down with that."

"I see." Patrick cleared his throat.

A soft knock sounded, and Margot pushed into the room with a tray carrying two IPA bottles, two mugs and a couple small bowls she put on the table. "Just a few nibbles." She smiled at him and gestured to the bowl of olives and one of nuts. "To soak up the beer."

"Thank you." Margot was a good woman, too sweet for him, but she and Patrick fit well.

Patrick waited for her to leave before he spoke again. "She told you about my reservations."

"Reservations?" Brett had to laugh at that one. "Man, the way I heard it you threatened to take her children away if she kept on seeing me." He intended to clear the air, not blow more smoke. "Way I see it, you stepped over a line there, but I've got two younger sisters, one of them not even in elementary school, and I would do anything to keep them safe."

"I only knew you by reputation." Patrick paled and sipped his beer. "You have an…er...colorful past."

There was no good dancing around it. "I'm an ex-con, Patrick. We both know that. I've been in and out of jail a good slice of my adult life. And I've never been falsely accused." His beer was sweating in his hands, so he put it on the coaster Margot had put next to her nibbles. "Short of rape and murder, there's not much I haven't done, and the way I was heading the last time I went down, God alone knew where I'd have ended up."

Patrick fiddled with the label on his bottle.

"My cell mate on my last stint was a lifer called Eli. You know they always say there's someone bigger and tougher than you? Well, he was for me. Eli made it clear from day one that he was there to serve his time, and anything I did to make that suck would not go over well." Brett had to smile at the memory. Him all bristling tough guy, so sure he couldn't meet a man he didn't scare the crap out of, fronting in that cell like he owned it. Eli had been lying on his bunk, ankles crossed, reading an Eckart Tolle book. The first thing Eli had said to him was, "Settle your stupid ass down, motherfucker. Nobody in here gives enough of a shit to fight you."

Not surprisingly, he'd tried to test that statement anyway. Eli had pretty much ignored him until Brett got the anger out his system.

"He was a wise man, who'd learned his lesson the hard way," Brett said to Patrick. "I owe him my life, because without him, I don't think I would have turned it around."

Patrick leaned forward. "What happened?"

"He got me thinking about some stuff, made me come along to some group sessions with guys like us. He helped me understand why I did what I did, and how to build the foundation to stop myself from keeping on doing those things." Brett had been a long way down a road to hell when Eli had intervened. It had taken months and months of patience and perseverance to break him down, and then even longer to build him back up again. Only for Laura would he lay himself bare for another person. "What you heard about me—" He met Patrick's gaze square as he owned his shit. "I'll go out on a limb and say it's all true."

Patrick frowned. "I heard you beat up your sister."

"You heard right." Brett hated that memory worst of all, but he'd done that shit, and he'd paid for doing it, but Blythe had paid too. That last part he hated most of all. "I was getting into drugs with some scary people, and I wanted Will —you might know him as Wheeler—to run product and money for me. Underage kids don't get the same sentences as adults if they're caught." He had thought he'd had it all worked out. "And they can slide under the radar better."

"How old was he?"

Brett couldn't remember. "Probably around ten. I didn't pay that much attention. But Blythe, she was paying attention, and she sure as sh—hell didn't intend me to use Will like that. She got in my face about him, and I decided to teach her a lesson." Sweat slid down his sides. "I was hyped up and in over my head, I'd been drinking all day as well, and the lesson got out of hand. I broke her arm in two places."

"Shit." Patrick flinched. "Laura knows this?"

"I told her." He nodded. "Not in as much detail, but if she asks, I will."

Patrick arranged his bottle on his blotter. "I'm not sure why you're telling me this."

"I'm telling you this so there are no secrets between us, and you know I don't lie, and I don't hide my past." Brett sipped his beer to help with his dry mouth. "But that's my past. I'm not going back there, and I'm no danger to Laura, or your daughter. I've looked into the face of my own private hell and walked away from it a better man. I've hurt a woman I love, and I know exactly what that feels like. She's forgiven me, and I'm most of the way to forgiving myself, but I'll never get there one hundred percent. Because when I look at my sister, a girl I near enough raised, I can never forget what I did to her, and I will never forget the fear and pain in her eyes when she looked at me."

Dropping his head, Patrick picked at the edge of his blotter. "You regret what you did."

"More than you will ever know." Strangely, the person who came near enough to understanding the depth of his regret was Blythe. With that beautiful, big heart of hers, she understood him. "I will also never do anything like that again. I can't prove that to you here and now, but I can make you that promise."

Patrick nodded, but Brett wasn't done yet.

"We have regret like that in common, Laura and me." Brett wanted to pace, but he didn't want to come across intimidating. A guy his size did that without having to try. "She lives with the regret of what she did to you and her children. She thinks that means she isn't entitled to be happy."

"That's not true." Patrick cleared his throat. "I don't want her thinking that."

"And she loves her children and came closer than anyone would like to losing them before. When you said she couldn't see me, there was no way she was taking a chance on losing them again." He took a careful breath before he let his soul through again. "And as the man who loves her, I would never do anything to hurt her more than she's already been hurt. Her kids are her world, so that makes them my world too."

Patrick's eyes flashed a warning. "You're not their father."

"No, I'm not. You are." Patrick had nothing to worry about there. "But I am the man who makes their mother happy, and I want to keep making her happy."

"What do you want from me?" Patrick spread his hands on his blotter.

"He wants you to say it's okay for him to be in Laura's life," Margot said from the door.

Brett had no idea how much she'd heard because he hadn't been aware of the door opening.

From the way he started, neither had Patrick. "Margot, you know why I can't do that."

"No, I don't." She sat on the edge of the sofa near Brett. "I know why you think you can't, but I also heard what Brett said, and I believe him. Also, he was the man who rescued Daisy and Laura. I can't think of many people they would be safer with." She took a deep breath and gave Brett a wistful smile. "But, sweetheart, this isn't really about Daisy though, is it?"

"Of course it is." Patrick bristled.

"No." Margot shook her head. "This is about your lingering anger with Laura."

Patrick jolted. "I'm not angry—"

"Yes, you are. You're angrier than even you know. Deep down, you don't think she deserves to be happy after what she did to you."

Brett would never have guessed the heft of the backbone on Margot, but the woman was not wrong either. "Take it from someone who knows," he said to Patrick. "Letting go is as freeing for you as it is for the other person."

"He's right." Margot shrugged. "We all deserve to be free of the past."

# Chapter Forty

Four days since Mom had told Brett to man up, and he'd walked out of her condo. Okay, that was doing the cause and correlation thing, but it still messed with her mind. Mom telling Brett to man up hadn't caused him to walk out, but he had walked out just after Mom had kicked him out so they could do girl time, Phi-style, which no sane man wanted to witness. There was her correlation.

Propping her chin on her hand, she stared out her office window at nothing in particular. Two squirrels played tag up the trunk of the aspen shading the front lawn of the rec center. With all that had happened, she felt wrong footed and not sure how to play what happened next with Brett. She knew she wanted Brett in her life, but she needed to know if he felt the same.

He could have called. At this stage she'd settle for a text telling her he was still breathing. And, maybe saying whether he was or was not going to man up and be with her. She'd left messages for him, texted to the verge of stalking, but so far…silence.

Maybe he had been in an accident or gone out of town for something. Perhaps he was even tracking down Pat somewhere and couldn't call. But she would have heard if he was hurt, and phones worked in all parts of the country.

Worst-case scenario was looking all too probable. Brett was done with her and her gnarled up reality of bitter exes and children.

Patrick had come around to her condo last night and apologized for his stance on Brett. He'd reluctantly conceded that Brett had paid for his crimes and that as her ex, Patrick had no say in her love life.

Great! Yay her! Except, at this precise moment, it appeared as if she didn't have a love life and wasn't about to get one anytime soon.

With his chest thumping and testosterone rumbling, Brett had snuck past her defenses and made himself at home.

He had liked her. A lot. She knew he liked her, and he'd certainly said so more than once. It made no sense, and it was beginning to piss her off that he'd made like smoke. She was beginning to think she might need to be the brave one.

"Hey." Daniel rapped on her office door and dragged her back to the present. "Got a minute?"

"Sure." Laura turned her chair to face him. It looked like she had nothing but time.

"I had some good news about Karstyn this morning," Daniel said.

Right about now, she could use some good news. "Tell me."

"He's got a scholarship to Blessed Sacrament," Daniel said. Daisy and Sam's school. "His teachers are happy to catch him up on any gaps, and they're putting him up for a college scholarship when he's ready for it. They're even talking national scholarship."

"That's great." Karstyn was the sort of kid who deserved a college education. "Daisy will be delighted."

Daniel laughed.

He really was such a good-looking guy. Why couldn't her heart have settled on him instead?

"What?" Daniel studied her. "You're looking at me funny."

Laura shrugged and tried to keep it light, but her face heated. "Just thinking."

"About?" Daniel tilted his head.

Waving a dismissive hand, Laura went back to the more important subject. "What about his foster family? Are they going to be able to swing that?"

"Absolutely." Daniel had the deep satisfaction of a good result written all over his face. In their work, when so many results were not good, they had to take the victories where they could get them. "His foster parents are so proud of him, and he has a little foster brother with him there. Karstyn wants to stay, and they're committed to doing everything they can to make sure he gets his ass to college."

"That really is great." Life hadn't done Karstyn any favors so far, but it looked like that was turning around.

Daniel chuckled and raised his eyebrows. "You say that, but you look bummed."

"No, I'm thrilled for him. He's a special kid, and I think the world of him. You know that." Her work with kids had pulled her through her divorce, and it would pull her through now.

Daniel folded his arms. "Hey, I saw a friend of yours the other day."

"Really?" Patrick had gotten most of their former friends in the divorce. "Who?"

"Brett Barrows." Daniel seemed to linger on the name longer than required. Even if he'd said it normally, that name would always get her pulse pounding.

Still, Laura went for cool and serene. "Really? How is he?"

"He's good." Daniel stretched his legs out. "Great even."

"Great!"

"Yeah, I thought so." Daniel smirked.

Good for Brett with his being great and all. She wasn't a petty person, and he'd not dumped her or anything. In fact, he'd done a selfless and honorable thing in stepping aside for her children.

He still had no business being great when she wasn't. And she apparently wasn't the bigger person she'd just been patting herself on the back for being.

"When I say I saw him the other day, I wasn't quite telling the truth." Daniel looked so smug she was revising her take on him being a thoroughly nice guy. "In fact, I saw him today."

So Brett was not lying at the bottom of an abandoned mine shaft without his phone. She kept it noncommittal. "Hmm?"

"About two minutes before I came here." Daniel stood. "Heading this way."

"What?" Laura shot to her feet.

Daniel grinned. "Yeah, that's what I thought."

"Hi, Brett Barrows." Uri called from the hallway outside her office.

Laura's heart pounded.

"Hey, Uri." Brett's deep voice tiptoed up her spine and made her shiver. "You good today?"

"Yes." Uri giggled. "Why are you carrying flowers?"

Brett had flowers, and suddenly she had trouble breathing.

Daniel stood there wearing his insufferable smirk and inviting her to smack him. Otherwise, she might have done the unthinkable and hidden under her desk.

She was nervous as hell, and now that he was finally there, she didn't want to see him anymore. What if he hadn't come to say what she wanted him to? What if the flowers were for Blythe, and she really had gotten the wrong message from him?

"Hi." Brett appeared in her office doorway.

Guess she was about to find out. "Hi."

He was in jeans and a button down that strained to contain his shoulders. Looking at Daniel, he nodded. "Daniel."

"Brett." Daniel cleared his throat. "Nice flowers. They for me?"

Laura giggled. She couldn't help it. She needed to break the tension somehow.

"Nope." Brett gave Daniel a level stare. "You still here?"

"Not anymore." Daniel sidled past him out the door. Over Brett's shoulder, he winked at her.

Instead of looking at Brett, Laura focused on the bunch of roses in his hand. They were beautiful, pink and cream and wrapped in brown paper with an enormous satin ribbon around it.

"Sugar?" Brett stepped into the office. "You gonna look at me?"

She shook her head. "Probably not."

Brett laughed and held out the flowers. "These are for you. Razor said that's how this is done, and for once in my life, I wanted to do shit right."

"Thank you." She stepped close enough to take the roses from him. "They're beautiful."

"Did you miss me?" Typical Brett, he got straight to the point.

Eyes still on the roses, Laura nodded. "Yes."

"Good," he said, his voice growing rougher. "Because I missed you every second. I counted them until I could be here with you."

"What took you so long?" The question got away from her before she could stop it.

Brett's boot toes nudged her Chucks. "I wanted a new beginning," he said. "I wanted to make sure that this time we do things right." He took a deep breath and tipped her chin up. "I went to see your ex."

His hazel eyes were open and vulnerable. He was giving her all that he had in that wide-open stare. "About us?"

"Yeah." His eyes warmed as he studied her face. "You're so beautiful, and I got no right to be here, and I sure as shit don't deserve you but I'm asking anyway."

Brett's visit might explain Patrick's change of heart. "What did you say to Patrick?"

"That the way I felt about you meant I wanted to be in your life for a long time," he said and slid his hand over her cheek and under her hair to cup her nape. "I said that I thought you felt the same. Was I right?"

"Yes." Laura nodded, and then spoke from the heart. "I'm scared."

He frowned. "Of me?"

"Not like that." She clasped the wrist of the hand holding her nape. "I know you'd never hurt me, that you'll never hurt anyone again, like you did Blythe." She took a deep breath to steady her nerves. "I'm scared because I want this so badly. I'm scared of what will happen if this doesn't work out, and I'm scared I'll screw it all up."

"Laura." Brett brought his other hand up and cupped her face. "We both know there is no definite in this world. Shit happens in a second that can change your life." He pressed his forehead to hers. "But that's exactly why we owe it to ourselves to do this."

She breathed him in and calm spread for her. "We do."

"Yeah." He nodded. "We've been given what neither of us thought we'd ever get. This connection between us, it's deeper than sexual, and it's richer than friendship." He kissed her cheek. "I've never been in love, sugar, so I don't know for sure if this is what I'm feeling. But yours is the last face I want to see at night, and the first face I want to see in the morning. I want to build something with you that includes all the days of the week and your kids too. I have never felt more like myself with anyone in my life. With you, I don't have to pretend I'm anything other than a thug from the wrong side of town."

Laura had stopped breathing on the part where he'd spoken of neither of them thinking they'd ever have anything like this, and she took a deep breath. "You're not a thug. You're a badass."

"Is that so?" A small smile tilted the corner of his mouth. "What do you say, sugar? We gonna give this thing a chance to grow?"

There really was only one answer to that. "Yes, we are." She slid her arms around his waist and pressed her cheek to his chest. With the strong drum of his heart against her ear, the heat and strength of him against her, and the smell that was all Brett, Laura finally felt like she was exactly who she should be and where she should be. "Although we do need to talk about you calling me sugar."

Brett drew in a deep breath and his voice rumbled through her. "Never gonna stop, sugar. Get your classy girl ass used to it."

# Epilogue

Brett had to give it to the diva. When she threw a party, she went all out. A huge tent had been erected in her garden, and the entire population of Ghost Falls must have pitched in to wish their most famous resident a happy birthday.

Bets were still flying around her exact age. Laura knew, and had told him, but he was part of the diva's clan now, and that meant keeping the secret. All his siblings had been invited, and Bo and Becker had shown up freshly showered in pressed button-down shirts and chinos. Blake had arrived with Ma and sat by her side at one of the beautifully decorated tables in the tent. Ma looked around her like a little girl at her first party, cheeks flushed and eyes sparkling. So far, her pregnancy was going all right, and Blake had even managed to talk her into doing some sessions with a local therapist.

"Evening." Simon slid into place beside him and handed him a beer. "Where is your gorgeous lady?"

"With Phi." He jerked his head at the house. "Phi is demanding all her girls make an entrance with her."

Simon chuckled. "This should be good."

"Laura's gonna need a big drink for sure." He and Razor and Simon had made good progress on their business in the two months following that first meeting at Cranks. Simon had mad contacts, and Razor and Brett brought in a steady trickle of business. Most of it from the ladies in their defense class, but gradually that circle was widening.

"Simon!" Bella, Nate's wife, pushed through the crowd with a fierce look on her angelic face.

Simon shifted. "Ah, shit!"

"You son of a bitch." Bella thumped Simon. "You've been in town for weeks." Her voice grew louder, and heads whipped their way. "Weeks! And you haven't been to see me once."

"I'm sorry, Bella girl." Simon gave her his lady-killer smile. Brett had seen him flash that concealed weapon more than once. "I've been busy setting it up so I can stay here long term."

Bella simmered down a bit, but still glared at him. "For real?"

"For real." Simon gave her a kiss on the cheek, followed by a huge hug. "Then you can yell at me any time you want."

"Right." Bella scowled at him. "Because I'm still mad at you, and so is Liz. I warn you she'll be here later, and she's not happy with you."

A ripple of interest ran through the partygoers, and all attention swung to the tent entrance.

Resplendent in gold lamé and diamonds, Diva Philomene St. Amor paused in the entrance and let the crowd get a load of her.

An appreciative murmur ran through the crowd, which quickly grew into applause.

The diva took it in stride, beaming and waving to her fans.

Brett kept his eyes on the women behind her. One woman behind Phi in particular. Looking sexy as fuck in a tight black evening gown, his Laura met his gaze and gave him a tiny eyeroll. She didn't like all the attention and the fanfare.

Standing next to her, Pippa looked as comfortable with the attention as Phi. Her daughter, Jasmine, grinned her gap-toothed baby smile at the crowds and waved. Emily looked cool and composed and nothing like the ballbreaker he knew her to be.

The town was there to celebrate their legend. Not just her incredible musical legacy, but her innate kindness. Brett couldn't say for sure, but he was willing to bet the diva's kindness had touched nearly every person there, either directly or indirectly.

He'd found out she'd also had a hand in Simon approaching him and Razor, and had put aside an education fund for Karstyn to go to college. When the time came, Karstyn would find himself the beneficiary of a full-ride scholarship from a company set up to hide his benefactor. Despite her outrageous daily antics, the diva kept her philanthropy much quieter.

Daisy and Sam stood to the left of Laura. Things there weren't always easy in their newly hatched version of a blended family, but they made it work one day at a time. He wasn't Daisy and Sam's father—a detail Daisy liked to produce when it suited whatever teenage rage fest she was on that day—but he was the man who loved the crap outta their mother, so loving her kids was part of the deal.

He turned his attention back to Laura, and mouthed, "You look beautiful."

"Thank you." She mouthed back and blushed, and then she said the thing he'd never take for granted. Every time she said it, it made him feel like the luckiest man alive. Laura looked at him and her lips formed the words, "I love you."

And he loved her right the fuck back and would spend the rest of their days making sure she knew that.

# The Ghost Falls series

For Pippa Turner there's only one place to go when her life self-destructs on national TV—home to Ghost Falls, and her heavily perfumed, overly dramatic, but supremely loving grandmother, Philomene. If anyone will understand how Pippa's hit makeover show was sabotaged by her vengeful ex, it's Phi. But she's not the only one who's happy to see her—and Pippa can't help but wonder if Matt Evans, her gorgeous high-school crush turned Phi's contractor, is game for a steamy close-up... Matt owes his whole career to Phi and her constant demands to embellish the gothically ridiculous house he built for her. Getting to see red-headed, red-hot Pippa is a bonus, especially now that she's no longer the troublesome teenager he remembers. He's willing to stay behind the scenes while she gives her own life a much-needed makeover, but not forever. As far as he's concerned, their connection is too electric to ignore. And the chance to build something lasting between them—before she can high-tail it back to Hollywood—is going to the top of his to-do list...

*This Christmas, a good reputation can really get in a girl's way . . .* As long as she can remember, Bella Erikson's been the unofficial sweetheart of Ghost Falls, Utah. And ever since Nate Evans dipped her braids in purple paint in the first grade, he's been her dream guy. Not that she minds the attention, but sometimes she wishes people saw more in her than just the girl who still has a crush on Sheriff Evans. She has a life after all, a new bridal shop to run, and more mature relationships to pursue . . . Nate knows he's not good enough for sweet Bella. But he's pretty sure the new guy sending her heart emojis and giant bouquets isn't either. And when Bella's suitor turns stalker, protecting Bella isn't just Nate's instinct—it's his duty. Crammed together for safety and really talking for the first time in years, Bella and Nate can't fight the moment their chemistry turns into pyrotechnics. Whether it will burn them out or light up the sky, only time will tell . . .

Eric Evans is about to discover that you don't know you love someone until you lose them, when town "bad girl", Blythe Barrows ends their long-term, on-again, off-again, friends with benefits relationship. Having finally gained independence from the disreputable Barrows family, Blythe wants more for herself. However commitment-phobic Eric never made any promises.  Unable to let her go, Eric must fight for what he's lost. But can Blythe trust him with her heart enough to give their love a second chance?

# About the Author

Born British and raised in South Africa, Sarah Hegger suffers from an incurable case of wanderlust. Her match? A hot Canadian engineer, whose marriage proposal she accepted six short weeks after they first met. Together they've made homes in seven different cities across three different continents (and back again once or twice). If only it made her multilingual, but the best she can manage is idiosyncratic English, fluent Afrikaans, conversant Russian, pigeon Portuguese, even worse Zulu and enough French to get herself into trouble.

Mimicking her globe trotting adventures, Sarah's career path began as a gainfully employed actress, drifted into public relations, settled a moment in advertising, and eventually took root in the fertile soil of her first love, writing. She also moonlights as a wife and mother. She currently lives in Ottawa, Canada, with aforementioned husband, filling their empty nest with fur babies. Part footloose buccaneer, part quixotic observer of life, Sarah's restless heart is most content when reading or writing books.

Medieval Romance

*Sir Arthur's Legacy Series*

Sweet Bea

My Lady Faye

Conquering William

Roger's Bride

Releasing Henry


*Love & War Series*

The Marriage Parley

The Betrothal Melee


Western Historical Romance

*The Soiled Dove Series*

Sugar Ellie


*Standalone*

The Bride Gift

Bad Wolfe On The Rise

Wild Honey